St Crispin

Book 6 in the Struggle f   ...wii Series

By

Griff Hosker

Published by Sword Books Ltd 2019

Cover by Design for Writers

Dedication

To Olivia Grace and her proud parents, Alex and Laura.

Contents

List of important characters in the novel

(Fictional characters are italicized)

- *Sir William Strongstaff*
- King Henry IV formerly Henry Bolingbroke
- King Henry V
- Humphrey, Duke of Gloucester (the King's brother)
- Thomas, Duke of Clarence (the King's brother)
- Edmund Mortimer, Earl of March
- Ralph Neville, 4th Baron Neville of Raby, and 1st Earl of Westmorland
- Sir Thomas Fitzalan, Earl of Arundel
- Thomas Arundel-Archbishop of Canterbury
- Bishop Henry Beaufort
- Nicholas Merbury- Master of the Ordnance
- Richard of Conisburgh, 3rd Earl of Cambridge
- Henry Scrope, Baron Scrope of Masham
- Sir Thomas Grey of Northumberland
- King Charles VI of France
- Louis, Dauphin of France (King Charles' heir)
- Duke John, 'the Fearless', of Burgundy
- Charles d'Albret the Constable of France
- John le Meingre, Boucicaut, Marshal of France

Royal Family Tree of England

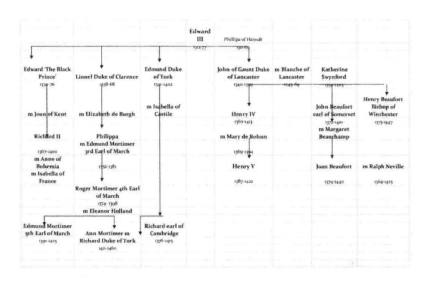

Prologue

Since my return from France where I had helped the Duke of Burgundy to defeat the French at the Battle of St Cloud, my life for the first time had been relatively peaceful. I had been fighting in one form or another since Spain when I had followed father and the Blue Company of English mercenaries. I came from common stock and my family were not in any way nobles. I was now a knight and held in high esteem but I was proud of the Blue Company and I missed those warriors more than anyone else. The Black Prince had hired me to train his son, the future King Richard and his cousin Henry Bolingbroke. Henry Bolingbroke had plotted his way to the throne but I had not broken my oath and I had defended both men from their enemies. Although he was not as old as me, King Henry was now dying and that was one enemy against whom I could not fight. When he died, I would not miss him for, unlike his son, he was not a likeable man. In contrast, I still missed the eccentric and erratic King Richard and his lovely wife, Anne of Bohemia. I think that I might have left the service of King Henry had it not been for his son. Henry Monmouth, or as he had been known when he trained with me, Prince Hal, was a warrior in the tradition of the Black Prince and the first King Edward. I had fought alongside him at the battle of Shrewsbury where Douglas and the treacherous Henry Percy had been defeated. It had shown me that there was nobility in this line and that he was a king worth following and so I continued to obey the orders of the Black Prince; I protected the King from all enemies, foreign and domestic. If we had thought that would end the treachery in England, we were wrong.

King Henry, who had been Henry Bolingbroke, was not a warrior, but he was a plotter and that was another reason I did not like him. He had used me too many times. When I had been sent with a small English army to help the Duke of Burgundy, he had had ulterior motives and he did not share them with me. I had been successful and helped the Duke to defeat the Armagnac faction at the battle of St Cloud. The result of the battle meant that the Duke of Burgundy was so pleased that he had offered me a Burgundian town, but I had declined for I was an Englishman and I wanted no divided loyalties! I did accept the revenue from a small French manor as there was no oath of allegiance involved. As the great and the good deferred to me when it came to matters of war then a new title meant nothing. My wife Eleanor, however, thought that I should have been made a senior lord, a baron or an earl; she, too, had thought me a fool for refusing Arles. We were rich for I had not only been given land, but we had also bought some and my wife had a good head for business. It was my family which was the most important thing to me. My sons, Harry and Thomas were both knights and Harry acted as Constable of Northampton for me. My life was good and with my son in law Richard living close by with my daughter, Alice, then I could see all of my grandchildren whenever time allowed.

Since my return from France, I had enjoyed visiting with my grandchildren as often as I could. I was now approaching sixty years of age and few men who fought in battle had lived as long as me. I was aware of my mortality and while I was no longer in the forefront of fights as often I used to be, I was in danger each time we went to war and I knew that Prince Hal would need me when he became King. He trusted me and my judgement. And so, for a short time before King Henry died, I did not have to raise my sword in anger. I enjoyed hunting, playing with my grandchildren and talking to my old friends of the wars in which we had fought. I still retained many of my men even though they were crippled. John of Aldgate had a crippled hand, but he still served me. Rafe Red Beard and James Jameson had suffered wounds at St Cloud, but I had not sent them down the road. They wished to serve me still and so I retained them as servants. When I went to war, the plate armour I wore took two or three people to fit it.

My sojourn from war and battle ended in the year of Our Lord, 1413; Henry Bolingbroke who had plotted his way to the crown succumbed to the illness which had plagued him since before the Battle of Shrewsbury. His funeral took some time to plan and it was many months after his death that the lavish funeral took place. I had known that I would be summoned to the new King's side, but the funeral was not held immediately. The new King was making a statement. He was a new King, but he would honour the past with a grand funeral which would be symbolic. There were still those who thought that Henry Bolingbroke had murdered King Richard. Canterbury Cathedral was the resting place of a martyr, Saint Thomas, who had also been murdered. Many pilgrims visited the cathedral and the new King Henry was ensuring that they would be honouring his father too. As the former bodyguard of Henry Bolingbroke, I was, of course, invited to the funeral at Canterbury Cathedral. From that day my life became one of war and intrigue and the time I spent with my grandchildren became a distant memory.

Chapter 1

Although the funeral took some time to organise King Henry had wasted no time in assuming the reins of power. He had been increasingly involved in the running of England over the last few years while his father's health declined. Along with his uncles, the Beauforts, he had been effectively running England. Now he could determine policy and not follow the wishes of his father. He was his own man. He had put in place plans to retake France from King Charles and I was part of those plans. It was after the funeral where we had interred his father and I was preparing to head back to Weedon with Harry and Tom when Sir John Holland, one of King Henry's oldest friends, sought me out. I knew Sir John well and had fought alongside him.

"King Henry would have a word with you, Sir William." He smiled somewhat sadly. We knew each other well, "I fear that your days of peace are over."

I sniffed, "As I expected. Is it to be France again?"

"You know the King better than any, William Strongstaff, and he will tell you all. I am just the messenger!"

The King had taken over Canterbury Castle. It was not a massive fortification for Dover and Leeds Castles, as well as the formidable Rochester Castle, meant that this part of Kent was safe from England's enemies and Canterbury was cosy by comparison. It suited the bachelor King. A tall and attractive King, despite the scar he had received at Shrewsbury, the King had yet to marry. I knew that he had already decided to marry the daughter of the King of France and that showed how much he wanted the throne of France. All of his advances had been rejected by the French King, but he would not give up until he had what he wanted. The third King Edward and his son had won France for England at the battles of Crécy and Poitiers. That it had been lost was the fault of King Richard. King Henry would remedy that.

I saw all the senior lords were there as well as his brothers and his uncle, the Duke of York. He smiled when he saw me and held out his arm, "William, it is good to see you." He used the back of his hand to touch my beard, "The grey suits you."

"The King is kind to say so." Appearances never bothered me and although we had that rarest of furnishings, a mirror, in my hall, I never looked in it. It was my wife who fussed over me when I left the hall.

"You will dine with me tonight for I wish to confer with the newest member of the Order of the Garter. Sir William Strongstaff!"

The honour came as a complete shock to me. "Order of the Garter, Your Majesty?" The order was the highest order of chivalry in the land and limited to a mere twenty-four members. To be elevated to it meant a knight was ranked with the royal family!

"Aye, for it is time you were elevated a little and there is now a space for we have just twenty-three members." That took some of the edge off for it sounded like I had been promoted to make up numbers. The knights, lords, princes and dukes in the hall, however, all began to clap and cheer. My first thought was that my wife had her wish; I had been accorded the highest honour in the land.

"We will hold the ceremony in St George's Chapel at Windsor when time allows. The King was a tall man and he put an arm around my back so that he could speak quietly and not be overheard. "I have a task which only you can perform, Will, for I need you to sniff out my enemies. You know my heart as well as any man. I have broken bread with you and your family and so, above all other men, I can trust you. I want France but I cannot go to France and recover my lost lands if there is trouble in England. I want you to find out who is disloyal to me! I am not a fool and know that there are many who wish me gone. They are the ones who spread these libellous tales of my drunken behaviour. They are not true but some believe them.

I turned, shocked, "You wish me to be a spy?"

His face kept the same expression as he said, "For your King and your country? Aye, of course I do! Whom else should I use? The Black Prince entrusted the protection of his son and my father to you. You guarded Kings against the blades of enemies and that is what you will do for me. We will speak more when we dine, for now, I have appointments to make." I was summarily dismissed. King Henry was always business-like. Some said he was cold, but I knew better. He just had the ability to make his life a series of rooms. He shut one door and then focussed on what lay in the next.

My sons waited without. They had our horses and our bags ready for we had expected to travel back home. They looked disappointed when I said, "The King has need of me and I shall be staying here tonight."

My eldest, Thomas, frowned. "I do not like you to travel on the road alone, father, for you have been attacked before on the roads of

Northamptonshire. We will take rooms at the inn here and accompany you home."

I shook my head, firmly, "There was a time when I would have needed such care, but times have changed, and this greybeard is no longer a threat to anyone. I will keep just Walter and Rafe with me. They will do." Walter was my newest squire. He was the son of Ralph of Middleham Grange and was really a page rather than a squire for he had yet to see ten summers but both his father and he were anxious for him to learn the way to become a knight. Walter's father had once been my squire and his father, Red Ralph, had been the man who made me the warrior who defended kings. Rafe was a servant but he had once been a man at arms until he was hurt in the leg and could no longer stand in a shield wall. He still practised with the men at arms and could handle a sword as well as any but a battlefield was no place for a lamed man. Others could die as a result and Rafe knew it. He was just happy to live in my manor. He shared the warrior hall with the other men who would, in times of war, help me to don my plate and assist my squire to prepare me and my horse.

Reluctantly my sons left me. Rafe had campaigned with me many times but Walter was new to the role he now took. Indeed, he had only been with me for a month. I had agreed to train him as a squire after the King had died for I knew I would have to go to war some time in the future. He was still learning, and I had to instruct him on his duties whilst we were in the castle, "Walter, tonight will be hard for you. As a squire, you will have to serve at table and there are the highest in the land at this table: dukes and earls, bishops and archbishops. Keep your eyes and ears open and try not to spill food."

Rafe laughed, "Aye, Master Walter, some of those knights think more about their precious clothes than they do about the men they lead. The King now, he is a proper soldier and he does not care about such matters!"

Rafe was right and had known the King when he had been the young Prince Hal who had been trained by my men and me. "You will sleep in the stable, Rafe, while you, Walter, will share my room!" That, too, would be a new experience for the young squire. At Weedon, he had his own room and he would have to learn a little more about his new lord.

As they took our animals to the stables, I returned to the antechamber of the Great Hall. The King rushed around in a very business-like manner, giving orders to two and three men at a time and as a servant brought me a goblet of wine, I watched liveried courtiers racing back and forth. Clerks and clerics with ink-stained hands were also summoned and then dismissed. King Henry had loved his father,

9

but I knew that Henry Bolingbroke and his policies had both been too cautious and lacking ambition for his son. Now that he was King, he was not simply mourning his dead father, but he was celebrating his opportunity to rule. Where Henry Bolingbroke had worried that raising taxes would make his people resent him the new King did not lose sleep over such things, he would make them happy about the extra financial burden and it explained the task he had given to me! There were men who would seek to take advantage of potential unrest in the land. As I sipped the wine, I worked out whence the treachery might come. There were, of course, Lollards in the land. This religious faction was opposed to both the Church and, by association, the King. They were led by commoners but they could be used by the real enemies, those who sought the crown itself. The figurehead that the enemies of King Henry could use was Edmund Mortimer. He had been King Richard's heir. If he was to be a ruthless ruler then King Henry could have him executed and eliminate the threat. That was not King Henry's way and, to be truthful, Edmund Mortimer appeared to be as loyal a knight as there was. The King had even rewarded him, and I knew that he believed that the Earl of March did not wish the crown. That would not, however, stop others using the man as the symbol of their struggle for the crown. I had to discover which knights also had an interest in fostering his cause.

Even before I spoke with the King, I had decided that I would look to the north first. Hotspur and his father had ever been enemies of the King and his father and the folk there still resented Henry Bolingbroke and his family for he had not only taken the lives of their favourite sons, but he had also taken land and power from them. The two of them were dead but they had tried to make a new England ruled from the north. There were many northern and Scottish knights who sought to reverse the result of Shrewsbury. It did not seem to matter to them that they had been soundly beaten; they thought that we had somehow cheated our way to victory. We had not; God was on our side. The northern barons had been quiet for a few years but that would be the first place I would try. I would visit with Walter's father who was a northern lord I could trust. I would begin my search for traitors amongst those that I knew I could trust. Of course, my task would not be helped by the fact that I was the knight responsible for the death of that hero of the north, Harry Hotspur!

When Walter arrived at the door to the Great Hall, he was laden with our bags. I had, of course, brought good clothes with me. I was a man of means and Eleanor was keen to show others that I knew how to dress. When I had been given my first manor, she had been angry with the way that the local gentry at Dauentre had looked down their noses at us and determined they would never have cause to do so again. I had a spare houppelande with me and I would be dressed as finely as the Duke of York himself.

A servant came over to me, "Now that your squire is here then I can take you to your chamber, Sir William."

I nodded, "Take some of the bags from my squire."

If the servant thought that he was too high and mighty for such a task, he was wise enough to hold his tongue and merely nod. Sir William Strongstaff was known as a man who expected commands to be obeyed. The chamber we were given was adequate although it was in a tower and the stairs taxed me. The castle was not a large one and only the King would have a large bedchamber. Walter helped me to dress and I made sure that his livery, which reflected on me, was also presentable. He was younger than my grandsons and I wondered if I should have had an older squire. He dutifully followed me down the stairs and I heard him sigh as we joined the other lords and squires. It was a daunting prospect to perform a new task under the scrutiny of the greatest in the land. I had never been a squire and my only experience of serving at table was as a recipient. The other squires would, in all likelihood, try to take advantage of Walter. When Tom and Harry had been my squires, they had told me of the games the older squires played. Walter would adapt and, more importantly, he would learn about their masters for squires could be indiscreet.

Just before we left the chamber, I told him that I would be seeking King Henry's enemies and I said, "Keep your eyes and ears open when you serve at table and keep your mouth closed whenever possible. As much as you may dislike it, this night will help to prepare you for the day when you become a knight! And, when we travel home you can tell me all that you learn about the lords the other squires serve."

"But surely their masters are above suspicion!"

"No one is above suspicion. There are some men at arms and knights whose words say one thing but whose thoughts speak differently." My voice sounded cold and I saw Walter almost recoil but it was true and I had seen too many people close to King Richard and King Henry who purported to be friends but, in reality, were trying to usurp them!

Walter nodded. He was inquisitive and was not afraid of looking foolish if there was something he did not understand, "My lord is a man-at-arms and a knight the same thing?"

I shook my head and I understood his confusion. I had men at arms who served me, and Walter spoke to them without having to show deference. "A knight has been given his spurs and a title. A man at arms

11

may be an esquire or a squire, not one such as you but one who is armed and attired much as a knight might be. Often if a man at arms does well then he might be knighted. When I was but little older than you, I fought in Spain and I was there when the great friend of the Black Prince, Sir John Chandos, died. Sir John had been given his spurs by King Edward when he fought with distinction in the Low Countries. It is expensive to be a man at arms but more so to be a knight. When we go to war I will need not only you but others to help me dress for war." I laughed, "I remember when it was not so, and I just donned a simple mail hauberk and helmet without the need for others to help me dress. Sometimes I yearn for those days!"

I was seated next to the King and that was an honour. He made much of it, welcoming a new Knight of the Garter but I knew just how astute he was. The honour meant we could meet regularly without suspicion and he also would have a bodyguard close to hand. As the first nibbles were brought before us and the wine served, he leaned closer to me so that he could speak confidentially. "We cannot invade France yet for we have not enough money and there is too much unrest. Sir John Oldcastle and the Lollards need to be neutralized and you, my old friend, must find those who seek to take from me that which I have barely attained."

I sighed and gave an honest answer for that would be what I would have expected if the roles had been reversed. "All men know, especially the lords of this land, that I am your man! I have defended you on battlefields and that is no secret. As soon as I visit with them they will know I do your bidding!"

He smiled, "I know but I also know that you know how to read men. King Richard was kind to me, and I remember, when I was his hostage in Ireland how he spoke of you. It was as a friend. He said that while you stood behind him, he feared no treachery for you could see the intent in men's eyes, and we both know that despite the rumours, my father had nought to do with King Richard's death." I nodded. "No enemy reached him except for the demons which tore him from within. Your eyes, your mind and, most of all, your experience, will help to sniff out these dogs who wish to take the crown from my head."

As I thought back to King Richard, I drank deeply from the wine which was an especially good one from the southwest of France, "It was when Queen Anne died that the monsters from within consumed King Richard. It distressed me to see it." I put down the goblet, "You are happy to take my opinion, without evidence?"

He spoke even more quietly, "I have lived in your home, William, and know you to be a good man. You are not a man to fight against on a battlefield but if you are a man's friend then he is the safest man in the Kingdom. I will trust your word for you have not a dishonest bone in your body!"

"And if I find no treachery?"

He laughed, "Old friend, do you think that is likely? However, you may be right and the presence of the bodyguard of kings might well make potential threats to think again. I will keep you apprised of my plans, but it is unlikely that we will be able to sail to France this year or, perhaps, next year. I have ships to find and then my uncle, Bishop Henry, has yet to complete the funding of the raid."

One of his brothers, Humphrey, stood, raised his goblet and shouted, "King Henry and damnation to the French!"

We all stood and repeated the toast. King Henry smiled as I sat back down, "My brothers are keen and should be above suspicion but..."

"If I hear a whisper then you shall know."

"And I shall need you at my side when we go to France as well as your sons, archers and men at arms. The other knights you trained may stay at home, but I need you and your familia."

I sighed, "I know but I fear for them."

The King looked puzzled, "You should not be afraid! You know that at Crécy my grandsire, King Edward and his tiny army slew over twenty thousand Frenchmen and only suffered the loss of two knights! I think that we will be as successful!" He was confident but I was a realist.

"The French may have learned from that!"

His voice became so low that I had to almost touch his head with mine to hear it, "You know you were sent to fight for Burgundy by my father and wondered at that?" I nodded. "We planned it thus. Duke John is the best of the French leaders. King Charles is mad, and his sons are incompetent. If the King of France or his sons lead the French, then we will win. Duke John, thanks to your defence of his person, has told me that he will not lead any men to oppose us. He has to provide men for the King of France but neither he nor his son will be on the battlefield! The best of the French leaders are the French Marshal Boucicaut and the Constable of France. They are not of royal blood! So, you see, William, you have already paved the way for victory although you did not know it and wondered at its wisdom!"

The Duke of York was on the other side of the King and he began to speak to the King. I used my knife to cut into the fish and then spear it with the point. It was a well-cooked pike and some of the pieces were so flaky that I had to use my fingers to lift the succulent beast into my mouth. As I wiped my fingers on a napkin, I looked around at the men gathered in the hall of the small castle. It was not a large number, but they were the heart of King Henry's leaders. I took some pride in the fact that the King had surrounded himself with men that he could trust. Some were family but there were others who had been selected because of their skills. His father had been too much of a plotter. I did not eliminate any of the men around the table, but I doubted that they would try to hurt the King. They had too much to gain by supporting him. If and when we won, then they would all be given large estates in France and Normandy.

Walter appeared over my shoulder with another platter of food, "Are you ready yet, my lord?"

I was an efficient eater. I had scavenged for the Blue Company and I never wasted food. While others took too much and left waste, I knew the size of my own belly. I had cleared the pewter platter of food and leaned back to help my squire do his duty, "Aye, Walter. How goes it?"

He smiled and, placing the wild boar slices on my platter, said quietly, "I play the northern country bumpkin and they are happy to mock me. They see me as a fool!"

I nodded. I had chosen my squire well. I had been well served by all of my squires and now that they were knights some of them would be in my retinue. I was obliged to provide thirty men at arms and eighty horsed archers when I went to war, a retinue of ten lances. The men at arms would not be a problem as my sons each had five men at arms, and my son in law, Richard of Kislingbury, had four. I had more than enough to furnish the rest. The King had said that he needed no other knights, but some might choose to serve with me. I was less sure if Sir Ralph of Middleham Grange would be allowed to come for King Henry would need to leave the north protected. The Scots were opportunist. When King Edward had defeated the French at Crécy the Scots under King David had attempted to take the north. Lord Neville had gathered a few knights and archers together and not only thrashed them at the Battle of Neville's Cross but also captured their King who died in English captivity. King Henry knew the story for I had told it to him.

When the King went to speak with his brothers the Duke of York leaned over to me, "You have heard what happened to Oldcastle?"

Sir John Oldcastle was a knight alongside whom I had fought in Wales and when fighting for Burgundy. He was a good knight in battle, but I knew him to be a Lollard. I did not mind if a man held views which opposed mine. A man's beliefs were personal. The Lollards opposed the Roman Catholic church and King Henry was duty-bound to rid the land of them. "Is he still spouting Wycliffe's dogma?"

"He is and the King has him in the Tower. They might have been comrades once, but no one challenges this King! Lincoln and Herefordshire, not to mention Gloucestershire are hotbeds of Lollardy! When you are travelling the roads, you should bear that in mind."

"Thank you for the warning, my lord!" I had even more to worry about now!

We left for home the next day. I intended to ride hard and to spend the night in my own bed. It meant using a ferry across the Thames, but I had a royal warrant from King Henry and securing our passage was easy. Now that I was a Knight of the Garter I had been elevated. We were using our hackneys which were good horses for riding and could run all day without damage. The hard ride would not hurt them. Walter, when we were alone on the road and with Rafe watching our backs, told me all that he had learned. I was patient with him for although much of what he told me was mere squires' gossip, there were nuggets to be gleaned. Some of the squires had travelled with their lords to tournaments and Walter told me of knights who were discontent. I had names already in my head and Walter's words narrowed the number I would need to investigate. I worked out a route which would allow me to speak to those malcontents. First, I would have to visit with Sir Ralph of Middleham Grange for he was my eyes and ears in the north. Walter would be glad to return to his family home.

On reflection, my decision to ride directly home proved to be a bad one but as I had learned over the years, hindsight was always perfect. I was no longer a young man and I required more stops along the way than when I was younger. To be fair so did Rafe and Walter had two old men to contend with. We were twenty miles south of Northampton and dusk was rapidly approaching when I heard the clippety-clop of horses behind us. We had slowed to a walk for, despite the fact that we were riding hackneys, they were tiring, and I did not wish one to go lame on us. The sound of the hooves behind us alarmed me a little for they suggested speed. One would think that was not an unusual event on the main road to the north but the nearest town where a man could stay was Northampton and the gates to the town would be closed by the time we neared it. The three of us would be heading along a side road to Weedon. Whoever was riding was following us and riding hard. Our four horses were walking. I could hear that the ones behind were galloping. Either they wished to speak with me urgently, or they meant us harm. Rafe had heard them too and glancing at him I nodded. He drew his sword as did I. We both did so surreptitiously so that the horsemen behind us would not see us do so.

Walter was blissfully unaware of danger until I said, "Walter, there may be danger. Draw your sword but do not turn nor let the horsemen behind see you do it." His sword was little more than a long dagger but it was a weapon.

"But."

Rafe snapped, "Just do as Sir William commands, Master Walter, and you will live a lot longer." He smiled to make the curt command less aggressive.

I held my sword down by my leg and I knew that in the failing light it would not be seen. I risked a surreptitious glance behind and saw that there were four horsemen and they were armed. That was not unexpected for the King's road had dangers along it. I could not see if they were mailed for, like us, they were cloaked, and their heads hidden in the cowls of their riding cloaks.

They must have seen my head turn for one called, "My Lord Strongstaff, wait; I beg of you!"

Innocent Walter said, "They must be from the King!"

I stopped and wheeled my horse around. Rafe placed his horse next to my left side. With Walter and the sumpter on my right, I was protected. I was under no illusions. In the schemes of the plotters, Rafe and Walter were unimportant, but I was a confidante of the King! I did not recognise any of them, but they looked to be working men rather than soldiers. The few words I had heard suggested that they came from the west country. As they reined in, I saw that their horses were lathered, and I knew then that we had been chased down. Perhaps crossing the Thames by ferry had been a wise move. They spread themselves out half a horse length from us and, as we were doing, they kept their right hands hidden. They meant us harm.

"You seem to know us, sir, but I am not familiar with either you or your companions. Why have you delayed us on the King's road?"

The leader whipped out his sword and pointed it at me. His companions did the same. I knew then that they were not soldiers for they were too far from us to be able to use their weapons quickly. Rafe and I kept our swords hidden but Walter held his nervously before him. I noticed that the four swords which faced us were not good ones and looked old. I was not even sure that they were sharpened. More importantly, they were both shorter than the swords which Rafe and I held.

"You threaten the King's counsellor and the man who is the law here in Northampton? You are either very foolish or very brave!"

The speaker was an earnest-looking man with a neatly trimmed beard. "We are friends of Sir John Oldcastle and he has been unjustly imprisoned in the Tower of London. We will hold you and the ransom will be Sir John's freedom!"

That it was an ill-thought-out venture was obvious even to a fool and I was no fool, "My friend, do you think that the King will give up a prisoner for me and, more importantly, do you think that the four of you are capable of taking us?"

My voice was so calm and reasonable that I made them nervous and the leader looked around to the others. One of them, a slightly broader built man with a lank and greasy beard snarled, "Jack, it is an old man, a cripple and a boy! We take them now and stop this debate!"

One of the others said, "Aye, Jack!" The slightly younger man dug his heels into his sumpter and, swashing his sword rode at Rafe. Both of us had been waiting for such a move and I spurred my horse to lunge at them and swung my sword hard at the leader, Jack's, hand. As my razor-sharp sword sliced through the glove and wrist of the leader, Rafe's sword came up and across the second, bold young man. My former man at arms' sword ripped off half of the man's face who whipped his horse's head around, dropping his sword in the process. He fled down the road. The man with the lank beard looked from the leader to me and back. The delay was all that Rafe needed and his sword hacked into the right arm of the Lollard, through to the bone. Dropping his sword, he, too, along with the fourth man, fled, following their leader whose hand, if he still had it, hung by a thread. There was little point in pursuing them for our horses were becoming weary and their capture was not worth the life of one of our animals.

I nodded, "Rafe, pick up the swords. We will be even later now for we must inform my son in Northampton that there are Lollards causing mischief!"

As we headed north along the road, now riding faster, Walter said, "How did you know what to do, my lord? You and Rafe were so calm but I thought we were dead men!"

"You will learn, Walter, to recognised men who are soldiers and a danger and others who are not. Look at weapons and horses. Your short sword was smaller but still superior to all of theirs. Show him, Rafe!"

My former man at arms took one of the swords we had taken and, placing it on his saddle, bent it. The lesson was an obvious one. The four men had been opportunists rather than real killers.

"The King will need to know of this for it means Oldcastle's supporters wish to effect his release. I do not think that Oldcastle would have sanctioned this attack for it was doomed to failure. Perhaps they heard I had been delayed in Canterbury and thought to ambush us after we had passed through London. There may have been more of them closer to London." The more I thought about it the clearer became the picture. They would have wanted to use more than four men to take us but had had to change their plans when I took the ferry. I pointed to Walter, "And not a word of this to Lady Eleanor or any of the servants. We need not bother her!"

"Aye, my lord." It was another lesson in being a squire; discretion.

The gates to Northampton were closed but I was recognised, and my son brought forth. I told him what had happened, and he sent a dozen men out to see if they could find the would-be kidnappers. I doubted that they would.

"Harry, keep this to yourself. I want your mother to be blissfully unaware of this!"

Harry nodded, "Next time, father, listen to Thomas and me. We predicted this!"

I laughed, "Ah, so you and your brother have become your mother! You sound like her. I am a warrior, as are you, Harry. Remember that!"

My wife was anxious as we entered my hall long after dark, "You have been on the road at night! There are brigands and bandits have you no sense? The older you get the more like a child you become!"

I had been attacked, many years earlier, by bandits and killers; I waved an airy hand, "I had Rafe with me!" I wondered what she would have thought of the attempted kidnap.

She sniffed as Walter took my cloak and she poured me some wine, "He is like you, an old man!"

I laughed, "Old or not we will be going to war again for the King."

She stopped, her hand holding the goblet in mid-air, "You? But you have done enough!"

"Eleanor, I am now a Knight of the Garter. You wished me to be elevated and now I am!"

"I wanted you to be given the title of Earl so that you could sit and grow fat and old!"

I sat down for I was weary. Eleanor was partially right, I did feel my age these days, "And you know that will not be for we cannot change that which is in us and makes us who we are. I am a warrior, a sword for hire and I am tied to the crown; we both know it. The fates which determine such things do not provide silk to bind us, I am bound with fetters of iron." I sipped the wine and then decided to get all of the bad news out of the way at once, "And Thomas, Harry and Richard will be with me too!"

She rolled her eyes, "And what does the young King want?"

"Nothing less than the Crown of France, the unpaid ransom for King John captured at Poitiers, the hand of Princess Katherine and a dowry of two million crowns!"

She could not help laughing, "You have to admire young Hal, he does not do things by halves! At least I have you home until then."

Shaking my head, I said, "I am sent on a mission by the King to uncover plots against him and the crown."

She sighed, "And, of course, no one else can do this. What would the kings of England do without Will Strongstaff? I am surprised that he does not have you waiting outside the garderobe!" She shook her head, "You will take a good escort of men at arms then!"

Most of the men who fought with me in France had used their money to buy themselves a life outside of war. I would have to employ either more men or ask my old men at arms to fight once more. When I had first fought as a sword for hire all that a man at arms needed was a helmet, sword and hauberk. Now he was called a lance and had to have plate armour, two horses, at least, and two or three men to service him. I had two men at arms who were still at Weedon. Both had a good warhorse each and I had servants who could come to war and help to put their plate on. Nat Washbourne and Matty of Street had not been my men originally but when their lords were killed in France at the battle of St Cloud, they took my coin to guard my home. All of the rest of my former men at arms lived north of me and I would visit with them as I headed on the King's quest.

My archers still lived either in my manor or in the castle at Northampton. I would not use Captain Alan of the Woods for he had a family of his own and much as I would want his experience, he deserved some peace. His son, Abelard, had been Sir Roger's squire but I had knighted him and that had pleased my old Captain of Archers. He would complain when I told him he would not be coming but I would give him the olive branch of ensuring that the mounted archers I took with me were of the highest standard! I spoke with my two men at arms and told them of our proposed journey. I would also take Rafe and James Jameson. James, too, had been wounded in my service, but he could still handle himself.

"We will head north and when we reach Middleham I shall see Red Ralph's widow, Mary, and buy some horses for we will need them when we go to France."

Matty of Street said, "And if you are to go to war again, my lord, then you need better plate!"

He was right. Weaponsmiths were improving the designs of their armour all the time and as I could afford the best then I would have it! "When we return from the north, I will have it made."

Matty shook his head, "If war is coming then weaponsmiths will be overwhelmed with work, lord. It would be better to get it ordered now."

"You are right. We will seek out William at Northampton Castle and I can speak with the archers there."

My son Harry was acting in my stead at Northampton as Constable and performing my duties as Sherriff. The role had yet to become a bore and he enjoyed administering justice and running the castle for the King. When I met him, he said that, following our attack, men had searched the London road. Although they had not found the four men they had found evidence of their presence. Those living along the road had heard the four men and some had seen the bloody evidence of their passing.

"I am sorry we could not find them, father."

I smiled, "We were unhurt, and I do not think that they will trouble us again and if they do then they will be recognisable. Two will only have the use of one arm and the other will be heavily disfigured. I think that they will slink back to the Lollard country in the west. We must be more vigilant. Have your men look for Lollards."

"That does not sit well with them for, Oldcastle apart, most are common men and their beliefs are harmless."

"They were harmless, but King Henry thinks otherwise and sees a threat to the crown. Now enough of that. I have other matters to discuss." I had already told Thomas of my task and before I visited William the Weaponsmith I told Harry. For his part, he was delighted and saw it as a chance for great honour and glory! "Tell Thomas that his son, Henry, is too young to come, even as a page. I know that with your nephew, William, accompanying your brother in law there will be a temptation for your elder brother to do the same, but this will not be an easy chevauchée." Sir Richard's firstborn, named after me, had been a squire for a number of years and this would be a good experience for him.

"I know and I will ensure that your new plate is ready by the time the King sends for us."

William the Weaponsmith took hours to measure me. This would be the first gorget I had had made although I had had versions of the other pieces, cuisse, solorets, poleyns, elbow-cops, faulds, vambraces and the like. The new plate was stronger and lighter offering more protection. It was expensive as I had known it would be. My wife would not quibble over the cost for it would keep me alive.

When we left for the north, we would wear mail beneath our surcoats and cloaks. Although the Lollard attack had not harmed us, we were heading into a part of the country where there was still much opposition to King Henry. We had been responsible for killing their favourite son. My new Captain of Archers, David of Welshpool, pressed two of his archers upon me. Christopher White Arrow and Jack Gardyvyan were both good archers and, like the two men at arms who came with me, were unmarried. I employed them all and should not have felt any guilt, but a man cannot change the demons inside him and despite my elevated position I still did not like to be a bother to others.

My wife fussed over me as I prepared to mount on the day of our departure. She brushed imaginary flecks of dust from my cloak, "Do not overtax yourself. Your health is important and who knows what pestilence lies in the north." My wife was suspicious of northerners. She looked pointedly at Rafe and James whom she knew the best, "And if anything happens to you then I know who to blame."

The two men quailed before my wife's words. They could face any number of enemies but not my wife.

"Wife," I kissed her on the top of her forehead, "I have done this journey many times before. I go to see Walter's father and his grandmother. We will buy horses and return."

"Do not try to fool me, Will Strongstaff! There is great danger as well you know! Return and return whole. I married a man with all of his limbs, and I would like to keep it that way!"

I knew that she was worried for the normally iron woman I had married looked tearful. I mounted and we headed for the road north. That was my lot in life to leave my family and serve my king!

Chapter 2

Our route would pass close by some of the places to which my men at arms had retired or bought land and I decided that we would visit with them. Since our service to the Duke of Burgundy, there had been little opportunity for men at arms to earn coin. There were always opportunities close to the borders, but my men had made too much money to risk their lives for the paltry pickings there. I knew that some would have hung up their swords and sought the reward of peace after a life of war. That was what Red Ralph, my mentor had done; he had become a horse farmer. Oliver the Bastard had surprised me when he had gone north to Lincoln. He had struck me as a warrior through and through. He had an inn close to the castle in the King's city, and rather than stay in the castle I chose to put coins in my old warrior's purse.

He was delighted to see me, "My lord! You should have warned me that you were coming."

The stables had been empty and when I looked around the empty drinking and eating area I said, "Because you are inundated with guests, Oliver? Come, this is me. What has happened?"

He shrugged, "Running an inn is not as easy as drinking in one. Let us say that this inn is drinking more of my coin than I would like."

"And your wife?"

He shrugged, "Left me after six months and ran off with a minstrel."

Rafe shook his head, "The old Oliver would have followed her and taken the man's jewels before dragging her back here!"

Oliver smiled, "I had no need. Within a month they were both dead of the pestilence. God punished them but I must confess that I wished I had used my rondel dagger instead!"

I could see little point in dancing with words, "Oliver, this life is not for you. The King needs me for a war and I am required to supply men at arms and archers. Would you return to my service?"

His eyes told me the answer before his words, "Aye and in a heartbeat! I would sell this and become that which I was intended to be, a bastard with a sword!"

I patted his waist which had burgeoned since he had left me, "Then sell it and lose the unborn child you carry! Resume your training and meet at Weedon in three months. You will need to have two horses, a squire and your own men to follow you." I looked at him to make the point. He would have to spend money.

"Do not worry, my lord, I have fellows in mind. It is to be France?"

"It is."

"Then whatever coin I spend will be well spent for the French pay good ransom!"

"Good, and now, while the others are taken to their rooms and your people have food and ale brought, then I will pick your brains."

Oliver's inn, whilst not as successful as he had hoped, was a mine of intelligence. Lincoln was one of the main places which men visited whilst on the north road and they were often looser with their tongues when drinking. I asked Oliver about the gossip. Oliver had always been a clever man and he told me much. None of it was admissible in a court and some of the lords he mentioned might have challenged his word with an offer of combat, but it provided me with some names that I could investigate. All had been critical of the King or his father. I knew that in some cases it was just because that was their nature but the others were men I had suspected before. The one common factor was that they all lived in the north and that I had heard their names before. I was surprised at one or two of the names for King Henry had been generous with them. Then I remembered King Richard who had, sometimes, made ill-advised decisions which had cost him dear. I did not think that King Henry had misjudged some of these men but, as de Vere had shown me, some men had ambitions far beyond any reasonable expectation and could be duplicitous and spin plots which would be the envy of a spider.

We headed for York where I hoped to speak with the Archbishop and, perhaps, find Dick Dickson who lived just north of the city at Easingwold. Archbishop Bowet was an old man, but for all that he was as loyal a man as one could wish for. He had been appointed by King Henry's father and replaced the Pope's choice. Despite his age and relative infirmity, he had his ear to the ground, and I hoped to hear confirmation of the names given to me by Oliver. I was better known in the south and west than the north, but my livery was still recognised and my close association with King Henry guaranteed me a cordial welcome when I reached the city. I was invited to dine with the Archbishop, and I let my men at arms, archers and servants, frequent the alehouses of York. I knew my men and they would gather valuable intelligence for me! Walter would not have to wait at the table as the Archbishop had servants for that.

The food we ate matched the infirm Archbishop and while that might have disappointed some visitors it was of no consequence to me. When you grew up scavenging in Spain then any food was welcome. I was open with Archbishop Bowet and he nodded, "I have heard rumours, too. Of course, some could be simply gossip but here we are close to the Scots and the Percy family have never been friends to the King and his family." He smiled, "Nor, I might add, the man who killed Harry Hotspur."

"The Percy family has been quiet of late; does that suggest that they are plotting?"

He shook his head, "The north, compared with the south, is poor. Most of the lords north of here cannot even grow wheat. There is much discontent. The raids from the Scots means that we use the full forty days of military service we are due each and every year. It does not take much to stir men to revolt."

"But the King cannot do much about the wheat and the Scots...!"

"Almost seventy years ago when King Edward defeated the French at Crécy the Scots took advantage and tried to invade the north. One of my predecessors and Lord Neville trounced them. If, as I have heard, the King plans to go to France then the north will be ripe for invasion. The malcontents will use that." He lowered his voice and leaned into me, "I have heard that some northern lords seek to place the Earl of March upon the throne."

"The Earl is loyal; I know that, and he would not be able to do anything about the Scots either."

"We both know, Sir William, that some men might seek to put one king on the throne just so that they could replace that man! I am a great reader of history and I believe that Simon de Montfort had just such a plan!"

He gave me some names and two of them were the same as the ones given to me by Oliver. I committed nothing to paper and I hoped that my memory would serve me. Before we left York, I visited the alms house where an old comrade, Peter the Priest had worked. He had died some time ago but, in his memory, I gave money each time I visited for they were old soldiers who lived there. Like Peter, I would not forget.

Dick Dickson had bought a large farm north of Easingwold. He had been married whilst he was still in Weedon and, as I rode into the walled courtyard of the farm, I saw that he now had four children. He had added to his family. I doubted that he would leave his wife, Anne, and their children.

When we rode in, he looked up and I saw delight upon not only his face but that of his wife. Lady Eleanor had always had time for the wives of my archers and men at arms. As I dismounted, I said, "I see that you prosper, Dick! Life is good?"

He bowed, "It is. Sir William. Will you stay the night with us?"

"I have business in Middleham else I would but when I return south, I may well take you up on the offer. I need to speak with you."

He nodded, "Anne, take Sir William's men into the kitchen. Give them some of your ale!" When they had left us, he said, "You wish me to go to war again." It was a statement and not a question. Like all my former retinue he knew my mind almost as well as I knew it myself.

"I do but I can see no reason why you should leave this... unless the farm does not prosper?"

"It prospers and I am happy, but I am an Englishman and you only go to war to serve your King and your country."

I nodded, "And yet it is not the Scots or the Welsh. King Henry wishes to have France returned to us."

He smiled, "I like this King for when he was a youth, he had neither airs nor an attitude. If my sons grew up like him then I would be a happy man! When would you want me?"

"Not for a year but you would need horses and men to accompany you."

He looked relieved, "I worried, for a moment if you needed me now. All is well. By next year, my son will be ready to go to war and I can ensure that I hire men to run the farm."

Dick's life in England's backwater meant that he knew nothing of lords or plots. That pleased me in too many ways to count!

We reached Middleham Grange just before dark. Despite our late and sudden arrival, Sir Ralph made us welcome. Now married and with sons, he looked more like his father than ever before. His waistline showed that he was not only growing older but was also comfortable with it. However, I knew that if danger threatened the north then there was no better man to defend it. Walter ran off to greet his mother. He was her favourite.

"A most welcome and happy surprise, Sir William. What brings you north? More horses?"

I nodded and said quietly, "That is one reason, but I am also here at the behest of the King who asks me to seek out his enemies."

His grim nod told me all that I wanted to know, "Then this is the perfect place to begin for north of the Tyne is a hotbed of unrest and this time it is not the Percy family."

I held up my hand, "And now is not the time to talk of such things for you are like family to me and I would enjoy this evening for what it should be. Tomorrow will be time enough and after I shall visit with your mother for it seems like a lifetime since I have seen her."

He led me into the main room and nodded, "Aye and now she is grey and shows her age. It comes to us all!"

Sir Ralph insisted that all of my men join us around the table. It was his mother's way and he had inherited good habits from her. Anne, Sir Ralph's wife who came from the powerful Willoughby family, was just delighted to see her son again. As we ate Ralph asked me how his son was faring. I know that, like all fathers, he wanted to hear good things but he was a friend too and deserved the truth.

I spoke quietly for my words were for his ears, "I believe he will make a good squire in time, but he is raw clay and he is young. It is good that he came to me whilst younger than most squires for I train him my way. When we go to war I will ensure that he is far from danger for he is too young to be able to fight men!" I told him of the incident on the road. "He did not run and was not afraid to fight but I have Rafe teaching him how to react more quickly."

Ralph nodded and laughed, "I confess that my wife brought him up gently and I was on the Sherriff's business too much when he was young. He needed rougher treatment."

"Your wife did a fine job, but he will need to learn new skills and quickly for I am to go to war for the King next year."

"Will we be needed?"

I knew he meant the northern lords, "I am not certain, but I will advise the King to leave enough men here in case we have another King David north of the border. The Scots prefer a knife to the back when they can manage it!"

Ralph looked over to his son who was laughing at something Rafe had said. Walter's mother looked happy beyond words. Ralph turned to me, "Whatever happens, for good or ill, I know that you will do your best for him. That is your way. If he needs aught then let me know for we prosper here."

"He will need a good horse for, although he will not be needed for the real fighting, we will have to ride far and wide. We still have your first mail hauberk and I am sure that will suit. Most squires ride to war with just a brigandine!" We then stopped talking war and I told him of my family for, as my squire, he had been close to them all.

The next day we all rode over to Middleham and it was there he told me of the knights he suspected. Most of the names were the same as I had already heard and centred on two men. There was, however, a new name and it was a knight called Sir Thomas Grey of Heaton or, as some men said it, Heton. As I already knew the other lords and could investigate them at my leisure, I needed to meet with this Sir Thomas. As Stephen of Morpeth lived quite close to one of his manors then I had an excuse to visit. Mary greeted me warmly and tearfully for it had been some years since Red Ralph had died and I was the last of her husband's comrades. She fussed over her grandson and when Ralph said that Walter needed a good horse, she became all business. The one she found for him was perfect. I could see a little of the courser in the animal. Sometimes, when Mary and her men used horses for breeding, they did not get the result that they sought. It did not mean it was a poor horse, but a courser had to carry a heavily armoured man and the one Walter had was just too slight. I had brought money with me and I knew the going rate for horses. I paid Mary for the twenty horses I would need, and she tried to return some of the money.

"I do not need charity, Sir William!"

"And you are not getting it. These are the prices I would have paid in Northamptonshire and I say to you that I need no charity!" She gave me a grateful smile for she had grown up if not poor then careful about every penny.

After promising to pick up the horses on our return south we left the next day for the ferry over the Tees at Stockton. Will of Stockton had returned to his roots with a young bride he had married in Weedon Church. Pippa's father was one of my tenants but she had fallen for my handsome man at arms. I knew that he lived in a village called Bewley which lay north of Stockton. I would visit with the lord of the manor but not stay in Stockton Castle. Sir Thomas of Stockton was not known to me, but he was a northern lord and the crossing of the Tees was a vital one. While his name had yet to come up it would not hurt to discover his loyalties.

The castle was a strong one as they had no bridge and, having just a ferry, it would be easy to deter the Scots and bar the crossing of the river. Of course, an invading army could head to Piercebridge or Barnard Castle but that would add time to an invading force of Scots and York could be warned. Leaving my men in the outer bailey I was admitted to the Great Hall to speak with Sir Thomas. He looked old and had grey hair but when I spoke with him, I realised he was younger than I was. It soon became apparent that the reason he looked old was because he had suffered a wound. He bade me sit and wine was brought.

"I am Sir William Strongstaff. King Henry has sent me north to speak with the Lords of the Northern March."

He smiled although the scar he had on his face made it a cockeyed smile. "You are here to test the loyalty of the men to the north, Sir William."

It took all of my powers of concentration to hide the shock on my face. "King Henry has just received the crown and buried a father. Should not a new king gauge the mood of the land?"

He laughed and quaffed the wine in one. I detected no sign of a lady of the house and I could smell the drink on the knight. I began to understand him.

"I lost my son at Shrewsbury and the scars you see, as well as the ones you cannot, were my reward for following Henry Percy. My wife died and I have paid the price for following the wrong side. I saw you at the battle and you fought bravely but I could see then that you were Henry's man. You not only protect the King you are his butcher too and if I were an enemy then you would happily end my life for the son of Bolingbroke."

"My lord, tread very carefully for the words you speak are treasonous!"

He refilled his goblet and laughed again. It was not a happy laugh. "You think I care? End my life now! You will be doing me a favour. I cannot go to war for I can neither ride nor use my right arm." It was only then I noticed that he had done everything left-handed. "I sit and I drink, and I wait to die! Now you have your message for your King! I might wish him harm as I might you, but I have not the means to do so. Leave me or take me in fetters to the Tower. I care not!"

I stood and, turning on my heel, left. A priest met me at the door, "My lord, do not be hasty. Sir Thomas has lost all and I can tell you that he is in great pain. He drinks to dull the senses and to make him forget!"

"Priest, he is a man and he made choices when he followed Hotspur. A man lives with those choices or he is not a man. I will do naught to him for he has given himself an early death, but I ask you a question. Is he part of a conspiracy to overthrow the King?" My eyes bored into him. "If you lie to me then you will die! Your cross will not save you!"

He looked sad, "I am a man of God and I cannot lie. You are the first noble to visit here these ten years. His steward keeps the manor paying taxes to the Bishop and I tend to his soul. He will not see another Christmas."

I nodded, "Just so, then I shall tell the King that he should advise the Prince Bishop to appoint a better lord of the manor next time!" Bishop Langley had been the executor of Henry Bolingbroke and was still at Windsor. I knew that when I spoke with King Henry, he would heed my advice. This was not the place to have a lord who was a potential enemy.

I mounted my horse and was silent as we rode through the busy port. My men knew better than to speak for one look at my face had told them all that they needed to know.

The village of Bewley was a spread-out affair and we did not know exactly where Will's farm was. I suppose I could have asked in Stockton, but my mind had been filled with anger and I had left it as soon as I could. Sir Thomas had lost and could not accept that defeat. They were the worst kind of rebels. Rafe took charge and stopped at the first farm we found. The land around here was low and close to the sea. Storms could wash in and inundate the fields. I wondered why Will had chosen such a place to farm.

"The man you seek, master, has a farm half a mile yonder up that track but he is not much of a farmer and I have not spoken to him this last six month."

"This way, Sir William." Rafe pointed and looking up I saw that we had been directed down an overgrown track heading south and east. In a way that helped to expunge the thoughts of Sir Thomas from my mind. There was no sign of wheels having gone down the lane nor horse droppings. I looked ahead seeking a sign of the smoke which would mark the house. I could not see anything ahead of me except, in the distance, what looked like a derelict farm. I wondered if we had been given the wrong directions.

When we reached it, I saw that the farm was not derelict; the door still stood but apart from a few fowl clucking and foraging there was no sign of life. The barn door swung on its hinges. In fact, the only sign that anyone had lived here were the two graves which were covered by wildflowers and mounted with two crudely made crosses. I dismounted, "Matty, Nat, go around the back and see what you can see. Walter, watch the horses. Rafe and James, draw your swords and come with me. I like this not!"

I did not draw my own sword. None of our horses had reacted to the silence. They did not sense danger, but I feared what I would find. I pushed open the creaking door and Rafe and James stepped into the darkness before I could. There was a smell which assaulted my nose. It was of dirt and an unwashed body. Suddenly something arose and charged towards me as I was framed in the open door. Rafe just reacted and he punched the figure to the ground with the pommel of his sword. It landed face down and James used the toe of his buskin to kick it over. It was Will of Stockton!

Rafe sheathed his sword and knelt down to see if he had killed him. They had been friends. "He lives, lord, but he stinks of stale ale!"

I looked around. There was no sign of a woman's hand or, indeed, any hand. "There is a tale here. We will spend the night. James, fetch Matty and Nat and then put the animals in the barn. Have Walter join us."

Left alone with Rafe, he said, "Where is Pippa, his wife? This is not the Will of Stockton I knew."

I nodded my agreement, "You fetched him a mighty blow, Rafe. See if there are candles and give us light. He will not awake soon."

"I did not know who he was, lord, and I did not wish you hurt on my watch!"

"And yet you did not strike to kill. Why was that?"

He looked down at his former friend, "I know not except that something stayed my hand and I thought to incapacitate him."

I smiled, "The bonds of brothers in arms, Rafe, that was what stopped you killing an old comrade."

We found tallow candles which burned with a thin light and gave off acrid smoke. What had happened to Will? He had had money when he left Weedon. I saw little sign of it in the farmhouse. When Walter came in, the two of us examined the farm while Rafe tended to Will. There were a number of rooms; it was not the mean property we had seen in the main village. The bedroom stank and it was obvious that Will had had accidents whilst sleeping. "Take off the bedding and throw it out!" The kitchen had little food. We had what I called our road rations: a ham, some dried beans, cheese and the like. We would make a camp stew. There was a barrel of ale in the pantry and that was half full. It was clear that Will had drunk himself into this state and there had been no Pippa to restrain him. The graves came to mind and even before I spoke with Will I began to form a picture of what had happened.

By the time we returned to the main room Rafe had cleaned up Will who was still out cold. Matty and Nat did not know Will and they looked down in disgust at the shell of a man before them. James saw their looks and snarled, "Do not judge this man until you have heard his story. Rafe and I have stood in a shield wall with him and there is no braver man. I may no longer be able to fight in a battle, but I can still give a good account of myself."

"James, peace. Matty and Nat do not know Will and are you not surprised at the depths into which he has fallen?"

He nodded and Rafe said, "The flowers and the graves, lord, I think Pippa has died. Will was besotted with the maid. He was not a young man, and this was his dream. I am lucky, I had no such dream and I am content to be a servant who serves you still. If my dream was shattered then I, too, might descend into a jug of ale. I have seen others suffer the ailment and few have the strength to climb out."

Darkness fell and we had a rough stew ready when Will awoke. We had brought the straw-filled mattress from the bedroom and placed it before the fire. We had found enough dried kindling and firewood to make a cheery blaze and it gave off better light than the tallow candles. Rafe had bandaged Will's head and as my former man at arms sat up his hand went to his head. I nodded to Rafe who spoke. Rafe and he had shared a hovel on campaign.

Rafe said, "Sorry that I fetched you such a clout, Will of Stockton, but I thought you meant to hurt Sir William."

Will looked up and saw the sea of faces. He shook his head and regretted it immediately, "That was Sir William? I saw the door open and thought it was an enemy."

Rafe held his arm out and pulled Will to his feet, "No, my friend, the enemy was in the jug of ale. You have fallen a long way!"

I said, "Walter, give your seat to Will and bring him some food."

"I need no food, Sir William."

"I command that you eat!" He nodded, "And when you have eaten then we can hear your tale and I will tell you why I have come here." He glanced up and saw the mailed Matty and Nat. "They are my men at arms, Will. Do you remember when you were like them and not this apology of a man who pisses his bed and lets his farm fall down around his ears?" I knew that I was being harsh, but I had heard the self-pity in his voice. Echoes of my father came to mind. When my mother had left him, he had been the same and he, too, had fallen into a jug of wine. Old Tom, Red Ralph and the others had had to show him harsh care to save him.

Matty said, "Nat and I will sleep in the barn, lord, we can keep a watch, and this is a place for old friends this night. We would not intrude."

That alone proved that I had hired good men and I nodded. Walter brought in the food and the five of us sat in silence as Will ate. That he had not eaten well became clear but the more he ate of the rough stew the clearer became his eyes. He nodded as he pushed away the wooden bowl and spoon, "I think I had forgotten the taste of food. That was good," he looked at my squire, "Walter is it?"

"Aye, I am the son of Sir Ralph of Middleham Grange."

"I thought you had the look of him." He shook his head, "I am sorry that you came, my lord. It would have been better if you had not and then you would remember me well and not the wreck of a man you

31

find." I said nothing. He would have to tell me his story in his own time. I saw his hands shake. He needed a drink and I nodded to Rafe who poured him a small beaker of ale. Will took it and sipped it slowly. "When I came here, I was the happiest man in the world and Pippa and I loved the life on the farm. Then, two years since she was with child and that made us even happier. I did not know that a cruel God would snatch happiness from me."

The other three clutched at their crosses. I put my hand on the back of Will's, "Will, we both know that God does not do such things. There are other forces at work."

He nodded, "Aye, well the baby came in the middle of winter and hereabouts they can be harsh. We were cut off and I could not seek help from the women of the village. Pippa was little more than a girl and…" he shook his head and relived that moment. "The women might have known what to do but I did not. I tried my best, but the bairn was born dead and then Pippa…Lord, there was more blood than at the battle of Shrewsbury. She died in my arms. The snow lay thick outside and I could not bury them for a sennight." He pointed outside. "Their graves are there."

He finished off the ale and I nodded, "Will, I came here to offer you the chance to fight for me again. I came with little expectation that you would choose to do so for I thought you would be happy and content. I see that you are not but, equally, you are in no condition to stand in a battle. I could not risk the men who stood around you and yet I would still have you with me." He looked up at me and his eyes were huge pools of sadness. He had lost his family and, it seemed, I was snatching away any hope of redemption in battle. I was not but I wanted Will to face the reality of his position. "You still have your mail and your weapons?"

He waved a hand, "They are somewhere."

"That is one thing at least. Rafe, you and James are his friends. If you would be willing, then I would leave you here with Will while I travel north to continue on the King's business. See if you can make a warrior of him. He may not be able to be a man at arms, but I need men upon whom I can rely, and Will of Stockton was once such a man."

Rafe nodded, "It is the least I can do but what of you, my lord, if aught happened to you then Lady Eleanor would make a necklace of my parts!"

I smiled, "I doubt that, but I am content with James, Walter and my two new men at arms. The question is, Will of Stockton, are you willing?"

"Aye, my lord. Pippa would not like the man I have become."

"Then while I am gone have the bodies reburied in the churchyard at St. Cuthbert's in Billingham." I handed Rafe some coins. "This will pay the priest. Then see if you can sell this farm and buy a sumpter for Will. He can have one of Mistress Mary's horses when we get to Middleham."

"Thank you, lord, I do not deserve this."

"Aye, you do for you were one of my men and Pippa was one of my people. Lords who care do not forget such things!"

Chapter 3

Our visit with Will affected us all. James was just grateful, I think, that he had a life untinged with such tragedy while Matty, Nat, Christopher White Arrow and Jack Gardyvyan saw a future they did not relish. They were both young men and had not thought beyond the campaign in France. Rafe and James showed them one future while Will another. Walter was just shocked at the fall from grace; he had never met Will but, as we had been travelling north, Rafe had told him of the warrior. I wondered how many other such stories there were. All of those who had left my service had parted on good terms and I had assumed that they were happy men. We headed north for the most difficult part of our journey and I was one man light! I was entering the borderlands of the north which were dangerous enough at the best of times, but I was the King's man heading for that part of England which did not like him. The very men who were sworn to keep the roads safe might be complicit in eliminating me. We rode as though we would be attacked at any time.

We passed Durham without incident as I knew that we would. The Bishop was the King's man and his knights would uphold the rule of law. I could have risked the bridge at Newcastle but that was a longer journey to Morpeth. Prudhoe was out of the question as the castle there was now ruled by the Percy family and that left the bridge at Corbridge. There was no castle there, but I knew, from Sir Ralph, that the hall had a pele tower as did the church. This was a favourite crossing of the Tyne for the Scottish brigands. I did not know who was the lord of the manor, but we would have to seek accommodation there. It was getting on to dusk when we approached the hall. I knew that we were watched as we approached for I saw movement at the top of the tower which would be a refuge in times of danger. I dismounted as the huge and solid-looking door was opened. It was an older man who answered the door.

He glanced down and saw my spurs, "Can I help you, my lord?"

"I am Sir William Strongstaff and I am here, in the north, on the King's business. My men and I seek shelter for the night." I saw the doubt on his face, and he glanced behind him. "We have little accommodation here, my lord. Hexham Priory has beds and it is not far away."

I shook my head, "That is four miles hence and darkness is upon us. I have a royal warrant from the King!"

"His lordship is not at home!"

I was tiring of this, "Christopher White Arrow and Jack Gardyvyan, check the outside and see if there is danger."

"Aye, lord!"

"James, put the horses in the stable. Walter fetch our bags." I pushed into the entrance chamber. I saw that there was a door to the right which led to the pele tower. I nodded at it and said, "Nat!"

"Aye lord." He shouldered aside the steward and headed up the stairs to find whoever had been watching. And Matty pushed past the steward who stood, defeated.

"My master will not be happy about this intrusion."

"And who is your master?"

"Sir John Grey."

I frowned for Sir John lived close to the Welsh borders and was a staunch supporter of the King. "I know Sir John and he would be unhappy with my treatment. Come, steward, for I am a justice and I am less than happy with your attitude. It was not your master who barred his gates to us was it?"

He looked unhappy but the threat of legal action made him speak the truth. "It was my master's elder brother Sir Thomas who told me that I was not to allow any lords not known to him to stay the night."

So the name of Sir Thomas Grey rose once more and added to my suspicions. "Your master would not be happy about that."

"My master rarely visits here, my lord, but Sir Thomas frequents it often. He has just acquired the manor of Wark, my lord and that lies just north of here."

I heard a noise coming from the pele tower and Nat emerged with a dishevelled looking man who had been roughly handled by my man at arms. "This one took exception to me, my lord."

The belligerent man did not seem cowed by my presence, "I serve Sir Thomas Grey and you had better be careful how you speak to me!" Nat silenced him with a blow to the stomach which had him retching for air.

I looked at the Steward who said, "Sir Thomas left this man here and he was commanded to see that all of Sir Thomas' orders were obeyed."

"Bind him and we will ride to Wark on the morrow and speak with this Sir Thomas Grey."

"My lord, he is not there. He is at Heton Castle which is close to Norham!" The steward was now a mine of information. Obviously, the man left by Sir Thomas had terrified him.

"Then we will take him back to Wark so that Sir Thomas knows that you had little choice in this matter, steward. And now we would be fed!"

Any protests from Sir Thomas' man were silenced by a second cuff from Nat. Our prisoner slept between my two men at arms and, strangely enough, proved to be of little trouble. The next day we rode, with the prisoner on the sumpter, the few miles north of the river to Wark. We gained entry to the castle, but the man had been correct, Sir Thomas was not at home. I spoke with his captain of the guard.

"This man tried to prevent Sir John Grey's steward from allowing us to stay in the tower at Corbridge. As we were on the business of the King, we brought him here for Sir Thomas' judgement. He told me that he was acting under Sir Thomas' orders, but I found that hard to believe as the castle does not belong to him. I will be in the area for a few days more if Sir Thomas needs me to provide further information."

The Captain of the guard had been at Shrewsbury. I did not recognise him, but he knew me and told me so when he answered. "Sir Thomas is at Alnwick, my lord, but I will inform him when he returns. Where shall I tell him that you will find him?"

"I have business on the border at Norham and then at Morpeth."

As we headed for Morpeth, Matty said, "I did not like the Captain, my lord. He took all that you said too readily."

I nodded, "And that is why I told him Norham first and then Morpeth. I think that men will be sent north to Norham and when they find us not, they will seek us at Morpeth. I have laid a trap for King Henry needs evidence of wrong going. We need Sir Thomas to act!"

Nat shook his head, "I am not happy about this, my lord, for it puts you in danger and there are but five of us now."

Walter butted in, "Do not forget me. My father spoke to me at Middleham and told me what I had to do. I am Sir William's man and I must show it!"

"Nat, I will not risk lives. I am confident that with two good men at arms, two of the finest archers in England as well as James and Walter we can handle whatever bandits they send at us. Whoever comes will not wear livery and will have little sign that they serve a knight but the fact that the only person who shall know where we go will be Sir Thomas Grey will damn him in the eyes of the King! We will be vigilant."

I did not know where in Morpeth my ex-man at arms lived. We stopped at the first inn we found and asked there. As I had expected he was well known, and we were given directions to a house just outside the town walls. Stephen had been one of my more successful men at arms when it came to hanging on to his hoarded coins, for he did not gamble nor did he use them to buy doxies. Consequently, the house he had bought for himself was an impressive one. As it was outside the walls of the town and the town was liable to Scottish raids the man who had built it had had a ditch with a stone wall behind the ditch. The gate was barred, and so James hammered on the door.

We seemed to be there an age and then we heard a distinctly northern voice shout, "Whoever you are we don't want any of what you are selling! Go away!"

I shouted, "Tell Stephen of Morpeth that Sir William Strongstaff is here to speak with him on the King's business."

"How do I know that you are who you say you are?"

James Jameson shouted, "Open the door and you will find out!"

I said, mildly, "Peace! This is the borderlands and we do not know what problems they have here which we do not."

There was silence and then the door swung open. I saw that there were five armed men and one of them was Stephen of Morpeth. He struck one of the men a blow to the back of the head, "Fool! This is Sir William!"

"I did not know!"

Stephen looked apologetic, "I am sorry, my lord, I beg you to enter. These are dangerous times." There was an edge to his voice which worried me. We rode through the gates and I saw that the wall had a fighting platform. The hall itself was also made of stone and the entrance was up an external staircase. This was a hall to be defended. Stephen pointed to a wooden building, "The stables are there. Harry, show his lordship's men."

I handed my reins to Walter and followed Stephen up the stairs. I could tell that this was a bachelor's home for there were neither wall hangings nor floor coverings and the goblets and platters on the table were simple wooden ones. Stephen still did not spend much of his coin. He waved me to a seat before a blazing fire and I warmed myself for the north was colder than Weedon!

"Is that Ralph's son who is your squire?" I nodded, "He has the look of his father. The two men at arms I do not recognise."

"So many of you left me, as rich men I might add, after serving with John the Fearless that I was forced to employ more men."

"And you wish to stay, my lord?"

"If you are happy to let us do so then yes."

He smiled, "Sir William, I owe all of this to you. Stay as long as you wish for we are a simple group of men but we live well."

"They are men at arms?"

"Better and more accurate to say they were all warriors. I am the only one with mail and a little plate but they all have weapons and know how to use them. I found most of them when I returned home and discovered that they had been let go by their lords. The ransoms from Shrewsbury meant that many families simply could not afford to pay for soldiers."

He poured us two large beakers of beer. Here in the north that was the preferred drink. He toasted me. It was a good strong beer, "And some fought against us?"

"Aye, but none bear a grudge. So, my lord, this King's business, what exactly is it?"

"Before your men return, I have to tell you that part of it is delicate. The King believes that there are men who seek his life and wish to replace him with the Earl of March!"

He swallowed all of his beer in one, "Then there is a simple solution; take the Earl of March's head and the problem is solved!"

Common soldiers saw simple solutions. I knew that such an act would divide the country but I, too, saw it as a way out. "You know Hal and he would not countenance such an act without evidence, and I believe that the Earl of March is innocent in all of this." I knew this for when I had served King Richard Edmund Mortimer had been his named heir and I got to know the boy. I did not believe that he would take the throne. "We have heard rumours of Northern Lords who are behind it. The Percy family?"

He shook his head, "If you think they are behind this then you are wrong. We took two generations of their family and they are broken. I am not saying that they would throw a feast the like of which the north has never seen if King Henry died, but they will not raise a finger to help conspirators. The ransoms and the punishments they received hurt them. But, my lord, there are others, and some are neighbours of mine. Sir Thomas Grey, Lord Scrope of Masham and the Earl of Cambridge, Richard of Conisburgh, are not to be trusted."

"You have evidence?"

"Not as such, they are too clever for that. But Grey is now tied to Conisburgh by marriage and he has gone into debt to do so. The Earl of Cambridge is descended from King Edward and if anything happened to the Earl of March…"

"My thoughts exactly. I had not heard Grey's name until we came north." I told him of the incident at Corbridge.

"The younger brother is a good man and a loyal one too." I already knew this. "Sir Thomas has a guest who is French!"

"You seem to know a great deal, Stephen, how is that so?"

"The lord of Morpeth is not a strong lord and he has to follow all of the commands of the Earl of Cambridge. There are many men in the garrison who do not like this for they are loyal Englishmen. I drink in the town and they talk. I do not give an opinion, but I listen."

"And this Frenchman?"

"I misled you for there is a knight and others arrived with him. They arrived about a year ago and they are guests at Alnwick. I am guessing that you would visit with the Earl there?"

I nodded, "I had intended to go to Heton close by Norham."

"You are putting your neck on the block, eh, to try to ensnare Grey. It will be dangerous. My men and I will come with you."

Almost by magic, our men entered, noisily. I said, "You have no need."

"I grow bored and it will be good to ride with you again."

"There is another reason I come and that is because I have to provide lances for the King."

"Not Scotland or Wales, I hope!"

"No, Stephen, France!"

He grinned, "Then we will follow your banner for it brings profit." I waved a hand around the room. "This place runs itself. It cost me most of my gold, but it is in profit and that is rare up here. I have a reeve and he is a good one." He stood, "I will get one of my men to cook some food. Hob, show Sir William's men to their chambers. Sir William and his squire shall have the room next to mine." He smiled at me, "The lord who lived here had one room and his wife the one next to him."

"What happened to him?"

"The plague and although I paid more than I wanted I almost stole the land from his heirs who feared the pestilence would remain! We cleaned the house and the buildings, and we are healthy"

My words with Stephen had done some way to making up for my anger with Sir Thomas! As we ate a simple stew washed down by ample ale, we formulated a plan. "You four are unknown to any who might wish us harm. We will not travel together on the road, but you will be a mile or so behind us."

Stephen nodded, "And which road, lord? The best road passes close to both Alnwick and Warkworth and they are Percy castles. They would

39

not harm us but word of our formation might leak to the enemy in addition to which that is a longer route to Norham and Heton."

"We will not make it easy for our enemies. We will take the Rothbury road and that will allow us to approach Heton from the south. I will use Christopher White Arrow and Jack Gardyvyan as scouts so that we will be spread out over two miles. Stephen, you know this land better than any, where do you think we might be ambushed?"

"Far enough from Heton so that Grey and his supporters can deny knowledge and involvement and yet close enough so that they can guarantee that we will have to use the road."

"Wooler!" We all looked at Hob. He shrugged, "I fought nearby with Hotspur and the road splits there. The road has two forks and both end up at Heton. It is ten miles from Heton. They would not know which one we took, and they could stay in the village. The Baron of Wooler has better lands further south and his estate is managed by a reeve. The Grey family are the powerful ones there and the reeve would have to do whatever they wanted."

Stephen nodded, "You have your uses, Hob! That makes sense to me for, as I recall, there is an inn and the ale there is not too bad. If I was hiring some expendable killers to rid me of a nosey lord, I would use Wooler."

He was right, the killers would be expendable. If you were gambling for a kingdom, then you had to be ruthless. I remembered others, like de Vere, the Earl of Oxford, who had gambled and lost. Henry Bolingbroke had been more subtle in his attempts to grab the throne. I was silent as the men around me discussed the ambush. I was thinking of Grey and the other two senior conspirators. None were close to King Henry. Sir John Grey was but from what I gathered he and his brother were estranged. They were relying on the impression many people in England had of King Henry. He was riotous and still too young to be king. The fact that he had not yet wed added to the illusion. I knew the King. He would marry but he was single-minded and he wanted France first! I did not know the three leading conspirators and that meant they did not know me. They would have heard of me, I was the protector of kings, but I was now so old as to be almost senile, in their eyes at least. I knew that William Marshall had been active long into old age but perhaps they had forgotten him. I would use my age as a weapon. If they thought me to be too old to fight then they were in for a shock. What I needed was to speak to the Earl of March. He was the key to all of this. How much did he know? I had enough to go to the King and give him my suspicions, but they were still unsubstantiated. The King and I believed that Mortimer would remain loyal but what if we were wrong?

I was suddenly aware that all those around the table were silent and looking at me. Stephen smiled, "My lord, are you tired? Matty here asked a question and you did not seem to hear it."

I shook my head, "Your ale is good, Stephen, and I have much to occupy my mind. Some of you seated with me know that I have been given the task of watching the Kings of England and that weight is heavy upon my shoulders."

Stephen nodded, "Then fear not because you will be protected not by fickle lords but the oaks of England!"

We finalised our plans. Wooler was twenty miles away and would take most of the day to get there. They would have men watching the road from the south. This was not the country to travel at night and the watchers would return to Wooler when it became dark. I told Christopher and Jack that when they spotted the watchers they were not to show that they had seen them.

"And if we do not see them, lord?"

"Then I am wrong, and we will have wasted a journey. If that is the case, then we will call at Heton Castle and speak with Sir Thomas. He will not be there unless I am completely wrong about him, but we will speak with his people and then carry on to Norham."

I doubted that I would be wrong. When we had finished our planning the others all went to sharpen their weapons and mine. In Stephen's case, he had to take out his mail and plate and examine it all. For the first time since France, he was going to war and from the way he sang as he did so he was happy.

This was not the flat and civilised land of Northampton. The farms here were small and the fields they tilled tiny compared with those south of the Tees. The land rose and fell, riven with small streams. Here men raised cattle and sheep. They kept both close to their farms and watched them carefully. The twisting, turning roads passed between dry stone walls and hedgerows, they towered over riders and made them feel enclosed in a maze. There were many woods, and, in the distance, we saw forests rising to the uplands of the west. To Matty and Nat, this was almost a foreign land and I was glad that I had, riding a mile behind us, Stephen and his men.

We had arranged a code so that we would have a warning of danger. When my archers spotted the watchers on the road then Jack would discard his archer's cap. If we saw that on the road then we would know that there was danger ahead. Stephen's men would pick it up. We were about two miles from Wooler when I spied the cap. We had Walter leading the two sumpters we now had to carry our goods. He was the least experienced and even a lamed man at arms like James Jameson was better protection for me than an untried youth. We all saw the hat, and all reacted in the same way. We slid our swords in and out of our scabbards. Our hands went to our helmets. This was where I missed a shield. Until that moment all of my fears could have been groundless, and I could have been making far more of the meeting with Sir Thomas Grey's man than it merited. Now that my archers had spied danger then it was confirmed, and I knew that men would die!

As we neared Wooler, with the sun slowly setting over the distant Cheviots, I began to smell the woodsmoke which told us that we were close to a village. The smell of animal dung in the fields grew stronger. My two archers had slowed a little as they neared the village so that we would all be closer together. Stephen and his men, having seen the hat, would even now be riding around the village to approach it from the north. We had assumed that any hired swords would know my reputation and I did not think it was arrogance to assume that they would try to outnumber us by two to one. When we had discussed the ambush, my men at arms, past and present, had shown their knowledge by guessing where the ambush would take place. They would want us in the open and they hidden. Wooler had a green, a common area for grazing in the centre of the village. We assumed that would be where they would try to take us. They would be hidden, and we would be in the open. Of course, our timing helped us for it would be darker than they would have wished.

I saw that, as we neared the two archers who were now less than two hundred paces from us, the village was largely one road passing between houses. I could see, in the fading light, one grand building and that would be the hall of the lord. Other, smaller houses spilt out towards the centre but what struck me was the absence of people. Normally, at this time of day, before men went to their homes for their evening meal, they would gather, for the weather was clement, to discuss the day. Places like Wooler were tightly knit communities. The absence of men was a warning. I used the shadows to draw my sword and hold it by my side. There would be no warning, and this would not be like the Lollard attack. Arrows would fly and the killers would try to unhorse us in the first attack.

Christopher White Arrow and Jack Gardyvyan halted close to the first house in the village. The light was so poor that I doubted that they could pick out details and my two archers dismounted to string their bows. Our horses and their clattering hooves kept moving closer to them and those waiting would just hear what they expected to hear; we were drawing closer. Matty and Nat, the ones with armour, nudged ahead of James and me. The two archers remounted and holding their bows and an arrow in their right hand followed. A nervous Walter brought up the rear.

It was one thing to expect an attack, but I knew that I was still a little fearful for we did not know when they would strike. Some of the houses had a sort of second floor to them and, as we rode through, we were level with them. The openings to allow wind through, wind holes, were dark. That in itself was not reassuring. There could be men with crossbows and as the openings were less than five paces from our heads then any missile would cause death. Of course, the only way that such openings could be used, and guarantee success was to have each one filled with a killer. As we neared the green, I knew that our attackers were waiting there.

That they were seeking my life became clear when the first arrows, sent prematurely, came directly at me and not the two men at arms who preceded me. I wore a cloak, surcoat and mail. Under the mail was my padded aketon. However, when the arrow hit my chest, I knew that the archers were not using bodkins and that meant they were not true longbowmen. I would be bruised, and my chest would hurt but that was all.

I spurred my horse and galloped towards the hidden archers. I knew that there would be other killers, but the archers were the ones who could hurt James Jameson and Walter. My archers had dismounted and nocked arrows. The rest of the ambushers raced from cover to come to get at me. I was more than happy to be the focus of the attack as I was the best protected. My bascinet and coif left just my nose and eyes showing. My leather gauntlets protected my hands and I knew that my sword skills would be superior to any soldier that we met. Another two arrows came at me, but they were hastily released and showed the poor quality of the archers for they missed me. In contrast, as the twelve killers emerged, my two archers showed what the best in England could do. I saw two of the ambushers knocked backwards by well flighted and powerfully drawn arrows. The two archers at whom I aimed my horse were sheltering close to a house and busy nocking another arrow when my sword hacked down to split the skull of one and then, as I turned my horse I bought my blade across the back of the other. I sliced deep into his back and, knowing that he was out of the battle, rode back to the open area. I was pleased to see that Walter had obeyed me and stayed out of danger. Even though four men lay dead we were still outnumbered and then there was a roar as Stephen of Morpeth brought his men to charge into the backs of our attackers. I could now see that the ambushers had been soldiers once or, perhaps were still soldiers, for they all wore brigandines and had helmets. Some had axes, most had swords and one, the leader, had a poleaxe. I rode at him as he raised his poleaxe to hack at Nat. My man at arms raised his shield to block the blow. It bit into the wood; the next blow would shatter it and the poleaxe was pulled back for a second strike. A poleaxe was a powerful weapon with a hammer head and a blade. When it struck and broke the shield it would either find flesh or break Nat's arm. I took no chances and as I reined in my horse and reared him to flail his hooves before the man, I brought my sword down across his neck. He had on a coif which afforded some protection, but my horse's hooves smashed into his skull and ended his life quickly and efficiently.

Whipping my horse's head around I shouted, "Yield!"

There were just four of them left alive and one shouted, "Never! Vengeance for Harry Hotspur!"

The four of them launched themselves at my men. Despite what people say there is no safe way to incapacitate someone trying to kill you. A warrior does all he can to stay alive and that means killing the man. It did not take many strokes before the four lay dead and I was able to look around. All of my men seemed whole but I asked, "Any injuries?"

James shouted, "A cut across my arm. It is nothing."

One of Stephen's men, Oswald, sat down, "I had a blow to my head. I will be fine."

"See to the hurts and then search them." I took off my helmet and waved over Walter. Cupping my hands, I shouted, "Men of Wooler show yourselves for I am the King's man, Sir William Strongstaff!" I dismounted and handed my reins to Walter, "Nat, go to the manor house with Walter and see if there is anyone within. We will sleep there this night."

Gradually light illuminated the common green as men walked over and the glow from their homes bathed the green in brighter shades The women would stay inside for they did not know us. One, a greybeard, approached me, "I am John the Smith of Wooler." His broad shoulders told his profession as did his name.

"Do you know anything about this treachery?"

He shook his head, "The leader, Gilbert of Alnwick, came three days ago and told us that they would be staying in the village and if we caused trouble our families would suffer. We are not warriors here unless the Scots come. We like the peaceful life and so we complied. Until they attacked you, we did not know what they wanted. They left us alone."

I walked closer to the blacksmith. Our eyes were on a level. "I want the truth, or I will haul every man to Newcastle and have the Sherriff try all of you for complicity in the attempted murder. You knew that they meant harm to someone!"

He could not hold my gaze and his eyes dropped, "Aye, lord, for these were Harry Hotspur's men. We did not know for whom they waited but we worked out it had to be someone from Shrewsbury."

My voice was laden with threat, "Then think yourself lucky that none of my men was hurt. We will stay in the manor house for I assume it is unoccupied."

He nodded, "The Reeve left when your men approached."

"Archers, take the road north and fetch back the Reeve. Dead or alive, I care not!" I did not want word of our survival to reach Heton.

Stephen of Morpeth came closer, he obviously wanted to talk. John the Smith turned and headed back, with the other chastened men to their families. There would be food provided. Stephen said, "We found signs of livery. These men fought for Henry Percy."

I sighed, "We have clever enemies, Stephen. The evidence I sought to link this attack with Grey is gone. The hired men who were identified would be seen as men loyal to Percy. It would be cheaper that way and there would be no link back to them. We have put ourselves in danger for nothing. These traitors know their business. Divide what they had in their purses and then take the rest to the manor house. Tonight we sleep under the roof of the manor house."

The villagers brought food and ale. We lit a fire in the manor house and were about to eat when my archers returned with a body draped over a horse. "We found him, lord, but the man was no horseman. The horse tried to evade us and, unable to control his mount, he fell and tumbled down a bank to the river. It took us some time to recover the body."

"You did your best now put the body with the other dead and then eat. Let us see the reaction of those in the castle at Heton when we deliver the news!"

Chapter 4

I had men watching all night but none of the villagers left to warn the castle. When we rose, the bodies, somewhat rat and fox ravaged, still lay on the green where they had fallen. I had no doubt that they would be buried by the men of Wooler for, despite their protestations of innocence, I knew that they had supported the action of Percy's men. With the trap sprung we could all travel together and it felt much safer. The two archers were just two hundred paces from us as we headed towards the Scottish border. There was neither ford nor bridge at Heton and, as we neared the castle, I saw the Scottish village of Coldstream across the Tweed. For once I would not have to worry about the Scots. When we had killed Douglas at Shrewsbury, we had torn the heart out of the Scots. I did not doubt that they would return to their warlike ways but not yet.

The castle at Heton, whilst made of stone, was a small one and I doubted that Sir Thomas would be at home. He had delusions of grandeur hence the betrothal of his young son to the daughter of the Earl of Cambridge. Through Sir Thomas' mother, he was related to the granddaughter of King Edward, Longshanks. Perhaps he sought to inveigle his family back into a position of power. We reined in at the drawbridge and, as the entrance was too low for horsemen we dismounted and walked across it. I smiled as the liveried men at arms parted to allow us entry. They knew who we were but it was still not evidence. The castle was held for Sir Thomas by a Captain of Arms, Giles d'Aubigny. He looked like he knew his business and I recognised a fellow professional soldier.

"Sir William, this is an honour." I did not trust his words and I studied his eyes. They showed surprise that I was still alive.

"You know me?"

"I saw you at Shrewsbury." Once again, he gave a false smile.

"From which side?"

He smiled, "Why the winning side of course." That made it worse for he had fought against Percy and was now part of the conspiracy to unseat King Henry.

"Is Sir Thomas at home?" Each question I asked was a further nail in the coffin of Sr Thomas Grey.

"No, my lord, he is at Alnwick Castle. There is some sort of meeting there." That I believed and I knew that it would be a meeting of conspirators. Perhaps I could surprise them there and then I realised that we would be murdered before we could get within ten miles of the Percy stronghold.

"A pity for I hoped to speak with him. I had a run in with one of his men at Prudhoe."

"I heard about that. The matter has been dealt with and I am certain that Sir Thomas, if he were here, would apologise for the incident." This man was smooth, and I guessed he had been well-rehearsed by Sir Thomas before he left for the conspirators' meeting.

"Good. Then we will water our horses and, if you do not mind, I will use your garderobe." I shrugged, "An old man's bladder and I am too long in the tooth to use the bushes when there is an indoor privy!"

He frowned for this was not what he had expected. I saw the dilemma. For some reason he did not want me in the castle and yet he could not refuse such a reasonable request. "Of course, my lord, I will just send a man to make sure that it is clean."

I waved a hand and strode towards the keep, "I do not mind a little dirt, Captain, for I have seen more campaigns than you have had women! Come, you can walk with me and you can tell me what brings a soldier like you to this backwater in the north."

"I serve Sir Thomas."

He could not leave my side now and we headed into the castle, "A simple answer, Captain which, I think, disguises the truth. I know that you could earn far more fighting for a company in France or Italy and the plate you wear is both expensive and well made. As far as I know, there are few tournaments in this part of the land and precious little coin."

He was uncomfortable and I could sense it. I had been around kings and their counsellors long enough to see a lie. I had also distracted him so that he forgot why he wished to keep me without and, as we entered the keep, I heard French being spoken. You do not get to guard the King of England without being fluent in French.

"So, the attack obviously failed! We should have used our men."

"Quiet, you fool. He has not left yet."

The Captain said, loudly, "The garderobe is to the right and up the stairs, Sir William!"

I nodded, "Thank you, and I can see that you have guests from France. Are they friends of Sir Thomas?"

I saw the lie in his eyes, "They are cousins of his wife and are travelling to Scotland."

I said, quietly, "Choose your friends carefully, my friend, for war is coming and you do not want to be on the wrong side of this one!"

I did not need the garderobe, but I went through the pretence of using it and then headed back to my men. The Captain awaited me. I saw no sign of the Frenchmen but then they had been warned and would be in hiding. I did not see the point in demanding that they be brought to me for I would learn nothing. We rode north to Norham which was a handful of miles away. I knew the Bishop's man, the Constable. He was not a knight but a man at arms, Roger of Tewkesbury, who had served the King at Shrewsbury.

He smiled when he saw me, and this was a genuine smile and welcome, "Sir William, what a surprise and a delight for if you are here then there is imminent action."

I shook my head, "Not really. The King goes to war next year and I am here…" I looked around. I did not know his men. "Our words were best spoke in private."

"Of course. This castle has a pleasant aspect and I have a solar with a fine view of the river. It is peaceful and the more pleasant part of Scotland."

My men would sort themselves out and leaving Walter to see to my things I went with the Constable. Once alone and with one of his most trusted men on watch I told him my task and the events which led to my arrival at Norham. "So you see, Roger, I am merely using Norham as a place to rest my head. I now have names to take to the King, but I only have suspicions and no evidence."

"I am not sure about that. The two Frenchmen you heard were part of a larger party of fifteen Frenchmen under the command of Robert, Lord of Beaumesnil. His livery is arms gules with two bars ermine. The rumour is that he is close to the Dauphin."

"So I look for a red shield with two bars." I helped myself to more of the wine, "That seems remarkably well informed for a Constable stuck out here on the edge of the world."

"The reason is, my lord, that I was out with my men, patrolling the road to Berwick when we met them. The man is arrogant and thought that, as I was not a knight, he could abuse me. When I pointed out that he was on the Bishop of Durham's land he threatened me with the Dauphin. However, they headed south, and we followed them. I did not know that two had gone to Heton. Perhaps I will ride down there and ask the castellan why they are there. I do not like Frenchmen at the best

48

of times and two in England at this time seems suspicious, to say the least."

"You say south, where do you think they went?"

"Not Bamburgh for that is a royal castle. If I was a gambling man, then I would say Alnwick."

"I have heard there is a meeting there of conspirators but would the Percy family risk the wrath of the new King by inviting Frenchmen?" It was good talking with a man I could trust and one who came from a similar background to myself. Speaking with lords and those who had inherited titles I was always wary of hidden motives.

"They are not in a position to stop this happening. When Hotspur, his son and his father died then there was a space left here in the north. The Earl of Cambridge was born here, and he uses his power well. If King Henry heard that there were French at Alnwick and that attempts on your life had been made by Hotspur's supporters, then what would he think?"

I knew King Henry and he would not make such a rash judgement, but the constable was correct. The evidence led not to the Earl of Cambridge, but the Percy family and I would have to find another way to gather the evidence.

The wounds to our two men meant that we were forced to stay for a week at Norham, but I confess that I did not regret one moment. My men and I enjoyed the company of good warriors who were far from home and without women and yet they did their duty surrounded by enemies. I admired them.

We consulted with the constable as we planned our route south. We had forty miles to travel to reach Morpeth and that was too far to reach in one day as this was not the flat lands of Lincolnshire but the rugged land of Northumberland. Stephen of Morpeth knew that the men he had left at his home could defend it against an attack, but we had to get there first. We decided to risk Wooler as our one stop and then to rise before dawn and ride as fast as we could. For my part, I knew that there would be combat before we reached Morpeth and I was not certain that we would all escape unscathed for they now knew our numbers and would plan accordingly. We acquired more arrows from the Constable and a spare sumpter. I promised that I would leave the sumpter at Durham, but Roger of Tewksbury did not seem concerned. We had enlivened his dull existence and our thwarting of England's enemies appealed to him. I would have liked to have had him at my side when we rode to France!

Stephen had two of his men ride as scouts with Christopher and Jack. The reason was clear. They were Northumbrians and knew the land. His other man, Hob, rode at the rear with Walter. I was still worried about my squire. His age had not seemed a problem when he had come to me for that was in a time of peace. This was war and was not the place for the young. When this was over, he would have learned much that would improve his skills, but we had a long way to go to achieve that! The manor house was still empty when we reached Wooler and so we occupied it. This time we searched it, but we found no incriminating documents. We ate well and the lord of the manor would be disappointed when he returned home for his wine cellar was also emptied. My men were good soldiers and did not allow a thick head to impair their judgement. We left well before dawn and headed down the road to Morpeth. The fact that Stephen of Morpeth lived north of the town helped us as it shortened our journey a little.

I confess that I was finding the long days in the saddle hard. I was the oldest by more than twenty years, but I would not show my men any weakness. My only concession was to ride with my helmet on my cantle. It weighed more than any other single piece of armour! It was good that we had men with local knowledge with us for the ambush when it came, was at a good site. We had to cross the River Coquet close to Thropton and the ambushers had chosen the spot with a keen eye. If we had not had Stephen of Morpeth and his men with us, then it might have gone ill with us. As it was John of Thropton was with my archers and he knew the village and the bridge. He halted us before we reached it.

"My lord, this does not feel right." He pointed to the trees by the river, "There are usually birds there, but I see none. I think that men will wait for us at the bridge over the Coquet. It is a wooden bridge and narrow. Crossbows and bows could make it a killing ground."

I had learned to trust these northern warriors. I turned to Stephen of Morpeth, "What do you suggest?"

"There is a ford to the east of the bridge. It cannot be crossed by men on foot, but horses can. We cross the river and then attack those waiting on the bridge."

"But you do not know the numbers!"

He laughed, "And I need not! In the first ambush, we slew them all and had two paltry wounds. I care not who waits for us; when we emerge behind them then they will fill their breeks and flee!"

With such confidence there was but one course of action. We left the road and headed across fields and through copses until we reached the ford. The river was not wide, but I could see that its speed meant a man on foot might be swept from his feet. Our horses had little trouble negotiating the obstacle for their hooves were on the riverbed the whole time. We could see the bridge upstream as we crossed, and I caught sight of metal as the sun glinted off the swords and helmets of the men waiting to attack us. John of Thropton had been correct and it looked like Stephen's plan might work. When we made the southern bank, we dismounted, and I left a reluctant Walter watching the tethered horses. Armed and ready my archers and John of Thropton led us towards the ambush. We heard their horses neigh as they sensed us, but the men seemed to ignore the sound. Stephen of Morpeth had trained his men well and we moved as one. Matty and Nat were keen to show that they were the equal of Stephen and James Jameson. My archers had bodkins nocked for we had seen metal. I led the arrow of men which moved up through the undergrowth. I glimpsed a livery and saw that it was arms gules with two bars ermine. There were some men on the southern bank but the majority were waiting in the woods to the north side. They were hidden from the road but not the river. The French were laying the ambush and I had to admire Richard, Earl of Cambridge. He was using allies and dupes to mask his trail. I was now convinced who had concocted this plot, but I had no evidence to give to the King!

My two archers flanked me with nocked arrows and when we were less than forty paces from the end of the bridge, I raised my sword to halt us and to indicate to the archers that they should draw. I did not need to tell them their targets. There were four mailed and plated men at arms at this end of the bridge. We could not see the knight but that did not matter. My archers would use bodkins to take out the mailed men and we would charge the others. As my men had said, it did not matter how many awaited us for this was our land and our country! The rest of the men I led were all waiting eagerly. They were all warriors and knew that a battle or a skirmish such as this one could be won in the first moments. The French were confident in their ambush and the fact that they had ignored the warning of their horses made them overconfident. We had to cross this bridge to reach Morpeth and they believed we would trot down the road like lambs to the slaughter. The knight and his squire were mounted on horses along with the others at the north side of the river. As two arrows slammed into two French men at arms, we ran. The knight drew his sword but his words were muffled for he wore a visor and was on the other side of the river, but the orders were clear and his men began to mount. Even as we clambered up the slope to the bridge the other two mailed men fell as Christopher and Jack used their skills well. I held my sword two handed and hacked through the leg of a mail-less warrior. The edge grated off the bone and I knew that he would simply bleed out. My men leapt up and slashed, stabbed and chopped into men who had no idea where we had come from.

Christopher and Jack made the road and began loosing their arrows at the men on the north side of the bridge. The French knight was lucky, a bodkin arrow hit his leg and a second smacked off his bascinet, but his squire was not so lucky. One of Jack's arrow struck him in the shoulder and stuck. They had almost twenty men on the north side of the bridge but the narrow bridge, as John of Thropton had said, was a killing ground, and they dared not cross it. Obviously, not all were French but, their plot foiled, they followed the French knight and his wounded squire and fled.

I cupped my hands and shouted, "Walter, fetch the horses, James, go and help him. Stephen, have your men collect the French horses and strip the bodies. We will guard the bridge."

Hob laughed, "They will still be running a week from now. Captain Stephen, I think I will enjoy following this man! Great rewards and little risk."

"Hob, you are a fool! Take the mail from the dead Frenchmen!" He shook his head, "Sorry, Sir William!"

Although it was late afternoon when we had finished, we feared no pursuit. Our archers had clearly terrified the French knight. The arrow which had clanged off his helmet could so easily, had the angle been right, penetrated and ended his life. Stephen sent one of his men to his hall to warn them of our imminent arrival and we rode through the dark to reach the sanctuary that was Stephen's hall.

It was only the next day that we realised what treasure we had. Stephen's men all gained a mail hauberk, good sword and helmet. We acquired ten horses; three of them were coursers. We had good swords which had been made in Bordeaux as well as a quantity of coins. I took none but shared the booty out amongst the others. I walked with Stephen while the booty was shared.

"So Stephen, will you still wish to join us in France?"

"Aye, Sir William, and with the money we have made I can buy more horses and hire two archers. I had forgotten how useful they could be!"

When we left, a week later, I felt happier even though I had still to find evidence of treachery. What I had done was prove that I was ready and still able to fight. Leaving Stephen to sort out his affairs we headed for Bewley, Rafe and William.

The farm close to the estuary of the Tees looked better already. I could see that Rafe had not been idle. The pit of self-pity into which Will had fallen would be a deep one but my old man at arms knew the remedy, hard work. As we rode into the yard, they both emerged from the barn. I noticed that the graves had both disappeared and I was pleased. The dead should be in hallowed ground. Will looked healthier too and actually smiled as he waved at us.

"I see you have worked hard eh?"

They saw the extra horses laden with mail and arms and Rafe said, "You have not been idle either, my lord. I can see there is a tale to tell here. Come inside for we have some interesting food to eat!"

Intrigued I dismounted and Walter and the others led the horses into the now repaired barn while I followed the two of them indoors. Straightaway I could see a difference. There was order and it was both clean and tidy. It did not smell of damp and soiled breeks. Will of Stockton must have seen my glance for he said, "I can only apologise again, my lord, that you saw the worst in me. I wish I could turn back time but..."

I sat at the table and removed my gloves for I was weary. "Do you remember the story from the Bible, Will, the one about the prodigal son?" He nodded, "Then you should know that redemption comes in many forms. You have a chance now to make something of your life. You lost one life you lived and now you have a choice and can make a new one."

Rafe brought over some freshly brewed ale and poured some for me. I looked at him and he nodded, "Aye, lord, he could be one of your men at arms. When we came then even a lamed man such as I would have been a better prospect." My men did not mince words and spoke plainly, even if that hurt. "We have worked each day and sweated out the poisons in his body and his mind. We could now sell this farm for it was derelict when we came and Will could equip himself as a man at arms."

"Good, then we have much to tell each other." I sniffed. There was an appetising smell in the air. "You said something about interesting food?"

Rafe laughed, "Have you ever eaten seal, my lord?" I shook my head, "A most interesting taste. A few miles south-east of here are mudbanks and an estuary where these beasts gather to sleep. Will and I went to hunt them." He saw my glance at Will. "What better way to test if a man was ready to become a warrior than hunting an animal which can hurt? They are a fierce and noisy beast. Their skin is thick, and a man must make a good strike with his spear if he is to pierce the skin. We killed three and we have been eating them. Their fat can be rendered down to make oil and their skin used to make buskins or capes. We have not been idle!"

I laughed, as my men came in, "That I can see. Let us eat this seal meat and we will tell you of our travails."

53

The meat was interesting, and we all enjoyed it although Walter picked his way nervously through the first few bites. As we ate, I told Will and Rafe of our journey. When the tale was over and we sat before a good fire with ale in our hands, Will asked, "Do I have a position as a man at arms then, lord?"

"You do but I am anxious to return home. I must visit with the King and give him my news. I do not think that I will please him for it is not conclusive news and I have no evidence. Will here will need time to sell his farm and follow us. You bought a sumpter?"

"Aye lord."

"Then we will leave in two days' time. It will allow us to finish the work on this farm and I can visit the grave in Billingham. I should like to pay my respects to Pippa." Will gave me a surprised look. "Do not look like that Will for Pippa was one of my people from Weedon. You, of all people, should know that it is not just my warriors who deserve my care."

"Sorry, my lord. You are right."

The graveyard in the parish church had few stones. The Black Death which had ravaged the land more than fifty years earlier had hurt Billingham more than most places. The priest knew a stonemason and I paid for a headstone for Pippa and her unnamed baby. I doubted that any would visit the grave for this was many miles from Weedon but a stone in a church showed that someone had lived, however briefly.

Leaving Will to sell his farm we headed for Middleham. While the horses were prepared, I spoke with Sir Ralph and his mother. "I leave one horse for Will of Stockton. He will be following before too long." They both nodded. "Any news of the three men I suspected?"

Sir Ralph nodded, "I have spoken with other knights. When the Earl of Cambridge inherited the title, he thought that it would come with an income, but it does not. Perhaps that is why his elder brother, the Duke of York, was so happy to give it up. The knight is poor, but he has aspirations, lord. So long as his brother lives then the Earl can have no claim to the throne, and that explains why he is backing Edmund Mortimer."

"From what you say this is common knowledge and evidence for the King. Can we not get depositions from these knights?"

He shook his head, "Much is opinion only and some of those who spoke with me owe allegiance to the Earl, Grey or to Baron Masham."

I shook my head, "He is the one I cannot understand. He fought with us at Shrewsbury. He accompanied the King's sister when she went to Hainault to be married. What is his motive? He has lands and money and he cannot gain anything from Mortimer being crowned."

Sir Ralph shrugged, "His uncle, the Archbishop of York, was executed when the Earl of Northumberland rebelled."

"That was eight years ago!"

Shaking his head Sir Ralph said, "Like you, Sir William, I am mystified but then I would never betray any man. All I know is that his name is linked to the other two. It may be that they need him to deceive the King."

Smiling I said, "You have done well and if you have presented me with a Gordian knot that is not your fault. There is a plot here and I can see only one solution. I must speak with the Earl of March!"

This time I did not head for York but went directly to Derby for that was where two of my former men at arms lived and it was somewhere I could glean more information about the Earl of Cambridge. Captain Edgar had been one of the first men to join my retinue and he was almost my age. I was not sure if he would be happy to come out of retirement. Harold of Derby was much younger, and I had been disappointed when he had left my service. My former captain had not kept in touch but that may well have been because he could not write. I knew that he had gone to his hometown and so we went directly there. We could have stayed in the castle but when I enquired about Edgar's whereabouts at the first inn we came to I discovered that he lived in the heart of the town. We found rooms and I went alone to the house he had bought. Rafe and James sought Harold.

Edgar's house was a modest one and that was in keeping with the man who had protected my back in so many battles. He was an understated man but totally reliable. An older woman answered my knock and, recognising my status, allowed me to enter. "My master is by the fire, my lord." She hesitated, "How do you know him, sir?"

It was not an unreasonable question, "I am Sir William Strongstaff and he followed my banner for many years."

"Then you do not know of his affliction?"

Fear gripped me for if this was the pestilence then I would have to leave the house without speaking to him. Often those who were struck down by the plague were cared for by women such as this. Sometimes they appeared to be immune from the disease. "Affliction?" I could not help gripping the cross which hung around my neck.

She gave a sad smile, "No, my lord, not the plague. The doctor who tends him said it is something to do with his head. He became almost paralysed one day and the doctor who came brought a priest for he thought he would die. He did not but when he recovered a little it was as though he was cursed. Half of his face is frozen, and he cannot use his left arm or leg. Job, my husband, has to act as a human crutch for him. Still, it will do him good to see an old friend." She paused, "I thought you should know, my lord."

I nodded, "You are a good woman…?"

"Joan, my lord."

I gave her a handful of coins, "For you. I am grateful that he has someone who cares."

"I do not need the money, lord, for Edgar is my uncle and he lets us live in this house."

"Keep the coins for they are easier to come by than loyal friends and family!"

It was good that she had prepared me for the shell of a man I saw before me was almost unrecognisable as the formidable warrior who had hewn heads at Shrewsbury. I smiled broadly and put a false joy into my voice, "Now then Edgar!"

He tried to rise, "My lord!" His voice sounded slurred and I saw that it only came from half of his mouth.

"Sit, old friend." I sat opposite him before the fire and held his useless left hand. It had been the one he used to hold the shield which had guarded me in battle. I owed that hand much.

"She told you then?" A man had to listen carefully to the words to understand them.

I nodded, "But you are alive and cared for. How many of those who fought with us would change places, eh?"

He shook his head, but it did not look right, somehow, "I wish I had died in battle rather than this living death where Job has to pull down my breeks for me to take a piss! It is not right, lord!"

There was little I could say to that. Until I walked in his steps then I could not judge. "You have all that you need? Enough coin?"

He nodded, "More than enough. Serving with you made me a rich man. How are Lady Eleanor and the children?"

I was on more comfortable ground and I told him of them. Joan came in with ale, ham, cheese and fresh bread. I went on to tell him of the King's campaign, but I did not mention the plot. That would not be fair for he was a loyal man and would make his own situation seem worse. He was sad to hear of Will's misfortune. When I told him of Stephen of Morpeth he became a little animated, "You should have him lead your men at arms, lord. He was the best of your men and that includes me. He deserves spurs."

"That he does and if I can manage it then he shall have them!"

We spoke for some time until Joan came in and asked, "Will you be dining with us, Sir William?"

I looked at Edgar who had pointedly not risked eating with one hand and I knew that he would not wish me to see him either struggle to eat or to be fed by Job. I shook my head and saw the relief on the half of Edgar's face which he still controlled, "I have another man at arms to find, Harold."

"He serves the Earl of Derby in the garrison, lord, and he will be glad to see you."

I frowned, "But he had money!"

"Harold was a gambler, lord. While he served you, I made sure that he was not taken advantage of but the world beyond your hall can be a cruel one."

"Thank you, Edgar, for all that you have done for me." I looked at Joan, "If he needs for anything then send word to Weedon. I do not forget those who bled for me."

She smiled, "I will, my lord, and now that I have met you, I can see that my uncle's stories were not exaggerated. You are a good man!"

I did not feel like a good man for at least three of my men at arms were worse off because I had let them go! I returned to the inn in a quieter mood. Rafe said, "We have not yet found Harold of Derby."

"That is because he is one of the garrison now."

That shocked Rafe and James for they knew that garrison duty was the last refuge of a man at arms. He took that up when all else had been tried. It had little prospect of action, the pay was poor as was the food and there was little chance of booty. The look they exchanged told me that they knew the reason. "And Captain Edgar?"

"God has dealt him an infirmity and he needs help to do almost everything."

Rafe smacked his leg, "And I complain because of this! At least I am able to earn a crust and to feed myself. I shall never complain again, lord."

James asked, "And what of Harold?"

"I will go tomorrow morning and speak with the castellan. It may be that Harold wishes employment with me again, we shall see."

I was quiet once again while we ate, and I knew the reason. The warriors alongside whom I had fought were, very largely, dead yet I was alive. I had trained so many knights that I lost count. I had fought my whole life without fearing death and I had outlived everyone but here I was still alive and now I feared death or, worse, to be afflicted like Edgar of Derby. More than ever good men at arms and archers were vital; I wanted men around me that I could trust.

One interesting thing we learned was that the Lollards, who had freed Sir John, were planning to attack churches and monasteries in the

New Year. They intended to target London. It was Matty who discovered this. He met an old comrade who had a brother who was a Lollard. It simply came up in conversation. The Lollard's brother was warning his old friend to steer clear of monasteries. I had three within twenty miles of my home! I stored that information for the King.

I went to the castle the next day. I recognised the sergeant for he had fought with us at Shrewsbury. "His lordship is not at home, Sir William, can I be of some help to you?"

I smiled for brothers in arms were always men with whom a man could speak openly. "You have a man at arms called Harold?"

He smiled, "He said he had served with you. Aye."

"I would ask him if he would rejoin my retinue."

The old sergeant rubbed his beard, "He would jump at the chance, lord but…"

My conversation with Edgar and my men had given me a better picture of Harold, "He has debts!"

He nodded, "He likes to gamble but he is not very good at it."

"How much?"

"Five florins would cover the debt."

"Make it ten and I will have a horse for him."

The sergeant nodded, "For you, Sir William, aye. I will fetch him. He is a good man, but gambling is like a disease for him."

"Then his family, my men, will cure him! Send him to the Lamb Inn. We shall await him there." I handed the coins over.

When Harold came with his horse, he looked shamefaced. He received little sympathy from Rafe and James, "As foolish as ever! It is a good job that our master is a kind man, Harold the Fool!"

I tried to make peace between my men, "Softly, Rafe, there will be time for recriminations later. Just think of Edgar and Will and think yourselves lucky that you were not struck down by such calamities. We have far to go for I would reach home by nightfall. We have been away from home long enough."

I rode with my two archers and Matty and Nat brought up the rear. It allowed the three former comrades to catch up on the news. I wondered as I rode if Uriah Longface, Kit Warhammer and Gilbert of Ely had had such a dramatic fall. Oliver, Dick and Stephen seemed to be the only ones who had prospered after leaving my company and that saddened me.

It was after dark when we reached my home and my men at arms and archers as well as Rafe and James seemed happy to return to the warrior hall they used. Walter, too, took his leave quickly. My wife was ever sensitive to such matters, "What is wrong?"

I smiled, "Everything and nothing for it is just life. A man plans and steers his course through life but events are often out of his control."

She laughed and linked me, "You speak in riddles; come within and I shall pull the cork on some good claret! I think you deserve it! I am just pleased that you have returned unwounded. You are without a wound are you not?"

"Aye, I am whole!"

When she had heard the whole story, she made the sign of the cross, "Poor Pippa. It happens but that does not make it easy. I shall tell her mother tomorrow and the priest can say a mass for her. And for Edgar to be struck down too. I understand your mood better. I shall have the builders come in next week to build more rooms for the men who will serve with you."

"Thank you, wife, I had not even thought of that!"

"And the King's business?"

"I know who the traitors are, but they are men of position and I have no evidence. I will write down what I have discovered and take it to the King in a few days."

"He is at Windsor. Oldcastle escaped! Men are hunting him." Her tone told me what she thought of the men who were guarding him. Incompetent at best and probably more likely to be corrupt. When I had lived in the Tower I had seen the type.

I shook my head, "The old fool! There is nothing wrong with having your own beliefs but to risk your neck for them seems foolish in the extreme. He could have feigned acceptance of the church and continued with his own beliefs!"

"It is blasphemy! I like Sir John and he seems like a kindly man, but his actions will bring disaster to his followers."

I nodded, "As the Cathars found to their cost." I kissed her on the forehead, "I will go say my prayers for I have many to pray for and then retire. It is good to be home!"

59

Chapter 5

While waiting for Will of Stockton to join us I sent Rafe and James to seek out my other men at arms. I realised that it was something they could do and would make them feel more like warriors. Neither could go to war again as men at arms, but they could still ride abroad. I visited with Thomas and Harry and told them what I had done and learned. I did not need to tell them to be discreet. Both had followed my banner enough to know that. With that done I sat in my solar and I began to write down what I had learned. When I wrote it upon parchment it looked impressive, but I knew that it was not for there were was not a shred of actual evidence; it was all conjecture. The presence of the French could be easily explained away as could the attack on me. I had done my best and if King Henry was not happy then there was little I could do about it. Ironically, the lack of evidence made me even more of a target and so when I rode, a week later, to Windsor, I took a good escort of my newer men at arms. I knew that the others would be arriving soon. War was coming and so the weaponsmith was busy making, not only my new armour but also mail hauberks, plate for my men at arms and swords. The King would provide the arrows and I knew that Nicholas Merbury, the Master of Ordnance, already had great stocks of arrows and bow staves. The bulk of the army would be made up of archers. France would be won not by the lance but the longbow!

On the road south we came upon many travellers and the talk was not about France but the threat to England from the Lollards. Lollardy was confined to certain areas. It had spread following the death of King Richard to Lincolnshire, Essex, Norfolk and Suffolk. Three of those counties bordered London and my lands. There was fear for we had managed to avoid civil war since the Battle of Shrewsbury and people liked peace. The fact that Christmas was almost upon us seemed to make the whole situation worse.

The King was at home and he immediately sent away his counsellors so that he could speak with me in private. I did not relish the conversation, but I faced the young King with all the courage I had faced the enemies of his father and King Richard. I laid my parchment before him and told him all. I did not exaggerate but let my simple words convey my message.

When I had finished, he said, "If I was my father then I could have them arrested and tried or even have them arrested and executed."

"But you will not do that, my lord."

He smiled, "No Will. You know me too well, but I must act soon, or people will think me weak. I have the Lollards ignoring my commands. However, your news about the Lollards may be just what I need. You have not yet finished with my quest. Come the Spring I would have you visit with the Earl of March. You know him well for he was close to King Richard and he knows you. I have made him and his brother, Roger, knights of the Bath and I believe that he is loyal but you and your keen insight into men's hearts may well divine the truth of it. I would like you and your men ready, in January, to come with me and deal with the Lollards. I thought I knew Oldcastle, but I was wrong. You are of an age with him and, if I can, I would avoid bloodshed. He might listen to you for all men respect you."

Inside I sighed for peace was a long way away, but I nodded and said, "We shall be ready. You will send for us, Your Majesty?"

"I have spies and I can use my mind. Your intelligence gives us a place to start. There are many monasteries north of London and I think it is there they will strike but I will send to you a week before I need you. Do not fail me."

"Have I ever, my lord?"

He patted my shoulder, "No, old friend, you have not!"

My wife was just relieved that I arrived back safe and sound. She was less keen on me being called upon to quell a rebellion especially a religious one. I could not bring myself to mention my attempted abduction for I thought that if the rebels were all of the same quality as the ones who had tried to abduct me then King Henry could manage it alone with just his bodyguards.

Will arrived the week before Christmas as did Gilbert of Ely and Uriah Longface. Both men had been wounded by crossbows and as that was the preferred weapon of the French then they were keen to wreak their revenge. Both brought a couple of archers with them. Neither had spent much of their coin and had taken occasional jobs for merchants and travellers. They had found that hiring archers and horse holders was profitable. The old warrior hall was filling up nicely and the new one would be ready by the Spring. My wife made a great fuss of Will. He, alone, had neither archers nor men to dress him. The latter problem was partly solved when he went to speak with Pippa's father and mother. He felt he owed it to them to explain what had happened to Pippa. They were understanding and Pippa's younger brother, Peter, asked if he could follow Will. It suited both the family and Will. Pippa's father had a smallholding and it did not yield enough food to feed them all. It seemed small recompense for the loss of a wife and a child but sometimes a man took what Fate handed out and got on with life.

My new plate and helmet were ready. William the Weaponsmith had done a good job. The helmet had been beaten from one piece of steel and there were no joints to split in battle. The plate was lighter than I had expected and, as I needed less mail, then it felt more comfortable. It cost me as much as one of my farms yielded in six months, but it was worth it. I had had a new courser from Mary, Fire was a reddish colour and big enough to intimidate Frenchmen. I had the weapon smith make a metal chamfron for his head although I did not think I would be riding him to battle. I was to be proved wrong.

It was the end of the first week of January when the message came from the King. I sent a message to my sons and son in law to ride to Clerkenwell where we would muster. I left half of my men at home for when there was unrest some men thought to make mischief while loyal men defended their country. They would get short shrift from mine. I led thirty men at arms, thirty archers and thirty others who could wield a weapon. David of Welshpool led my mounted archers. As some of my men were not mounted, we simply marched, camping in the grounds of St John's Priory. The King was there already and between us, we had just five hundred men. It did not seem much, but he had sent his brothers and other lords he could trust to the other religious targets of the Lollards. Even if we were outnumbered, we were soldiers and they were not.

Word came that the rebels had made a camp at St Giles' Field and were laying waste to the churches close by. The King wasted not a moment. We did not bother with horses but marched the two miles to their camp. They had many mailed warriors, Oldcastle and Walter Blake amongst them. There were even a few foreign mercenaries. As we neared the camp the Lollards formed ranks and I saw that there were almost two thousand of them. It said much for my men that they were not daunted by such numbers. I had Walter wait with the spearmen and warned him to stay out of the fighting. Watching would be a good lesson.

I went to King Henry, "Do you wish me to try to talk to Sir John?"

He shook his head, "Had they not destroyed churches and property then I might be willing to talk. They have incurred my wrath. Lay on, Sir William, and do not spare them!"

Altogether we had two hundred archers and I shouted, "Archers, draw!" It had been some time since I had heard the creaking yew bows being drawn in numbers and it still made the hairs on the back of my neck tingle! "Loose!" Even as the arrows fell the archers nocked and drew another arrow. "Loose!"

Instead of waiting for a third flight for I could see the effect of the first two I nodded to the King who shouted, "Cry God, St George and England! Have at them!"

I ran with my hand and a half sword held in two hands. I had not fought like this for some time, but the new armour felt light and although I could not keep up with Thomas and Harry, I was not far behind them. Instead of standing and fighting, Sir John Oldcastle turned and ran. He disappointed me. He had been a leader of this rebellion and was held in high regard. To turn and run, leaving behind those who had followed you, was inexcusable. Thomas and Harry laid about them with their swords and cleared me a path. Matty and Nat were behind me along with Walter. I saw a Swabian with a two-handed sword. I would not risk my sons and I ran to him shouting, "Swabian, face an old man if you dare!"

He must have recognised my livery for he ran at me swinging his mighty weapon. He had a longer reach with his two-handed sword and he began to swing. I was not as fast as I had been, but I still had a few tricks. As his sword came at my new gorget I swung the opposite way. The end of his sword almost grazed the new steel plate, but it did not, and I swung my sword hard into his side. As I had expected he wore good plate and I merely left a mark on the metal, but I was behind him and I swung again at the same place. This time I hurt him. As he tried to turn, I drew my rondel dagger. He needed room to swing the longer sword and my movement stopped him. I rammed the rondel dagger up under his arm. Not a killing blow, it incapacitated him for he could not use his two-handed sword one handed. As he tried to swing at me, I rammed my sword into his eye, twisting as I did so. There was no point in asking for ransom, he was a mercenary. He fell dead at my feet and then I saw that it was over, and the rebels were fleeing. They did not get far for our archers were as fast as the men they chased, and they were deadly.

Matty and Nat were shaking their heads and Matty said, "I saw the Swabian and thought, 'I hope Nat takes him and up you step and despatch him as though he was a French peasant."

I nodded as I took off my helmet, "I have been fighting for forty years and I have crossed swords with Swabians. They are more useful against horses for once they are committed to a swing, they cannot reverse their action. Walter, take his armour, sword and coin. I am sure that one of my men at arms can benefit from the plate."

A grinning Walter hurried off to obey me. The rest of my men were busy stripping the dead. They had little enough and, I think, had disposed of their treasures before they came to battle. The King walked over to me, "I made a wise choice in the man I wanted with me this day, Will Strongstaff. You know I am disappointed in Sir John. He was a rock at Shrewsbury!"

"Aye, my lord, but there he was fighting for you and your father, the King. That is the difference. Men who fight for religion, as the Cathars discovered, inevitably lose."

He frowned, for he, too, had taken off his helmet, "And what of the Crusaders? Do they not fight for Christ?"

I laughed, "No, my lord, they fight for land and coin."

I saw in his face that I had surprised him with my answer. "I will see how our other men have done but there will be executions."

"I will return to my manor, lord, if we are to fight this year…"

He leaned in to me and said, quietly, "Do not forget to visit with the Earl of March. I would know the depth of the treachery before we leave for France. It would not do to have me assassinated in France!"

King Henry was a hard man and a strong King, but he was also the bravest King that I knew. I had served under three and this one, the fourth, was without a doubt the best.

My other men at arms began to return as soon as the weather improved. Kit Warhammer returned having served as a mercenary in Spain. He did not like the clime for it was too hot. He brought with him two men who were handy with weapons and he also had good mail bought in Cordoba! When Oliver the Bastard, Stephen of Morpeth and Dick Dickson arrived I had my full quota of men at arms, but I was still light on archers. I had David of Welshpool travel across to Cheshire to recruit more archers. Cheshire had good archers and was close enough to Wales to attract Welshmen. Surprisingly enough even though I had been responsible for so many Cheshire archers dying, many wanted to fill my ranks.

David explained it away, "Lord, you are a winner. You did nothing in the battle that was dishonourable, and you were seen to be fair in victory. The men I brought follow you and not King Henry. They believe that he will win but that victory will be due, largely, to you."

I laughed, "And that is foolish nonsense."

"That may be, my lord, but we both know that such confidence can only help a man in battle!"

The influx of new men meant that we needed more surcoats and my manor was a flurry of activity. I confess that I immersed myself in it for it delayed my departure for Suffolk. I had promised the King that I would speak with the Earl of March and, thus far, I had failed to do so. The muster for the crossing to France would be in the next months and I had to act. I gave myself a week and then I would ride to Suffolk with a handful of men. Suffolk had been a hotbed of Lollardy. Whilst those who had rebelled had been publicly executed, Sir John Oldcastle was still at large. Some said he was hiding in the Welsh Marches. So long as he remained a free man then there would be many Lollards who would be desperate to wreak their vengeance on one of the men who thwarted their uprising.

Every town and village, not to mention the cities, was full of the talk of the invasion of France. When the Black Prince had defeated the French at Poitiers even I had yet to be born and that had been the last successful incursion into France. Everyone on the other side of the Channel knew that we were coming but the King was being very clever. As we had yet to muster, he was disguising our numbers and he had told no one our destination. The French had similar problems to the King. It cost money to keep an army in the field and the French had almost bankrupted the country when King Edward and the Black Prince had raided. With luck, we would land unopposed.

As my men and I rode towards the Earl of March's hall in Suffolk we passed through a land which was busy not only with growing crops and animals but making all that the army would need. Every town had to provide arrows and bow staves. Every weaponsmith was turning out arrowheads by the hundreds as well as all the other weapons, helmets and armour which would be needed. My own weaponsmiths had begun early and were now almost finished. I had heeded the advice of Edgar of Derby and Stephen of Morpeth was now the captain of my men at arms. The men he had brought with him were as good as any men at arms who served me and it was they along with Matty and Nat who escorted Walter and me. Four archers acted as scouts. Back at Weedon the rest of my men practised. In Will of Stockton's case, he had more to do than most although Harold of Derby had squatted in a garrison too long and needed to be toned up too.

When I had first met the Earl of March, he had been but a boy. He had been kept close to King Richard who had chosen him as his heir. I had always felt sorry for the boy. He had been a pawn used by others. Henry Bolingbroke had kept him closely watched and he had been kidnapped by his uncle and the Welsh. To be fair to King Henry he had always treated him fairly and making him a Knight of the Bath had shown England that the rift was healed. The Earl, however, had made an error of judgement. He had married without the King's permission. He had married Anne Stafford, the daughter of Anne of Gloucester and Edmund Stafford, 5th Earl of Stafford. As such, she was also descended from King Edward III. It gave him an even stronger claim to the throne for he now had two direct lines to the crown. King Henry was furious and had fined the Earl of March ten thousand marks! I think that was the real reason that the King had sent me. He was displeased with the Earl and he needed to retain distance. I was the perfect go-between.

The Earl was at home and I found him in his courtyard practising with his men at arms. We had always got on and I had been the one who had first instructed him in swordsmanship. "Sir William, it is good to see you! How are my strokes?"

I smiled as I dismounted, "You need to vary them more, my lord. Keep your opponent guessing!"

He laughed, "Sage advice from you is always welcome." He seemed to notice my men for the first time and his face clouded, "Am I in trouble, Sir William?"

I walked over to him and shook my head, "Suffolk has many Lollards and I am close to the King. It seemed judicious to come through Suffolk with protection, but I do need to speak with you and in private."

He nodded and I wondered if he was hiding something for his eyes became almost hooded, "You will stay the night, of course."

"If that is not too much trouble, my lord, for I am of an age where I do not particularly enjoy riding great distances."

He waved over his steward, "Have Sir William's men accommodated. He and his squire can have a room in the west wing. Tell Lady Anne that we will have guests this evening."

"Yes, my lord."

The Earl of March's manner and voice were smooth and easy, and I wondered if I was being duped. He had grown up in a court filled with intrigue and plots. He knew better than most how to navigate the dangerous waters of English politics. I would do as I had always done and assume guilt. It had kept two kings safe from assassins. I now had a third to protect. I wondered if he would be the last.

"Come, I have a small chamber where I like to sit and reflect." He smiled, "It is like the one King Richard used at Eltham."

"I remember it well, my lord, I stood many a duty there."

He stopped and looked at me, "I remember for, to me, you seemed like a rock. I never felt in danger or threatened when you were close by for none could pass you. Should I feel danger now?" He lowered his voice, "You defend the crown from danger still. Do you think me a threat?"

I did not smile for I felt no joy and I would not be false, "Let us speak in private, lord, for I have much to say. You are safe from me. I have never murdered in my life and I shall not begin now! My day of judgement is too close for me to risk my soul!"

The hall was a large one and I wondered why he did not live in a castle. Then I realised that a castle might imply that he was a threat to the King. The Earl of March was not a fool. We passed through opulently furnished rooms. The Earl might have had to pay a huge fine to the King, but he and his wife were incredibly rich, and they used their gold well. The room we entered was south-west facing and he had glass put in to allow light in the room. A large fireplace showed that in the winter it would be cold although I suspected he would have hangings over the glass. Now that it was early summer it was a perfect place to sit bathed in sunlight.

Once we were seated, we did not speak until his servants had brought us wine and closed the door. The Earl looked nervous as he said, "Well, Sir William, what is my crime?"

"I am a bluff soldier, Earl Edmund, you know that, and I speak plainly. Word has come to the King that there are men in the land who plot to remove him and place you upon the throne. What say you to that charge?"

He was assured but my bluntness took him by surprise, and I saw the hint of guilt on his face before he recovered and shook his head, "I have no aspirations to be King."

I nodded and tried to hold his gaze, "I did not say that. There are men who seek to place you upon the throne. If you wish to know who told the King of the plot, then it is me!"

That completely unsettled him. "My lord, you cannot…"

I used the voice I had used when instructing him in the use of a sword, what my sons called my teacher's voice, "My lord, do not tell me what I can or cannot do! I am an emissary from King Henry, and I speak with his full authority. We are to sail to France and King Henry needs to know who is loyal and who he can trust. Before you lie to me again know that I have been studying the eyes and voices of those who would harm the King of England since the time of the Black Prince. I know that you know something about this plot." I allowed that to sink in and drank some of the wine. "I do not say that you concocted it or even that you are happy about it, but you know something and by keeping silent then you become a conspirator!"

I saw him pale. "But I am innocent!"

67

I shook my head, "None of us are innocent and if you know anything about a plot and do not tell the King then even though he has every sympathy for you and wishes to believe well of you then it would be the block for you!" I let that sink in and then continued, "If it makes it any easier for you to speak I know that Richard, Earl of Cambridge, Thomas Grey, knight of Northumberland and Baron Henry Scrope of Masham are the triumvirate who are behind this plot."

Sometimes those you think should have more sense do not. Had this been one of my men and they were facing punishment for a major crime then they would have thought it through and recognised the ramifications. It was as though I had to state what was to me blindingly obvious before the Earl of March understood. As I stated the names his eyes widened, and his mouth opened making him look like a fish gasping for air.

He finally nodded, "There is a plot to put me on the throne and you are right those three are behind it. I have done nothing to encourage it. In fact, when it was mentioned to me, I said I did not wish to be king! My cousin, Cambridge, said that it was my duty and I owed it to my family to do so. I swear that I did nothing."

"And doing nothing can result in your execution." I walked over to him and slid his sword from its scabbard. I saw not just fear but terror in his eyes for he thought I was going to execute him. I held the blade in my hand and proffered it to him. "Take this symbol of knighthood and the Holy Cross. Kiss it and swear by Almighty God that you do not wish to kill the King and take his crown."

He greedily grabbed the sword and kissed it, "I swear by all that is holy that I am a pawn in all of this and wish no harm to my liege lord and I do not wish to be King of England!"

I sat, "You should have told the King."

"I feared to do so for I thought that he would order my death!"

I became angry, "Then you are a fool and do not know your King!" I sat back and poured myself some wine to cool my temper. It was rare for me to do so but March's foolishness had managed to do what few others had done. I drank the wine and controlled my rage. "I could go back to King Henry now and tell him all. You would be arrested and taken to the tower." He nodded knowing that he was in my power. "However, I will not do so. I will ride to the King and tell him that the plot of which he has suspicions is very real and I will also tell him that I believe you are innocent but I would urge you to ride to him and confess all and trust in his mercy."

"But if you are wrong and he does not show me mercy?"

"We all make decisions which change our lives and we can do nothing about them except live with them. I believe he will let you live but I cannot guarantee it. No man can."

"You have been honest and fair. I thank you for that."

"I will leave first thing on the morrow and ride to Windsor. Do not be tardy for the King will soon go to Southampton to begin to organise his ships." I suddenly stopped, "Do you know when the assassination is planned?"

Shaking his head. he said, "I know not but I would assume when he is alone."

"Scrope and Cambridge are close to the King. They are involved in the planning of this war. They would have the opportunity to get close to him." I did not tell the Earl that I had already warned the King of the conspiracy and I doubted that any of the three would get close to him.

I left almost before the sun had risen and we rode hard. I believed that the King should have acted earlier for he had suspicions. This was evidence or, at least, if the Earl spoke it then it would be. Had I miscalculated and was the Earl of March involved? My heart said no, and I would trust my judgement. I barely made Windsor in time for even as we galloped into the inner bailey his men were packing wagons with weapons. I was whisked into his presence and, as it was me, all else were dismissed.

"Well?"

"There is a plot, but the Earl of March refused to help the traitors."

"He confirmed their names?" I nodded. "And yet he did not tell me. Why?"

I sighed, "He was afraid that you would not believe him, lord. I can understand that fear. He was a prisoner for most of his life."

"Yet I gave him freedom and honours, and this is the way he repays me?"

"King Henry, he will come to you and confess all. Look into his eyes and judge him then. I know that you are a good judge of men as well as a fair one."

"You would let him live?"

"I would let him live and also I would have him prove to me his commitment by taking him to France!"

"And I trust you but let us lay a little trap. Say nothing of this and I will let the three think that I am fooled. I will offer them senior positions in the army, and I will spring the trap before we sail."

"Is that not dangerous, sire? Should I stay by your side? I did so for your father and King Richard."

"I am not that foolish. You shall be there. Go now to Weedon and fetch your men to Southampton. That way you shall have the best of rooms and be on hand should they attempt anything, but my plan will keep them apart. I would know if there are others involved. I learned much from you, Strongstaff, and I have men who serve me who are not noble-born. From the moment they arrive in Southampton, I will have them followed. When March has spoken with me, I will decide what to do with my foolish cousin!" I nodded and bowed. "I thank you for this. Once more I am in your debt!"

Chapter 6

When I reached home, I was like a whirlwind for that which should have taken weeks to organise now had to be done in days! There were not enough hours in the day to do all that I had to do! For my sons, this would be something new; they were going to fight in a foreign war and that would be different from anything they had experienced before. They were both warriors but when I was their age, I had fought abroad more than I had in England. The Channel would separate them from their families. This would be a hard parting and I could do little to help them for my experience of fighting abroad had been my whole life until I had met Eleanor. There were many knights who owed me fealty, but the King had asked for my sons and my son in law. All of the others, Sir Henry, Sir Peter, Sir Alan, Sir John, Sir Abelard all of them could stay in England. Now that I had grandchildren, I could risk my sons. I knew that both of them were eager. Sir Richard, my son in law, was harder to gauge. I had not trained him, and it was many years since I had fought alongside him. This campaign would tell me much about him and my grandson, William.

I led my men towards the great road which led to London and thence to Southampton and we were waved and cheered by wives, families and tenants. They each had an interest in our success. If we came back laden with ransom and treasure, then the manor could afford a couple of poor harvests. We had been lucky with the seasons but all of us knew that it could change quickly. The people wanted us to win and they wanted the French to lose! It was nothing to do with wanting their land, it was simpler than that, it was economics! As we were serving the King then accommodation, food and grazing would all be supplied by lords along the way. King Henry was not taking all of his knights and lords. In fact, far more would be staying at home. It meant that they paid King Henry to hire men at arms, archers and spearmen instead of either sending their men to fight or fighting themselves. I did not mind for it meant we would be fighting alongside professionals and that suited us.

King Henry was right, our early arrival meant that we were able to acquire rooms and stables close to the port and, as they had been taken over by the King, our costs were kept down. He had his headquarters at the Three Red Leopards and the first thing I noticed when I arrived was that as well as his two brothers and the Duke of York, there was the Earl of March and the Earl of Cambridge. Edmund Mortimer had done as I had suggested and the fact that he still had his freedom meant that the King had believed his story. I was relieved. However, I wondered at the presence of the Earl of Cambridge.

The King smiled when I entered, "Good, Strongstaff, you will be my Chamberlain! I hope that you are not too old to sleep behind my door. Cambridge here offered to perform that duty but as I knew you were coming, I told him that you would do as you had done for my predecessors." He nodded at the Earl, "You and Mortimer can enjoy yourselves while you may for once we are in France then there will be neither time nor opportunity for carousing and wenching!"

I nodded, "Never too old, my lord, for I was born in a camp and sleeping on the ground is second nature."

I knew the Duke of York well and he laughed, "Aye, Strongstaff, you are the toughest man I know. I thought that when you won your spurs that you would change but you never have. I find that reassuring. I am just glad that you are on our side for you are a terrifying enemy!"

The Earl of Cambridge tried hard to disguise his feelings, but his eyes flashed a look of pure hatred. I knew why he had offered to be chamberlain, he would have his chance to be an assassin. I had my mail beneath my surcoat, and I knew that I would need it. A knife in the night might be a likely prospect once the Earl's cronies arrived! I wondered who else might be a potential killer. There might only be three lords involved in the plot to assassinate the King, but they might have hired men. I would have Rafe and James, who had come as servants, to look for any familiar faces. Matty and Nat looked like what they were, men at arms but Rafe and James, with their thinning hair and flecks of grey, looked just like yeomen and none would give them a second glance.

I sat in the corner of the room while the others discussed strategy. I listened and learned that King Henry had commissioned over three hundred and fifty ships to take us to Normandy. He had used the Cinque Ports first and then simply commandeered any other suitable vessel which happened to be in harbour regardless of nationality. He was also planning for the future for he was having built three huge carracks! Southampton harbour was already full and I wondered where the rest would anchor. We were taking two and a half thousand men at arms and eight thousand archers. We had gunners with their guns and gunpowder as well as engineers and miners. That would add more than a thousand men to our army. Yet that was a fraction of the army that the French would bring to fight us. The Duke of York was the most experienced in the room, except for me and he estimated between thirty and fifty thousand men would be mustered to repel us. Of course, they were not as well led and well over half would be their levy. They might have a shield, helmet and a weapon but they were just numbers. Our men at arms would be outnumbered by up to five to one by the French most of whom would be knights. We had but eighty-odd knights! I would have said it was a daunting prospect but as King Edward had shown at Crécy it was not about numbers, it was about the quality of the men and, of course, the longbow.

I listened and I watched. I kept my eyes on the Earl of Cambridge. He had the least to say and it was obvious he had no interest in the campaign, but he kept as close to the King as he could. He also agreed with all that the King had to say. He was trying to appear as a loyal supporter, but it was a wasted act for the King and I knew the truth. The King worked hard, and it was dark when he ended the meeting.

"Uncle, tell the landlord that we are ready for food. Sir William and I will join you when I have shown him his room!"

The Duke of York nodded, "Aye for I could eat a horse... with its skin on!"

We all laughed dutifully at the old joke. I was nearly twenty years older than the Duke, but he was the elder statesman. The senior lords of England and the royal family did not have a long expectancy of life, it seemed.

When they had left us King Henry said, "The Earl of March spoke to me. You are right, he is a fool, but he is an innocent one. He has no more aspirations to be King than you. Cambridge arrived a day after Mortimer and I wonder if he has a spy in Mortimer's household. He has rarely left my side. I do not fear him, but he makes my flesh creep for he toadies around me in such an obvious way that even had you not warned me of the danger I would have suspected him. Now we await the other two. I want them all here in this room when I accuse him. Only you and Mortimer know and I can trust you both to be silent. My uncle cannot keep a secret and his face would give him away!" he smiled, "You need not sleep behind the door, Strongstaff. I said that just to warn Cambridge."

I smiled, "And I meant what I said, King Henry, I slept behind King Richard's door and I thwarted an attempt on his life. I will sleep on the floor behind the door. When we are in France, I think we shall have more floors than soft beds!"

He clapped me about the shoulders, "God's Blood, but it is good to have a real soldier. My brothers think we should have more knights with us. I am happy with the men at arms for you showed me their worth! Come let us descend and eat."

I nodded, "First, Your Majesty, I must speak with my sons so that they know what I am about." He raised his eyebrows. "I will tell them naught about the plot, but they need to know where I will spend my nights." I smiled, "I do not want them to think I have a doxy here!"

By the time July arrived most of the army had arrived and Henry Scrope seemed attached to the Earl of Cambridge by some sort of invisible umbilical cord. It was almost amusing to look at the expressions on the faces of the King's brothers and uncle when he attended all of the meetings. Of course, the King did nothing to discourage it; he wanted all three together so that he could arrest them but, for some reason, Sir Thomas Grey was conspicuous by his absence. By the time he did arrive, the whole army was ready to embark. The King's brothers were already at the harbour beginning the loading of the artillery and siege equipment. Perhaps that determined the three plotters' plan for there would be fewer men close to the King.

The Earl of Cambridge ostentatiously introduced Sir Thomas Grey, "Your Majesty, here is an old friend returned from the North, Sir Thomas Grey."

The King nodded and I saw the perplexed look on his uncle's face. The Duke of York wondered why a lowly knight deserved to be at the meeting. "Welcome, Sir Thomas." He nodded to me, "Sir William here visited your home recently." I had spoken to the King and told him all that had occurred.

The Northumbrian knight tried to look innocent but I saw the panic in his eyes, "Really, my lord? I am sorry that I missed you."

I noticed that the three of them were standing close together and they had the Earl of March to the side. I knew that they intended to take us by surprise if they could. Their left hands were behind their backs. It was an old assassin's trick.

The King had what he wanted, the three plotters together and so I took the offensive, "Oh come, now Sir Thomas, of course you knew for that was why you sent those killers after me!"

He made a mistake, "They were Percy's men!"

I leaned forward, "And how do you know for we killed them all and their bodies were burned."

He looked in panic at the Earl of Cambridge, "I must have heard it from…"

My men had been waiting for Sir Thomas to arrive and I knew that, within earshot, were my men at arms. My sons would have been too obvious but my men at arms could blend in anywhere.

"The three of you are here to kill the King and put the Earl of March upon the throne! Throw down your weapons!"

The King and I had spoken of this and I had been given the task of distracting them so that the King and the Earl of March could draw their own weapons before the conspirators. They made the mistake of pulling out their daggers. The King and Edmund Mortimer had their daggers at the throats of the Earl of Cambridge and Henry Scrope before the two traitors could pull around their hands. As my men ran in, I grabbed Sir Thomas' dagger hand with my left hand and then punched him in the mouth so hard that a tooth flew from his mouth and his nose exploded across his face.

The King's voice was venomous, "You are traitors and you shall be tried and executed before we leave for France."

"My lord! Let us explain!"

"Richard, Earl of Cambridge, do not try to talk your way out of this. The three of you were trusted and honoured. You have betrayed me and tried to use Edmund Mortimer for your own purposes."

Henry Scrope shouted, "He was the one who came up with the plot and we went along with it so that we could tell you!"

The King backhanded him across the mouth, "You are not only a traitor you are without any honour at all. Sir William, have your men bind them and keep them safe before the trial on the morrow." He smiled as he recognised Stephen of Morpeth, "And, Stephen of Morpeth, if they should fall down the stairs of this inn then it will be an accident or an act of God!"

Stephen grinned. He had helped to train Prince Hal, "Aye, Your Majesty, for my men are clumsy buggers!"

The trial was brief and held in Southampton Castle. There were three dukes and three earls on the jury. The King was the judge. They were found guilty and all begged for mercy which, of course, was not forthcoming. They were paying the price for their greed. Had they been loyal knights then there would have been a reward for King Henry was a generous man but he was an unforgiving enemy. Sir Thomas was the first to be executed on the second of August at the Bargate. The other two followed three days later. The army could sail to France knowing that the traitors had all paid the price for their treachery.

Before we left the port, the King addressed all of the men. He visited each group as they prepared to embark and gave them exactly the same speech. This was not his father who spoke to his men as little as possible. This was King Henry Vth who wanted every man to know exactly what was expected of him. "Englishmen, we go to France not to take another country but to reclaim that which is ours. The French King and his knights have forgotten that we have a lawful claim to the land. To that end, there will be no looting. This is not a chevauchée! We pay for food and we take nothing! I will hang any man who steals, robs, rapes or abuses. We fight the armies they send against us and that is all!"

I saw some disappointment on the faces of others, but I knew that we would make enough from ransom and that which we took from the battlefield to make it worth our while. I also knew that there would be land to be had. When the Duke of Burgundy had offered me a town for my own, I had seen what could be had. I was unconcerned about lands in France for I had enough in England but my sons and men at arms might well wish income from France. It never occurred to me that we would lose. I had yet to be on the losing side and this King did not appear to be a loser to me. The wound he had carried on the battlefield of Shrewsbury showed me that he had steel for a backbone. There might be setbacks, but King Henry would overcome them.

The boarding of the ships seemed almost like an anti-climax after the drama in the inn. I was no longer needed as a Chamberlain and I rejoined my men. I was assaulted by questions from my sons who had observed all the events from a distance. I satisfied their curiosity not least because it was a lesson they needed to learn. We were Englishmen and we protected our King and our country. The Earl Marshal, William Marshall, had known that King John was a bad king, but he had supported him and thank God that he had for if he had not then the French invasion would have succeeded. William Marshal was my ideal and I sought to be like him.

The King sailed in the largest of our ships, the *Trinité Royale*. She was five hundred tons and the largest ship I had ever seen. My men and I had two ships for us and our horses, the *Maid of Harwich* and *The Rose of Whitby.* We had a long two or three days at sea for the King intended to land on the north bank of the Seine at Harfleur. The French might have known we were coming but they had no idea of where.

I sat with my sons and my two captains. Walter waited on us as I discussed the campaign. "I have been privy to much of the planning. We take Harfleur and garrison it. We have Calais in the north and the King intends for us to have two ports at which we can land men. The French will probably expect us to land at Calais and head for Paris. This way we steal a march."

Looking back, I can see that the plan, which looked flawless, was riddled with holes. The King assumed that we would take Harfleur quickly. Indeed, he thought we would not have to fight. The campaign would begin badly but, of course, we were not to know that for we were all in high spirits having thwarted a plot to kill the King. The army was in a positive frame of mind and the men in my ship, because I had been pivotal in foiling the plot, were in even better spirits. My star was once again on the rise and my men appreciated that. My two sons were keen to emulate my exploits and, as one of my grandsons was with us, I was at pains to point out that I had never deliberately done anything heroic. The one who appeared the quietest was Sir Richard, my son in law.

Before we boarded the ships I gathered them on the quayside and addressed them, "Just do your duty and do not try to win the battle. That is the surest way to death." I retold all of them the story of my father's death. "He was a mighty warrior but there is always another warrior on the battlefield who may be better."

"And will we fight on horseback, father?"

"I doubt it, Thomas. We have plenty of horses, but our strength lies in men like David of Welshpool. We will fight on foot as our forefathers did at Crécy."

"Was our grandfather at Crécy?"

"I believe so. That was before he joined the Blue Company and before he met my mother. From what Red Ralph told me my father was a young man not much older than Walter here, but he had a talent which all could see. He made money in that battle for the French were massacred. Perhaps that bodes well for us but let us take each day as it comes. Our archers will fight with the other archers, but we will be one body. We fight for each other and I am pleased that we have so many men at arms returned to fight for us. We know each other and how we fight. Since our last battle, we have changed and some whom I wish were here are lost. We are stronger for that. Harold of Derby and Will of Stockton have passed through their own fires of hell and that makes them stronger. Others like you two, Harry and Tom, now have families and there is something to live for."

Walter's eyes were wide with excitement, "And we go to win France for the King!"

"That is the King's purpose, but we fight to ensure that he does not die but, more importantly, that neither do we and, with luck and if God is willing, then we come home in profit."

Stephen of Morpeth said, "Amen to that lord, but fear not, Walter, for the squires will just guard the baggage and there you shall be safe!"

I think my squire was disappointed at that. He had hoped, I suspect, to be behind me with spare weapons and ready to defend his lord's body.

We set sail on August the 11th and I kept to the deck. I needed to be close to the men who sailed with me. While some men spent money they had yet to win, I wandered amongst those men at arms who had not fared well since they had last followed my banner. Will of Stockton had two men who were in his lance. Joseph and Wilton were young lads from Bewley who wanted a life of adventure. Both were young; Wilton was the same age as Walter, and they had no experience of war, but their task was to help mail Will and to watch his horses. When we fought, they would be close by in case Will was hurt and had to be fetched from the field. I had given Will one of the suits of armour we had captured on our way back from the border. He and his two men and Peter, his squire, were alone.

"So, Will of Stockton, you are recovered now?"

He smiled, "Aye lord and I am at peace. Speaking with Pippa's parents helped me. The priests have told me that my wife and child are now in heaven. I shall live a good life so that guarantees I will see them."

"Do not be in a hurry to join them." I nodded meaningfully at the three boys. "You now have a different responsibility."

"And I know that, lord. Until you found me, I was buried in a pit of self-pity. I have seen the light and I would not wish to descend again. Pippa and her voice are within me and she will keep me on the straight. Do not fear for me, lord."

"I will not. I just wanted to see your eyes when you spoke with me."

I next spoke with Harold. He was watching others throw dice. Stephen of Morpeth was also close by and watching. "Well Harold, is this better than life in the garrison at Derby?"

He grinned, "Aye lord. The men there called themselves warriors, but they were not. If an army had come then they would have filled their breeks and wet themselves. It is good to be amongst real men again." As with Will of Stockton, I was staring into his eyes as he spoke. He held my gaze, "And I will not slide back into my foolish ways. Watching others lose their money is a better occupation and besides, Stephen and the others will not let me become the shadow of the man who followed your banner.

Stephen nodded, "And that is the truth, lord. We are your company and we have standards."

The last man I spoke with was Oliver the Bastard. He had been the last to join me. After selling his inn he had found four good men to follow him and, along with Stephen of Morpeth was one of the stronger lances in my company. He smiled as I approached, "This is better than running an inn, Sir William."

"But less certain, Oliver."

"With you and Hal, I mean King Henry leading us? The Duke of Burgundy recognised you for what you are, lord, a leader. When we were in Southampton, we heard that John the Fearless will not fight alongside his liege lord, King Charles. He knows that he cannot defeat you. When we fought for him it was us who won the battle and there were just one thousand of us. We have ten times that number now."

I liked his confidence. It was not because I feared we might lose but because it showed a change in him. When his wife had left him, it was as though he had lost part of himself; the part which made him a man. Now that he was amongst warriors again his confidence returned. I went back to the stern and my sons happier. This was not the Blue Company, but it was my company and I think old Captain Tom would have relished the opportunity to lead them into battle.

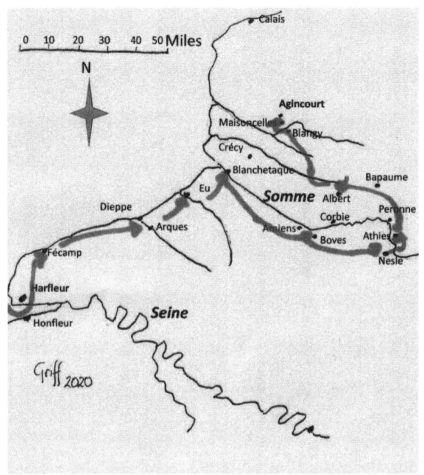

Normandy and the route, in red, taken by the English army.
Map by the author

Chapter 7

Harfleur was a well-defended town. As we approached up the narrow channel from the sea, I saw that they had surrounded the port with water leaving the south-west gate as the only one we could assault. It did not look to be a large port and was certainly smaller than Calais, but I could see that we had to take it for we needed a port. It took two days to unload the horses and men from the ships. The gunners and the engineers had to set up their guns and begin to build the stone-throwers which would reduce the walls. All of this took time and we needed to surround the port. To that end, he entrusted his brother, the Duke of Clarence with the task of encircling the town. He left and two days later sent the message that he had succeeded and captured a relief train which had been taking men and powder to the town. However, and this was to prove crucial, three hundred men had managed to reinforce the garrison and we now had four hundred soldiers to fight instead of one hundred.

As we made our camp Harry wondered at that, "We outnumber them by many hundreds to one! They should surrender soon."

Stephen of Morpeth overheard my son, "Sir Henry, we have to get close to their walls and that is no easy thing for they have flooded the land around it. Our archers can clear a battlefield in a few flights but here the crossbow is king. The crossbow was made for such defences."

I nodded, "Richard the Lionheart discovered that to his cost for he was slain by a bolt when he besieged a castle. I do not like such warfare." I waved a hand at the ground. "This is a disease-ridden pestilential hole. It is almost September and when the autumn rains come then we will suffer." I pointed to the land to the south of Harfleur. The tide was coming in and soon it would be flooded. "We fight not just the French and the town but nature and the sea!"

"September? But we should take it in days!"

I laughed, "Harry, it will take days for the engineers to build the siege tower and the machines. Those fowlers, the King's cannons, can reduce walls, but they take time to set up and they do not send their stones rapidly. Keep you and your men dry. Drink none of the water. Ale and wine are the safest and keep your eye on your men. If they are bored, then they can do foolish things."

I was summoned to the King's tent to discover what we were to do. The King had a plan, but the whole was in his head and each of us were given our part. He waved me to a seat, "The French have flooded the north and east sides of the town. It means that the only way we can maintain contact between us and my brother is to use boats. I want you and your men to find as many boats as you can. We can then attack the huge bastion which guards the Loure Gate." I nodded. The bastion was an earthwork which protected the only gate we could attack. Finding boats was hardly glorious work, but I knew that this would not be a quick siege and so long as my men were occupied I would be happy. "My brother has mines begun but it is here that we will win the town. When you have the boats, I would have you defend the gunners. They will take some time to set up their fowlers. It will be noisy and dirty work, but I can rely upon you to keep them safe. Their task is to break down the walls of the bastion which guards the bridge and the Loure Gate. Until we have the bastion in our hands, we cannot effectively assault the walls. At best our fowlers can drop haphazard stones into the port, but it will not win the siege."

"Aye, King Henry." I hesitated, "And when we have taken Harfleur? Paris?"

He shook his head, "No, Normandy. We drive south to Bordeaux and take the rich farmland then we can winter there before taking Paris next year."

It was a clever plan for the French would assume that we would head for Paris. We had just enough men to achieve victory, but we would have to take Harfleur quickly.

I had ensured that our camp was on the driest piece of land we could find, and I had men making it secure by digging a ditch and building a palisade. I then took my archers and men at arms to find the boats that we would need. We did not wear armour while we did so. This work was both dirty and tiring. It took three days but we managed to find twenty boats. Not only did that allow our army to keep contact with each other it denied the French their own means of communication. It also showed me the extent of the defences. If we took this port, then the French would struggle to reclaim it.

By the time our first task was done the guns were in position and, taking the pavise we had constructed we went to defend them. The guns were going to break down the defences of the bastion whilst also raining stones on the town and the town wall. We joined the pavise so that the gunners could be protected while they reloaded. This was hard for my men at arms not to mention my sons. We had to stand and be deafened by the booming fowlers as they battered the walls. The sound hurt our ears and the fumes and smell made men vomit. How the gunners stood it I will never know. At least the archers would have something to do. When the pavise were lifted up they sent arrows towards the men with crossbows on the bastion. We just had to stand and endure it. We could not fight back. Halfway through the first day my son, Thomas, said, "Father, you need not endure this! Go back to the camp and wait there."

"Son, this is a lesson for you. If a man leads, then he does just that! He endures that which his men do. I told your brother that this would take time and it will."

The dangers were made clear on the second day when one gunner was killed and a second wounded by crossbow bolts. David of Welshpool took exception to the death. I had accepted that we would lose men but David hated all crossbowmen and he and the archers worked even harder and although we were uncertain if any crossbowmen were actually killed we had neither deaths nor serious injuries from then on. The guns had begun to fire after a week but they were extremely slow to reload. We had worked out that if we used the men at arms and pavise we could protect the gunners while they reloaded, and it also gave the men at arms some purpose. That inevitably slowed down the rate of the bombardment for we had to wait until every fowler was loaded. This was unsatisfactory and so we used fascines to protect the guns and made simple devices made from pavise which could be raised when the guns fired and lowered while they were reloaded. It also afforded protection for my men. The archers no longer needed the pavise, but they could not use their bows as often.

When the stone-throwers were built then other men at arms protected them as they began their attack. The heat from the guns added to the heat of the hot late summer days and we envied the gunners who were stripped to the waist. The worst part of our duty was the stink from the gunpowder. I did not know how the gunners could abide it. That and the thick smoke which enveloped us each time we fired. However, those two factors may have helped us for the rest of the army soon fell prey to pestilential diseases and dysentery, the bloody flux which soon claimed the life of Thomas Courtney, Bishop of Norwich. Countless others fell victim to the two diseases but my men and the gunners seemed immune. Perhaps the insects which caused the diseases could not abide the smell and the smoke either. We stopped complaining about the stink and the smoke for they appeared to protect us. The master gunners had tar with them and we watched as they soaked the stones in the tar before loading them. The result was astounding. The heat from the gunpowder ignited the tar and made it a flaming missile which set fire to the wooden buildings of Harfleur. Sadly, they had enough water to douse the flames, but it must have made life as unpleasant for the French inside as it was for us outside.

It was one day when we were watching the guns batter the bastion that I met an old friend. Davy Gam was a Welshman who supported England. He had served both King Henry and me well. I was delighted to meet him and his two sons. He was a man at arms but as dependable as they came. As soon as I spied him my spirits soared for that was the effect the Welshman had upon people.

"We hope for great reward in this campaign, Sir William. It seems my star and that of the King are intertwined." He smiled and I returned it for his was infectious, "It seems that I have good luck when I serve with you. Perhaps tonight we can share a jug of wine."

I frowned, "You have not been looting have you?"

He adopted an innocent look, "I am a God-fearing man and the jug sort of fell into my possession. It would have been a crime to abandon it."

Later that night I took my sons and son in law and we shared the wine with Davy. Walter was quite taken with the Welshman who had a seemingly bottomless fund of stories. We would see him intermittently during the campaign and I think those meetings kept me sane.

The Loure Gate led to the bridge and we knew that we must have been winning when, one morning in September, as dawn broke and the gunners prepared to fire their fowlers, horsemen rode from the town intent upon killing the gunners and destroying the foul-smelling weapons. King Henry's decision to place my men there was justified for my men were alert and as soon as they were seen by my son, Sir Thomas, he ordered the men at arms to stand to and to form a shield wall. Walter handed me a poleaxe as I ran from my tent to join the others. The guns had been set up a little way from the bridge to avoid the counter fire from the French. It meant that the French had the length of the bridge to ride before they could fan out. My son had our shield wall in place before they reached it and a wall of spears, cut down lances and other pole weapons greeted them. Our archers sent arrows into them, but it was our pole weapons which defeated them. I used the poleaxe twohanded and, standing between my sons, hacked through the chamfron of the French horse which came at me to crack its skull. The mighty warhorse fell at my feet and Harry swung his war hammer to crush the skull of the French knight. I think the Frenchman might have surrendered but Harry was too concerned about my life to worry about money! The survivors retreated back and that proved to be the only attempt from the garrison to stop the barrage.

My men butchered the horse and we ate well. The chamfron was ruined and so it was taken to the weaponsmiths we had brought to be melted down and made into arrowheads. The knight and the other men at arms had money too. We divided it equally. The gunners did not seem to mind that we had not shared it with them as they knew that but for us, they might have been butchered themselves and their guns destroyed.

Later in the day the King came to see us, "I fear, Strongstaff, that this siege will not end as quickly as I might have hoped. The walls are taking too long to destroy. This pestilential hole is claiming too many lives. The Earl of Suffolk is now at death's door and my brother, Clarence is weak from the bloody flux!" He smacked his right fist into the palm of his left, "I have had enough of this, Master Gunner."

John Guidon knuckled his forehead, "Aye, Your Majesty!"

The King pointed to the bastion which lay at the end of the bridge. It had been damaged already. "I want all the fowlers to concentrate their missiles on that bastion. Forget the town and the walls, I want that destroyed!"

No one argued with the King when he was in that sort of mood. The gunner nodded, "Aye, Your Majesty. Right lads, I want all the fowlers turning."

I knew that it would take hours to realign the guns.

The King said, "Your men are fitter than most. Tomorrow, after the gunners have weakened the bastion, I want you and Sir John Holland to lead an attack on the bastion and take it. Once we have it, we can move the guns inside it and destroy the gate!"

"We will be ready!"

I knew Sir John Holland; he was a reliable knight and more than capable of leading the assault despite his youth; he was but twenty years of age! I knew why he had been chosen to be the figurehead for he was the King's cousin and related to both King Richard and King Edward. I was there to give advice. I did not mind that I was being used for that was my lot in life. While the fowlers pounded away, I gathered my men around me. The archers would not be needed. This would be my knights and men at arms. During my talk, Sir John Holland arrived, and I saw that he was listening. That was a good sign for it showed that he was not an arrogant noble who thought he knew it all.

"Tomorrow we have been given the honour of helping Sir John Holland to take the bastion and to help us end this siege!" They did not cheer as many might have done for that was not their way. I saw my son, Harry, and my son in law, Richard. Both looked nervous. "We will not need shields for they will encumber us, and I would recommend a weapon you can use with one hand for we may have to climb over fallen stones." I was speaking as much for Sir John as I was my men. Most of my men at arms had done this before and would know exactly what to do. "I shall use my hand and a half sword, but I will carry an axe in my belt." I smiled, "Those of you who do not have metal-backed gauntlets, manifers, may decide to acquire some after tomorrow, but you will need your leather gloves. The French will try to make us bleed for every inch of their bastion. When it falls the town will soon follow!" I looked at their faces and saw no reason to worry. They were like greyhounds ready to slip their leads. "We attack with fortitude and know that I shall be at the forefront. If this old warhorse can scale the bastion then you young tigers should have little problem and remember, the King will be watching you. I have never let down a king yet and I do not intend to begin on the morrow. The cry will be God, King Henry, and St. George! Now get some rest and prepare yourselves. Those who feel they need to be shriven twice can see the priests tonight but before we leave I, for one, will confess all of my sins!"

The King's cousin joined me. I had been present when his father had been executed on the orders of Henry Bolingbroke. I wondered what he thought of me for his father had been a supporter of King Richard. Did he view me as a traitor or merely a pragmatic and practical man?

His question answered my own, "I am pleased that my cousin has made you my lieutenant for I feel that I am young for this command."

"You will succeed, Sir John, and your father, no doubt in heaven, will be proud of you." I had said the right thing and he stood a little straighter. "The secret is to keep going and assume that all of our men will follow us. It will be a fierce fight, of that I have no doubt, but you have good plate and, I can see, a good sword. And I meant what I said when I spoke with my men, I shall lead. You may have all the glory of our victory but the bulk of the men we lead will be mine and they will follow me. Tomorrow is about victory at all costs!"

He looked at me and smiled, "Aye, Sir William, and it will be a lesson in war for me."

Walter polished my plate until it shone. That was not simply for appearance only. We would be attacking as the sun rose and from the west. The rising sun would catch the metal and help to blind our enemies. Blades were also more likely to slide off the highly polished plate. He sharpened my sword until I was satisfied. I used the edge to take some stubble from my chin.

"Sir William are you not afraid that you will die tomorrow?"

I shook my head, "A man who is afraid to die should not go to war for death is always a sword thrust or arrow away. I will confess my sins knowing that if I die doing King Henry's will, the deaths I cause will not bar me from heaven. I have many friends there. I do not think I will die for I am skilled in war. That is why it will be many years until we risk you in war. You will fetch and carry; you will sharpen weapons and lead horses until you are trained enough to fight. It helped your father become the warrior he is, and I will not change my methods for his son. I know that you wish to fight but that will not be in this campaign."

I had not lied about my prayers and I spoke them aloud before retiring. I would be the first awake but that was my old man's bladder and not the fear which made my son, Harry, start as he woke in the dark. Before I woke Walter, Rafe and James joined me for some stale bread toasted at the night watch's brazier. Smothered with butter it was one of the delights of the day. We washed it down with good ale, we still had a couple of barrels and then, as a guilty Walter leapt from his bed, they prepared me for war. I had learned that clean garments next to the skin helped to prevent infections and, as it was early in the campaign, we had clean ones available. The hose was close-fitting. Then Rafe slipped my aketon over the top and James fastened it. I still wore a mail coif for I liked to feel its weight. With the new gorget I had had made it was unnecessary but it was an old habit, but they were the hardest to lose. Then it was up to the three of them as they fitted first my breast and backplate and the fauld, or skirt over the cuisse which protected my thighs and as they were all fastened Walter fitted my greaves before fitting the poleyns over the knees. I sat while they fitted the sabatons on my feet. The last item to be fitted was the gorget. I would carry the helmet, my new bascinet until I began to advance. It was the heaviest of my pieces of armour. Rafe would carry my sword and James my axe. Walter would carry my gauntlets with the metal lames protecting the backs of my hand. The sun had yet to rise as we made our way to the front line. The rest were still behind me and I knelt before the Bishop of Ely who knelt close so that he could hear my confession. Other priests were waiting for the rest of our men. When I had been given absolution Sir John knelt and the Bishop shrove him too. I saw when I stood, having confessed, that Will's squire, Wilton, was speaking with Walter. That was good for they were of an age and Walter would not miss the company of his young brothers at home in Middleham.

As soon as the first rays of the sun appeared behind Harfleur the fowlers all opened fire and the noise was so loud that I jumped. Rafe laughed, "That is you awake then, my lord."

I laughed too, "Aye and it is a good job I emptied my bowels before I dressed or poor Walter here would have had a terrible mess to clean.

Come, squire, don my manifers and then get back to the camp. I will be hungry once we have sent these Frenchmen packing."

Rafe smiled when my squire ran off, "Kindly done, my lord. Send him to safety."

I took the axe from James and hung it from my baldric and then the sword from Rafe. "And you two will join him! You have nothing more to do today except groom my horses so you can wash some clothes. Let us take advantage of all of this water and the hot days!"

I moved forward as the two left, albeit reluctantly. "Thomas, Harry, Richard, you will be behind me."

"Aye lord."

"A good day eh, Sir William?" I saw that Sir John had a poleaxe. He had not heeded my advice. He would learn.

"Aye, Sir John!" I saw that the bastion had been badly damaged. Stones had fallen from the top and there was a natural ramp. I suspected that they had hand gunners who would be waiting for us. I had yet to face these weapons. It would be interesting to see if they could hurt men in armour or were just noisy toys to frighten the horses!

I waited until the smoke had cleared and the sun shone, as though God himself had ordered it, and I raised my sword, "God, King Henry, and St. George!"

I was the oldest man there, but I was determined to be the first up the ramp. Perhaps I was being a coward for the French were taken by surprise and their first bolts, arrows and handguns sent their missiles either too high or short. Something clanged off my plate, it could have been a stone from a handgun or a bolt, but by then I was halfway up the slope and I had my sword pulled behind me ready to strike. Now it was a race between the missiles and me. The only weapon which could reload in time was the bow and the archer who aimed at me panicked and sent not a bodkin but a war arrow which struck my plate but did not harm me. I swung at the unfortunate hand gunner who was touching his linstock to the fuse. Without helmet and mail, I cleaved his head from his body and then I was amongst the defenders. They had few men at arms in the bastion and Sir John and I, backed by my sons, son in law and my men were among the French like wolves in the sheepfold.

I used my sword twohanded and swept all before me. I was confident for I had my sons close by and they would allow nothing untoward happen to their father. Sir John Holland also fought like a man possessed as he was fighting alongside a man three times his age and he was desperate to prove his ability. I began to tire and that was not surprising, but I could not let the others see that. "God, King Henry, and St. George!" My cry spurred the ones lower down the breach to hurry towards us. More importantly, it disheartened the French defenders who fled back across the bridge into Harfleur. It was an admission of defeat for, as the last men were slain, we could begin to drag the fowlers onto the elevated bastion and rain death into the walls of the town. The end of Harfleur was upon them.

I took off my helmet and surveyed the breach. Two of Sir John's men had been slain but none of my men. That was the difference between inexperienced novices and veterans. Sir John himself was fulsome in his praise, "Sir William! It was an honour to fight alongside you this day. You belie your age!"

"You did well, Sir John, for what we did was not easy but shows what courage and Englishmen can do."

King Henry sent men with his brother, the Duke of Gloucester, to secure the bastion for we had done that which we had been ordered. Leaving some of the men at arms to strip the dead of whatever they had we headed back to our camp. I knew that the French were defeated. No matter what happened from now on they could no longer hold Harfleur. They had held us longer than the King had intended but we had our port and could now begin to reclaim France.

Rafe and the others had watched our victory and they were cooking a feast for us. We still had some choice horsemeat and that would be the centrepiece of a feast for Sir William and his men. We had fought with Sir John and his men, but we would celebrate our victory with our brothers in arms. That was our way. We had managed to loot some wine from the bastion. That was another difference between a novice and a veteran. My men knew where to look! I drank the rough French wine and listened to accounts of the fight. Every man saw it differently and that did not worry me. We had not let down the King and we were all alive. Sadly, dysentery and disease were sweeping through the camp and our casualties from the attack were nothing compared with the bloody flux!

As we ate one of the King's esquires came to tell me that the King was delighted with our success. When I asked him how the camp stood his face fell. "My lord, we have been here but a few weeks and fought little yet two thousand men have died and a further two thousand will have to be sent home to England for they are too sick to fight. Our army is almost halved. King Henry is gravely troubled."

"Tell him that, on the morrow, I will come to give him counsel."

So, while the rest of my lances celebrated, I was silent and downhearted. It felt like a victory to my men, but I knew that we were now in a worse position than we had been. I tried not to let them know and when they approached, I smiled and looked happy but inside I was not for I had fought longer than any man on the battlefield and the truth could not be hidden from me! Some days later when it became obvious that no help was coming to the garrison, De Gaucourt, the constable, surrendered. King Henry kept his word and the town was neither sacked nor pillaged. The Duke of Clarence and the others too ill to fight any longer were sent home and the Earl of Dorset was appointed to command our new port. King Henry did not want to lose what had cost us so much to capture and so he gave the Earl a garrison of five hundred men at arms and a thousand archers. With the losses to disease and those sent home that left us with an army of just nine hundred men at arms and a little over five thousand archers. Our army had shrunk dramatically, and I could see no way that we could do that which the King had planned. We could not conquer France.

I was invited to the council of war convened by the King. He looked downhearted. "Tomorrow I shall release the French prisoners. They are too few to make a difference to our progress and we will not have to feed them." There were nods all around, but that decision was not a major one. We all waited for the King to come up with a plan. If this had been the King's father then I might have made suggestions myself but King Henry was not his father and whatever he came up with would be a starting point. He gave us a rueful smile, "It seems that only Sir William and Sir John have had to draw their swords in anger. For the rest of us, we might as well have wielded ploughshares." He received dutiful smiles for his humour. "To that end, I have decided that when I release the French tomorrow, I will send a message to the Dauphin for single combat between the two of us to settle the matter before God."

It was a bold idea and I saw some of the younger lords nod appreciatively. I felt honour bound to speak, "He will not accept, Your Majesty. It is known that you are a warrior and few men could face you in any kind of combat. As you know, King Henry, I do not gamble but I would happily place my family fortune on the outcome for Prince Louis is a weak and vacillating heir to the throne. If he accepts…" I shook my head. "He will not!"

"And I fear that you are right, old friend. If he does not, then we have no alternative but to march to Calais and take ship for England."

His younger brother frowned, "If that is all that we have planned then why not simply take ship from here? We have the ships in harbour already."

King Henry's eyes narrowed, "Because that would encourage the French and would be seen by those at home and here in France as a defeat for me and we shall not have that. We will do as King Edward did and march north. We will cross the Somme at Blanchetaque and take ship. The campaigning season is almost over, and I will not have my army starve to death in Picardy. Harfleur held us up too long." He did not say so but he blamed his brother for that. His tardiness in surrounding the walls had allowed the French to quadruple their defenders. Had they not done so then we would have had the port in less than a week. King Henry said nothing for he was the commander and he took responsibility for the setback. I had trained him well.

The Duke of York shook his head, "My liege this is foolishness. Your brother is right. We have a port, let us sail home and return next year."

King Henry's voice was commanding as he spoke to his most senior of advisers, "Uncle, we raised money for this attack. If we sail home with our tails between our legs then those enemies, like Cambridge, Scrope and Grey whom we executed, will use it to rally opposition to us. If we return home without crossing swords with the French, then it will be seen as a weakness."

"Then you still hope for battle? Even though we are a shadow of the army which landed here?"

He laughed, "Of course for we are English, and we have the right! God intends for this land to be returned to English rule and I, for one, will not thwart that plan!" He had not convinced the gainsayers, but King Henry was a stronger man than his father had been and he knew his own mind.

We had a week in the port and my sons and I had a roof over our heads. No message came from the Dauphin and, as October approached, King Henry took the fateful decision to march north to Calais. The night before we left, he came to visit with me. He looked to have aged since that day in August when we had confronted the traitors. He had lost valued advisers and he had endured his first failures. "Old friend, things have not gone as I would have wished."

"And they were events which were not under your control."

"I should have dealt with the traitors earlier than I did and I should have trusted your judgement."

I shook my head, "The law had to be upheld or you would have been seen as a tyrant. Trust me, King Henry, I know of what I speak. That was King Richard's downfall. Others portrayed him as a tyrant. It is very easy to criticise and not to make a positive suggestion. Too many men do that. That makes me angrier than almost anything. Right now, in England, there will be many who will pick holes in your plans. Not one of them would raise a hand to help you and they would not have the first idea how to do that which you do."

He laughed, "Anger, Sir William! I hear the anger in your voice!"

91

I nodded, "That is because I have been close to three kings and there are too many I have watched and heard who have brought them down or tried to bring them down. It is good that I have little power for if I did, they would have lost their heads already!"

"You would be a tyrant?"

"To save England?" I snapped my fingers, "In a heartbeat!"

He sighed, "It is good to speak with you, but I fear I cannot walk that road. When we leave on the morrow, I want you with Sir Gilbert D'Umphraville and Sir John Cornwall and act as our vanguard. Both are good knights, but you have forgotten more than they will ever know and besides that, your men are in the best condition. We need a passage across the Somme. If memory serves King Edward and his men found a ford at Blanchetaque before they fought at Crécy. Perhaps that is a sign and we shall face the French again where my grandsire slew so many!"

I laughed, "I think, Your Majesty, that Crécy is the one place that they will not face us for it is filled with too many ghosts from their past!"

"You may be right."

"We have little food, King Henry, and the French, I think, will not, of their own volition, give us food. They will wish to starve us."

"I know what you are saying, Strongstaff, but this is not a chevauchée. I give you permission to take food and those animals we need for meat but there will be no pillaging." I nodded, "But you will kill all who oppose our passage!"

I had my clear instructions and I would carve a path to Calais for this shadow of an army!

Chapter 8

Our first obstacle was the town of Fécamp. The town had been razed to the ground five years earlier, but the French had been busy since then rebuilding it. I rode with the archers and a handful of my men at arms ahead of the rest of the vanguard. We left before dawn as I wished to surprise the town. The King had charged me with making the route safe from the French and I knew that meant using my sword and the arrows of my archers. I would not be negotiating a passage. I had four hundred archers with me, and I had appointed David of Welshpool to command them. We rode hard and fast to reach the town before they were alerted. In the five years since the English had razed it, they had managed to build a wooden palisade and a gatehouse, but we arrived before the town had risen. I dismounted my men and while my archers nocked arrows, I led my twenty men at arms with axes and pole weapons to the gate. I had my shield with me and as we ran towards the gate I raised it for the shouts of the sentries told us that we had been seen. Of course, the cries of the sentries were soon silenced by a shower of arrows, but the walls and the gate would soon be manned. My men at arms hacked and chopped at the newly built gates. This was not their first time and their blows were not haphazard. I heard cries from the walls as, with the rising sun, my archers were able to see and to hit the newly arrived defenders. My men, who wielded their axes better than a woodsman, made short work of the bar holding the gate and we poured through.

They did not need to be told to spare the women and children as well as those who did not wield weapons for my men would not waste a sword stroke or risk blunting a weapon. My men knew their business. Stephen, Oliver and Dick led my men at arms as they formed a human shield before me. David of Welshpool led the archers as they raced through the wrecked gates. They had already cleared most of the fighting platform and now they aimed their arrows at the armed men who were on the walls which lay further away. There was a constable in the town, and he must have taken the time to arm and don mail. He and a dozen men at arms ran towards us. That they outnumbered us did not worry my men. The ones who ran at us wore mail hauberks only; we had plate.

My men at arms spread out to bring as many of the French within range of our weapons as they could. I still had my shield and I stepped up to take on the constable. I shouldered Harold of Derby out of the way to do so. The Frenchman had a poleaxe which he swept towards my head. He must have thought my white hair made me slow, but it did not, and I stepped to the side as I angled shield to allow the axe head to slide down the side. I swung my hand and a half sword in a long sweep towards his side. Stephen and Oliver had cleared space for me by dispatching their opponents. Walter had sharpened it well and it sliced through some of the links and into the aketon. As I sawed it back it drew blood.

"Yield for you are wounded and resistance is futile! We have your town!"

I saw that I had hurt him, but he still spat defiance at me, "English cur, I am a Frenchman, and this is my land!"

In answer, I punched him hard in the face with my shield and he was too slow to react. He fell in a heap at my feet, his sallet falling from his head. Placing my sword at his throat I said, "Once again I ask you to yield for it would be the work of a moment to end your foolish life."

Dropping his poleaxe, he said, "I yield!" With his surrender, we had the town. The King and the rest of the army rode in as we began to empty the storerooms of food. We had had to leave supplies at Harfleur, and we carried with us just enough food for the next few days.

I had taken the town and so the ransom from the constable came to me and my men. We had taken the risks. It was little enough but my men deserved a reward. We ate well and we destroyed the defences of the town. The next day we headed for the crossing of the River Bethune at Arques. This time the walls were more substantial than at Fécamp. The bridge over the river could be defended. I waited with Sir Gilbert and Sir John and sent my archers upstream to find a ford and to seal off the town. King Henry was not far behind us, and he surveyed the bridge and the walls.

"Come, Sir William, let us debate with the castellan and see if we can cross without a battle. We have too few men to be careless with their lives." We rode bareheaded towards the bridge. When we came close enough he shouted, "I am King Henry and I have come to liberate my land from French oppression. I ask that you allow us across the river and provide sustenance for us."

A French knight with a good helmet appeared on the wall over the bridge gate. "This is France, my lord, and I will defend the bridge and the town for my king."

"Then you are an enemy to me, and we must use any means at our disposal. I ask again but this time I offer the promise of death and destruction. If you fail to do as I ask, then I will unleash my dogs of war upon you. We will destroy your walls, take your food and then burn your town to the ground." He turned in his saddle and pointed at the army which was arraying for battle. "Do you think you can weather this storm, Castellan? Do as I ask and then we shall leave your homes and women alone."

I was not certain that King Henry would have allowed our men to harm their women, but the threat worked, and the gates were opened. We took food but King Henry did not take all. His words before we had begun this increasingly ill-fated campaign were still at the heart of our quest and we pushed on to Eu which guarded the crossing of the River Brestle. My archers, having found the crossing of the Bethune, now found a crossing of the Brestle. Leaving Sir John and Sir Gilbert to bring the bulk of the vanguard to the town I went with my archers and men at arms and crossed the river upstream. Using my archers as scouts we made our way around the walled town of Eu and they reported that the northeast gate to the town was still open. The French paid for their oversight when we galloped into the town. Sir Gilbert and Sir John attacked the river gate while we fought our way through their defences to reach the town square. My archers did not use their bows. Each one had a good sword and David of Welshpool had ensured that they all knew how to use them. We may have had few men at arms, but my mounted archers hacked, sliced and chopped at the defenders as they followed my men at arms and me into another French town.

I only found one man who had the courage to stand before me for the rest surrendered when they saw the mailed knight on the enormous horse. The man was braver than the rest. He was not a knight, but he wore plate, a full-face bascinet and a poleaxe and, as such, would need to be treated with respect. I used the speed of my horse. Fire lived up to his name for he was fast and he was fierce. I galloped towards the man at arms and used the speed of my horse, rather than my speed to defeat him. Perhaps the man had been in a garrison for too long, I know not but he swung too soon and clumsily, striking the fresh air which my horse had just occupied as I jerked his head away from the blow. It allowed me to swing my sword over the top of Fire's head and strike the man at arms on his helmet. It was a good helmet, but my sword was also heavy, and the man fell in a heap. Had I used a war hammer like Kit then he would be dead. We reached and opened the other gate. The town surrendered rapidly and, once again, the King showed his mercy, and we took the food they had, leaving them enough to get by.

The result was that, as we headed for the ford at Blanchetaque, we had enough rations for a week but only if we tightened our belts. My men and I were sent out early the next day and fortune favoured us. We came upon a patrol of six Gascon light horsemen. My archers were all well mounted and not having to wear mail meant that they were faster than the Gascons. My archers outnumbered them but the Gascons chose to fight. Heeding my orders David of Welshpool ensured that we had two prisoners.

Sir John and Sir Gilbert arrived as I began to question them. I know that if the two young knights had questioned them then they would have asked the wrong questions. The fact that they were on horses and Gascons told me that they had not come from Eu. I nodded, to the east, "You strayed too far from the advance guard eh?"

One nodded, sadly, "Aye, lord. We had been to visit with the piquets at Blanchetaque."

I nodded to David of Welshpool who rattled off some orders and Christopher White Arrow led five men to ride to the ford. "Then your advance guard will soon be at Abbeville."

I made it sound like we knew everything already when, in fact, we knew nothing. I assumed that the French must have sent men from Rouen to shadow us. This was merely confirming it.

They both nodded and the chatty one said, "Constable d'Albret leads the six thousand men to stop you from crossing the Somme."

I saw the surprise on the faces of the two young knights whom the King had asked to lead the vanguard. "Sir John and Sir Gilbert, I would suggest that you take these two prisoners to the King so that he may question them further."

Happy to be able to claim the credit for the news they rode off.

I turned to my son in law, Sir Richard, "I want you to wait here for Christopher White Arrow. It is my belief that he will report that the ford at Blanchetaque is barred to us. It was too much to hope that they would forget Crécy! I will take some archers and half of my men at arms and I will try to scout out the enemy vanguard. The prisoners may have the numbers wrong. I prefer the judgement of my own eyes."

"Aye, my lord, but surely one of us could do this?"

I was blunt, "You could but your young eyes might miss something which my rheumy ones would spot! I have done this for longer than you have been alive, Richard, I will be fine for I will take the best of my men!"

Taking all of my own archers we headed for the Somme. I had my archers string their bows before we set off. If we found trouble, then I wanted to be able to get out of it fast. We had too few men to risk them.

Once we reached the Somme, we followed the line of the river. I knew that Abbeville lay on the northern bank of the river and that they had a barbican bridge. The town was close to us and we needed to avoid being seen. We saw the towers of the churches before we saw the walled town. Leaving most of my men hidden in the shelter of some trees on the riverbank I went with David of Welshpool and two other archers. With my cloak wrapped around my armour, I hoped to be invisible. We stopped just a mile from the bridge as we needed to go no further. I saw the advance guard of the French army as it was crossing the bridge. The French had taken the direct line and that meant that we could not use the ford at Blanchetaque. I knew now that when Christopher White Arrow reported back he would tell us that the ford was guarded. We sheltered behind the wall of a farmhouse. That it was occupied was clear from the smoke which rose from the fire, but, equally, there was no way that a Norman farmer would take on a knight and four of the dreaded English archers. They would wait and watch. When we had gone then they would tell the French commander in Abbeville what they had seen.

The youngest archer was Geraint the Arrow. "Geraint, you have young eyes. What can you tell me of the banners which you see?"

He stared into the distance, "There is one looks like red with white bars and what look like arrows, lord." I nodded. That sounded like Beaumesnil and the knight I had wounded in Northumberland. "Then there is a big banner with quarters of red and the blue fleur de lys in the other."

"Well done, Geraint, you have good eyes." I turned to David of Welshpool. "That is the Constable of France and confirms what the Gascon told us. This is the advanced guard of the French army. The question is where are the rest of them?" I stared at the seemingly endless snake of soldiers as it tramped across the bridge. The Gascon appeared to have told us the truth and I estimated more than five thousand men were in the advanced guard. We had no siege equipment and not enough men. We might fight an open battle, but we could not risk being trapped against town walls. We would have to find another crossing over the Somme and that meant heading upstream and deeper into France. It was a dangerous strategy. I looked south. The French did not use as many mounted men as we did. Their men at arms were mounted but the rest, as the advanced guard demonstrated, tended to move on foot and that slowed them down. We had the chance to slip between the advanced guard and the main army but only if we moved quickly!

We turned and headed back to the rest of our men. The King was already there and he was speaking with the Duke of York and his brother, the Duke of Gloucester. Christopher White Arrow rode up to me, "I have reported to the King, Sir William. The French have embedded stakes in the ford and there are some two or three thousand Frenchmen waiting on the north bank by the ford. We cannot cross."

"Thank you."

The King waved me over, "Well Strongstaff? Tell me you have good news for this day seems filled with dire tidings."

"I have none, Your Majesty, but I spy some hope. The French Constable has occupied Abbeville with the vanguard of the French army. They outnumber us but I saw no sign of the main body. If we were to move quickly then there is a chance, we might slip between them."

The Duke of York interjected, "And be trapped! This is madness nephew! Let us negotiate a passage home rather than risking being caught in a trap."

The King shook his head, "You might not have noticed, Uncle, but we are trapped already." He then turned to me as though his uncle had left us, "Strongstaff, find me another bridge. Amiens and the large towns are not suitable, so we need somewhere quiet, a ford or a causeway."

I nodded, "I will just take my lances. Sir John and Sir Gilbert can revert to acting as the vanguard."

"You know best; just get me north of the Somme!"

This meant that I would have all of my men with me. Rafe, James and the others could ride with us. I felt safer that way. We headed, first to Pont St Remy but there was a force of over a thousand men there. We might have been able to force it, but they would be able to hold us up enough to trap us between their two armies: the advance guard and the main army. Speed was our only ally and so we kept up a good pace. I sent a message to the King that the village of Bailleul, close to Pont St Remy would be a good place to camp and we pushed on, deeper into French territory. By the time we reached Amiens we saw that the French had destroyed all but the major bridges and they were defensible. To cross them we would have to fight and then assault walls. Dysentery had ended any chance of such a strategy. We camped at Pont de Metz which was close to Amiens. The people fled at our arrival and crossed over to Amiens. It meant that there were animals for us; spoils of war. We were hungry and although my men were used to such privations, I doubted that the main army was. We had one advantage. Every single man capable of bearing arms was either with the advanced guard at Abbeville or on the road somewhere. Amiens would just have enough men to defend the walls and that was all.

We headed for Boves before dawn. I left four men, under the command of Matty, with the animals we had taken and instructions to see that the King himself was given them. And it was at Boves that we found a defended castle. However, as we wearily dismounted, just out of range of missiles from the castle walls, I noticed that there was no attempt to shift us and that suggested that the castle was garrisoned by the men of the village. My men and I were weary and I saw heads dropping. Even my sons and son in law were not immune from the depression which gripped us.

"We will wait here for the King. David of Welshpool, come with me and we will scout. Sir Richard, make a good camp and use stakes! I would not have us attacked from the castle."

"Aye, lord."

They had ceased trying to dissuade me from such acts. Walter rode with us as did Rafe and we followed the river. Walter had adapted well to life on the road and took the privations better than many others. He had formed a good friendship with Wilton, Will of Stockton's squire, and as we rode used his eyes well. It was he who spotted that the river headed north. It was at Corbie and I saw that we could continue to follow the river but in the far distance, I saw signs that the river made a great loop. I realised that we could get ahead of the French by not following the river and cutting out a forty-mile ride along the river. We might miss opportunities to cross but would gain a whole day. Although it would soon be dark, I pushed our weary horses on to the large village of Nesle and there I spied some hope. There was a mile-wide marsh close to the river and that suggested to me that we might be able to cross. It was too late at night to risk it and so we headed back. The last mile or so we were guided by the fires my men had lit. We had almost exhausted our rations and I knew that the stew we ate would be wild greens, a few dried beans and the last of the ham bones. The great and the good would turn their noses up at the plain fare but my hardy men would make the best of it.

Rafe said, as Walter unsaddled our horses, "Lord, we had better have a late start tomorrow for these horses have little left to give and even an hour or so of extra rest might help them to survive."

Rafe knew his horses. I was also weary. I would await the King and give him a glimmer of hope. Matty and my four men arrived just after we did. "There is to be a trial tomorrow, lord. The King found one of his brother's men stealing a pyx from a church. He is to be tried here."

"Then it is good that I stay for he will want all to witness his discipline."

I had men watching all sides of the castle and village. They must have had few horses for there was no attempt to send a rider for help. To be fair to the French it would have been a hazardous ride as the French had cut all of the bridges thus far. They were inconveniencing their own people as much as they were preventing us from crossing. Rafe had the rest for the horses and in the morning, we added water to the pans which had held the stew and had that for breakfast.

The King arrived before noon for it was a short journey from their camp. He dismounted close to me so that he could speak with me and the prisoner was brought, tethered to a wagon and in full view of the castle. I wondered at the mind of the King.

"So, Strongstaff, you have a bridge for me?"

"Perhaps, King Henry." I pointed to the east. "If we cut the loop of the river we can get ahead of those following us and those who are across the river and shadowing us. Just before dark, I spied a piece of land which looked marshy and flat. Such places are normally close to places where the river can be forded."

"And are there any French close by?"

"I believe there is another castle at Corbie on the river but by heading east we can avoid it."

"You have done well and now let us get this unpleasantness over with." He mounted his horse and, bareheaded rode over to the wagon. "John of Southwark you have been found guilty of stealing a pyx from the church. Did you not hear my explicit command that there would be no looting?"

"It was just a small pyx, my lord!" I heard the panic in his voice. He had stolen something which was small in the hope that no one would notice.

The King raised his voice, "Does any man here, in this army, wish me to show this man mercy? Are there any of his friends who think I am being harsh? Speak now and do not let it fester."

A voice called out, "The man is a fool and would take the pennies from a corpse's eyes! Hang the bastard!"

The King shrugged, "So be it. Brother, he is your man, hang him!" The King was showing his hard side. It would be a lesson for his young brother. He would learn that he was responsible for his men and their actions. A rope was thrown over a tree and, with his hands tethered behind him the Duke of Gloucester had his men haul the thief, his legs kicking, into the air. It would not be a quick death. His neck was not broken, and we all watched, mesmerized as his legs kicked and thrashed until they slowly stopped, and he choked to death. His body would be left there overnight.

"Uncle, Strongstaff, fetch your horses and come with me!"

Intrigued the two of us followed him to the castle and town of Boves. We reined in before the walls, "I am King Henry of England and France, I am here to claim back my land. I would have bread, food and wine brought out to me and my men."

The French castellan did not sound confident as he said, "We have little enough, my lord."

"Then send out what you have." There was silence. This was wine-growing country and the town of Boves was known for its produce. "You have just witnessed my justice. If you do not comply with my request, then I will send my men to tear out every vine that they can find and then use them to burn down your walls." He smiled. "It is your choice."

It worked and bread and wine were brought forth. I wondered if the King had planned this when he had captured the thief and kept his justice for a place where it would do some good. We all knew of the vines for we had drunk the wine of Boves before now. The men wanted to fill their water bottles with the wine for the burghers of Boves brought it out in great quantities. They knew the effect it had on Englishmen. King Henry refused their request and said that only water could be kept in water skins. The wine, bread and food held off starvation, but the mood of the men was growing increasingly ugly.

While we awaited the food, the King sent every archer into the small wood which lay between the castle and the river. He had them all cut a six-foot-long stake. It was a wise move for if we were attacked on the road then each archer carried the means to make an instant fort. Every archer always carried a small hand axe or hatchet. They were useful for foraging timber and in a battle could be used to deadly effect against fallen horsemen. As we ate warm bread washed down with good red wine he said, "In a way, I hoped that the men of Boves would have refused my request. The men need to fight and to kill. If they do not, then they may look closer to home." I nodded, for he was right. "Tomorrow, we will take this short-cut of yours, it looks like it is our only hope."

Once again, the pressure was on me. It had been the same with his father, especially when we had been in the Baltic. The difference was that I knew I would not be blamed if I was wrong. This King Henry understood the vagaries of war.

I had slept well the night before and we rode before dawn. Corbie was on the river and so we were able to stay out of crossbow range. I sent a dozen archers ahead to Nesle while I awaited the King who was hard on the heels of the van. Our column was like a ship dragging a sea anchor. The wagons with the baggage, the engineers and the priests and healers dragged us and held us back. We were mounted, in the main, but we were held back by wagons and slow marching priests. The men who fought on foot were tough men who could keep up with horses, especially for short distances and we needed speed. The French army was slower than we were, but they had horsemen who could race ahead and destroy bridges. As we waited for the King, I knew that our only chance was this one. We would find no bridges standing and so we would have to ford the river.

It may have been that we delayed too long but, more likely, we probably presented a target which the French could not ignore. The garrison at Corbie suddenly erupted from their castle. We were outnumbered and isolated. David of Welshpool did not hesitate, "Archers dismount! Horse holders take the horses. Embed your stakes."

I shouted, "Men at arms, to me! Squires! Hold the archer's horses!"

To a watcher, it would have looked like confusion but it was not. The stakes were quickly driven into the ground as one archer in four held the horses. As the squires and servants, like Rafe and James, arrived so the archers holding the horses were able to release them and join the other archers. The three quarters of a mile the French had to cover meant that the archers were ready with a strung bow and nocked arrow before the leading French horses had covered half of that distance. To my left I heard a horn as Sir Gilbert and Sir John, leading the van saw the attack and raced towards us with the rest of the vanguard.

The archers drew back their bows, and I raised my sword. We would attack the mass of men coming towards us. I had to assume that my men at arms and knights were better protected than many of the garrison. "Keep to the west so that the archers can rain death. We will charge them and hold until Sir John and Sir Gilbert arrive."

None of us was dismayed by the attack and I knew that King Henry would relish the opportunity. If anything, this played into his hands as it might persuade the French that we intended to force a crossing of the river at the castle of Corbie. I saw as we charged towards the French that Sir Gilbert and Sir John had kept their men as close to us as they could. However, their archers would not be of any use as they were mounted. My archers would have to thin the French ranks while the two groups of men at arms did battle. I saw that many of the knights with the vanguard had their banners flying. We did not. My men at arms, knights and I struck first, even before the arrows had fallen. I had my shield strapped to my left arm where it would act as an extra piece of armour. Fire was also well-rested and he powered ahead of the others. I knew that my sons, not to mention Stephen of Morpeth and my men at arms would be cursing me for doing so. It meant that we were an arrowhead and I would strike the French first. I saw that, to the west Sir Hugh Stafford, Lord Bouchier, who was carrying the standard of Guienne was ahead of Sir Gilbert. The young knight would reach the French at the same time as I did!

I leaned forward in the saddle and held my sword behind me. The knight against whom I would fight had a lance and I could see that he was not experienced with it. The head rose and fell as his horse galloped over the uneven ground. I angled my left arm as I began my sword swing. My arm was unencumbered as I was ahead of Harry. The wooden lance shattered and splintered when it hit my shield. It might have hurt me more if I had not angled it but the smack I received was loud rather than disabling. I swung my sword over Fire's head and connected with the back of the French knight's head. He slumped over his saddle, held in place by his cantle. One of my men at arms would finish him off.

Sir Hugh Stafford had been foolish. Carrying a banner meant that you could not defend yourself well and I saw the standard wrenched from his hand and the French man at arms who did so began to head back to Corbie. I cursed Sir Hugh. Losing a standard would tear the heart from our men.

Already our archers had thinned the enemy ranks and my men and I were winning the skirmish but the standard was heading back into the French castle. "Sir Thomas, Sir Henry! Recover that standard!" The falling French knight I had defeated had created a hole and my sons had a clear line to chase down the Frenchman with the standard.

"Aye!"

The two of them, with four of their men at arms, poured through the hole and I turned my attention to the Frenchmen before me. Sir Gilbert and the rest of the vanguard were now applying pressure to the French right and with our archers on our right, we had them contained. It was now a battle of men at arms and we were winning.

My son in law had joined me, and Stephen of Morpeth filled the gap vacated by my sons. The three of us drove towards a French knight and men at arms who looked to be from the same familia. The knight had a war hammer and in a confused mêlée such as this, it could be a deadly weapon. As luck would have it the knight was between myself and my son in law. I could not risk Sir Richard. He was a good horseman, but he did not have as much experience as I did in such skirmishes. I spurred Fire who leapt at the chestnut ridden by the French knight. Mary's men in Middleham had schooled Fire well and he snapped and bit at the French courser. It was just enough to make the French horse veer away slightly and allowed me to get in the first swing as the French knight readjusted his swing. My strike was not a clean one, but it struck first and that was important. I hit his right shoulder and the edge of my blade slid from the mail to hack into the wooden haft of the war hammer close to the knight's hands. Higher up there was metal to protect it. The blow slightly weakened the war hammer but, more importantly, sent the head to the left of the French horse. A war hammer is heavy and as he pulled back his arm for a second attempt, I rammed the tip of my sword up towards his helmet. He wore a coif, but the sword went between the coif and the helmet. The helmet flew from his head. I stood in my stirrups and swung my shield so that the edge connected with the side of the French knight's head. I stunned him and his war hammer dropped. One of his men at arms grabbed his reins to lead him from the battle while Sir Richard hacked into the shoulder of a second. It was a crucial moment in the skirmish for the French heard the horns as King Henry led the bulk of our men at arms to come to our aid and they began to flee.

Then I heard a cheer and, looking to my left, I saw Harry slay one man at arms while Thomas wrenched the standard of Guienne from the dead hand of the man he had just killed. The potential disaster had been averted. As the French fled back into their castle there was a collective cheer. The spirits of the army had been at a low ebb, but the French attack and our response had given the army heart, once more. We would fight on.

A chastened Sir Hugh was grateful to have his banner back and I knew that there would be words from Sir Gilbert and Sir John. The King, in contrast, was in high spirits. "Would that every French garrison came at us piecemeal. Well done, my lords." He pointed east, "Sir William, you have work to do. Find me the crossing of the river!"

I nodded, "Aye, my lord. Archers, pick up your stakes! Let us ride!"

Chapter 9

Gill of Wetherby was on the north bank of the Somme when we reached my scouts. He had his bow strung and an arrow ready. I could see how he had crossed; there was a causeway. Will Straight Shaft pointed, "There are two causeways, lord, but they are narrow, and it will take time to cross."

I stood in my saddle so that I could see better. "Harry, ride back to the King and tell him there are two narrow passages across the river we can cross. We will secure the north bank."

I followed Will as he led me over the slightly wider of the two causeways. The water came to Fire's belly and that meant it was fordable, however, just next to my horse I saw that the water was deeper. When I made the other side and while my men crossed, I looked and saw a small farm. The people had fled when my archers had arrived. "Begin to demolish the wooden buildings. We will widen the crossing. If we can only cross two men at a time, then it will take us days to cross."

I dismounted as my men began to obey my orders. I waved over David of Welshpool. "Send the archers in patrols. I would know what is close by. The army will be heading north and west; find the King a route to Calais. The French will be to the east of us. I believe that there is a castle at Peronne. Have the men stay hidden."

He gave me a wry smile, "Aye, lord, and shall I also teach them to suck eggs?"

I smiled back for I had insulted my archers, "If they need the instruction then aye!"

I saw that the King himself had ridden with the vanguard. He looked elated when he saw my men on the north bank of the river. I waded back towards him. It was to show him that work needed to be done.

"Well done Strongstaff. This may be just the advantage that we need although the French may be close by. We will make the causeway wider and begin to cross the men. You have sent scouts to find a route to the coast?"

"Yes, King Henry, but once we cross this river there is no way back to Harfleur."

"I know but we have many routes we can take to reach Calais and we shall keep the French guessing." He turned in his saddle. "There are two causeways! The soldiers will use the narrower one and the baggage the wider one." He turned back to me. "I shall stay here to ensure that there is good order." This was King Henry's army and he would take command! The baggage had not only the wagons but the priests, minstrels, surgeons, engineers and servants. Not all the servants were soldiers like my men and their passage would, perforce, be slow.

He was in good spirits and he stayed by the causeway, which was constantly being improved to make certain that there would be no panic amongst the men. He joked and bantered with those that he knew, especially my men at arms who had now demolished the farm buildings and had doubled the width of one of the causeways.

The archers I had sent east returned first. David of Welshpool pointed, "You were right, Sir William, the French army is at Peronne, but they have men billeted in the nearby villages and we saw some arming. We will have company soon."

"Spread the archers out in a screen. Sir Richard, tell our men to stop work and mount their horses." I rode to the King to tell him the news.

He waved over Sir Gilbert and Sir John, "Have your men at arms support Sir William. If the French try to dispute our crossing deal with them. I will get the men across." As they rode off, he said, "Who did you send to find a passage home?"

"Christopher White Arrow."

The King nodded. He knew most of my men, both archers and men at arms by name. "He is a good man I will watch for him. Deal with the French for I spy hope here. Perhaps the hanging of the thief has changed our fortune. If we can steal a march on the French and put daylight between us then we might be able to find somewhere to turn, as King Edward did. I like not this running before the French!" King Henry was a warrior and not a politician as his father had been.

By the time I joined the two hundred men at arms and fifty archers I saw movement to the east. It was the French horsemen David had warned me of. I doubted that they would be the mailed knights but there would be men at arms amongst the hobelars and if they fell upon men wading through the river then they could harm our already much-depleted numbers. I noticed a chastened Sir Hugh had now given the standard to someone else and he had a sword and a shield. Banners were for battles and not skirmishes at inconsequential halts!

The French were coming at us in small groups. Perhaps the farmers who had seen my archers approaching had fled and warned them. The question was would the main army seize this opportunity to bring us to battle? If they did then we were lost for even though it was gone noon less than a quarter of the army had crossed. I saw Christopher White Arrow ride towards the river and he rode directly to the King who still stood in the river directing the flow of men. I turned back to the French horsemen who approached. David of Welshpool was using the remains of the farm buildings for cover and they began to loose arrows at the approaching horsemen. We had too few archers in place for them to have a dramatic effect. By the same token, there was little point in us charging them until they had more men. Our horses were too valuable to risk and so we waited. After losing ten or twelve men to our arrows the French withdrew to await greater numbers. I took the opportunity to glance behind where I saw that the Duke of Gloucester was directing men to follow Christopher White Arrow. The King must have approved of his news. Now we had to hold on to the crossing until darkness. When night fell, we would be able to lose the French for in this marshy land we could go in any direction. Daylight might show the tracks which night would hide.

I saw light glinting off mail as some French knights arrived. I could see much gesticulating and I guessed that whoever had arrived had realised the problem they faced. This was their chance to win and they had to engage us. I saw a sword raised and then the ragged line of horsemen charged. The King had said for Sir Gilbert and Sir John to support me and so I shouted, "We wait for our archers to thin them a little and then we charge, hurt them and withdraw! We are here to slow them!" I added, "No heroics, Sir Hugh!"

"Aye, lord, I have learned a lesson!"

David of Welshpool knew his craft and he had his men arrayed so that they could all release at once. He waited until the French were just two hundred and fifty paces from us and then had his men send arrow after arrow. After they had sent five flights each I shouted, "For God, King Henry and St George!" I spurred Fire and my eager young horse took off as though stung

David had heard my words and, as we passed them, I heard him command his men to send their arrows into the rear of the French host. The arrows had thinned the enemy and I headed for the plated knights who led the French. The range had been too great for the bodkin arrows to have much effect and the riders, with their armoured horses, were unharmed. Again, I had my shield strapped to my arm and with Thomas on my left and Harry on my right, I was well protected. I knew that Stephen of Morpeth and my other men at arms would have preferred to be guarding me, but my sons would not allow it. Walter, Rafe and James rode some forty paces behind in case I was unhorsed or hurt. I hoped that they would not be needed but I knew that Rafe and James would watch out for Walter. He would come to no harm so long as they lived. When heavily plated horses and men meet there is a din so loud that it sounds like a sudden thunderstorm. Often that first collision, without the use of a single weapon could result in death or injury. A knight could plan what he would do but he could not know what his enemy would do. I had seen in the past two riders charge each other and both turn the same way resulting in both riders falling from their mounts and being trampled. Shrewsbury had seen men fighting on foot and that was a more assured way to fight. This charge, whilst necessary, was unpredictable. The leader of the French must have been inexperienced or like Sir Hugh had been over-keen. He committed to an attack too soon. He was going to engage me sword to sword. I jinked my reins to the right. Had he emulated me then we would have collided, and the result would have been in God's hands. As it was, he was too slow to react, and his sword was on the wrong side. I swung my sword at the back of his head. The way it jerked told me that I had hurt him and when he slipped from the saddle that was confirmed. Thomas' horse trampled and crushed his body while my son used his war axe to hack through the arm of the man at arms he faced. Harry's sword had found the open helmet of a second knight and then our line was amongst the hobelars and lightly armoured men.

"Turn and cut them up!"

We were impervious to their blows for they were trying to strike at plate. Our swords could penetrate their brigandines and their edges hacked into mail. The French stood until it was clear that every knight was dead or badly wounded and then they fled. As we made our way back to the causeways, I saw that almost all of the army was across, and the light was fading to darkness and night.

The Duke of York rode up to me, "Well done, Strongstaff. We ride to Athies. It is a hamlet just a few miles up the road. We will spend the night there and leave on the morrow."

We waited until our archers had mounted and then, leaving the rearguard to take from the dead, we headed to our temporary home.

We were exhausted and there was little food to be had. My men were luckier than most, Rafe and James had seized the opportunity to hack the hindquarters and rumps from one of the hobelars' small horses. We ate, at least, and as my scouts had chased the French from the hamlet it was they who had acquired the wine and ale that was there. The hamlet was defensible and so, while our horses recuperated, the King convened a council of war.

"We have saved a week thanks to the scouts of Sir William Strongstaff. Now we push on to Calais."

His uncle said, "If the French will allow us."

"We know that they have men at Peronne, but they did not come forth in force. We will leave as soon as we can. Once we cross the River Ternoise at Blangy we will be close to Calais. Our ordeal is almost over."

Sir Walter Hungerford said, "Aye, Your Majesty, but if we had the ten thousand archers who are still in England then we could turn and rout this French rabble!"

King Henry laughed, "I would not have more than we have even if I could. Do you not believe that the Almighty will help this humble little band overcome the pride of these Frenchmen who boast of their numbers and their strength? Our losses have not been in war they have been through disease. When we have crossed swords and exchanged arrows with the French then they have lost. I had thought to fight them here but as they have not obliged yet then we will push on!"

King Henry was the very heart and soul of the army. We had had to hang one man but he was the only one and it made better soldiers of the others. The rest all believed that if we had to fight the French then we would not lose. It seemed impossible but that was the mood of the whole camp. I know that I was luckier than most men for my men, all of them, were close to me, and I knew their feelings. At the same time because I was the senior knight then other lords confided in me.

When we took the road, I led the van once more and it was I who discovered, on the Amiens to Bapaume road, the huge swathe cut by the French army which had passed north. Leaving my sons to lead the vanguard I rode back to the King and told him what I had seen. The French army is ahead of us but they cannot know where we are or they would have waited for us!"

"Then the Almighty does, indeed, wish us to win and I take great heart from your news. Had they turned then they could have surrounded and trapped us. They are heading for St. Pol and trying to cut us off from Calais. We have a chance to reach Calais before they realise. Push on Strongstaff and we will be right behind you."

We rode hard, as we had been commanded but the populace seemed outraged that the English were still abroad in their land. The King had told us that civilians were to be left unharmed but that was hard, especially when they not only cursed and abused us as we rode through the villages but hurled stones at our horses.

"My lord, let us teach them a lesson and they will stop!"

"I am sorry, Jack, but we have our orders and we cannot hurt them. Just then a huge blacksmith came from his forge and, in his hands, he held tongs which gripped a blazing coal from his fire. That was too much for me to bear and so I reacted instinctively as I did not wish him to throw it at my horse. It was only later that I remembered my horse's name. I pulled back on the reins and stood in the saddle. Fire reared and so took the smith by surprise that he took three steps backwards and tripped over the leg of a boy, I assumed was his son. The tongs and stone flew over his head and stuck in the thatch on a low, one-storied building. The summer dried thatch burst into flames and all thoughts of abusing us ceased as everyone in the village grabbed pails of water and tried to douse the flames. We passed through without any further abuse and my men were greatly cheered by the action. I had no idea what the King would say but I had had no choice in the matter. If I was to be punished, then so be it.

One advantage of being the advance guard was that we were the first at any encampment. In fact, we chose most of them. We were able to find the driest piece of ground and to refill our water bottles before horses had tramped in it and those upstream spoiled it. While we were forbidden to take from the villagers there was nothing wrong with foraging and we were usually able to find wild greens. Occasionally we were able to hunt a rabbit or squirrel or two and they went into a pot which would otherwise have been wild greens and water! The village of Acheux did not try to abuse us but there was no food to be had and so we set up a camp. I sent a couple of archers north to try to find the French. The vanguard always left camp an hour before the rest of the army and therefore we camped an hour earlier. There would still be enough daylight for the scouts to find the enemy if they were close.

The King arrived and I was summoned to his tent. His servants were adept at erecting it so quickly that it almost appeared to be the work of a magician! "Strongstaff, we passed a burning house. What do you know of it?" I did not tell a falsehood but gave him the truth and he smiled, "You obey my orders, yet you still manage to chastise our foes. I constantly tell my young knights to watch you for there is much to learn."

I was still speaking with the King when Jack Gardyvyan rode in. He dropped to one knee and addressed the King, "My Lord, the French and their army are ten miles north of us. It seems that they follow a parallel course."

"Then it will be a race to Calais, eh? You will keep a sharp look out on the morrow, Strongstaff. I think our two roads combine although I am unsure of that."

After leaving the King, I spoke with the other knights of the vanguard and warned them what was likely to happen. Unlike the King, I was convinced that the French would catch us before Calais. The English island in France lay more than fifty miles away and our horses had been hard ridden for more than half a month. Added to that was the fact that the people of this part of France had been feeding their own knights and half of our army was starving to death. Now it would not be a pyx which caused a hanging but the theft of a loaf of bread! We sharpened swords and checked equipment. As we prepared to ride, I heard hooves and stopped. I gripped my sword but as I peered into the distance, I saw that it was Davy Gam and his sons.

He grinned and held up his hands, "It is us, Sir William. I pressed the King and asked him leave to ride with you. He knew our history and he allowed it. I hope that you do not mind?"

I shook my head, "Just keep silent, you garrulous Welshman."

"It will be hard, Sir William, but for you, I shall try!"

It was dark when we rose and headed to the bridge at Blangy. This was the last river we would cross before we reached Calais and I was anxious to secure it for the King and the army. The villagers there might be like the ones who had hurled abuse and stones at us and the sooner we reached it the better. I also woke Sir Gilbert and Sir John for I wanted their support too. I suspected that we might meet the French vanguard and I wanted the support of as many men at arms as I could! The narrow twisting roads would have been hard enough to navigate in daylight but in the half-light of pre-dawn, they were a positive danger. I was with my archers this time. David of Welshpool was as experienced as I was, but four eyes were better than two. We both smelt the wood smoke long before we reached the bridge and that was a worry for it was before dawn and any fires in houses would not yet have taken.

I reined in and spoke into David's ear. "I like this not, David. That wood smoke may mean that the bridge is guarded."

He nodded his agreement. He said nothing but dismounted and handed his reins to the designated horse holder. He pointed to four of his archers and they loped off into the dark.

Sir Gilbert joined me as did Sir John. My sons and son in law were there but they knew better than to engage in conversation. I watched Gilbert open his mouth and I put my hand over it and shook my head. It was almost amusing to watch his expression. I pointed to the bridge and mimed, '*The French*'. He nodded.

The sun was just rising behind us when my archers ghosted up so quietly that Sir John started. David spoke quietly but urgently, "The French hold the bridge, my lord. it is less than half a mile up the road.

They will hear your hooves on the cobbles. I would say no more than a hundred of them, but they have a barrier across the road."

I nodded, "Take the archers, cross the river and flank them." As he and the archers led their horses off, I turned to the men at arms close by me. "We will charge the bridge. Matty, Nat, Harold and Dick I want you to dismount now and leave your horses here with Walter. Go on foot and, when we advance, and David of Welshpool sends his arrows, I want you to remove the barriers so that we can charge across."

"Aye, my lord."

I knew that we were making more noise but that could not be helped. As I drew my sword, I saw the questions written all over the faces of Sir Gilbert and Sir John. I had not the time to explain that I knew my men and I could rely on all of them to do that which I asked when I asked. I spurred Fire and with my two sons and son in law flanking me began to ride towards the bridge. As David had predicted the noise of our hooves made the French sound the alarm. Then I heard the first cry as my archers aimed their arrows at short range. The sun seemed to suddenly erupt behind us as we neared the bridge. I saw the brazier and it illuminated metal. I had my sword drawn and watched as a crossbowman with an arrow in the side of his head pitched into the river. My four men at arms were fearless and they grabbed the first of the barriers to hurl into the water. There was a second. A French man at arms ran towards them with a sword drawn. My men were weaponless, but I watched Harold of Derby run towards the man and as the sword came down to split his skull, he used his strength to block the blow and hurl the man over the parapet. The other three cleared the bridge for us just as we clattered noisily across. I knew that Davy and his sons had inveigled themselves behind us. They were good men but my men at arms would be less than happy!

The archers had cleared the bridge but not the village side and the men who had been asleep had now roused and were racing at us with their weapons drawn. Until we had a bridgehead then the four of us would be vulnerable. As usual, Fire was the first across and the slight drop to the road surface enabled me to almost fly through the air. His hooves smashed into the chest of the first Frenchman and my sword swept into the side of the skull of a second. Harry and Thomas wielded their weapons with great skill and two more Frenchmen were knocked to the ground. Davy and his sons were so close to us that they risked crashing into our horses. He led them to the right into the blackness that was there. It was a brave thing to do. We had now created enough space for more of my men at arms to pour across. Kit Warhammer lived up to his name and he crashed between Thomas and me to smash his weapon through the helmet and into the skull of a luckless Frenchman.

"Push them from the village! We need a perimeter!"

Davy and his sons pushed to the right as Kit and the other pushed to the left. We were an unstoppable force and showed the power of well-used men at arms on heavy horses.

All of the men at arms and knights of the vanguard were now in Blangy and soon, any Frenchmen who were left would be dead or prisoners. David and the archers had scrambled up the bank and they were loosing arrows at close range. Even plate could not withstand them and that made the French flee. As they did so I looked to the north and saw, to my horror, the French advance guard. They were ahead of us and would be able to cut us off from Calais. We were trapped. Now it was even more imperative to get as far north as we could. I turned in the saddle, "Harry, ride to the King and tell him that the French vanguard is ahead of us!"

He waved his hand in acknowledgement and made his way back over the bridge now clear of the vanguard. It was not as bad as the causeways had been but the baggage would take an age to cross it and if the main French army was behind us then it would end very badly for us. I took off my helmet and rode through the dead and dying Frenchmen to spy out the enemy position. There were at least five thousand men in the French vanguard, and they outnumbered not just our advanced guard but our whole army!"

"Stephen of Morpeth, take four men and ride along the road. I think I spy a village not far ahead. Hold it and send a man back. "

"Aye, lord." He was, amazingly, grinning. "Don't worry Sir William, our luck has to change soon and besides all that French armour will bring us all great booty!"

That was the English warrior in a nutshell. Until his sword was taken from his dead hand, he would not believe he was beaten.

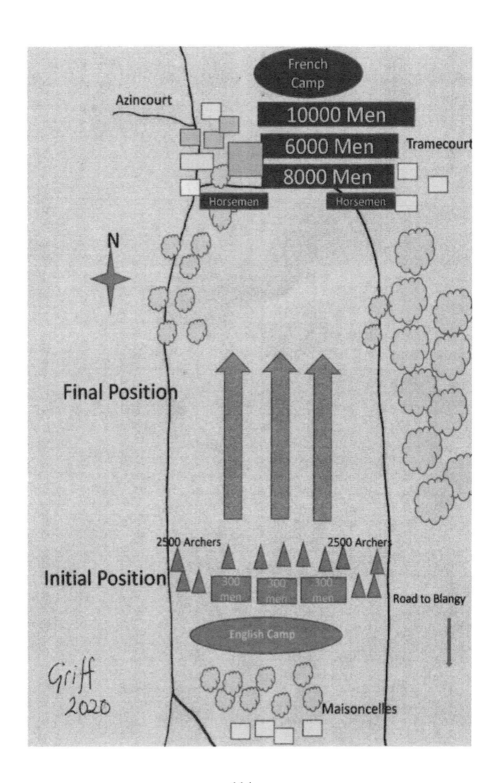

Chapter 10

The hamlet we had found was Maisoncelles and it was on a hill with a wood before it. The dozen or so houses were just a mile from Azincourt which was a much larger village sporting a castle. Of course, none of the English could pronounce the French word and so we all called the village, Agincourt. The King rode through the army to join me and together we rode hard with the vanguard to the wood just north of Maisoncelles. The people had fled to the castle and villages north of it. for it was quite obvious that a battle would take place and the villagers knew that was no place for bystanders. I saw the French vanguard begin to position themselves on the high ground just below the other two villages.

King Henry was a practical man and not given to histrionics. King Richard would have ranted and railed about his ill-luck and Henry Bolingbroke would have been looking for a political escape route but King Henry was a better man, leader and king than both of them. Even as he viewed the French while they filled the ground opposite us, he was thinking of a way out and how to defeat the French. As he had shown at Shrewsbury, he was not afraid to die. "Well Strongstaff, if that is their advance guard then we can assume that they will have six times that number when it comes to battle."

He was inviting a comment, "Aye, my lord, I would guess closer to thirty thousand men." I waved a hand at the ploughed field before us. Recently harvested it looked like it had been ploughed to sow the next crop. It was bordered by the road to Blangy and beyond it was the Forest of Tramecourt. "This could be a killing ground for our archers." I glanced up at the sky where the clouds were increasing. "And if it rains…"

"This will become a muddy morass." The King nodded and looked behind us at the trees, "If it went ill for us, we could slip through those trees behind us." He pointed across the field to the larger village the French were using as their base. "That castle and those houses mean that they will be concentrated between it and those trees there." He nodded towards the hamlet of Tramecourt to the east of the French position. "This is as good a position as we could have wished, and the

French have chosen it. Honour is satisfied. We dig in here and plant stakes. We will put our camp here close to the trees. We will put our three battles here with a line of archers before them. The bulk of the longbowmen will be on the flanks. I will echelon them so that we can pour arrows into their flanks. Let us wait for them to attack us and then use our greatest weapon the archer. We will keep our men on foot and test the valour of these French, but I know that God is on our side and I doubt not that we shall prevail. Your men shall be on the right. Have them embed their stakes to discourage their advanced guard from harassing us. I will ride back and direct the battles to their allotted positions. I will not be caught with our breeks around our ankles, Strongstaff. We shall be ready whenever the French come."

"Aye, my lord."

He nodded to me, "I hear Gam did well at Blangy!"

"He did, my lord, as did Kit Warhammer."

He nodded, "But Gam has served us well before. He shall have his spurs for it will raise the spirits of the loyal Welshmen who follow us." I confess that I had never thought of such things but he was right and we needed all the help we could get in this battle. It was not fair on Kit, but I could knight him when we returned to England. The King had a greater responsibility than I did.

As he and his squire left, I waved over Walter and dismounted; I handed Fire's reins to him, "This will be our camp. When Rafe and the others get here choose a good place for our tents and baggage."

My young squire looked fearfully at the increasing numbers of French who were filling the ground between Agincourt and Tramecourt. The light glinted off their mail and in contrast to our mud-spattered tunics they looked like peacocks in their bright surcoats. "There are so many, my lord. Will the king negotiate?"

I laughed, "King Henry? Never. Fear not, Walter, you shall be safe here with the French prisoners, the other squires, the baggage and the spare horses. Even if we lost, which I doubt then you would be safe. Now go and choose a good spot. You know how to do so now."

"Aye, my lord,"

"David of Welshpool, come with me and fetch the archers along with their stakes. Sir Gilbert, this will be the camp and the men at arms are to fight dismounted. The King would have us on the right by the wood of Tramecourt. The men at arms will be behind and to the right of the stakes we are to embed."

"Aye Sir William! At last, we have the chance to fight!" He seemed eager to get to grips with the French. The skirmishes we had enjoyed had shown our superiority, but I knew that this would be a much harder test.

I know of no other army which would have faced such odds so eagerly. Certainly, in the vanguard, none were dismayed by the odds. In the case of all of my men, they were viewing the French much as a wolf views a flock of sheep. They were already calculating how much they would get for mail, plate, weapons and ransom. David and the archers had already dismounted, and the men designated as horse holders were leading the mounts to Walter and the other squires. They would fasten lines in the trees and tether the horses there. One of the tasks those in the camp would have would be to feed and water the horses. If we had to run, then the horses would be the only way to escape.

I led the archers to the highest point in the ploughed field. The summer crops had been harvested and the field harrowed. It was not smooth. That would not matter to archers, but horses would not be able to maintain a straight line and even men on foot would struggle. The French farmers had, unwittingly, aided us.

"I want the archers here. Embed and sharpen the stakes. Leave space on the right of you close to the wood for the King intends to have two strong wings of archers. When the other archers arrive have them make a new moon with their stakes. The King will invite the French to take him in the centre."

"A good position, my lord, and it is good that we have wagonloads of arrows," he pointed to the skyline which was now filled with French horsemen, "for we shall need them." David was not being downhearted, merely realistic. He also knew that even though the archers were a much easier target for horsemen to attack the French would send their men towards the men at arms for there was more honour in that.

The King's battle arrived, and I watched the King's brother, the Duke of Gloucester, direct them to the left of us. The Duke of York had dismounted his horse and walked over to me. "I am to command the right." I nodded. He gave me a wry shake of the head, "My nephew seems to have drawn every French lance here to this inconsequential part of France."

"It saves us having to seek the others out when we have won this day!"

The King's uncle lowered his voice, "You think we can win this day?"

"My lord, I have fought in too many battles where the odds appeared too great to speculate. We should have lost at Shrewsbury, but we did not. I believe that if every man does his duty then we shall win for our men are better. All the hunger of the march north will disappear. My men are already eating, in their minds, the meal they will garner from the French camp. They are eager to fight."

He nodded, "We will each have to slay four of their men at arms to do so."

I smiled, "Then I shall need a spare sword!"

He patted me on the back and went to direct more archers into their positions. Our smaller numbers meant that the three battles and the attendant archers were in position before the French. Our squires and servants had erected the tents and our camp was finished. I saw the King change into a clean surcoat and don a great helm topped with a crown. He was one of the few who had such fine clothes left to him and it made him stand out. I knew that was deliberate. King Henry would have preferred a single combat with the greatest of all of the French knights to decide the outcome of this conflict. It had been refused once and he would not offer again. He was, instead, drawing the French to him and he would be in the centre. His household knights and his bodyguards would be hard-pressed.

I walked along the line of archers speaking to those I knew. I had been a camp follower with the Blue Company and the Black Prince had always spoken to his men before battle. When I led men then I did so too and I wandered amongst my own men. I spoke about personal matters with the men from my manors and with the others, I spoke of weapons and battles. It was late afternoon when I returned to my position and still the French had not attacked. I knew that they were still arriving but, already, the slopes below Azincourt were a sea of plate festooned with bright surcoats and banners. I could see on the two flanks more than two thousand mounted men at arms and, in the centre more than eight thousand dismounted men at arms. We had nine hundred to face them. I wondered what made them hold off. As I viewed them, I could see which of the archers had either had or still had, the bloody flux which had claimed so many lives. They wore half hose and a loincloth. It was easier and quicker to remove a loincloth than attempt to take off hose or breeks!

Sir Thomas Erpingham came over to me, "Sir William, I am to command the archers and your man, David of Welshpool, is known to be the best captain of archers. I would speak with him."

I pointed him out, "He is there."

"The King would speak with you; he wonders why the French do not attack!"

I turned to my son, "Thomas, take command of my men. The King needs my counsel!"

"He always does. Take care father! I would not be the one to face my mother's wrath if I returned with news of your demise!"

"I do not think that day is here yet." Even as I said it, I clutched at the crosspiece of my sword for it did not do to tempt fate in such a way.

The King was surrounded by his senior lords. His brother and uncle were at his side, but they made way for me. Perhaps it was the white hairs, or it may have been that I had fought more battles than any two knights on the field that day.

"Strongstaff, what think you?"

"I think that the French are superstitious. Each battle in which they have attacked first they have lost. I think they hope to tempt us to attack up that slope."

They all laughed but King Henry waved them to be silent with an imperious wave of his arm. "But we will not do that! It would be foolish."

I nodded and pointed to the castle, "And when we do not the Constable and the French leaders will dine in the Great Hall of yonder castle. The villagers will have baked bread for the army. They will eat well this night and drink wine. We will make nettle stew and drink the water we collected from the bloody river at Blangy. The French are counting on the fact that we are starving and have to attack to reach Calais."

"You are saying that we are beaten?"

"No, King Henry, you of all people know me better than that. You asked me why the French were not yet ready to attack, and I have told you. Of course, in a day or so they may think that we are weak enough to risk an attack." I nodded at the blackening skies behind us. "The point will soon be moot for it will rain ere long. Our archers cannot loose in rain. If they attacked when it rained, then that would give them a chance."

I had given the King much to ponder and he said, "Stay by me, Will Strongstaff, for what you have said makes sense. Uncle, return to your battle and we shall see what the next hours bring."

They brought rain and as darkness fell it became obvious that no battle would be fought. The French heralds would have approached us to ask us to surrender had battle been imminent and it looked like my assessment was right. The Duke of Gloucester was sent to our prisoners. We had captured many on our journey north and could no longer feed them. They were given their parole. They were sent from the camp and they would return if we won. They happily left and headed back to Blangy. They were confident that they would win. We lit fires and listened to the laughter from the other side of the field as the French

119

army drank and ate well while we sat huddled around fires which sputtered in the drizzle which fell. The King's minstrels tried to rouse the spirits of the men by singing popular and patriotic songs. Men sat in groups which reflected their past. They were brothers in arms. Matty and Nat sat with the newer men at arms while the older ones gathered around Stephen of Morpeth's fire. I sat with my sons and son in law.

Walter and the other squires served us. William, my grandson, had grown up a great deal on the campaign. My wife would have been appalled at the conditions he had had to endure and before we returned home, we would have to advise him to keep the secrets of the battlefield to save offence. Our weapons had been sharpened and our plate polished. There was little left to eat and so when they had taken away the platters and cleaned them then they joined us by the fire. We were largely silent, but I sensed questions and worries bubbling just below the surface.

My son, Harry, also had concerns, "What if the French do not attack, father? I know that the men we lead are resolute, but I have heard murmurings and some of those who follow other knights speak of fleeing and heading for Calais."

I shook my head and threw another branch into the sputtering fire for the rain was falling harder now, "Then they are fools. The French will catch them and hang them. If they are to die, then better to die here where they can serve England."

William said, quietly, "I do not want to die. My life has barely begun."

Thomas put his arm around his nephew, for they were close, "When you took the opportunity to be a squire then death was always a possibility. Your grandfather here had been fighting for six or seven years when he was your age. It is what our family do."

"And yet, grandfather, there are many men abed in England who chose not to fight and if we win then they will reap the reward."

I nodded, "That is true and, as your uncle said, we all make choices. Do I think that makes those abed in England lesser men than we? Then the answer would be, aye. They are like leeches who suck on our blood. London is full of them and if we had a tenth of the men who live in London and profit from our endeavours then we would have the same number of men as the French! We cannot change that although we have, in King Henry, a king who might be able to do that!"

The King's voice came from behind me and made me start for he must have been listening there awhile, "You are right, Strongstaff. The leeches, as you call them, are sucking our land dry. They are the ones who moan and criticise all that is done and yet offer nothing in return."

He looked at William, "Your grandfather knows what he is talking about and when France is won, I will set about shaping England into a land which is fit for heroes like William Strongstaff."

I smiled, "You are not abed yet, Your Majesty? It is not many hours until Laudes."

"There will be time enough for that. Tonight, I speak with as many soldiers as I can for tomorrow, who knows how many will survive."

I smiled, "And tomorrow is an auspicious day, King Henry." He frowned, "Why, it is the feast day of Saint Crispin and Crispinian. It was on that day that the Armagnacs sacked Soissons killing many churchmen and civilians and God will surely be on our side to punish them for that act." I held my hands palms up, "For see he has sent this rain to make the field before us a quagmire and the French will surely struggle to pass it."

The King laughed, "It is good speaking with you, Will Strongstaff, for there is not a pessimistic bone in your body. Sleep well, my friends and especially you, Strongstaff. I have been a member of your band of brothers and I like to think that though we are small in number, this English army is a band of brothers and we will fight for each other!" He looked around and spied Davy Gam and his sons. "Come we shall take this opportunity to give Gam his spurs. The army expected a battle, let us give them something else to celebrate.

It was a spontaneous act and although witnessed, largely, by my men and Gam's Welshmen, the word soon spread. The King must have had spare spurs for he handed Davy a set. When he was knighted the King hugged him and departed,

As the King left us, I saw the faces of the young squires and the Welshmen. They were lit up with joy. Their King had spent time with them, and they now believed that we could win. In addition, he had knighted a commoner and in that, they spied hope. William, Walter and all of the squires were filled with zeal and, more importantly, confidence. I knew that confidence was a key part of any victory.

I turned to Davy, "I am pleased for you, Davy, Sir Davy, it is an honour well deserved."

"And I owe much to you and the luck you bring. Tomorrow I will be on the right with you and I am sure that by the end of the day I shall be an earl!" He had an infectious humour. He and his sons left to celebrate. I had no doubt that they had secured more wine.

"Walter, go and fetch Rafe for me. He will be gambling somewhere and if he complains tell him that Sir William is saving him money!"

Rafe soon arrived and looked suitably offended, "I was not gambling, Sir William, I was settling debts for that is what a man does before a battle. It does not do to die owing money."

I waved him closer to me, "And you will not die tomorrow. I want you and James to watch over the squires as they guard the camp. We will not need horses tomorrow and will not require lances. They can stay in the camp."

"They may be asked to fetch arrows, my lord."

"Then you and James can bring them. The two of you know the dangers. These young lads do not."

He nodded, "And you too should stay from the front line, my lord. You and your sons have played your part already. Let some of those who flocked around the King do some of the fighting."

"Tomorrow, Rafe, there will be no place to hide! The French have handed the King a good battlefield, but it is small and constricted by trees. Those very factors which give us aid are also a prison to trap us should we lose."

"Aye, lord, but we shan't lose! The King was handy when he was Prince Hal and now that he is a man, I fear no Frenchman!"

Leaving my camp, I headed to the men at arms and my archers. The archers' camp was closest to the French for the archers were our piquets. I stood and listened to them as they chatted. The older ones were trying to tell the younger ones what to expect. They had all fought in this campaign, but this was the first real battle and it would be totally different. I stood in the shadows between fires and listened.

"You have to choose your arrows well. Bodkins for men at arms and war arrows for archers, crossbowmen, and spearmen. The bodkins will just annoy the men at arms until they are so close that you will feel the thunder from their horses' hooves. We will send so many arrows that your arms and backs will burn, and Sir Thomas will still demand that you send more. When they are so close that you can smell the garlic on their breath then you drop your bows and use whatever you have to hand." I watched David of Welshpool draw the bodkin dagger from his buskin, "This is the weapon to have. Even a full-face boar's snout helmet has to have eye holes and this beauty will slip into it and take the eyeballs from any Frenchman. They will not yield to us and so there will be no ransom. Kill the bastards. If they come on horses and breach our line, then hamstring their horses."

"But Captain, there are so many that we have not enough arrows to kill them all!"

"Oh, we have enough arrows, but you are right, Peter, some of us, maybe many of us will die tomorrow. When the priests come then confess your sins for some of you will meet your maker before the day is out. The ones who survive will remember you. We will have a mass said for you and we will make sure that your widows and children are cared for. Remember that we serve the Strongstaff family and there are no better lords. There are many lords who will forget their men, but you will not be forgotten."

I saw that his words had reassured them. Christopher White Arrow said, "Keep your bowstrings under your hat and your arrows covered until the last moment and stay close to your stakes."

I stepped into the light and they all leapt to their feet, "Sit. I just came to tell you that I will have Rafe and James fetch your arrows on the morrow. They know their business. They will keep you well supplied and David is quite right, many of us may die tomorrow but we are warriors and if we wanted to die in our own beds we would have become mercers or cordwainers!"

That made them laugh. David said, "They will hold, lord, but if the French do not attack, what then?"

"They will. King Henry will make sure of it."

I headed to my men at arms and I saw that they were sharpening weapons. Approaching from the dark I was unseen, and I heard their words again. It was one of my new men at arms, Martyn, Jack's son. "We should have taken the ship at Harfleur when disease took so many."

Stephen of Morpeth spat into the fire, "What made you want to be a soldier, eh? You have whinged and moaned all the way here."

"I am a good soldier and my dad was a soldier in Pontefract Castle."

"Aye, you can fight, and you are handy but that was not what I asked. What did you think a campaign would be like?"

"Not this! When this is over, I shall seek a life in a garrison."

I heard Harold of Derby snort, "Then you don't want to be a soldier. This is the only life for me. We are all comrades together and tomorrow, no matter what happens there will be no regrets from me. I knew when Sir William offered me the chance to follow his banner, I would jump at it!"

Martyn was not convinced, "I still don't see why it has to be us though."

"Because we are here and nobody else. We follow a real soldier. I could have stayed on my farm in Morpeth but as soon as Sir William asked me then I jumped at the chance to follow him and King Henry. We helped to train him and tomorrow you will see a real leader, two, King Henry and Sir William!"

I felt guilty as I stepped into the light. Harold and Stephen might die the next day and that would be my fault. They had followed me. I waved them to stay seated and spoke. I saw Martyn looking guilty, "I came here to thank you all for what you have done thus far. Tomorrow will be hard, but I know the mettle of the men I lead and when we head home to England, we can reflect on what we have achieved thus far. I am proud of you," I looked pointedly at Martyn, Jack's son, "All of you!"

Chapter 11

It was pitch black when I was awakened by the night guard. The rain still fell but not as heavily. The ones who had not had the luxury of a tent would wake cold and wet. My men had built good hovels and used their oiled cloaks. They would have fared better than most. Rafe and James were there to dress me. They had not woken Walter. I think they regarded him as almost a grandchild. The three of us fitted every strap and plate as though our lives depended upon the fitting. In my case they did. When they were done, they placed my sword and helmet in my tent and returned to the baggage area to begin to cook our breakfast. We would eat after services. I wished to attend the service of Laudes with the King. Some of the men in our camp were awake but most were still asleep. I could hear occasional bursts of laughter from the French camp. The King's Chaplain was waiting to begin the service. He would wait until the Dukes of York and Gloucester arrived before he began.

As we knelt the King said, "From the laughter, the French must be confident, Strongstaff."

"If numbers only won battles then, if I were the French, I would be in high spirits too, but they have no leader. The Constable is the best general they have here and I do not fear him. Duke John the Fearless might be a different prospect."

The King shook his head as his uncle and brother arrived, "It was you won his battle for him, William. Remember that!"

By the time the service had finished, our camp had been roused and the chaplains and priests were busy hearing confessions. Men paid off old debts and confessed to all manner of sins before a major battle. If a man died, he did not want to burn in the fires of hell. I went to see the squires and impress upon them the need to stay close to the camp and the baggage. We had a very shallow line and I wanted none of them risked. Walter and Wilton were the youngest but many others were little older than they were. The servants there, Rafe and James amongst them, nodded that they would ensure that my orders were obeyed. They then carried on making a frugal breakfast of hot food which would fool our stomachs into thinking that we had eaten well. I then went to visit with Fire and my other horses. It was sentimental but I said goodbye to them in case God chose to take me. By the time I had returned to the camp dawn was about to break and Rafe handed me a wooden bowl with some sort of stew. I think they had retained a few bones from the horse we had butchered after we hurt the hobelars, and they had split the bone so that the stew was enriched by the marrow. The greens they had picked gave it some sort of flavour.

As I sipped it, I detected an unusual taste. It was not unpleasant. I looked up at Rafe, "Chestnuts?"

He grinned, "Aye lord, we found some fallen on the road. Roasted and ground they give a bit of taste to the stew. I am pleased you like it."

I nodded, "The first two swords I take today are yours!"

"Thank you, Sir William, but we would just as well you came back emptyhanded but safe."

I strapped on my sword and held my helmet. It was too soon to put it on. "Rafe, fetch a poleaxe, will you. I may well need it today."

"We have one sharpened already." Rafe and James anticipated my every thought, it seemed

I made my way down to the King who was mounting a small white horse. Looking down at me he said, "So far they have not made a move and appear happy for the sun to dry out the ground!"

I shook my head, "It will not be dry until November, my lord. it did not stop raining until after we had been confessed." Rafe handed me my poleaxe and as I took it, I said, "Where will you want me today, King Henry?"

He laughed, "Where would I want the man the Black Prince asked to protect his son and my father? The man who trained me and stood by me through more battles than I care to remember? I would have you next to me! The French will come for me and my standard this day. You will hew them down!"

I nodded, "It will be my honour." I knew that Davy Gam, not to mention my sons, son in law and men at arms would be less than happy but I knew that it was my lot in life. I was the defender of kings!

I saw that he had with him the men who would carry the standards of St George, Edward the Confessor, the Trinity and his own personal arms quartering the lions of England with the fleur-de-lys of France.

Our pathetically small line meant that the King could speak to the whole army as he rode up and down.

"Lions of England know that our cause is just and on this day of St Crispin Crispianus God smiles upon us for he inflicted a defeat upon the French on such a day as this. Your forefathers who were at Crécy and Poitiers are looking down upon you. I know that they will be proud when we emerge victorious. At Crécy the tiny army led by King

126

Edward and the Black Prince lost just forty men and half the noble families of France lost a loved one. We shall emulate their great deeds this day!" He paused. "Many of you think that those of us with titles have the chance to yield and pay a ransom. I will not yield and if it is my lot to die then I forbid any Englishman to pay ransom for my body. If I am to die, then what better resting place than amongst the yeomen of England! You should know that when I spoke with the French heralds, they told me that when they are victorious, they will cut two fingers from the right hand of every archer!" There was a huge jeer at that. The King held up his hands, "It is an empty gesture for they will never win against our army. We may be small in number but each of you is worth ten Frenchmen! Heed your captains and know that I will not yield one inch of this French field to the French! God, St George and England!"

The cry was taken up and echoed around the field as every single man, boy, chaplain, engineer, minstrel and cordwainer cheered. King Henry had chosen the perfect words. He dismounted his small horse and as it was led away, he joined me and his brother in the centre. "Now we wait. Let us hope the Constable is not too long I do not want the fire in my men's bellies to be dampened."

We could see the French plan now. They had shown us their battle plan when they formed up. There were two ominously large bodies of horsemen forming up on their flanks. "I confess that I am at a loss to understand their delay in attacking us. That they outnumber us is clear for all to see. A slow and steady approach after their crossbows have thinned our archers might just work!"

The King nodded, "Ay, I can see their plan, Strongstaff, they will advance with their vanguard, protected by bows and crossbows while two bodies of horsemen outflank us. It is a sound plan and will negate our archers. Why have they not done so?"

I shrugged for I was as confused as he was, "Perhaps they are waiting for the field to dry but it is clear that the day is too damp for that. It is good growing weather!"

It soon became clear that the French had no intention of doing anything except to wait. Many of the French cavalry had dismounted.

The King turned to his brother and me. "Have they outwitted me, Strongstaff? My men are starving and cannot endure another day without food. What do we do?"

I am not, by nature, a gambler, but I knew when to take a chance and when not to. The French seemed to me slow to react and as I surveyed their lines, I saw a weakness. They had cavalry on their flanks, but they were dismounted. In the centre, they had eight thousand men at arms

127

who were also dismounted. Many were seated on the ground or lying down. There were bows and crossbows too, but they were not standing; they had taken the opportunity to lie where they could. Behind the dismounted men at arms was their second battle of six thousand mounted men at arms and finally there was their third battle: an enormous line of ten thousand mounted men at arms. None of the horsemen was mounted.

"King Henry, let us advance to bow range. We outnumber their crossbows and archers by many thousands and their horsemen are dismounted. We can up stakes and move seven hundred paces towards them." I pointed, "That is where the field narrows, and they will not be able to get around our flank! We will rain arrows on them and they will either have to endure it or charge us. The village of Tramecourt will protect our archers on that flank! I know the French, King Henry, and they will charge!"

King Henry had many faults, but indecisiveness was not one. He had heralds and pursuivants with him. "Tell my lords that upon the command, 'In the name of Almighty God and St George Banners advance', the whole army will up stakes and move seven hundred paces. Tell Sir Thomas Erpingham that as soon as his archers are ready, he is to loose and keep loosing arrows until the French are forced to attack!"

He gave the command and our eager army moved quickly to their new positions. We began to move and I found it difficult to make progress. It was fortunate that we were so few for our feet churned up the mud and the men who followed us sank deeper into the slimy morass beneath our feet. I fear that I slowed down our progress and I did not have my sons and son in law to help me. My men at arms were to my left and I, once more, was the King's bodyguard! I hurried, as best I could, to keep up with him as he moved as quickly as he could to our new position.

The French Constable and the Dukes who led the French, in contrast, seemed frozen as they watched us move forward. Perhaps they were confused as to our intentions. Then was the time to send their horsemen sweeping down as our English archers, vulnerable without the protection of stakes, walked towards them across a muddy field which sucked and dragged at buskins, boots and sabatons! When they did react, it was too late for the archers who could move far quicker than we could in plate had their stakes in place even while the French horsemen were mounting. The French could have used their bows and crossbows or even the few handguns that they had while the archers hammered in and then sharpened their stakes but they were unable to do so for the horsemen, incensed no doubt by the audacity of the English mounted and formed hurried lines to charge us and punish us for our impudence. The three battles were slower to reach the newly embedded stakes than the archers were but we were still in position well before the French men at arms charged.

As we reached our position all of us, the King included, knelt to taste a piece of the French earth. It was symbolic and represented the mass we had all enjoyed earlier that morning except that the host was now soil. I heard Sir Thomas Erpingham's Norfolk voice as, after throwing his baton into the air, bellowed to the archers, "Now strike!" It was not the command which David of Welshpool would have given but it sufficed, and five thousand arrows soared into the air. That was more arrows than the men who now advanced on our lines. The bodkins our archers used tore into French plate. Not all arrows killed or even incapacitated for an arrow in the thigh could be borne and as the horsemen would be unlucky to have to dismount it would not impair his fighting too much but more than a third of the men who charged at our lines were hit and that had to have an effect on their ability to fight. The French were also hurt by the mud. We had struggled to wade through the knee-deep mud to reach our lines but a heavy, plated horse with a mailed man on top sank even further. The charge was not at speed. At best it was a walk and a slow walk at that. Horses fell and men slipped from horses. If the French intentions had been to rid the battlefield of our most deadly weapon it was failing and, even though I could not see it, I knew that when the French horsemen drew close to our stakes David of Welshpool and the other archers would race forward to hamstring horses and drive short swords into the unprotected groins of helpless horsemen.

I heard a horn and saw that the French vanguard was coming. The horsemen's first attack had failed or, rather, was failing, for the French compounded their tardy start by feeding more of the cavalry in piecemeal. The archers' rain of arrows succeeded in thinning their numbers and stemming the tide. The huge line of dismounted men at arms marched down the slope to meet us. Ironically, the slope which should have aided them proved to be an obstacle as there were so many men pushing from behind that some of those leading the line slipped and fell in the mud. They were trampled by those following. The archers before us also managed to hurt many men at arms and this time, when a man at arms was struck in the leg, he fell and was trampled. Hundreds fell as they inexorably made their way closer to us. The Captain who led the archers before us would choose his moment to leave the stakes and run behind us.

King Henry was using his voice as a weapon exhorting all of us to fight for England. His brother, Humphrey, Duke of Gloucester had not been in a major battle before and I could tell that he was nervous. He was also standing close to the King and I wished that it was someone like me, a man with more experience. In the race to the new position, I had left my shield behind. Many others had done the same, but it mattered little for the French had not used missiles of any description. Our change of position had upset their plans and, it seemed, driven military sense from their minds. I held my poleaxe in two hands. The French who advanced had as wide a variety of weapons as we did but most had not used them in such a conflict. There had not been a battle for a generation for many of the noble families of France. This was the first such major battle for many men. When I had fought alongside Duke John the Fearless it was not the lords of France we had fought at St. Cloud, it was the Écorcheurs who had fought against us. Many of the nobles and men at arms who slipped and slithered through the mud had not fought in a battle. They had taken part in tournaments or had read of what seemed like chivalrous exchanges between knights. As they drew closer to our lines, they were about to realise the reality of war!

Despite the numbers who had fallen already as more than eight thousand men had begun the laborious charge down the field there were still many more French men at arms approaching than we had to greet them. There would be more than seven French men at arms to each one of us. I braced myself as the archers raced through our lines to stand behind us as the French made their way through the embedded stakes to close with us. I held my poleaxe above my head with the small spiked hammer head ready to smash into the skull or shoulder of the first man who came close to the King. I risked a thrust to the chest and neck, but I counted on the fact that it was unlikely to penetrate my plate. The French were too closely packed to allow a sideways swing and even an axe needed power to penetrate plate.

"Now is your time! For God and St George!" Even as he raised his sword to begin the battle King Henry was leading by example. He was telling the French where he was. His bright surcoat would draw them like bees to nectar. I stood as close to his left as I dared.

I recognised the colours of the Duke of Alençon as he, too, exhorted his men. He was not in the front rank, but I saw the red shield with the eight silver roundels. Before him were lesser nobles who were eager to claim the honour of killing King Henry. Only a few men would be close enough to hurt the King and I had enough experience to choose the target I thought presented the most danger. It was a knight with a war axe, and he was already trying to swing it laterally to hack across the breastplate of the King. King Henry was already using the skills which I had first taught him at Weedon. He lunged with his sword through the eyeholes of a boar's head bascinet. Neither the King nor I liked such helmets as it limited vision and reactions. Even as the King's opponent fell, I was bringing down the hammer head of my poleaxe on to the helmet of the knight with the axe. It was my first blow of the day and all of my venom was in the blow. As I had told my sons when I trained them, a blow half struck could kill you! The Frenchman's helmet was a good one but the top crumpled like parchment and the head of my poleaxe smashed into the bone of his skull. He was stunned briefly before the head demolished his brains. He fell before the King and me. The poleaxe also had a spearhead and as the body fell from my weapon, I lunged at the next man at arms who came at me. He too had a poleaxe and like me, a heartbeat ago, he had it raised for he intended to smash the axe head into my helmet. I rammed the spearhead into his screaming open mouth. The hammer head and axe caught on his jaw and I tore them out sideways. The very act of pulling it sideways caused the axe head to tear into the side of the helmet of the next man at arms. It stunned him and as he stood, momentarily frozen, the King dispatched him.

The sheer weight of the men facing us forced us to take a few steps back. In my case, it was to allow a better swing with my poleaxe. In the case of the King and his young brother, it was because there were so many French knights and men at arms trying to get at them. The three of us, and the other knights in the front rank, all had good plate and practical helmets. Many of the French appeared to have chosen art over functionality and their helmets restricted vision and did not afford good protection. The King had esquires who were guarding his person and I saw at least four had already fallen so desperate were the French to get at the King. As I stepped back and raised my now gore covered poleaxe, I saw the sky ahead blackened by the arrows sent from our flanks. The French who were trying to reach the King of England were paying a terrible price. On the skyline, I saw the next French battle preparing to attack. The red Oriflamme, the sacred banner of the French normally housed in Saint-Denis, was going to lead what the Constable must have assumed was the attack which would finally defeat us. The archers who had been before us were now sending arrow after arrow over our heads. Although they were not directly aimed, as they fell from the sky the bodkin heads would drive through plate and even if they did not kill would wound. The French were already weary from their tramp through the mud in heavy plate and the falling of the arrows was like a death knell on their plate!

Our step back must have encouraged the French and I saw the Duke of Alençon step into the breach and shout, "We have them! For France and St Louis!"

He lurched towards King Henry with a French knight at his side. I swung my poleaxe sideways to hack its head into the side of the French knight's helmet. The knight was doing what I was doing; he was protecting his lord, Charles of Alençon. He died doing so but a second knight stepped into the breach caused by his death and I barely blocked his sword with my poleaxe. Suddenly, I was face to face with the Frenchman, or I would have been had he not had a boar's snout visor on his helmet. I knew what he intended even before he attempted it. He pulled his head back to butt the pointed visor into my face. Still holding my poleaxe before me I stepped to the side and his momentum made him trip over my foot. He fell face down in the mud. I suspect that had I left him he would have suffocated or drowned in the muddy morass. I raised my poleaxe and rammed the spearhead into the back of his neck.

The Duke of Alençon was beginning to realise that King Henry was a better fighter than he was, and I saw that the King would soon win. When the Duke's sword fell from his hands he shouted, "I yield!" The King nodded and turned his attention to the next man he had to fight. I know that many men who were not there said that I murdered an unarmed man, but it was not true. Even as the King turned, I saw the Duke slip a dagger into his hand and stab at the King. I had been a bodyguard for so many years that it was pure instinct which made me lift my poleaxe and slide it under his raised arm. The head came out of the top of his shoulder and the Duke fell dead.

His death marked a moment when the French stopped, seemingly stunned. King Henry shouted, "Push! We have them."

It was then that Humphrey, Duke of Gloucester showed his inexperience. He was facing a man at arms and as he stepped forward to bring his sword over his head the cunning man at arms blocked the blow with his sword and then rammed his dagger up into the groin of the Duke. The King's brother fell but, before the man at arms could end the royal life King Henry had skewered the man at arms with his own sword and stood astride the prostrate Duke.

"Strongstaff!"

Stepping forward I swung the poleaxe in a large arc to keep the eager French at bay. I heard the cry go up that the King had fallen. They mistook the Duke of Gloucester's surcoat for the King's. My poleaxe created a space and placed me before the King and his brother. As the

Duke's men began to drag the wounded knight away, I faced five men at arms, two of them knights. The King was in danger and my life mattered not a jot. I rammed the spearhead of my weapon at a similarly armed Frenchman. He had a visor on his helmet, and I did not. His spear came for my open face while mine came up under the fauld to spear his groin. I saw the spearhead coming for me and I moved my head to the side. A line was scored along the helmet while the Frenchman fell, bleeding. The King brought his sword into the side of the head of the man at arms who tried to skewer me in the side as I blocked the blow from the war axe of another Frenchman.

Others had seen our dilemma and men ran to our side and we pushed back the men eager to take advantage of our brief isolation. The result was that King Henry achieved his push. As arrows soared above us, landing dangerously close to the King and me, we found space and as we moved beyond our original start point the French battle took to their heels and headed back up the slope.

"Take my brother to the healers! Search the French for prisoners and reform!"

"Aye, King Henry." The archers raced forward for they were the ones who were in the best position to obey the King's command.

I looked along our line which looked remarkably intact, in contrast to the bodies of French men and horses which littered the ground before us. "Thank you, Strongstaff."

"We held them but," I pointed to the high ground close to the castle of Azincourt, "their second battle will soon be here." I pointed to his helmet and crown, "You have lost fleur-de-lys and your helmet will need repair!"

He laughed, "If that is all that I lose this day then I will be a happy man!"

The prisoners were taken to the area between us and our distant camp. I saw Rafe and James fetching arrows for the archers and I was glad that Walter and the squires were a good half a mile from danger! While the archers cleared the ground, we heard French horns and saw their second battle heading down the slope. It was now even worse than at the start of the battle for it had been churned up by thousands of feet. Dying men had fallen and littered the ground. Some of the archers were now protected by a wall of French dead bodies. During the next attack, they would not have to fall back for they would have their own personal fort. This time more of the French bore shields and that meant that there were fewer with pole weapons.

The King looked at the line of bodies before us and smiled at me, "Very good of the French to give us an additional barrier, Strongstaff."

"Aye and the archers can use them to gain elevation."

I heard the whoosh of arrows as the two huge blocks of our archers sent their next flights towards the advancing French. While many of the arrows struck shields men still fell. Some Frenchmen would find their shields were heavier due to the number of arrows which had hit them. When they reached the archers before us fewer archers ran back for some stayed, protected by the stakes, and that meant that the French would have arrows coming from every direction. More knights now flanked the King on his right side and there were fresh men to my left. While other knights and men at arms were able to rotate, the King had to stay in the front rank and I had to guard him. I knew that my men and family would be fretting about me. They would see the King's banners and know exactly where I was. They would see the huge press of men and fear for me.

When the archers had passed through us, they were closer to us and their arrows could be sent on a flatter trajectory. The plate had not been made which could stop a bodkin at a range of forty paces. This time there was no rush when the French came to close with us. There were too many bodies in the way and sabatons slip on plate armour. As one knight slipped, I brought up my poleaxe and brought it down on his back. I achieved enough speed and power to hack through the plate and break his spine. There is a technique in the use of a poleaxe for apart from the axe head there is a hammer head and a spear. I did not pull the poleaxe up vertically but at an angle and was rewarded when the hammer struck a man at arms on the side of the head. As he stumbled a sword from my left found the gap under his armpit. He had no besagew to protect it.

It was not just the King who drew the blade of every Frenchman. There were also the fluttering banners held by the King's standard-bearers. The French Oriflamme was still on the ridge but ours were there for the taking. As I had discovered at Shrewsbury the act of carrying the standard was not to be undertaken lightly. The arrows continued to fly both from the sides and over our heads. I knew that soon they would run out. I hoped that they had saved enough for the third battle which would come if and when we defeated this second battle. For me, the battle was a small one. I could only see ten men on either side of me. I had no idea what was happening to the Duke of York to my right, or Lord Camoys to my left. Our three battles were all the same size but all that I knew was that we were assailed on all sides and keeping my feet was the most important thing I could do. As I skewered another French knight who had fallen at my feet, I felt the burn in my arms. Archers were used to this. I was not.

Then I saw a familiar livery. It was two ermine bars on a red shield: it was Robert Lord of Beaumesnil, the knight who had tried to ambush us in Northumberland. He looked to have recovered from his wounds. He came directly for me and not the King. This was personal. I needed every ounce of energy I possessed for he was fresh and, as yet, his sword had yet to be used. It would be sharp and, unlike me, he would not be weary. He also had a shield and he came at me using it offensively. I had been taught too well to be taken in by such a move and I used the butt of the poleaxe to swing at the shield. The shield and the shaft neutralised each other but I used the blow to pivot my poleaxe towards his head just as he tried to swing his sword at me. His blade grated against the hammer head of the poleaxe.

"You will die at my hands, old man, and then I will kill the King!"

I was too experienced to return the banter and I used my breath for something infinitely more useful. I put all of my effort into my next blow. A poleaxe can be swung but it can also be used as a spear and he was expecting me to use the axe head. I rammed the spear point at him. I took him by surprise and his visor impaired his reaction. The spear point caught in one of the eyeholes and my strength dragged his head around. He began to lose his balance and so he stepped backwards. Once again, I swung the shaft of the pole weapon and smacked his knee. As he began to fall, I inverted the poleaxe and rammed it down. He had good plate and the spearhead slid off it. The head of the axe, however, struck his plate. It was not the edge, but the weight of the weapon which dented the breastplate. I pulled the spear up again and this time aimed it at the dent. The spearhead penetrated the breastplate and found his heart. The blood gushed making his surcoat red and the man who had attacked me in England now died in France!

It was then that the French began to surrender. "I yield" was an increasingly common cry. They were tired after wading through mud, blood and bodies. They had come up against men who were, quite simply, better than they were. Each time a Frenchman surrendered then the prisoner had to be escorted to the rear of our lines in the area between our camp and the last men at arms. Healers tended to the wounded; chaplains gave the last rites and our men guarded the ever-increasing number of prisoners.

I contemplated switching to my sword as the axe head became blunted and a piece of hammerhead was broken off, but I realised that I was having a greater effect with my poleaxe. I had been able to clear a space before the king many times. That was my job for I was there to guard his body and without a shield his left side was vulnerable. I had not escaped unscathed for my new helmet and plate were dented and scratched but they had served their purpose. I could feel blood trickling down from my scalp. I could not remember the blow to my head which had resulted in the wound, but it did not surprise me. When you are fighting your only aim is to kill your opponent before he kills you. Often you do not even notice when you are struck.

The French who had not died and had not surrendered did not want to fall back and so they made a concerted effort to win the battle while they still could. They were led by two men whose arms I recognised, Charles d'Albret was the Constable of France. Behind him came the Oriflamme carried by Guillaume de Martel. This told me that this was an attack by the best left to France. When I saw the distinctive silver roundels on blue with the red two-headed eagle on the knight behind then I knew that it was Boucicaut, Marshal of France. This would be a hard fight for they were three of the best warriors that France had to offer. The King and I were already tired and now we would have to be at our best.

It was just then that William, my grandson, with a bleeding scalp, burst through the lines and shouted, "Grandfather, French knights are attacking our camp! They are killing the squires!"

I was a grandfather and my initial reaction was to forget my task and go to my grandson's side. But I was a bodyguard to the King. Even as I swung my poleaxe at the knight who was clearing the way for Boucicaut I shouted to William, for I could see that he had a wound, "Get to the healers and stay there!"

I heard King Henry roar, "Treachery and dishonour!" He renewed his attack on the Constable. The Constable was fresher and had weapons which were still sharp, but I knew that he stood little chance against the King as he was angry about the dishonourable attack on our squires. I advanced to meet Boucicaut who was as widely travelled and experienced as I was. He was a little younger than I and I would take no chances with him. The Oriflamme fluttered above our heads and Sir John Codrington who carried King Henry's banner advanced to battle with the French standard-bearer. It seemed to me that we three were the whole battle encapsulated in one small portion of French earth. I had to ignore the King and Sir John for my enemy was one of the two best warriors we faced. His jupon hid his armour, but I knew that it would be well-made. On his head, he had a hounskull or pig-faced bascinet which obscured the vision of the wearer, especially on ground like this. That gave me a slight advantage for the ground upon which we fought was slippery and sabatons were not the most secure footwear. In his hand, he wielded an axe.

He stepped almost gingerly towards me and that told me he was keenly aware of the footing. He waited until he was balanced. I allowed him the first swing not least because I was tiring but, more importantly, to see his technique. He knew how to use the weapon. I flicked up the head of the poleaxe and the two blades rang and clanged together, sparks flying from the steel. I used the bottom of the poleaxe to crack into his thigh. It was to disrupt his attack, but he knew his business and took the blow easily. He then showed his skill by bringing his axe to strike between my hands for there it was just a wooden haft. He hacked through the shaft below the langet, the metal which protected the head. I now had an unwieldy weapon but, rather than disposing of it, I used it with my left hand while I drew my sword. The French Marshal struck again quickly but my left hand flicked up, the poleaxe partly blocked the blow and the French axe slid down my side, tearing my surcoat. My sword was sharp for I had not used it. My poleaxe was not only much shorter, but part of the hammer had also been destroyed and the axe head was blunt. The spear point, however, although covered in blood and gore was still pointed and I jabbed it at him. The defect of the pig-faced visor became evident when he failed to see the sudden strike of the spearhead. It clanged off the metal and had it been narrower would have penetrated the eye hole. As it was, he had to take a step back and he slipped. On such tiny matters are life and death decided. Even as he slipped, I saw King Henry end the life of the Constable. I raised my own sword to strike down the Marshal as an arrow slammed into the leg of the French knight who bore the Oriflamme. Boucicaut held his axe in both hands as he forced himself to rise. My sword came down hard and although it bit a chunk from the shaft it was still a deadly weapon.

The Oriflamme fell to the ground as Sir John used his own standard in two hands to punch the standard-bearer in the mouth. As the Frenchman lay there, Sir John killed him. The deaths of the standard-bearer and the Constable made the French halt in their assault. Arrows were still flying and thinning their ranks. Many formed huddles with shields to protect them. Arrows still pierced legs and arms and I could hear the French cries of 'I yield!'

It was time to end my own battle to the death. I feinted with my poleaxe and the Marshal, now thoroughly shaken, reacted with a flick of his axe. His stronger right arm easily deflected the blow, but I had already been swinging my sword and I struck him hard on the couter which protected his elbow. The plate did its job and stopped my sword from penetrating his elbow, but the blow was so hard that I hurt him, and I watched his left arm drop as though he had no control over it. I raised my sword again and I think that he feared the same strike. He brought his axe to block my strike and failed to stop the spearhead on my poleaxe finding the gap behind his poleyn protecting his knee. I pushed hard, and my spearhead penetrated the mail beneath the poleyn. I heard the muffled scream from beneath his visor as the spear struck into his knee. He dropped his axe, sat on his backside and, raised his visor, "I yield! I yield!"

I dropped my ruined poleaxe and held my hand out for his sword. He handed it to me. The attack of the second battle had ended and the survivors limped back to the castle at Azincourt. The King was looking at the ridge. Already the men who had yielded were being taken back to join the prisoners who now numbered more than fifteen hundred. They outnumbered our surviving men at arms.

I saw that many of our archers had run out of arrows and were now joining the fray using their swords and captured weapons. The French were exhausted. Marching into the low winter sun they had kept their heads down to avoid its blinding rays and the English arrows. When they reached the English line, they were battered and beaten so that when the archers leapt eagerly to slit their throats they had no defence. The King shouted, "Reform!" As men wearily shuffled into position, he turned to me, "What do you think?"

"I think that eight thousand men on horses could walk down here and simply ride over us, King Henry." I pointed to the archers risking the battlefield to collect arrows.

Just then my son, Harry, ran up. My heart sank. Was this more bad news for me? You could not see his surcoat for blood and guts. I realised I must have looked the same. However, it was not me he sought but the King. "King Henry, Sir Gilbert sent me, your Uncle the Duke has been slain and there has been a great loss of life on the right." He looked at me, "Father, Davy Gam is dead and his sons!"

The King nodded and pointed to the bodies of the eighteen esquires who had begun the battle as the King's bodyguards. Only I remained of them, "Here too the fighting was the fiercest!"

The King's shoulders slumped. He had lost an uncle and his brother was wounded; we knew not how badly. I could see the French horsemen on the ridge forming lines and it was I who gave the command, "Harry, go back and tell Sir Gilbert to hold. The French will attack once more."

The King shook his head, "No they will not! They broke the rules when they slaughtered our squires. I will repay them." He turned and shouted, at the top of his voice, "Kill all the prisoners! I will hang any man who disobeys me."

To say it was draconian was an understatement. Not a single knight nor man at arms wished to obey the order for it was like dropping sack loads of gold into the sea. There would be no ransom! However, King Henry gave orders and we obeyed. The French we had captured could not believe what was happening and their screams must have reached the French at Azincourt. Without weapons, they were butchered where they stood. It had the desired effect. Even though they outnumbered us with an untried battle, they turned and yielded us the field. We had won!

I put my sword to the throat of the French Marshal who looked aghast at the King.

"Hold, Strongstaff. We will keep the most senior French lords in case we need to bargain with the French!"

His decision proved a wise one and the French lost almost a third of the men who supported their King, but he showed a hard side of him I did not know he possessed. It was one thing to kill a man in battle but quite another to slit his throat in cold blood. I would have done so had I been ordered but the King had not made me carry out his order. Leaving his personal bodyguard to guard the prisoners and while the rest of the army was taking the mail, plate, weapons and loot from the French we headed through the wounded to the camp. I found William and saw that he had been bandaged. His wound had not been life-threatening and he would have a scar to go with his tale of the day that King Henry trounced the French and won back France.

As we headed to the camp, which we could see had been looted the King asked my grandson what had happened. "A column of mailed and armoured men rode into camp. Most of the servants were taking arrows to the archers or fetching the wounded from the field. There were just squires and pages there. We tried to defend the camp, but they were ruthless. I was knocked from my feet by the spear of a horseman and when I came to I saw that the others had all been butchered and I could do nothing." His eyes welled up as he said, "I am sorry, King Henry! I did not protect your valuables! I am a coward!"

The King put a kindly arm around my grandson, "No, William, the cowards are the ones who broke every rule of chivalry. Tell me what you know of the men who did this. Can you describe their livery?" From his description, we deduced that it was the local lord, Isembart d'Azincourt and Robinet de Bournonville. "Their names and deeds will be added to the reparations we demand."

When we reached the camp the sight which met our eyes was even more pitiful than we had anticipated. The squires had at best a brigandine and some of the bodies had been so badly mutilated by weapons and by horses' hooves that they were almost unrecognisable. I knew Walter from the dagger his father had given to him. It had belonged to Red Ralph and my squire had died with that and his short sword in his hand. He had died bravely but to what end? He should have run. And then I realised that he was trying to emulate me. The stories his grandfather had told his father had been repeated to Walter. They spoke of my heroic deeds when I had been a boy. I had been lucky, and I had a natural skill. No other could have done as I had done. There would be no more tales of Will Strongstaff to turn young boys' heads! We found the other squires and some of the servants too. Will of Stockton and my two sons had lost squires. Walter and Wilton had died together as they fought back to back. They had died as little more than boys and I was wracked with grief and guilt.

Chapter 12

The next day, after we had packed the booty away we had the grim task of burying the archers and the squires, burning the unknown Frenchmen and, the hardest job of all, of boiling the bodies of those who had fallen for we would take their bones home for burial. The Duke of York and Davy Gam and his sons were amongst that number, but I intended to take Walter's bones for his father. I owed it to Red Ralph. Rafe and James undertook that task. They blamed themselves for Walter's death even though they had been obeying my orders and taking arrows to the archers. Poor Will of Stockton had one of those young men he had brought from the north to bury. Wilton would not be forgotten but he would be buried in the cemetery by the church close to the castle of Azincourt.

I had wandered the field with the King on the morning after the battle. "We were lucky, Strongstaff. I know that we grieve for the loss of the squires but my uncle, the new Earl of Suffolk and Davy Gam, so recently knighted, and his sons were the only losses amongst those with titles."

He was right, of course, but another two hundred of our men who were neither nobles nor squires had died and there were many who were so badly injured that they would bear Agincourt scars until their dying day. It was the King himself who named the battle. When we met with Mountjoy, the French herald, to demand ransom for the few prisoners we had taken, he had told the French herald the name he had chosen. It was partly to remind the French that we would not forget the treachery of the Lord of Azincourt and he would be held to account! We also told the herald the names of the dead we had identified. More than two and a half thousand could not be named as their liveries were despoiled or had been removed. It was understandable. Some of those who had trawled the battlefield for treasure had taken some of the surcoats as a souvenir which would not be sold but brought out when tales of the battle were told. The death toll amongst the French was terrifying: three Royal dukes were dead, eight counts, an archbishop, the Constable of France, the grandmaster and steward of the royal household, the grandmaster of the crossbowmen, the bearer of the Oriflamme as well as sixteen hundred named nobles and knights, and more than five thousand men at arms and esquires had also died. The ordinary soldiers of France were not even counted.

The two of us had stood on the ridge and looked down at the sea of corpses, "And what now, King Henry? Many of the men think that we will march to Paris to claim the crown."

He laughed, "You of all people know that will not happen. It is the wrong season to campaign, and we have not enough men to reduce a castle let alone the great city of Paris. No, we leave and head for Calais. The wagons we have taken will be laden with both treasure and our wounded. We sail for England and celebrate there. You do not win a kingdom in battle. You win it by holding on to territory. Harfleur was bought at a terrible price and I lost dear friends there, but we now have a toe hold in Normandy and we can use Harfleur to launch an attack next year." He waved an arm around the battlefield which was still littered with the dead. During the night locals had emerged and begun to strip the bodies of their clothes. Our appearance had scattered them but when we left, they would continue to take all signs of the identity of the brave men of France. I had no doubt that there would be some families who would come to identify and claim their fathers, brothers, and sons but most would end up ploughed into the earth upon which they fought. Our own dead had already been buried. "The French have lost their leaders, but the French are a proud people and they will resist us. We shall return with a new army and take the jewels of Normandy. It will take time, but we shall succeed." He looked at me, "And I hope that you will be with me for your advice has been sage and I know that while many lesser men fell defending me you protected my left side like a human shield."

"I will, if God allows, return with you, King Henry, but I fear I shall never see you crowned for I am old. Only Sir Thomas Erpingham is of an age with me."

"Yet you are like human plate which neither bends nor yields; I am lucky to have you. Let us return to the camp and begin the journey home. This time Sir Gilbert and Sir John can have the van alone for they have learned from you. You and your men have earned the right to allow others the harder task of seeking a passage to Calais."

We had not only lost Walter and Wilton, as well as Harry and Thomas' squires, from my company, five archers and two men at arms had also fallen. Hob and Matty had died bravely. With no families, their treasure was split amongst the others. Some had terrible wounds: Nat had lost an eye, Dick Dickson two fingers from his left hand and broken toes which might not heal properly. My men were, generally in good spirits for they had won and were all rich. The dark clouds which hung over us all were the deaths of Walter and the other squires. Only William remained from the ones who had formed a bond during the campaign and I hoped that he would recover. I believe that the King and I had persuaded him that he had no reason to feel guilty, but we were not inside his head and could not see the demons with which he wrestled.

Rafe and James stayed close to William as we headed north on the three-day ride to Calais. He was the last of the squires and as they had not saved Walter, they would ensure that my grandson reached home safely. It meant I rode between my sons. Sir Richard stayed close to William. The near-death experience had brought them closer together.

Thomas said, "I shall have to rethink taking Henry with me as my squire. Edward's death came as a blow to me."

"It surprised all of us, and the Lord of Agincourt will be brought to account for his actions." I looked at Harry who was also silent. "And you will have the same problem when your son is of an age to ride to war. I shall give you both some advice which you can take or you can ignore for you are men and lords. I do not tell you what you should think and do."

Thomas smiled, "Yet we will heed your words for you have yet to give us bad advice."

"Then here it is, your sons need not be warriors. They have your mother's blood in them, and she has shown a skill for the management of the land and the making of money. We are a rich family and thanks to the battle we are even richer now. The ransom for the Constable alone will be the same as many dukes earn in a year."

Harry said, "Father, that is your coin. You defeated him and it is yours."

"Do you not know me yet, my son? What is mine is yours, your brother's, Sir Richard's and all the men who fought with us. I was lucky enough on St Crispin's Day to capture a fine prize but had you and the right wing not done your duty then we might have lost all."

Chastened, Harry nodded.

"You say you do not know if you want your sons as squires and then knights. That may be out of your hands. Let me ask you a question. What if I had not allowed you to become warriors? If I had forbidden you to train with Edgar of Derby and Harold Four Fingers?"

Thomas looked into the distance and then shook his head, "It is a rhetorical question for you would not have done so!"

I smiled, "Then humour me and assume that I would have listened to your mother who did not wish either of you to go to war!" They both looked at me in surprise. My smile became a laugh, "You think any mother wishes to lose her son in battle? So, Thomas, what would you have done?"

"Defied you, I think, and trained in secret."

"And if I had punished you for disobedience?"

"Then I might have run and joined a Free Company." He stared at me, "I would have followed the same path as you!"

"Exactly. Now I do not say that your sons will wish to go to war but I believe that the odds are that they will and so you have your answer. You must wrestle with the problem. I know I did. My solution was to make you the best that you could be! You are both fine knights and the King thinks well of you. He has yet to marry and have children but when he does then I believe that you will be chosen to be mentors to the princes." Lowering my voice, I patted my hackney, Maud, "I am not sure that Sir Richard invested enough time in making William a warrior. However, that is in the past and your sons are young. That bridge is a long way in the future. We have to get to England, celebrate with the King and then go home. Know this, though, come the Spring you will be called upon again. You can refuse and the King will not think the worse of you, but you have the winter to decide what it is that you will be. I fear I have set your feet on a path which is hard to leave."

I knew that I was right for Stephen of Morpeth had told me how my two sons had fought like lions on the battlefield and they had tried, in vain, to save the life of the Duke of York. He had also told me, in confidence, that my son in law, Sir Richard, had fought in the second rank behind his own men at arms. His last comment was eloquent and told me all I needed to know, "You could still slice meat with his sword at the end of the battle, Sir William."

Sir Richard was a good man and husband. My daughter adored him, but he was not of my blood and I knew that he went to war out of a sense of duty to me. I was not certain that he would go to war with me again. I would find time, when we were in Calais, to let him know that he did not need to go to war and his son, my grandson, had the same choice. Rafe and James rode with a sumpter. On it there were a couple of chests. Although one contained coin there the most valuable treasure which they guarded was the chest containing Walter's bones, his sword and his dagger. They would come with me when I rode to Middleham Grange. They were never cowards and would face Sir Ralph and tell him of the death of his son. They were men and that was what men did.

Some of the men, not mine, chose to sell their treasures in Calais. I knew that they would find better and richer buyers in England. More than half of the men at arms and knights that we had slain had come from Artois and Picardy. Any money people had would be kept either for ransom or, more likely, to feed families who had lost the ones who earned the coin. The King arranged for ships to be sent from England. We would need a huge fleet to take us home, despite the fact that it was so close to Dover, we would also need favourable winds. Not only the campaigning season was over but also the sailing season would soon end. It was now November and cold and wet. I was lucky in that I was favoured by the King and my men and I were housed. Many others had to use the fields around Calais and, once more they camped in the cold autumnal nights. I spent some of my coin in Calais for it was known for its lace as well as having a thriving market. I made purchases for my wife, daughter, and daughters in law. Rafe and James were my constant companions. This was not England and they were mistrustful of everyone; this might have been the Pale but we were too close to France to take chances. On a couple of the excursions David of Welshpool, Stephen of Morpeth and some of my other men at arms accompanied me. It was pleasant to be able to wander, even in the bad weather, and take shelter in a tavern. When we were seated by a warm fire then, inevitably, talk turned to the battles we had fought and the men who had died. It was but a short leap to the future and wars as yet unfought.

"You know, Sir William, that while none of us needs to venture beyond our homes, we are quite happy to do so if you need us." Oliver the Bastard was a strangely sentimental man for one who could kill so easily. "I thought after St Cloud that I would sit and become old and fat. I believed that I would never go to war again and yet as soon as you asked then I knew that I would follow."

Will of Stockton nodded, "Although my wife is dead, I believe that I too would have left Bewley to come with you, lord."

"And what will you do now, Will? Return to the north and start again?"

"That was my home but there are too many memories and they are not all good. The pit of despair in which you found me is not a place I choose to revisit. No, Sir William, I will use some of the money I have earned to make life easier for Pippa's family, perhaps I can make up for taking her away."

"And you Stephen?"

"That is easy, my lord. I shall gather what remains of my men and go back to Morpeth. I like the house there and with the coin I have accumulated I can make it even better. Who knows I may even find a bride!"

Harold of Derby laughed, "Then make sure she is short-sighted for the scars you earned this campaign have done nothing for your looks!"

145

And so, the men bantered. That was their way.

I saw little of the King for he was busy. He had letters to write and messages to send. He reiterated his request for the hand of Princess Katherine. The King of France would refuse but King Henry was dogged and would not give up. He had orders to send to our men in Gascony. He feared that the French might try something there in the south. He also wrote letters to England for he wished a victory parade through London. The people had paid for this war and they needed to know that it had been worthwhile. The prisoners we had, while fewer in number than we might have expected were all nobles of the highest order and they would be led through the streets before being imprisoned to await ransom. The ransom would be very high and would be another humiliation.

I was invited, a day or two before we sailed, to dine with the King and his brother who was now recovering well from his wound. I learned much in that meeting not least that the two brothers of John the Fearless, Duke of Burgundy, had perished in the battle. The Duke of Brabant and the Count of Nevers had been in the second bloody attack on our lines. I wondered how that would affect the Duke of Burgundy. We had helped him to defeat the Armagnacs, and he had been an ally of England, but blood was blood. Indeed, his absence might have helped us win the battle. How would we fare in a battle against him?

"You shall have the winter at home, Strongstaff, for you have earned it. The hard part will come when we work our way through Normandy. I have learned that the French are not beaten, and the Dauphin is still defiant. I will need you at my side. My uncle has been taken from us as has the Earl of Suffolk. I will need all the sage advice I can get."

I nodded, "And I will follow you, King Henry, but can I ask that my sons stay at home? I would use the lances who owe me fealty. Knights like Sir Henry of Stratford, Sir Abelard, Sir Ralph of Middleham Grange and the like."

He frowned, "Your sons are made of the same steel as you, Strongstaff. Stratford has not fought for many years and Sir Abelard is young. I need men who can fight."

"I have yet to let you down, King Henry, and I promise you that the men at arms I lead will be worthy of your banner."

He sipped his wine and then nodded, "I have spoken with Sir Gilbert and Sir John. They praised many of your men and wondered why they were not knights already. We can remedy that. I will dub Stephen of Morpeth and Oliver the Bastard at the victory ceremony."

"Thank you and Will of Stockton also showed great courage."

146

"Then him, too. I have manors now at my disposal. I have not forgotten the three traitors. So, Strongstaff, you will stay at my side until after the parade and then you shall have the winter in Weedon! Use your time well!"

We were delayed by the wind for fourteen nights and then we sailed, not to Dover but up the river to London. Most of the others disembarked at Dover but we carried on with the King and a handful of ships to the great city of London. There were enough palaces and residences belonging to the King to accommodate the men at arms who were to be knighted and myself. The archers, my sons and Sir Richard left for home. The three men to be knighted were far more nervous than I had expected them to be. After all, they had been around kings, dukes and earls most of their working lives. Then I remembered when I had been knighted. It is a huge step and men address you differently. Inside you believe you are still the same but the mere address of, 'my lord', is a powerful one. As much as they each wanted it, they knew that their lives would change.

The victory parade was on the 23rd of November. The ceremony of knighthood would take place at Eltham Palace. It had been a favourite of King Richard and I had been happy there. It seemed appropriate to me as I felt more comfortable there than almost anywhere. I had spurs made for each of them for they were my men and now when I went to war, I would have more lances following my banner. The King had made me more powerful. He was a practical and pragmatic man and I knew he would have weighed that up. It showed that he trusted me and that gave me huge satisfaction.

They held a vigil the night before the ceremony. Poor Davy Gam had not had the same ritual when he had been knighted and he had enjoyed his knighthood for less than a day. I mourned his loss more than any other for his sons had died too. I kept his memory alive for he was the embodiment of loyalty. Born in Wales he was loyal to King Henry and his son and that took real courage. It was he who was in my thoughts as King Henry touched their shoulders with his sword. His ceremonial sword had been stolen, along with a crown, when the camp had been sacked but I thought it was fitting that he used his Agincourt sword to dub them. That sword had helped to win the battle and France for the King.

After the ceremony, as I expected, the King and his brothers were closeted together. The ceremony had been a political act showing other men at arms that if they were lucky then they could be knighted. I knew that every one of my men deserved the honour, but I would take three of them being rewarded.

"Our lives change now, my lord."

"Yes, Sir Stephen!" He smiled as I was the first to use his title and I think he enjoyed it. "It is not just the wearing of the spurs but there are other responsibilities. When we go to war again you will count as a lance and that means you have to provide two more men at arms or spearmen and two archers. You will need servants and a squire. Even a simple act such as marrying is no longer as simple. The King has to approve the marriage." I saw the look of horror on their faces and I hurriedly added, "I doubt that your choices will need sanction but the Earl of March was fined ten thousand marks for marrying a lady from a powerful family without the King's permission." I shook my head, "I am painting a blacker picture than I should. Enjoy the moment, enjoy the day and relish the title. You will no longer be at the beck and call of nobles who are half the warriors that you are." I smiled, "And from now on you may enter tournaments. I know your skills and there is another way for you to make money!"

Will shook his head, "I have more money now, my lord, than I can ever spend and when we have our share of the Marshal's ransom then…"

I smiled, "Then all is well!"

Chapter 13

We shared the road north and it was a wet one. England at the end of November is never a pleasant place to be unless you are inside your hall with a blazing fire and ale which has been heated with a red-hot poker and infused with butter! Oliver and Stephen parted when Will and I headed for Weedon. Our farewells, to some, would have looked perfunctory. They were not for we were brothers in arms and had buried comrades. We had shared danger and fought as one. We needed no words for we knew the minds of the other and soon would fight alongside each other again.

Will went to stay with his father in law. I would see him almost every day for his farm was not far away from mine. My wife had been expecting me and James had ridden ahead to announce my imminent arrival so that forewarned, she had had hot food and mulled ale awaiting me. It was the best of welcomes. After I had eaten, we sat before the fire and she said, "Well husband, what tales are there? Our sons told us of Walter as well as Matty." She made the sign of the cross. "That will be hard to bear for his mother and grandmother not to mention poor Ralph."

I retold the campaign and I had learned, over the years, to speak the truth to my wife, however, it was a version of the truth which would be acceptable to her. I did not wish her to have the nightmares which sometimes came to me. I did not mention the butchery. She saw her sons as noble knights and did not need to know that when King Henry had ordered the prisoners slain, they had slit the throats of the men they had captured. I did not speak of the Frenchmen who had been crushed to death beneath bodies piled so high that it was as though a wall had been built before us. I did not tell her of the thousands who had died of the bloody flux, I just said that disease had taken many men. I told her how we had fought against two superior battles of the French and that I saw no reason why we should not take France when next we returned.

She poured me some more ale, "But to what end? I can see that King Henry achieved that which he wished but from what you say there are many who will not return home. How does their loss make England stronger?"

There was but one way to explain it to my wife; in terms of money and profit. "When we were in Calais, we saw the amount of trade with England. That trade is taxed and represents one-third of all the income which the crown receives. Now that we have Harfleur to go with Bordeaux and Calais then, when we have more of France under King Henry's thumb there will be more tax and the King will not need to tax English farmers."

She smiled, "Then that is no bad thing. If the King had to raise animals and grow crops, he would see how hard it is." She patted the back of my hand. "And the treasure you brought back means we can buy another manor or two."

"Will of Stockton seeks to buy a manor here closer to Pippa's parents."

She nodded, "He is no farmer but there is one I can think of which has a fine wood within it. Will could hunt, have his men gather timber and there is a fine house. The wood he had gathered would also bring a profit. That would suit Will!"

"Sir Will!"

She smiled, "It took years for you to be knighted and now others achieve it overnight!"

"Not true and Stephen, Oliver and Will are not young men. They deserve it and I do not begrudge them the honour."

"And that is because you are a good man!"

"If it is any consolation to you, I do not believe that Sir Richard and our grandson will go to war again." She gave me a questioning look. "William came within a handspan of death and it frightened him. My men at arms told me that while our sons fought at the forefront Richard did not." I shrugged, "It will be good that he stays home with Alice."

She did not see that as a weakness, as my men did, but as a sign of sense, "And what of our sons? Will they be in danger again?"

"The King says that they need not come with us when we retake France. I will take other knights. I just have to provide lances. No names are specified." I smiled, "Except, of course, mine!"

"Of course!" My wife could not keep the irony from her voice.

After we had retired and I had said my prayers and asked God, once more, to watch over my family, I tried to sleep but could not. I would have to take on another squire and I knew, now, what a big decision that would be. Walter was the first squire I had lost, and I knew the reason. It was my fault. I had spent longer with all of the others training them to be warriors. I had practised with them and they had practised with my men at arms. The years after St Cloud had been peaceful ones for me and when Walter had come, I had just used him as a servant. Perhaps if

I had trained him better, he might have survived. There were many lords who would wish their son to be the squire of a Knight of the Garter. I would refuse all such offers. I needed a young man at arms. I would seek someone more like myself when I had been with the Blue Company. I had the winter to seek one out. I would not take a boy the next time.

Whilst I was not looking forward to the journey north I knew that I had to go sooner rather than later. That was not just because of the roads but because any further delay would make it look as though I was a coward who could not face Mary, Ralph and his wife, Anne. Rafe and James were also keen to make the journey. Will of Stockton came too for now that he had a manor and was a knight, he needed horses, in addition, he had to tell Wilton's family that their son had died in France. Bewley was a day north of the horse farm. Joseph, who had survived because he was carrying arrows, would also come with us along with Peter. Pippa's younger brother, he had now become a squire and served his brother in law. He had served as a servant and because he too had been carrying arrows he had survived St Crispin's Day. Ironically, had he been a squire on that fateful day then he might have died. The six of us left Weedon on the last day in November when the winds were blowing from the northeast and there were flecks of sleet and snow in them.

Rafe chuckled as we wrapped the cowls of our cloaks tighter about our faces, "Here is one of the great lords of England and when he should be seated before a fire drinking claret and eating well, he is riding along an empty road with us!"

I laughed, "I must be atoning for some sin I committed, Rafe! I confess that we shall treat this journey as though the French were chasing us for I do not wish to tarry on the road!"

Will said, "And yet we must for God has made these days the shortest in the year!"

He was right and we rode hard for the five or six hours of daylight we were allowed and ensured that we paid for good grain for our horses which were housed in the best of stables. My name was well known and each inn and castle at which we stayed made us doubly welcome for we were a form of entertainment. We were able to tell them of the remarkable victory which had been achieved against all the odds. They had all heard of Crécy, but Agincourt had been just as astounding, and they wanted us to tell them of the battle first hand. Even though it hurt I owed it to the dead, Walter, Wilton, Matty, Hob, Davy Gam and his sons, to tell of the heroic fight. What I realised, as we left the Great Road, was that the victory had united the land behind the King. The

Lollard rebellion had fizzled out like the fuze on a damp handgun. Sir John Oldcastle was a hunted man and his supporters had either been executed or they had fled the land.

The news of Walter's death had not been written down and none of my men at arms, returning north, would have told Sir Ralph of his loss. I would be the one who would bear the news, but I knew that when Ralph saw that his son was not with me he would know the worst. We rode directly to the hall at Middleham Grange. It was dusk as we arrived and, cloaked and cowled it was hard to make out who we were. Ralph's hall had a small watchtower and a voice called down, "Who is it that calls at this ungodly hour? Identify yourselves."

"It is Sir William Strongstaff!" That was all that I said and all that I needed to. I heard bolts on the doors as they were pulled back and muffled orders. The courtyard was bathed in light as the door opened.

Ralph stood there grinning, "I am sorry, Sir William, we did not expect you. Edgar, take the horses to the stable. Come, my lord, and get yourselves inside in the warmth. Anne is busy organising food. Come, for it is a cold black night and not fit for a Christian to be abroad."

We piled in and each of us dropped the cowls on our cloaks. I saw the expectant look on Ralph's face change in an instant when Peter dropped his cowl. Rafe held the small chest with Walter's bones but he kept the box hidden. Ralph looked at me and said, in a small voice, "Walter?"

I shook my head, "He died at Agincourt. He was murdered by the Lord of Azincourt who sacked the camp. He died with his sword and dagger in his hands." I gestured for Rafe to step forward. "Here are his bones, his dagger and his cross. We brought them for burial."

Ralph took the chest and, his voice thick with emotion said, "It feels so light. It is as though he was a newborn." I think he would have wept had Anne not come from the dining hall.

"Why do you keep our guests out here, husband? I would see my..." as she emerged, she saw the chest and our faces. She looked at Peter and tried to peer behind him as though her son was hiding there. The wail she gave chilled me to my very soul. I can still hear it at night. It was a mother mourning her dead son.

Her cry made Ralph speak, "Here is our son, come home from war and he died a man. We will speak of this later, wife, for now, we have guests." She fled.

I shook my head, "We will go within and warm ourselves by your fire. Do not worry about us. He was your son and you do not need us." Ralph's other son and his daughters were helping the servants to lay out the table. They looked at us with fear on their faces as we entered. I sighed and spoke, "Your elder brother, Walter, died at the battle of Agincourt. Let your parents mourn. When the time is right, we shall tell you all."

Old Edward had been with Red Ralph and acted as Sir Ralph's steward, he said, "Give me your cloaks, my lord, and I will dry them. Agnes, fetch mulled ale for our master's guests."

His words broke the stillness which filled the hall. Everyone seemed pleased to have something to do. When the door opened it was just Sir Ralph who entered, and he had no chest with him. "My wife will join us later for now she…"

I waved my hand, "No explanation is necessary, Ralph."

Agnes fetched us the ale and I raised mine, "To Walter son of Ralph who was a brave squire and would have been a good knight had time allowed."

"Walter!"

Ralph drank his entire beaker and then said, "Tell me now while my wife is absent and do not spare me." His son Ralph and sister Margaret came in and Ralph snapped, "In the kitchen! I will send for you when we are ready!"

I put my hand on Ralph's shoulder, "Peace, Ralph, they are your children too." I nodded to Edward to refill his master's beaker. I sat in the chair and when Ralph was seated, I told him of the campaign and Walter's part in it.

When I had done his eyes narrowed and he said, "So, this Isembart d'Azincourt and Robinet de Bournonville escaped punishment?"

"Thus far, aye, but the King has not forgotten and next year we go to France to retake his lands there. Retribution will catch up with these men and those who obeyed their orders!"

Ralph nodded, "Aye and it shall come at the end of my sword. When next you go to war, Sir William, I shall be at your side. I will have vengeance for my son. That is my quest. When I became a knight, I swore an oath. This Isembart swore the same oath and I will punish him for his breaking of that most solemn of vows."

I nodded for I understood him.

We did not see Anne for the rest of the evening. Walter had been her eldest and named after her father. I learned that her grandfather, who had also been named Walter, had fallen in the Battle of Neville's Cross. Fate has long threads.

After sending for Mary, Walter's grandmother, we buried him in the small parish church and, as we did as they always do in the north we drank to celebrate the life of the dead we mourned, I spoke with Anne. I was gentle with her as I spoke of the joy Walter had enjoyed in the campaign and how he had grown. I told her that the King thought well of him. It did not take away her pain, but it dulled it. I then sat with Mary.

She held my right hand in her two, "Red Ralph would have understood but I confess, Sir William, I do not. From what you have told me many older knights and men at arms lived, in fact, few died and yet many boys were taken. They had yet to bud and they were destroyed. Can you explain that?"

I shook my head, "I was not yet born when the Black Death devastated this land but, from what I have been told by men who are far wiser than I am, that it killed indiscriminately. Some villages were completely destroyed, and others lost but a couple of people. God seems to send his reaper and we know not the reason. And you are wrong, neither Red Ralph nor myself understand this slaughter. Your son will go to France and he will seek out this Isembart and his accomplice. That will not bring back Walter, but he needs to do this. You understand?"

She nodded, "You are saying that my son may not come back. I do not like that prospect, but I believe in the Bible and there it says an eye for an eye." She gave me a sudden look, "You will be with him?"

"Aye, of course."

"Then he will be safe."

I did not argue with her, but Walter's untimely death proved otherwise. We could not stay long, for it was coming up to Christmas but we stayed long enough for Will to buy horses and then he, Peter and Joseph travelled up to Bewley for they had business there too. We waited at Middleham but we did not have to wait too long for Will and his boys did the journey in two hard days.

When we left Ralph I spoke to him whilst holding the reins of my horse for I was anxious to leave, "I will send to you when the King lets me know when we shall be needed." He nodded. "I will not be taking my sons but those knights who owe me fealty: Sir Henry of Stratford, Sir John of Dauentre, and Sir Abelard. With your men at arms and archers, I will fulfil my commitment to the King."

"The men I bring will be good ones, Sir William, for we have a hard border to guard, and we know our business."

"I doubt it not!" I stood outside the doorway to the hall with a wild wind blowing from the east. I clasped Ralph's arm in a warrior grasp and, I know not why, I pulled him to me and held him close. I said in his ear, "I am so sorry that I could not save your son."

His voice was husky as he said, "Sir William, you were doing that which you have done all your life, you were protecting the King. If he had died and Walter lived then we, in this little corner of England, would have been happy, but the rest of the country would have mourned, and we would have been plunged into anarchy. It was not your fault."

As we rode into the teeth of the storm I reflected on Ralph's words. He was right, of course, but that would not help me to sleep at night. I wondered if we had left it too late to return home as the sleet had turned to snow and we barely made the Great Road before the smaller ones disappeared. If it were not for the milestones jutting up through the snow, we would never have kept to the road. We had to stay in Ripon which was well short of our planned destination that first night on the road home. There were many other travellers trapped in the city, but we were warriors and while merchants and others who used the road stayed another night, we pushed on, leaving while it was still dark and what passed for the sun had still to put in an appearance. The snow had stopped but it was now freezing, and the wind still whipped towards the west! We pushed on and reached Pontefract after dark. If we had not had Will's new horses, then we could not have made it for our hackneys and palfreys would have been too exhausted to carry us. We stayed in the castle there and heard disquieting news from the lord of the manor. The forests around Doncaster, Sheffield and Nottingham had once been the haunts of bandits and outlaws. King Richard had begun the policy of purging the parasites from them but the failed Lollard rebellion and unsuccessful forays from Scotland had drawn every wrongdoer back there. The road was considered unsafe. We, it seemed, had been lucky while travelling north as the bodies of several merchants had been discovered there.

Pontefract Castle was a royal castle and King Richard had died there. The castellan was Sir Geoffrey D'Arcy and I knew him from Shrewsbury. It was why I gave his dire news such credibility. "I had intended to take my men to scour the forest of these men, but half of my garrison was with the King at Agincourt and have but recently returned. Now the weather has closed the road I cannot guarantee your safety." I was a Knight of the Garter and to lose a confidante of the King would be unacceptable.

"We all wear mail and we are all warriors. We will take our chances, but I confess that I am grateful for your warning. Had you said nothing then we might have ridden through the forest with our cowls around our ears."

"It is sixty miles to Grantham and once you reach there you should be safe. The castle at Worksop or the one at Retford would give you a safe bed for the night but beware the road."

155

When we left the next day we changed our formation and placed Peter and Joseph in the middle with the line of horses tethered to their saddles. I made it quite clear that if there was trouble, they were to use the horses as equine shields and the rest of us would do the fighting. I regretted not bringing archers, but we would have to make do with what we had. We reached Worksop safely and Sir William Lovetot welcomed us. He was an old, childless knight and his castle and land would revert to the crown upon his death. He had few men at arms and I understood how the bandits had gained such a hold on the road. Sir William was responsible for this section and he obviously did not venture forth nor send his men to keep the King's Highway safe. I would need to tell the King of the situation.

Having said all of that he was a charming host and keen to know of the battle in which we had fought. He was older than I was and that meant he had not been born in time for Poitiers and was too old for both Shrewsbury and Agincourt. It was as I told him of the campaign and the battle that I fully realised just how lucky we had been. There were three or four catastrophic decisions taken by the French and we should have been stopped. I think King Henry was right. God intended us to have France!

When we left we found that the road was still icy but there was also a fog. Such weather conditions were common in this part of the world. As we headed towards the safety of Grantham all the sounds from the forest were muffled. They were perfect conditions for an ambush for the murky fog swirled around us and made shadows of all that we could see. We rode with our cowls around our shoulders. Will and Rafe both had sealskin hats they had made from the seals they had hunted at Bewley. They wore them over their helmets and would be warmer than the rest of us. We used our eyes and our noses. Outlaws rarely had the opportunity to bathe and although we bathed infrequently at least we changed our clothes. An outlaw changed clothes when he killed someone the same size. If I smelled humans, then the odds were that they would be outlaws. The villages and hamlets which lay between Worksop and Grantham were small, inconsequential and, more often than not, off the main road. We met not a single traveller.

When we did hear noise, it was not one we expected. It was a single scream and came from ahead of us. If we galloped towards the noise, then we would be heard for the hard ground beneath our horses' hooves amplified every hoofbeat! I pointed to Peter to make him and Joseph slow and then drew my sword. We headed into the fog with every sense strained. There was a sudden clash of steel and a shout. Someone was being attacked. Throwing caution to the wind I spurred my horse and galloped towards the fray. The noise of the battle increased and, perhaps, hid the sound of our hooves from the ambushers.

I saw the first body with three arrows in him. By his dress and his weapons, he was a man at arms but a poor one for he wore only old-fashioned mail. I saw shadows ahead and they were fighting. We had to ensure that we fought for the right side. That was made easier when I saw the surcoats of the bodies of the men fighting the others. I had seen the surcoats at Harfleur. That made it easier for it meant they were friends and I saw a large bandit draw back on a bow intending to send it into the back of a spearman. His arrow flew straight and true just a heartbeat before I ended his life. My sword hacked across his shoulders and grated off the bone. The spearmen fell with an arrow through his head.

"Watch out!" The words came from a bandit who had a sword and a small buckler.

I rode at him and shouted, "In the name of the King put up your weapons or I shall have you hanged."

A hurriedly released arrow came at me and struck me on the metal clasp of my cloak. The blow hurt but that was all. James brought his sword to hack off the arm of the archer. He would bleed to death. More arrows flew but none came close to me. When Peter, Joseph and the string of horses trotted through the fog I think the bandits thought they were all ridden by more men and one of the bandits shouted, "We have enough! Let us flee!"

Even as the bandit shouted, Will slew another bandit and I slashed across the back of a brigand who was turning to run. Rafe and James hurtled into the woods after the bandits who appeared to have taken the horses from the men that they had ambushed. I looked around. There were at least six dead bandits with four, including the one who had lost his arm, who were about to die. I dismounted and kept hold of my horse's reins. I saw men in surcoats, but most appeared to be dead. Rafe and James returned leading two of the horses taken by the bandits.

"See if any are left alive. We must leave quickly for they will soon realise how few we are."

Will shouted, "My lord, here is one who lives but not for much longer."

I ran to him and saw that he knelt next to a man at arms who had been struck in the stomach by an axe. He was holding in his guts. A tendril of blood dripped from his mouth. "Thank you, Sir William. Those bastards have done for me but they shall not feast on my flesh and I can confess my sins."

"You know me?"

He nodded, "We were in the company of Sir Geoffrey Fitzwalter who died of the bloody flux at Harfleur and then followed Davy Gam. We were two of the lances." He nodded at Will, "I know Will of Stockton."

Will looked closer and nodded, "Aye, lord, this is Edgar of Hutton Rudby. What happened, old friend?"

"Hear my confession, Sir William, for while you are not a priest you are close to the King."

I nodded and handed him my sword, "Hold this for a cross. Will, see if any others live."

His confession was brief and could have been every soldier's last words. He confessed to killing his fellow man and of not always speaking the truth. For what it was worth I said that he would be forgiven. "Now, Edgar, what happened?"

"We were paid off after Agincourt but without a lord, we did not receive as much as some others. When we reached England, we sought employment but found none and so I said that we should head to my home and my mother and father would let us spend the winter in the barn."

"How many were there of you?"

"Eight. Four men at arms and four spearmen. We were a good company, but we had no luck. From the moment our lord died things went badly. We lost eight to disease in Harfleur and two more on the road. I …"

His voice had been getting weaker and he simply expired. I prised his dead fingers from my sword and stood, "Are any left alive?" They all shook their heads. "Then put them on the horses and we will take them to Grantham. They deserve a decent burial. Let us be quick about this."

I helped by lifting Edgar's body on to the back of one of the two horses recovered by Rafe and James. It was Rafe who made the discovery. "My lord, this one breathes!"

I ran to the young man Rafe had just draped over a saddle. Sure enough, he was breathing, He had a head injury. "Quickly tie him to the horse and put two cloaks about him. The dead will not mind, and they would want us to save this man. Perhaps Edgar was wrong, and their luck is about to change."

Chapter 14

I took the reins and went to my horse. After mounting I led the horse with the wounded young man. Grantham might be too far for head wounds were always dangerous. The man might be dead from the jolting within a mile or two. The fight meant that we were delayed in any case. The already short day was almost over and we would be riding in the dark. It was the tolling of the bell ahead which told me there was a church and that it was close by. It spurred me on. A church meant a priest and most priests had some knowledge of surgery. Even if they didn't, they had a church and light as well as clean water. It turned out to be an Augustine Monastery. It was not a large one, but Augustine monks were known for their skill in healing.

I banged on the door and a querulous voice from inside answered me, "Go away! We are just canons who wish to worship God!"

"I am Sir William Strongstaff, Knight of the Garter and defender to the King. We have a wounded man who needs tending. I beg you to open up."

A hatch opened and a tonsured head peered out. The hatch closed and then I heard the bars on the gate opening and we were admitted to the courtyard. The man who had spoken to us was obviously a monk who acted as a gatekeeper. The Friar came out and took charge, "You are Sir William?" I nodded, "I know of you. Canon Paul and Canon Matthew, fetch the wounded man into the hospital. He saw the bodies on the other horses and made the sign of the cross. "If you bring those poor men into the church, we will bury them in the morning. This night they can enjoy the peace of our church." He pointed to the church and I hurried after him while the others saw to the dead and the two monks who carried the corpselike body into the church. There were eight beds in the small hospital but only two were occupied. As the two monks laid the body on a table which was covered by a white sheet, the monk said, "I am Prior Richard. We keep these beds for travellers. The woods around here teem with bandits. In the time of King John, they had a reason to fight against his tyranny but the ones there now prey on the weak. Our gate is strong, and our walls are high. You will be safe." He washed his hands and went over to the youth. "What is his name?"

"I know not. We arrived in time to stop the bandits from causing further harm to the dead. We do not know them."

He smiled as he examined the wound, "Then you are like the Good Samaritan. God will smile upon you, Sir William, for such an act." He turned to one of the monks, "Canon Matthew, I can see nothing for the blood and matted hair, shave the head." As the monk went for a razor the Friar said, "There will be hot food in the refectory."

"If you do not mind, Friar Richard, I will stay. I am a soldier and I have a professional interest in all wounds and their healing."

He seemed to scrutinise my face, "And that may explain why you have lived so long my lord. Just stay out of the way."

The monk who shaved the injured man seemed to know his business. I suppose shaving heads on a regular basis gave a man an unusual skill. The skull had blood seeping from it, and it was not the result of the shaving. The Prior kept washing the blood away so that he could examine it.

He peered closely at it and sniffed. Seemingly satisfied he said, "Canon Matthew, fetch vinegar, honey and rosemary. Pound the rosemary with the honey add a little vinegar and have some bandages brought as well as gut and a needle." He glanced up at me as he wiped his bloody hands. "The skull had been broken and there is a piece pressing inside. The brain is a marvellous work created by God and we know not how it works but a lump of bone which is intended to protect the fragile brain cannot be meant to press inside. I will cut away a flap of skin, bring out the fragment and try to replace it. After using the honey and rosemary to help the healing I will sew back the skin and then we shall pray for nothing can be achieved except that God helps us." He smiled as the Canon returned. "Bone can regrow you know. Remarkable is it not that something which is so hard can yet be supple enough to reform."

I watched in fascination as the Prior used his long fingers to carefully and patiently, remove the bone and examine it. He washed it in vinegar and laid it in a bowl. Then he used a bunch of rosemary to wipe the wound with vinegar. He then meticulously replaced the bone in position. I was not close but, to me, it seemed to fit perfectly. He then delicately covered the whole injury in a very thin layer of the rosemary paste and finally replaced the flap of skin. His stitches were as small and delicate as I had ever seen. Finally, he poured some holy water over the wound before nodding to Canon Matthew to bandage it. He made the sign of the cross and murmured some Latin.

"Now it is in the hands of God, as it always is. He is breathing easier and, if he is to live then we shall know by the morrow. I will have my canons watch him this night." Wiping his hands, he said, "Come, let us eat and we can speak." As we walked, he said, "Where is your home, Sir William?"

"Weedon, close to Northampton, Prior."

"Then you still have a journey, eh?"

"Two days, but in this weather, who knows."

"And what of your plans for the young man? I take him to be no more than sixteen years of age and that bodes well for the younger a man the quicker he heals." He chuckled, "Men of our age know that all too well, eh, Sir William?"

We entered the refectory and the first thing which struck me was the calm. Even my men, normally chatty and noisy were silent. This was a peaceful place. As we went towards the table which housed my men I thought about the Prior's question. I had not thought beyond saving the youth's life. The dying sergeant at arms had made me think about the others who had fought in the great battle. My men and I had been successful and, with the exception of Walter, Wilton, Matty and Hob, had emerged without harm. I had studied the young man while I watched the Prior seemingly work a miracle for he had taken away part of the skull and the youth had not died. The youth appeared at peace and looked like he might recover. I had examined his face for the Canon had not just shaved his skull, but he had removed the wispy growth from his chin and cheeks. The Prior was right, he was a young man, but he was a man and had fought on Crispin's Day with a spear. I knew from my time in the Blue Company that when a life was saved then there was a bond, a tie, if you will, between the ones who saved the life and the one who was saved. Christmas would be upon us in days and I would be in the bosom of my family. My men would all enjoy the festive season in warmth and comfort. Could I abandon the youth here and expect the canons to care for him?

"Sir William?"

I looked up and saw that all of the table was looking at me and the Prior was smiling at me. "Sorry, I er…"

"You were thinking of my words. I am sorry I should have let you eat before taxing your mind. Canon John asked if you wished wine or ale with your food."

"Er, wine." I nodded, "You are right. The youth was upon my mind. Your words about the Good Samaritan struck a nerve. In the Bible, the Samaritan pays for the man to be cared for. Could I do that here? Could I give you coin, and you care for him?"

The wine came and the Prior said Grace. When he opened his eyes, he raised his chalice. "To a life saved!"

We all repeated the words and I sipped the heavy red wine. This was unwatered. I knew that the Canons would drink watered wine. This was for us.

The Prior put down his chalice and wiped both his mouth and the rim of the vessel with his napkin. "Such a financial gift would be most welcome for we are not a rich order and we could care for him but I believe that the youth is tied to you and your men. When he wakes, he will look around and seek the men alongside whom he fought. They are all dead. Will he be happy with monks? I think not. I say again, Sir William, what would you?"

"I have a dilemma, Prior, for I wish to reach my home as soon as I can and yet, you are right, there is an unseen shackle now which ties each of us to this youth. Had Rafe not noticed that he breathed he might have been placed with the other dead and would, even now, be beyond help. They fought alongside my men at Agincourt and that makes him a brother in arms. If the weather was perfect and, if the youth could travel, then I would take him with us and have him recover at my home and then when he was healed, I would give him coin and let him choose his own path."

The Prior nodded and sipped his wine again, "Much as the Samaritan did. I cannot change the weather but if he wakes in the morning then I see no reason why he should not travel. Less than thirty miles south of here is Laundes Abbey and it is also an Augustine Priory. Prior Gilbert who is there has skills for he was a Knight Hospitaller in another life. He could give a better opinion than I. Does that solution offer hope?"

I smiled, "You are a wise man, Prior, for you can read my mind. If he wakes, then it means God wishes him to travel and we shall take him." Although they had said nothing my companions all looked relieved. Perhaps they were thinking of Walter. If someone had come, as we had, then perhaps his life might have been saved.

We all slept in the hospital and a canon kept a candlelit vigil over the youth. I was unused to sleeping with a light and I did not sleep well, in addition, the bells sounded to summon the canons to prayer. I was also thinking of the men at arms who had lost their lord and now had lost their lives. There would be many such men in England. It was all very well for King Henry to plan for the next campaigning season but there were men in England who, through no fault of their own, might be cast upon hard times. I would take this youth home. I had months before I needed to leave England by which time my wife and I would have prepared him for life alone. I suddenly realised how lucky I had been.

162

The Blue Company had been my family and I had had enough fathers and others to care for me.

When the youth awoke it was not yet dawn, but my sleep was so shallow that I was alert in an instant. I rose and donned my cloak for the air in the hospital was so cold that it formed a mist before me as I walked to the canon and the injured youth. The canon was cradling the youth's shaven head and pouring honeyed wine into his mouth. The youth's eyes were closed. The canon smiled, "God has smiled upon this one. His heart beats well and he can drink. I will fetch the Prior." He laid down the youth's head and left.

The eyes opened and the youth's piercingly blue ones stared up at me, "Where am I? Where is the monk?"

"He has gone to fetch the Prior for it was his skill saved your life after the attack."

His eyes darted to the side and he tried to rise, "Where is Richard? Edgar?"

I gently pushed him back to lie flat, "Peace, for they are dead, but they will be buried here in holy ground."

He closed his eyes and I heard a sigh so deep that it seemed as though the earth had opened and swallowed him. "Then I am now alone, once more."

"What is your name?"

"Michael of Kildale."

"You were at Agincourt with my men?"

He looked up at me and appeared to recognise me, "You are Sir William. I saw your sons fighting under the Duke of York."

I nodded, "Edgar spoke to me before he died. He told me of your misfortunes."

The Prior appeared in the doorway with Canon James, but they did not intrude, "Edgar was taking us to his family's farm. It is not far from where I was born. My family had a small farm, but the pestilence took my mother, father, brothers and sisters. I was spared. Why was that, lord, for I bring bad luck to all that I meet?"

"I do not think that is so. You have no family there now?"

"My family was our company. They watched over me. I had few skills when I went to war, but I learned to prepare Edgar and the others to fight and to use a spear and a short sword. I think I killed some Frenchmen at Agincourt."

"And what would you do now?" The Prior had said that he thought the youth looked to be no older than fifteen or sixteen summers. In that moment he looked young, almost like Walter.

He looked at me fearfully, "I am alone! I know not."

"You are not alone for you fought with us on St Crispin's Day at Agincourt and you are our brother in arms. You shall, if the Prior deems it right, come with us to my home until you have decided what it is that you wish for your life."

The Prior came over and smiling said, "Aye, Michael of Kildale, for you have been given a rare opportunity. You were dead and now have been reborn. There is a chance of a new life and that is not to be scorned. The Good Lord has given you a clean tablet of wax. Your life can be whatever you wish it to be. While Sir William joins the brothers at the refectory, I will examine the wound and see if you are fit to travel."

I said, loudly, "Time for you to make a move, gentlemen." Men at arms could sleep standing up and neither the bells nor my conversation had disturbed them!

The food was simple but wholesome fare. They had bread ovens in the priory, and I enjoyed warm bread smothered in fresh butter. The runny cheese and the slices of ham made it a feast fit for a king. I am not sure if it was my commands or the smell of freshly baked bread which drew my men but I was only on my second piece when they arrived.

"We will take Michael back to Weedon with us. There is a prior at Laundes Abbey who can look at the wound."

Peter said, "Michael?"

"That is the name of the youth we saved. He is an orphan and the men who died were as close to family as he has. He said he remembered fighting on the same part of the battlefield as my sons."

Will nodded, "I vaguely remembered the men at arms but not this, Michael."

"From what he said he fought with just a spear and a short sword. I think Edgar of Hutton Rudby and the others took sympathy on him."

Rafe smeared a large dollop of butter on his bread. It began to melt almost immediately, "It is not just our Christian duty, my lord, when we fought for King Henry, we were all one family. James and I are happy to watch him while we ride south."

The Prior pronounced Michael well enough to ride but, before we left, we interred the dead men at arms in the Priory graveyard. It was well done and had we not come along the road then their bones would have lain there until they became dust. Their spirits would have wandered the road. That the bandits who had killed them would have been haunted as well as ordinary travellers brought no sense of comfort to me. We each put a spadeful of earth on Edgar's grave and Michael knelt to say his own goodbye. We stood back for such a parting was private. Wrapped against the bitingly cold wind we bade farewell to the canons and headed to the next priory.

Rafe and James rode on either side of Michael and chatted to him as we rode along the deserted road. Only fools or those who had to make the journey would be out on such a day. I think that Michael found it easy to talk to Rafe and James for they were older versions of Edgar and they spoke the same language. I rode ahead with Will of Stockton.

"Do you think that Michael was sent to replace Walter?"

Sir Will's words made me whip my head around in surprise, "What?"

"We buried Walter and Wilton's bones and within a day we find Michael who is almost dead." He shrugged, "I believe in God, my lord, but since Pippa died, I have heard her voice at night. A man can believe in God and spirits, can he not?"

"I am not sure but we all believe in the Holy Spirit so who knows. When we reach the Priory ask Prior Gilbert. He may be able to enlighten you."

"No, lord, for he might prove that the voices I hear are not my wife and that would break my heart for a second time. I think that Walter's spirit entered Michael's body. Look how well he gets on with Rafe and James. They were both close to Walter."

I shook my head, "I am not certain of anything anymore. The death of so many squires and pages is hard to come to terms with. Yours is a comforting thought but I would not wish to delude myself. We will do our best for the youth and see what happens. I was rewarded well enough after the battle. I can afford to fit out Michael so that if he wishes to become a warrior he can. Who knows, he may choose another path for as Prior Richard said, he has the chance to choose a new path for his new life."

Prior Gilbert was older than even I was and a more kindly and knowledgeable man I have yet to meet. He reminded me of Peter the Priest. He sent us to the refectory so that he could examine Michael in private. They both joined us and the Prior waved me to his side, "Brother Richard has done a good job, but the boy is lucky. The wound was a finger's width away being fatal. I believe that the bone will mend and he will heal. I see God's hand in all of this. From what the boy told me had you not come along then he would have died and died unshriven!"

I remembered Will's words, "Tell me Prior, is it possible for a spirit to pass between bodies?"

He was a clever man and he did not answer me but asked me to explain. I told him of Walter's death and our journey to his family. He gave me a sad smile, "In all honesty, Sir William, I know not but I have lived, as you have, for a long time and there are many things I do not understand. I served in the Holy Land and witnessed things there which are hard to explain. I have given up trying. If you and your men choose to believe that Walter's spirit lives in Michael then I see no harm in it." He added quietly, "Just do not say so before less enlightened priests than me. What I will say is that you have performed a good deed. I know your name and that you have defended kings and princes. That is laudable but I believe that the act of saving this boy and giving him a home is even nobler. You are a good man."

Coming from the venerable prior that was the greatest compliment I could hope for. When we left the next day for the last leg of the journey, I took hope from the change in the weather. The wind had veered in the night and came from the south and west. It was warm enough to begin a thaw and while it made for a slush filled journey, it was a sign of a change.

When we reached Weedon I let the others take the horses to the stables so that I could explain the arrival of Michael to my wife. She was a kind woman and would understand why I had brought him but this was her house as much as mine and she deserved some sort of consultation.

She greeted me warmly, "You have been longer than I expected. I feared that you might not return before Christmas and that would have disappointed us. I have asked Harry and Elizabeth to host the Christmas feast at Northampton Castle this year. I think it is time the whole family gathered under one roof to celebrate the fact that we are all whole!"

The look she gave me dared me to object. I did not and I hugged her, "A splendid idea and we will have an extra guest."

She frowned and so I took her indoors to explain. As I expected her maternal instincts wanted the best for this youth she did not know. "He will sleep in the hall?"

I was on uncertain ground, "Regard him as a squire. He can have Walter's room. I am unsure what he will wish for himself but until winter is over then he will stay here with us and we will heal him from within too."

Just then Rafe and James arrived with Michael and Michael's few belongings. When she saw the bandage around his shaven head, I thought she would burst into tears. "Rafe, take our guest to Walter's room. There are some clothes there left from when Abelard had the room. They may fit Michael." She smiled at the youth. "I am Lady Eleanor and you're welcome!"

166

Michael ensured his place in her heart when he dropped to one knee and kissed the back of her hand, "Thank you, Lady Eleanor. I will try not to be a bother!"

Rafe grinned and said, "Come with me, young man. I think that you will like it here!"

Bearing in mind that Michael had come from little more than a hut and had nothing I was certain that Rafe was right. It was as Michael disappeared up the stairs, something he had probably never done in his life before, that I saw the similarities to me. Will was right; Michael was meant to come to Weedon.

Chapter 15

The first thing we had to do with Michael was to stop him from apologising all the time. He seemed to think that he was doing everything in the wrong manner. I think it endeared him to my wife more. We discovered that his family had all been taken by the illness which had struck the village when he was eight and now he was sixteen. It explained a great deal. He had been taken in by Edgar's parents, but they had been too busy to give him the care and attention he needed and that was why Edgar had taken him to war. While living there he had shared the barn with the animals and when he had lived with his own parents, the hut had but one room for sleeping. The concept of sheets on the bed and freshwater to wash in was something he had never experienced. My wife spent the five days before we went to Northampton for Christmas explaining how things would be done. This was not out of any sort of embarrassment about Michael's behaviour but just so that he felt more comfortable. My wife was the matriarch of the family and none, me included, would argue with her. While Michael waited for the new clothes my wife's seamstresses made for him, he wore Abelard's old clothes. There was nothing wrong with them and had he lived then when he had grown Walter would have worn them too. Nothing was thrown away until it had no purpose at all! As he had been a warrior, we also fitted him out with a brigandine, short sword, spear and a shield. If he chose not to stay with us, then he would be able to make his way in the world as a mercenary. When the weather improved Rafe and James would help him improve his skills.

The day before we were to leave and as I was checking the horses we would take with Rafe and James, Michael asked, "Am I like Rafe and James, here, lord? Am I to be a servant?"

"Until you are healed, and the doctor says that you have overcome the wound then you are our guest. What happens after that will be up to you."

He was silent for a while and then said, "I do not understand, lord, up to me?"

"You have choices to make. If you no longer wish to stay with us, then we will give you a horse and some coins and you can choose your own future."

He suddenly looked terrified, "I would be alone?"

"If you chose to be."

"And I could choose to stay here?"

"Of course."

"Then I will stay!"

Rafe laughed, "Then the blow did not rob you of your senses, Michael."

I scowled at Rafe and explained gently to Michael, "Lady Eleanor and I do not wish a rash decision. There is no hurry. I will not be leaving until late spring. By then your wound should have been healed and your hair regrown. I have no doubt that Lady Eleanor will feed you up and so you will be larger than you are. Weedon may seem too small for you then."

He gave a rueful smile, "Lord, this hall seems like a palace to me and I would not wish anything which was grander. You have all been kinder to me than I could have hoped. When I fell on the road in the forest, I thought my life was over and the only sad part was that I was leaving my brothers in arms. Lady Eleanor and the women of the house are the first women I have seen since Hutton Rudby and they have shown me the same kindness I had before my mother died, for I was her favourite."

Rafe said, quietly, "And you miss her."

Nodding he said, "My father was hard working and with a large family had little time for any of us. He was not a hard man by any means but he was always trying to put bread on the table and that sucked kindness from him. My mother more than made up for it. She was the last in the family to die and she died in my arms." Silence filled the stable and no one broke it. We did not look at Michael for we heard the emotion in his voice. A wrong word or look, however well-meaning, could unman him.

It was Matilda, one of my wife's women, who broke the spell, "My lord, Lady Eleanor is ready for you to fetch the luggage to the wagon."

I had sent messengers to Northampton so that my sons knew we had a guest. They could be discreet and, as they had fought alongside the dead men at arms, I knew that they would go out of their way to show him kindness. The most embarrassing moment came when we were served by the squires and Michael could not grasp the idea that my grandson was waiting at the table while he ate. It took my wife to put him in his place, "Michael, this is not a punishment for William. He is training to be a knight. His two uncles did the same and I do not doubt that their sons will too. Enjoy it!" My wife understood how to talk to people, and it was one of her many characteristics which endeared her to me.

We stayed until twelfth night and then headed home. The days we had spent in the castle had been an education for the youth who had almost died on the Great Road. His confidence had also improved. My sons and their squires had helped as had their children. I was lucky for I had a kind family and they were not, as so often happened in royal and noble families, trying to kill each other!

When we reached my home, I set about preparing for the coming campaign. I wrote letters to Sir John of Dauentre, Sir Abelard and Sir Henry of Stratford. I let them know how many lances I expected of them. Sir Ralph and my men at arms knew already. Michael asked if he was to come with us for he had a spear, a horse and a sword.

I spread an arm, "It is as I said, Michael, that is your choice. Do not rush into it for I know that if you do go to war again it will be hard for there will be ghosts at your shoulder."

And then I received the summons to ride to Windsor. The esquire who brought the summons was new and I did not know him. It took quite a while to discover that the reason was my investiture into the Order of the Garter. Although it was an honour it would mean a great deal of fuss and would take not only me but also my sons away from our home for ten days. I would need an escort of knights. For once my wife did not mind my absence. Rafe came to me the day before I was due to leave. "My lord, take Michael with you."

I shook my head, "Rafe it is an affair of the high and the mighty. It would be cruel to inflict it upon him."

Shaking his head Rafe said, "My lord, he would like to go and you need a servant for the horses. Take him. He will be honoured to be so close to the King. Trust me in this matter. I know the boy and James and I are close to him."

I had to trust Rafe for he had been closer to me than my sons in the last few years. I agreed and I confess the look on Michael's face confirmed Rafe's opinion.

Winter had yet to turn to Spring and although the days were marginally longer it was still cold but, thankfully, we had no snow. We travelled to London and we stayed at Eltham Palace. The short ride to Windsor meant we reached the castle by noon. Windsor is a magnificent castle and more of a castle than the Tower. I would be housed in the round tower and a herald and a pursuivant spent the first afternoon going through the details of the ceremony. King Edward had formed the order two years after the Battle of Crécy and not a detail had been changed. We had barely arrived in time and the ceremony was to be the next day. King Henry was not one to waste time and the day following the ceremony would be given over to planning the Normandy Campaign.

The ceremony was every bit as daunting as I had expected but I had been well drilled and I managed to avoid making any mistakes. The honour was conferred and that night we dined in the huge building which King Edward had built to emulate the legendary round table. I confess that when I retired that night I felt as though I had joined an elite. It was a remarkable journey for the son of a camp follower.

The next day, however, was all business and I was summoned to King Henry's chamber to meet with his brothers, the Earl of March and John, Duke of Bedford. It was an august body and I was honoured to be included.

"Know you all that I have been making plans since before we returned from Agincourt. The Duke of Bedford summoned parliament and has the funding not only for a new war but also a fleet. The Earl of Dorset who commands at Harfleur will command the fleet eventually. Come the summer we will assemble an army at Southampton and use Harfleur as a base from which we can launch our attack on Normandy. I would take Honfleur and then Caen, I have the support of the Holy Roman Emperor and the Pope. At the moment it is in the form of a promise, but the Emperor will visit England later in the year and then it will be confirmed."

He then went through the details of the actual campaign and the men who would lead it. As with all of King Henry's plans, it was meticulous and well thought out. I realised that it would be a series of sieges: Caen first and then the other strongholds. Sieges, as we had discovered at Harfleur, could be costlier than a battle and I did not relish the prospect. He also had an idea of a chevauchée from Calais to draw forces from Normandy. It seemed a bold plan, more importantly, I saw a way to allow Sir Ralph to lay the ghost of his son to bed. By the time we had finished, I was exhausted, but I begged leave to speak with the King in private. While he had been speaking, I had been thinking of the men I would lead and what they would hope from this campaign in France. Since speaking with Sir Ralph I knew that this day would come, and I had to broach the subject of vengeance. I was not sure how it would be viewed by the King.

"King Henry, I have to tell you that my knights are still incensed about the attack on the squires. The Lord of Azincourt has yet to be brought to account for his actions."

"Not true, Will, for the Duke of Burgundy has sent back the sword which was stolen. He confiscated it from the knight and I have my crown returned too. All is well."

Had he changed so much that swords and crowns meant more than men? I sighed, "With respect, King Henry, I care not for crowns, jewelled swords and treasure. You cannot buy back the lives of the boys and squires who were killed, can you?"

He reddened, "Be careful, Strongstaff, for I am no longer the boy you mentored."

"I apologise, Your Majesty, I meant no offence. Perhaps this old warhorse should be put out to grass. I tend to speak my mind these days and I would not show you any disrespect." I was not doing myself any favours for I was digging a deeper hole. "What I ask is this, when we are in Normandy, I would like to take my lances and apprehend and bring to justice the two men who ordered the attack on the camp. Have I your permission to do so?"

I do not know what he thought I had meant when I first spoke but his face broke into a smile. "Is that all you ask? Of course. We leave for France in June. If you wish you and your men can land at Calais." He sipped some wine and then smiled broadly, "In fact, this might be the very diversion which our campaign needs. If you were active in the north of France it would divert attention from Normandy; you could draw men from our attacks. And when you capture him you have my permission to try him. I shall give you written authority!" He clapped me on the back, "You had me worried there. I thought your elevation to the order had given you ideas. I should have known better."

That was a relief and I enjoyed the last two days at Windsor. I discovered that my elevation made a difference to many senior lords and I did not know why. I was still the same man I had always been. Nothing about being a Knight of the Order of the Garter made me a different man but the new fur on my cloak seemed to make them forget that my parents had never been married and my mother had been, in essence, a camp follower.

When we left, I had a clearer idea of the dates. The invasion was planned for July and that meant I had some months to prepare. I would present myself in Dover at the end of June and there would be ships waiting to take us to Calais. The King would embark the army in the newly commissioned fleet in July. I would now be the catalyst to set in motion the plan to retake Normandy and then France. The King still hoped to marry Katherine Valois, but he knew now that might be as the result of a military victory. King Henry was single-minded! Of course, events did not follow the King's plan, but it says much of him that he was able to adapt when Fate and other kings intervened. For my men and me I was happier, for we could avenge Walter and still follow the King!

My sons and I discussed the plans as we rode home. Surrounded by our men we could talk freely for they were all completely trustworthy. Thomas was the more concerned of the two, "Father, I know you meant well to leave us at home for the coming campaign, but it seems to me that you need the two of us."

I noticed that he did not include Sir Richard in his comments. I nodded, "And why is that?"

"We are experienced knights!"

"Ah, and Ralph, John, Will and Henry are not? I will have six knights with me this time and not the three I took to Harfleur."

I could tell that the two of them had not thought this through. Harry added, "We are your sons." Even as he said it, I saw that he realised that it sounded lame.

"And surely, all the more reason that you stay here. The Earl of Suffolk died at Harfleur. His son was given the title and died less than a month later on St Crispin's Day. I have thought this through well and the two of you will stay at home. You will keep the King's Road clear of bandits and brigands and you will uphold the rule of law." They were silent and I added, quietly, "I fear that this will be my last campaign."

They looked at me with concern written all over their faces. Thomas shook his head, "You are not ill, are you? You have done too much travelling!"

I shook my head, "No but it will be a six-month campaign at the very least and I am no longer a young man. I do not find myself in the heart of the battle any longer but there are other dangers on campaign. Whatever the outcome I shall beg leave of the King to stay at home when next he needs warriors."

Harry laughed, "Not in the heart of the battle? The king lost so many esquires at Agincourt that he lost count and yet, at the end, you were still there guarding his back." I said nothing. "Who will guard your back? Who will be your squire? The campaign is mere months away and you have none yet to ride behind you."

He was right, of course. It was not as simple as walking up to a youth and asking him to serve you. A knight needed a squire with potential. I saw now, in hindsight, that I had made a mistake with Walter. He would have made a good page, but I had asked him to do too much too early. The premature death of King Henry had caused the problem. Had Henry Bolingbroke not died when he did then we would not have fought at Agincourt and Walter might have learned more skills.

"I will be your squire, Sir William, if you will have me."

I turned and looked at Michael. I had almost forgotten that he was riding close behind me. Thomas and Harry also looked surprised. I nodded, "It is good of you to offer and I do not dismiss it out of hand, but do you know what you do? My wife and I have told you that when you are ready you can have coins, clothes and weapons and you can be your own man and make your own decisions. As my squire, there is no such thing as time off. You will be at my beck and call at all hours of the day. You will have to serve at table. You will need to help me to dress, care for my horse, keep my weapons sharp, be close by in battle with a spare horse…" I waved a hand around as though there were many other such arduous tasks.

He smiled and shrugged, "Sir William, I was dead and reborn but not as a babe. I was reborn with memories and experience. I know that I am raw clay, much as the first man was but already James and Rafe have given me skills. Besides that, I believe that I was sent back to this earth to replace Walter. I have listened to all that has been said of that youth and know that he had a future. I have yet to meet his father but from what others have said, Walter would have been a knight like Sir Ralph. I do not say that I would become such a man, but I can protect your back. Edgar and the others taught me loyalty and also how to see when a man deserved that loyalty. Even before you found me, I knew that you were such a man. We all knew that it was you watched King Henry at the battle. Edgar admired you almost as much as he admired the King. He said you were well named. You were the staff which would neither bend nor break." I was silent and thinking about the matter. "Give me a month, lord, while you seek another. If I have not impressed you in that time then I will take you up on your offer and seek a life elsewhere."

I had no idea how Michael would adjust to life as a squire but it seemed to me that if I had to choose a squire then he had many of the abilities already. He had stood in battle and killed a man. He had campaigned and was used to a harsh life. The skills he lacked were not the ones I valued. I cared not if he could serve well at table nor if he could play a rote or sing a song. I needed someone like me, someone who had a hard life and was resilient.

"Very well. We shall begin your training now. You shall groom my horse and, this night shall sleep across my door. Michael of Kildale, you are now my squire! My son's squires will begin instruction when we stop for the night and it will continue at Weedon."

I had no idea what my sons thought of the idea and, to be honest, I cared not. The decision felt right.

My wife, ever the practical woman, approved and was pleased for the young man but she also knew that there was a cost for us. He needed to be fitted out in my livery. I was a Knight of the Garter and I was close to the King. My squire would have to reflect that status and be dressed accordingly. Not surprisingly Rafe and James were delighted and took great pleasure in training him in arms. They had both been wounded and could no longer fight but that did not stop them from passing on their skills as warriors. They were both the best trainers of men. Michael was also helped by the fact that Will of Stockton lived close by and Peter, his new squire, was also undergoing training. Peter had a humble background too although not as humble as Michael and that helped them both. They bonded and that made my task easier for I had much to do before the campaign began.

The King kept me informed, not in writing, but by messengers. He was now training esquires who would replace those killed at Agincourt and riding his roads, delivering his messages was a way to prepare them for the task they would have when the war began. I got to know them all well as a rider would arrive every few days. I learned that the Dauphin had died and the new one was married to the niece of Duke John the Fearless. King Henry had lost an ally and, even more importantly provided the French with a better general than the ones we had defeated. Then the French blockaded Harfleur. Men were being gathered at Southampton ready for the campaign, but our ships were not yet ready. I wondered if all that we had achieved would be lost. If Harfleur fell, then we would have to begin again. The King told me that the campaign would now be delayed until later in the summer and that helped me for Michael's training could be a priority for my men at arms.

Michael knew how to ride but not how to fight on horseback. I remembered back to the ambush by the Lollards and how Walter had almost frozen with fear. Now Nat worked, in the afternoons, on Michael's riding skills. The fact that he was aching and black and blue from his morning workout at the pel with Rafe and James must have made Michael regret his decision to be my squire. However, he stuck at the task and all three of them were impressed with his improvement. With good, regular food, his lean framed filled out and my wife complained that the clothes she was having made for him would be too small!

Then I had a message from the King. This time it was written, and it was sealed. It was a long letter and told me that he had been forced to alter his plans. It was all to do with the politics of the papacy and the Holy Roman Emperor. The new Dauphin had died, poisoned apparently, and there was the third Dauphin in a year. As with all such matters, it changed the political landscape. As Harfleur was still under siege then I was asked to sail with my men to Calais and use my men to threaten Picardy. It was hoped to distract attention from Harfleur so that the Duke of Bedford could relieve the siege with his new fleet and crewed by many men at arms and archers. That would allow the King to launch his invasion albeit somewhat later than he had intended. Our action in the north-west of France would still draw men away from Normandy. My raid would be a chevauchée but the carrot he dangled before me was that he would allow me to capture Isembart d'Azincourt and Robinet de Bournonville. The King asked me to send my answer in writing.

I went alone to my solar to consider my decision. I had extra time to prepare for the campaign. My men at arms and knights had been expecting the summons for months. They would be eager to go. I would be able to leave within a fortnight. However, I would be alone in Northern France with little expectation of support. I would have no more than three hundred men and that would include servants. I would have to find Isembart d'Azincourt and Robinet de Bournonville in their heartland where they were well supported, and I would be a tempting target for my many enemies. I knew that I had no choice in the matter. For my knights, this would mean that they were absolved from having to serve in the next campaign and they would be happy to be serving under me. I wrote the letters, first to the King and then to my knights. Sir Ralph, who would have the furthest to travel would be keen to ride and with the horses at his disposal would arrive within a week. Stephen of Morpeth would have the longest journey of any of my men at arms. That could not be helped and if he did not make the muster then he would have to remain in England. He had served me well enough. Although I did not want to have to use David of Welshpool, I knew that I would have to for he was the best at what he did. This would be his last campaign too.

The esquire joined us at table, and it was as we ate that I made the announcement, "Strongstaff goes to war once more! We leave in ten days for Dover!"

My wife made the sign of the cross and I saw the beaming smile spread across Michael's face.

Chapter 16

I sent Sir Will of Stockton and some of my men at arms and archers ahead of the rest of us to Dover. They would ensure that the ships promised by the King would be ready and waiting. I sent other riders for my knights and men at arms. Sir Abelard and Sir John would be with me within a day while Sir Henry might take a day or two. The northern knights and men at arms might take longer. This was Michael's first real lesson in becoming a squire. My wife took him in hand and showed him how to pack my clothes. That done he was given lessons in erecting my tent. Rafe and James taught him how to attach my armour. They used a wooden dummy to do so. Michael knew how to help a man at arms don mail, but plate was a completely different matter. He was given one of Abelard's mail hauberks. Before that it had been Ralph's and before that Sir John's. It had seen sterling service but as it was the first the youth had worn it felt special to him and Rafe showed him how to clean it using a bag of sand.

Sir Abelard and his squire, James, arrived first and that helped Michael. I saw Abelard smile as he watched Michael cleaning the mail links. It had been some years since he had had to do so. Sir John had been my first real squire for I had been hired to help Sir Henry become a knight. Sir John managed Dauentre for me and that was the jewel in my manors. My wife had been snubbed by the burghers of the town and although they had seen the error of their ways my wife could not abide the place and so we had stayed in Weedon. Sir John and his wife enjoyed a grand house, but I did not begrudge it him. He had served me the longest and if I was to be honest, was the best of my squires. It had been many years since I had fought alongside him and Sir Henry. I wondered how they had changed in that time.

When Harold of Derby returned it was with the sad news that Edgar of Derby's condition had worsened and he was now bedridden. Harold was not sure that he would see another Christmas and that saddened me. He had returned home yet had he stayed at Weedon with Rafe and James, his life might have been more enjoyable. Sir Stephen of Morpeth and Sir Ralph of Middleham Grange arrived together having met upon the road. Stephen had obviously used his money wisely. He had with him ten retainers, five archers and five men at arms, including Oswald, Harry and John of Thropton. He also wore good plate. He looked, to all intents and purposes, like a knight. Indeed, his plate was better than Sir Henry's. The first man I had trained had not been to war since Shrewsbury and it showed! When all of my warriors arrived, I invited them to dine with me so that I could explain our task. Sir Henry also brought with him, two healers. They were from his manor and healers were always welcome.

"It is twofold: the King wishes us to draw men from Normandy. We need to make the French think that we are the vanguard of another invasion. The illusion will be helped by the fact that before Agincourt I led the vanguard. However, we must avoid entanglements with larger forces of the enemy. Our second task is more personal. We seek Isembart d'Azincourt and Robinet de Bournonville. We will try to bring them to justice."

Sir Ralph's eyes flashed fire, "And that they shall receive at the end of my sword."

"Sir Ralph, that may well be but, if we can then we bring them back to England to be tried." I held his gaze and he nodded. "If they retreat, as I expect they will, to the castle at Azincourt, then we may well have to take it and, as we all learned at Harfleur, that may not be easy."

Stephen of Morpeth smiled, "It may be easier than you think, my lord."

My curiosity was piqued, "How so, Stephen?"

"When we cleared the battlefield, Oswald and I found the castle. It was empty for the garrison had fled and there was little to take." He grinned, "Although we did find a chest or two which they had forgotten. However, we also found a hidden sally port in the wall. It was overgrown with ivy. We found it while we were searching the grounds for freshly turned earth." Stephen, like all good scavengers, knew that people still liked to bury treasure when danger came, and we always sought out freshly turned soil. "We know where it is to be found, and it is unlikely that they will have cleared the ivy. We could sneak through their defences."

I spied hope in this quest. Since I had spoken with the King, I had realised the enormity of what we planned. That would not stop us attempting it as we owed it to Walter and the other squires to punish their killers. I had almost resigned myself to failure and hoped that the mere effort of trying to take Isembart d'Azincourt and Robinet de Bournonville might be enough.

Sir Oliver cautioned us, "As soon as we arrive in Calais then these killers will know of our presence for you are not an anonymous man;

you are the King's bodyguard, my lord, what if they flee and find refuge where we cannot get at them?"

Sir Ralph said, "I know not about the rest of you, but I will hunt them down to the ends of the earth if necessary."

The rest of my knights and men at arms said nothing. With Ralph this was personal. We had all mourned the dead squires and boys, but Walter had been his son. We understood but I would not allow us all to die just because of one dead squire.

I almost ignored Ralph's words, "I do not intend to be in France above a month. In fact, a month may be too long. The longer we are there the more chance the French have of bringing us to battle with superior numbers. So long as we alleviate the pressure on Harfleur we have fulfilled our commitment. We will try to take these child killers but I will not risk other men's lives recklessly."

With that warning in place, we planned what we would need to take, and we left a day later in the middle of a hot July. It felt strange to be going to war when the rest of the country was waiting and, seemingly at peace. The Duke of Bedford would be loading his great ships, the new five hundred-ton carracks: '*Trinity Royal*', '*Jesus*', '*Holy Ghost*' and '*Grace Dieu*', at Southampton. The men who were to have been sent to France to fight on land would, instead, fight aboard these new floating fortresses. They would take a week or more to load and then it would take them a week, at least, to sail to Harfleur. If I timed it right, then we would be in Calais before the end of July and Harfleur would be saved.

As we rode south to Dover I realised that Sir Henry was now almost middle-aged, or he appeared so compared with the other knights. Sir John had not fought since Shrewsbury either, but he appeared to be fit. Their conversation, as we rode to the port, was of the profits their manors had made. In contrast, Ralph, Abelard, Stephen, and Oliver looked lean and hungry and they spoke of war. Sir Abelard had been at St. Cloud and there he had fought hard. All had fought recently and while Sir Ralph had not been at Agincourt, he had had to fight Scottish raiders more than enough. I would have to watch Sir Henry and Sir John; it would not do to have to report their deaths to their widows. Their men, too, were not of the same quality as the rest of my men at arms, spearmen and archers. They were not professional soldiers and would be numbers only. My strength lay in those who had been at Agincourt. I would be leading seven knights, a hundred and thirty archers, one hundred of them mounted, sixty men at arms and a hundred and ten spearmen. The servants and squires added thirty men to our number. I intended to requisition wagons at Calais to speed up our journey.

As we rode, I saw the other men at arms who served me looking enviously at Stephen of Morpeth and Oliver the Bastard. They had now been knighted and they would hope that they, too, could be given their spurs. Some of the older squires, too, like Edward, Sir Henry's and William, Sir John's son, would be hoping to attract my attention and be given their spurs. While their lords might have been happy not to have to go to war a squire knew that it was his best chance to be knighted. Edward was older than Sir Abelard and had yet to fight in his first battle! Michael, my new squire, was just happy to be riding to war. He had had to march when we were in Normandy. One of the first presents he had received from my wife was a fine pair of buskins. Northampton was known for its cordwainers and bootmakers. He had told me that only the men at arms in his company had ridden to war and the rest had walked or run. The horse he had been given after we rescued him was Edgar's.

"Sir William, when you ride to battle then I will be close behind with another lance or will I have your spare horse in hand, Blaze?"

I smiled, "Both! Although I prefer a spear to a lance. It is unlikely that I will need a horse for Fire is a powerful animal and with his armour would be hard to hurt but battlefields are often littered with holes and I could be unhorsed. I am hoping to avoid a pitched battle but who knows."

"Then how do you hope to catch these murderers?" He was asking me more pertinent questions than Walter had ever asked and that showed the difference in ages and experience.

"We have permission from the King to make a nuisance of ourselves. That means we can raid animals and burn buildings. I hope to draw our foes to us and then use our greatest weapon, the longbow. We will disguise the numbers of bows we bring and hope to tempt the French to attack us. It is more than likely that we will not charge them but let them charge us."

"Why would they do that?"

"Because I am Sir William Strongstaff and I have a reputation. The two men we seek had their honour tarnished when they killed the squires and the boys. I hope that by raiding the lands around their castle they come for us in the hopes of being lauded as heroes and ridding themselves of the stigma of the slaughter of the squires. If they suspected that we came for vengeance, then I fear that they would simply squat in their castle and let greater lords rid the land of us."

He nodded for he was always learning, "That is what the King did at Agincourt, and you helped him. He drew the French to him so that the rest of us had a greater chance of victory."

"It is what good leaders do."

He lowered his voice, "Rafe told me that at Shrewsbury, the King's father,"

"Henry Bolingbroke?"

"Aye, he had men dressed identically to him." I nodded. "You were one."

"I was his bodyguard. Why should I not have dressed like him? I fear no man on the battlefield although I confess that now that I am older, Michael, I am more aware of my mortality. If I let others do more fighting it is not cowardice which makes me do so but the knowledge that I am no longer the knight who was able to defend kings."

Sir Will had shown that he had overcome his grief and he had taken charge of the situation in Dover. We had four ships at our disposal. They were not the huge carracks which the Duke of Bedford used but the small cogs we had used to sail to Harfleur. It would not matter for the voyage across the short stretch of water would take just half a day at most although as we had discovered before, adverse winds could hold us up. I had tried to eliminate that by enlisting the aid of Saint Thomas Becket. I had prayed at his tomb in Canterbury Cathedral and made a sizeable offering in the poor box. Such things could not hurt. There were large numbers of arrows there in preparation for the coming campaign and we loaded those and the horses. It took a day to load all that we would need, and we took the evening tide, for the winds were in our favour, and we headed to Calais.

As I had expected some of those unused to the sea, both men and horses, suffered in the crossing and we had to wait for three days once we were in Calais to allow them to recover. I did not waste that time and I consulted with Richard Beauchamp, 13th Earl of Warwick who was the Lieutenant of Calais and commanded Calais for the King.

I had known him since he had been a child for he was King Richard's godson. "Sir William it is good that you have been appointed to this task but I fear that with the paltry numbers of men you have been given you will find it hard to achieve that which the King wishes."

"So long as we create a sense of threat here then the French will have to send some men north to deal with us and that means the Duke of Bedford has more chance of success."

"And what of your mission to apprehend Isembart d'Azincourt and Robinet de Bournonville?"

"I intend to raid just north of Agincourt and hope to draw them to my banner. I will disguise the numbers of my archers. Is he in the area?"

He nodded, "The two of them and some of their men visited with the Duke of Burgundy in the hopes of ingratiating themselves with John the Fearless but that failed and he confiscated some of the treasure they stole and he has returned them to the King. I believe that the two of them are in the castle at Azincourt."

I did not like to criticise the Earl but if I had been the Lieutenant then I think I might have used spies to discover the truth. I smiled and said, "We will leave in a day or two. I will need wagons and horses to enable us to move quickly and it might be useful if you had patrols out in case, when we return, we have to do so quickly."

He nodded, "As the Duke of Brabant was killed in the battle then many of those in Brabant and Flanders are not disposed to be friendly towards us."

"I intend to assume that all the warriors we meet will be enemies!" I liked the Earl and I was pleased that he commanded the castle. I was being selfish for I knew he liked me and would not see harm come to me or mine if he could help it. Had the King known this when he commissioned me?

"Beware the garrison at Saint-Omer. They are the closest French force to this port, and they are vigilant."

Once the wagons were ready, we prepared to leave. David of Welshpool selected Christopher White Arrow and Jack Gardyvyan as our scouts. They had more experience than any other archers in my command. They would act as vintenars and each would command twenty men. It meant we had forty archers ahead of us. Their bows would be carried in cases and they would only be needed when we had to battle. I kept Sir Henry and Sir John with the wagons and the dismounted archers and spearmen. Although they were our weakest arm, I had a plan to make them stronger. The wagons would become mobile forts and if we were attacked, they would form up and make structure within which we could shelter if we needed to. Rafe and the other servants would also be with the wagons. In the case of Rafe and James, it was to give a stiffening of backbone and experience. Finally, the two chaplains and two healers we had would also be with the wagons. The rest of our archers would precede the wagons and the other knights and the men at arms would be the main body. My whole battle plan relied on every man obeying my orders.

While in the castle at Calais I studied maps. There was, to the east of the road we would be using, a castle at Saint-Omer but, having been warned by Sir Richard, I intended to avoid it. Close by, however, was a village called Arques which controlled a small river. The river could be forded but I had decided to raid the village and destroy the bridge. I intended to panic the garrison at Saint-Omer. Of course, if I could draw them from their walls and defeat them in battle then that would be a good result but at the very least I would draw attention away from Agincourt. Once we had destroyed the bridge and gathered ourselves some supplies, we would disappear in the vast forests which lay between Arques and Agincourt. The populace would see my surcoat and I would be recognised; I hoped that would be enough to tempt the Lord of Agincourt to seek me out.

The village was just twenty-five miles from Calais, and we left before dawn. The long days would give us an advantage for we could attack towards late afternoon when many people would be preparing to eat and their work day would be over. A column of heavily armed and mounted men would cause panic as we headed south and east. Our route took us along small roads through hamlets and tiny villages. Word could not be spread for these were not the kind of farms which had horses that could outrun my scouts. My archers passed Saint-Omer without being noticed. For that section, we left the main road and took a side road which passed the hamlet of Longuenesse. This was a risk but an acceptable one. When we passed the villagers might well run to Saint-Omer and warn the garrison but by then we would be beyond the danger. I planned on leaving my mobile forts and two rearguard knights to watch the road from Saint-Omer.

Cedric of Herrteburne rode back to tell us that the scouts had found the village, the bridge was unguarded and that the village was less than a mile away. Leaving Sir Henry and Sir John to block the road with the wagons I led the rest of my men to the village. As we thundered towards my hidden archers, panic set in amongst the villagers. I heard screams and shouts as the entire village fled across the wooden bridge. There was no reason why we could not follow them, but civilians often panic, and they fled.

I reined in, "Archers, search the houses for food then fire the village. Sir Oliver, have the men destroy the bridge!"

This was far easier than anything we had done more than half a year earlier but then we had been forbidden to raid. I heard squeals as a couple of pigs were captured. We would eat well when they were slaughtered. I waved Sir Abelard to my side. "Come with me and we will return to the rearguard. There is no danger here."

"Aye, lord."

"Sir Stephen, take charge. I will send Michael back if there is a problem."

Even as we galloped back up the road, I heard shouts which told me that there might be such a problem, but I refrained from sending

Michael back. It was better to see the scale of the trouble. I saw that the wagons were under a determined attack. The garrison from Saint-Omer had emerged. There were at least ten mounted men at arms, and I saw the spurs of four knights. Already the French had success and a couple of servants were nursing wounds from crossbow bolts. Had it been a mistake to have Sir Henry and Sir John in command? Had they changed so much since last they had fought for me? And then I realised that I had asked them to do something with which they were unfamiliar. The situation was not beyond remedy.

As I rode up, I shouted to the men in the wagons, "Archers, concentrate your arrows on the crossbows. Spearmen use your shields. Sir Henry, Sir John, fetch your mounted men at arms." I could see that the French had come en masse but that their mounted men were together in the centre of the road. The woods held their archers, crossbowmen and spearmen. I turned to Michael. "You will follow me with your spear and your shield. Guard my back and when you see a crossbowman reloading his weapon, then is the time to charge him!"

"Aye lord." His only sign of nerves was that he licked his lips.

Sir Henry and Sir John arrived, and I could see that Sir Henry was flushed. He was out of condition. "Flank me and have your eight men at arms follow. We charge their four knights and your squires can support Michael!"

"Sir Henry said, "But we are outnumbered!"

I laughed, "Aye, Agincourt we were outnumbered by ten to one and we still won." Drawing my sword, I raised it, "For God, King Harry and St George!" I spurred my horse and Fire almost leapt into the air. As he did so two bolts slammed into my breastplate. It was relatively close range and they hurt but did not penetrate. The weaponsmith had made them well and they had been worth every penny I had paid. I was ahead of Sir John and Sir Henry. Indeed, three of the men at arms were closer to me than the two knights. It was a combination of slow reactions and horses that were not up to the task. My sudden attack had taken the French knights and men at arms by surprise. They were still weighing up their options. The wagons contained only spearmen, servants and dismounted archers.

The archers had obeyed me and some of the crossbowmen, spearmen and archers in the woods were hit by well-flighted arrows. Our best archers were in the village. As the French realised what I intended they charged towards me, but we had momentum and they did not. They were still getting up to speed when Fire clattered amongst them. My shield was held tightly to my chest and, having no one to my right, I was able to give a full swing and strike the knight in the chest with my sword. He wore a breastplate and it was well made but my blow was so powerful that he began to fall back towards the cantle of his saddle. It meant my sword slid up the cuirass and struck him under the chin. His helmet had a boar's head snout and my sword ripped it from his head. I heard a cry a heartbeat later which I learned after the skirmish was over, was the man at arms behind me hacking across the French knight's face.

My unexpected charge had totally disorientated the French knights. One was down and a second followed as I lunged over the sword of the next Frenchman and the tip of my sword slid across the Frenchman's chin, tore into his mouth and the side of his skull. His sword scraped across my gorget. Then I was amongst men at arms who wore largely mail. A war axe hacked into my shield. It was a well-struck blow and the edge of the axe penetrated to the manifer on my left hand. The metal held and more importantly, as the axe head stuck there, I swung my sword around in a wide arc. The man at arms was so concerned with his axe head that he did not see the sword which swept into his back and, after severing some mail links ripped open his flesh.

Sir Henry and Sir John had finally followed me and the men at arms behind me had widened the gap we had made so that the two of them dealt with the two French knights. As Sir John disarmed one who fled, the other turned tail and followed him. It was the signal for a general flight. I managed to wound another man at arms as he passed and was able to watch Michael lead the other two squires into the woods to pursue and hack down the fleeing Frenchmen who had been using crossbows and bows. We had done all that I wished and so I shouted, "Stand fast! Stand fast!"

It took a few moments, but eventually, the men at arms and the three squires stopped chasing the French and returned to me. The three squires looked elated and I praised them, "You did well, now take all that there is to take from the dead. Those two horses look worth taking. Sir John, see to our wounded and then when all is done here bring the wagons to the village. We have a pig!"

I rode alone back to the village. The bridge was destroyed, and the buildings were burning. Some might have waited until the next day to burn the buildings for we could have used them for accommodation. However, it was the start of August and we needed no shelter. It was more important to alert the region to our presence and nothing did that like a fire. It would burn long into the night. The outraged villagers would head for Lens where there was a castle with a garrison. From there the news would be sent to Paris. It was like throwing a stone into a pond. The ripples kept going and when they reached those at Harfleur besieging the Earl of Dorset, their resolve would begin to weaken. They would look over their shoulders for the English army coming to relieve the siege. That it was an incredibly long way from Picardy would not matter. Our numbers would grow in the retelling of the story!

The slow reactions of the two knights worried me but I would keep that to myself. I knew we had lost men but that was inevitable, and my timely arrival had stirred them to action. Darkness was falling already as I rode towards the burning village. I could smell the burning skin of the pigs as they were cooked. The servants were still with the wagons but my men at arms and archers knew how to cook and understood the importance of cooking food as soon as you could. Who knew when a meal might be disturbed?

Sir Will and Sir Abelard greeted me as I dismounted, "We did not manage to gather a great deal of treasure, my lord, but we have plenty of food and we lost no one. Sir Stephen and the others are searching the farms and buildings which lie just outside the village." Will of Stockton handed me a beaker of wine.

I nodded and told him of our action, "The garrison emerged but we sent them hence and killed two knights. I think that the garrison will send for help and squat within their walls. The foot archers at the rear did not do as well as I might have expected but that may help us. The presence of David of Welshpool and his mounted archers may still be a secret."

They nodded and Will said, "When we pulled down the bridge, we saw the villagers fleeing along the road. They will not stop until there is a solid wall behind which they can hide."

I looked up at the sky, it looked to be clear. "We will not bother with tents this night. I would be away before dawn. I wish to be as close to the castle of Azincourt as possible by tomorrow. It may well be that the men of Saint-Omer sent there for help. They will have seen my surcoat and the fact that they saw but three knights might make us an even more tempting target."

Just then we heard the creak of wagons as the rearguard arrived. I cupped my hand and shouted, "Put the wagons to make a square and place them well away from the burning buildings. Take the horses to the horse lines."

Sir Abelard shook his head, "We should have done that Sir William! It is as though we are children waiting for instructions!"

I quaffed the last of the wine, "Abelard, to me all of you are like my children! I am too old to change my ways now. However, I will find Michael and have him remove my armour; the day has been long."

Will asked, "How did he fare today?"

"Better than I might have expected. He obeyed orders instantly and looked to lead the squires of Sir Henry and Sir John."

I saw that Rafe and James were helping to organise the wagons. My knights looked to be happy to let them do so. This did not bode well for we had been lucky and had to deal with a handful of soldiers. I anticipated much sterner tests before we returned to Calais. Until a large force came to shift us then we would have to stay in the region or else we would have failed the King. Abelard took it upon himself to set the sentries for the night and that made me smile. He was the youngest of the knights and yet he had grasped the reins which others had not.

Michael, Rafe and James came over to help me remove my armour. Michael seemed in especially high spirits. "I will see to Fire after this, my lord." He seemed unable to remain silent and was like a chattering magpie. "I now see why Edgar liked to fight from a horse. I know that I am no horseman but the Frenchman I skewered looked terrified as my spear found flesh."

Rafe shook his head, "Be wary, young Michael. The men we fought today, the knights apart, were not the best." He gave me a look which told me that he had seen the hesitation from our knights, "Had not Sir William done what he did then it might have gone ill for us."

"Did we lose many, Rafe?"

"Half a dozen men, lord, and another eight wounded. We heard the French horses, but the men were not ready." He would say no more for it would be a criticism of the two knights. I nodded.

Michael seemed oblivious to the unspoken words. "And I have coins, a sword and a dagger."

"There will be more before all of this is over. You did well Michael." They undid the last strap and I said, "Now go to see to Fire and, James, see if the food is ready. The smell of roasting pig is too much to bear!"

"Aye, lord, and I shall fetch us each a goodly portion."

Alone with Rafe, I asked, "What could have been done to save the men we lost?"

"We should have had sentries watching the road, but we did not and the men of the rearguard are unused to action. James heard the horses and alerted Sir Henry. He consulted with Sir John and by then the six men had fallen for the French were in the woods and used their crossbows and bows to great effect."

I nodded, "Then next time just give the command yourself!"

"You forget, my lord, that I am no longer a man at arms. I am a lamed servant. Who would listen?"

I laughed, "You said yourself, Rafe, that these men are not used to battle. I have heard your voice on the battlefield and had you shouted then they would have obeyed."

My knights and the men at arms from my household along with David of Welshpool approached my fire. Only Sir Henry and Sir John did not look elated. Sir Stephen rubbed his hands together, "Who would have thought it to be so easy a victory and that we would enjoy freshly cooked pig as well as ale and wine on our first night? This is better than tramping through Normandy, Sir William!"

"Do not be so cocky, Stephen. We caught them unawares and now it becomes harder. This will soon be a game of ducks and drakes and we will need all our wits to avoid becoming trapped. We will have to move quickly and react even quicker." I was looking at Sir John when I spoke. I now knew that it had been a mistake to bring Sir Henry, but Sir John had fought with me relatively recently and that worried me too.

David of Welshpool nodded, "But they do not know we have mounted archers lord. The villagers saw just armed men on horses. When we are discovered they will see our teeth. We head for Agincourt on the morrow?"

I nodded, "We leave before dawn. By the time the sun peers over the horizon I would be five miles closer!"

"I will have White Arrow and Gardyvyan ride ahead and ensure that the ground ahead is clear."

"And have four of your best men ride a mile behind the wagons so that we are forewarned to any pursuit."

All eyes looked at me except for Sir Henry and Sir John who stared at the wine their squires had brought. Those who had fought at Agincourt and Harfleur did not need telling that we had to be aware of the danger.

I smiled, "And now let us devour this food for Stephen is right, this is a rare gift which should not be spurned."

Chapter 17

As we rode towards Agincourt, I saw that Michael had strapped on the sword he had taken from the battlefield. I realised that it had not belonged to the crossbowman he had slain but one of the men at arms for it was of good quality. It told me much about him. He was the same as I had been, he was a scavenger and he was not afraid to take on an experienced warrior and win! He had also taken a sallet helmet from the field. I wondered why another had not done so and then it came to me, Michael was a real soldier and the others who were with the rearguard had been pressed men. They were fulfilling their duty and that was all. Michael knew that this was his life. It made me feel better for we had both made the right decision and he now had a purpose in his life.

I rode with David and his archers at the head of the column. I wanted to know what Christopher and Jack found first. Captains Edgar and Wilfred had both been men who could make instant decisions. One was dead and the other as good as. Stephen was the nearest to them, but he was still learning to be a leader of men. One day he would be able to ride where I did and make the right decision at the right time.

I was listening for trouble as I knew the closer we came to the castle the more likelihood we had of meeting danger. I heard thundering hooves and knew that it meant trouble. When all of the scouts came galloping along the road, close to the hamlet of Delettes. then I knew that word had reached our foe and the prey had decided to become the hunter. I held up my hand to halt the column. Even as they hurtled towards us, I was looking for somewhere we could fight. The hamlet lay less than half a mile behind us. I could see the last house and we could use that for the wagons and the rearguard. To the right and left of me were some fields which had once been used for animals; I saw the piles of sheep droppings and animal dung. Then the forest encroached upon the edge of the field. There was a ditch which ran along the road, but it was largely overgrown and would be no obstacle.

"Michael, ride to Sir Henry and have him leave the wagons in the village as a fort once more. The servants can guard them. I want the rest of the men here! Tell Rafe to hoist my banner above one wagon!"

189

Michael stared up the road but all that we could see were the scouts, "But what…"

"Michael, just obey the orders. David, have the archers dismount and tether their horses behind us." As he shouted his orders, I waved my hand in a circle and the knights and men at arms galloped up. "From the speed our scouts are coming I fear that there are enemies ahead. Let us prepare. We will fight dismounted with our archers behind. The French may not expect us to have so many archers." I dismounted and handed my reins to Sir Oliver's squire, Alan, while I held my helmet in my hand. My shield still hung from my saddle.

Christopher White Arrow reined in, "My lord, we found a host marching along the road. There are knights, men at arms and crossbowmen. They have raised the levy. I recognised the colours of the Lord of Azincourt. I think they had men watching the road, lord!"

Sir Ralph had a wolfish grin upon his face, "He comes to his death!"

I ignored the bravado. I had learned that a battle was never won until it was over and better to assume a hard fight which you might not win than such overconfidence. "We will have the knights here in the road and the men at arms on the two flanks. David of Welshpool, place the mounted archers behind us." I heard hooves as Sir Henry and Sir John reined in. "Michael, fetch me my shield and my spear. Knights stand here, filling the road and the squires behind. Men at arms flank us!" I shouted, "How many are coming, Christopher White Arrow?"

"We counted ten banners!"

That meant ten knights and that would imply ten men at arms for each knight and, perhaps another two hundred in the levy. There would be unlikely to be more than forty crossbows. That meant there would be three hundred and fifty men coming down the road. I knew my archers and if they chose not to be seen then the French would know nothing of us. When they came around the bend of the road, they would be one hundred and fifty paces from us but they would know where we were before that as they would catch glimpses of our surcoats as the road twisted and turned. Sir Stephen was the first knight in place, and he stood to my left, as I knew he would. Sir Ralph stood on my right and he was flanked by Sir Abelard and Sir John. Sir Will and Sir Oliver were to the left of Sir Stephen and Sir Henry anchored the line at the left. Michael handed me my shield and spear. I saw that he had a spear too.

Turning I said, "Squires, today I have to ask you to fight. Stand behind your knight and protect him with your spear. If your knight falls then you must step into the breach!" Most looked happy at the prospect of fighting, but not all.

David of Welshpool ghosted next to me, "The archers are in position, lord. I have sent the foot archers and spearmen into the eaves of the forest."

It was the right decision. That way they could run if they were afraid and it would not harm our position too much. If they stood then they would be able to pick off the French on the flanks. I hoped that they would not be needed. I smiled, "Do not loose until they are less than one hundred paces from us."

"That is close, my lord. We will not get off above three or four flights in that time."

"But the arrows we send will each find the target for even the foot archers can hurt them at that range and I want them hurt in that first, eager attack!"

I caught sight of a colourful surcoat and then, a heartbeat later, I heard a horn. We had been spotted. The elevated wagon and banner behind us would draw the eye of our enemy and he would try to get the banner. Of course, that meant he would have to get through my knights and men at arms. When we had fought at Agincourt there had been some, like the Duke of Gloucester, who had been nervous. Here too I sensed nervousness from Sir Henry and his men at arms. I saw them looking nervously at each other while the rest of my men stared steadfastly at the French who were advancing slowly towards us. Sir John looked a little more confident but then he was closer to my sword this time. The French plan was clear. Their mounted men would charge down the centre of the road and along the edge of the field. That meant there would be a gap, albeit slight, where the drainage ditches ran. We had them too but a man at arms stood in the dank and pungent water. A horseman could not risk standing in an unknown hole. A man at arms had no such fears. Their men on foot and their crossbows would advance along the fields. As they formed up, two hundred paces from us, I realised that they were not sending men into the woods and they intended to use their weight of numbers to sweep us away. My gamble might pay off. The lightly armed spearmen and dismounted archers could fight from the shelter of the woods and that would only bolster their courage. This time I was not using a poleaxe but a spear. We were packed tightly together, and Sir Stephen and Sir Ralph also had spears as we would not have room to swing. I had forgotten to bring caltrops with us. If we had brought them then the cavalry charge would have been ended before it reached us. Age does that to a man. Ten years earlier I would have remembered.

When they were in position a horn sounded and they charged. I saw that Isembart d'Azincourt and Robinet de Bournonville were in the second rank next to squires who held their banners. The front rank was made up of the other knights. All wore visors and I could not see their faces but if I was to guess I would have said they were young knights. The majority of knights in this part of the world had been slain on St Crispin's Day. The ones we had slain at Saint-Omer had been younger knights too. Their youth explained their eagerness to get at us; so it was with these knights as they galloped towards us. Isembart d'Azincourt and Robinet de Bournonville must have thought we had few archers when no arrows descended as they made their charge. David and my dismounted archers would be crouching behind the line of men at arms. The eyes of the French would be drawn to the wagons. Isembart d'Azincourt had shown that he liked to attack weak targets. At Agincourt, he could have chosen to attack our left flank and fought warriors. Had he done so then, who knows, he might have turned the tide of battle, but he did not and went for the easier and more profitable target of baggage and wagons.

I heard David of Welshpool shout, "Release!" and there was a whoosh as their arrows soared into the air. The second flight was in the air even as the first one struck. From the flanks came a slightly more ragged volley as the foot archers sent their arrows into the French. The third flight hit when the French were just fifty paces from us and I heard David of Welshpool shout, "Choose your own targets!" For the men on the flanks that was an easy order to obey as they had a clear line of sight but the ones behind us had to use a flatter trajectory and hope that one of our own men at arms or knights did not move their head at the wrong moment. They would err on the side of caution.

The arrows had the desired effect and horses and men fell. Almost all of the knights and some of the men at arms remained in their saddle but some had arrows sticking out of their cuisse and some of their horses had been struck in the shoulder. Few had avoided the arrow storm. Still, they came on until they reached our wall of spears. Harold of Derby and Gilbert of Ely were the two men in the ditches, and, with space to swing, they had chosen poleaxes. The French lances and spears were aimed at those of us in the road and the men in the field. The two men were able to swing freely. When the knights crashed into our spears there was the sound of thunder as the wood shattered and splintered. The horses stopped and reared. Men screamed. Our front line was pushed back, as it had at Agincourt, for four feet but it held. More importantly, our spears had found more flesh than the French and both Harold and Gilbert's swings had hacked through horse armour and into the sides of the horses. As the two knights they struck fell to the ground so my men at arms raised their poleaxes and ended their lives in a heartbeat.

Even had the knights and men at arms in the centre had the will to fight on, the levy had taken so many casualties already that not only had they stopped their advance, but they had begun to move backwards. "Switch to the men on the flanks!" David of Welshpool saw his chance and as every bow moved and rained death on the levy, spearmen and crossbows, the French broke and fled leaving just the knights and men at arms in the centre.

My spear had broken when they had crashed into us and so I whipped out my sword to face the French knight whose horse was wounded and lumbering towards me. Michael's spear darted out and jabbed at the Frenchman's horse. It turned its head to avoid the blow. All along our line, the squires were adding their spears to our attack and the hedgehog of spears had an effect. I punched at the horse's crinet, the metal which protected its neck, and the animal, already wounded, tried to rear out of the way. I lunged with my hand and a half sword up towards the knight's middle. He aided my blow by standing as he tried to keep his balance. The tip slid through the jupon and between the fauld and the cuirass. The gambeson beneath the plate offered no resistance and my sword entered the middle of his body and I watched as his weapon and shield fell from his dying hands. Two other men at arms and a further knight fell and the French horn sounded the retreat. The men at arms and knights did not survive their flight unscathed. Arrows struck them as they ran but their cantles held them.

Even as they ran, I shouted, "David, mount your archers, follow them and surround their castle. Let none escape. If those in the village try to enter the castle, then let them! I want all of them trapped inside its walls."

"Aye lord."

I took off my helmet and looked to my left and right. My knights were blood-spattered but it looked as though they had all survived and then after I had seen Sir John raise his visor and looked down towards where Sir Henry had fought I realised I could not see him. Throwing down my shield I ran.

Sir Will and Gilbert of Ely were leaning over him and, as I came up to him Will shook his head and pointed to the helmet which was caved in. "The French knight had a war hammer and Sir Henry was too slow to react. I do not think he even saw the blow coming and I do not think that he felt anything."

I nodded. His death was clearly my responsibility. I should never have brought him but having brought him and seen his reaction to the first fight I should have left him with the wagons. In trying to help him regain some honour and dignity, I had killed him. I turned and saw Sir John. He had helped me to train Sir Henry and they were close in age. Although he had fought more recently than Sir Henry, I knew, as I looked at his ashen face that he, too, no longer wished to go to war. His father had been my steward and he had died some years ago. John's mother lived in Dauentre with her son and if he died here too... I did not need Sir John, and, in fact, he might be a liability. His slow reactions might get a good man killed. I knew that I did not need numbers to take the two dishonourable knights, I needed cunning.

I put my arm around Sir John and led him away so that I could speak alone with him, "John, you were my first squire and followed me in the Baltic and when we served Henry Bolingbroke. That was then and this is now. You gave up war after Shrewsbury and that was more than ten years ago and I shudder to think how long it has been since Sir Henry followed my banner. His death is upon my head. I do not want another, and I would not deprive your mother, your wife, your sisters and your children of you. You are Lord of Dauentre and there is none better at what you do but you and I know that you are a warrior, like these men at arms, no longer." His eyes told me that I spoke the truth, "You are afraid of each opponent you fight."

He looked relieved as though he had been at a confessional, "I do not lack courage, my lord, but I do not train every day. If I am to be honest then sometimes, not even every week. I am slow and I do not react quickly enough. When I fought alongside Sir Henry I did not feel so vulnerable but now that he is dead..."

"I know and for that reason, I would have you take Sir Henry's body back to his family."

"What will the others think? How can I look them in the eye?"

"John, you owe none of these men anything and you have fulfilled your obligation to me many times over. You know that the men you and Sir Henry brought are not the same quality as the others who are here." He nodded, "If you stay and they follow you even if you survive, they might not. Would you wish that on your conscience?"

"No, Sir William, but I feel I am letting you down."

"You are not and there are enough of us to do that which I intend, and we should, already, have drawn men from the south. You brought the spearmen and the archers who fight on foot. If you leave and take them with you then I have a fully mounted force and we can move more quickly and if we are forced to, flee." I could see from his face that he wanted to leave, "Go, for we need to catch d'Azincourt."

194

He nodded, dully, "And it is not your fault, Sir William. It is we failed you. You trained the two of us and we forgot too much of that training. We should have had the courage to say that we did not relish the campaign and paid for another to take our place."

"And that shows that you are both noble. Now go and I shall visit with you and Sir Henry's widow when I return."

No one said a word as the two retinues packed up their wagons and trudged north-west towards Calais. We just mounted and, as I raised my sword, we headed towards the battlefield we had quit almost a year since.

We reached the field just after dark and I led my men to camp close to the village of Tramecourt. The villagers had all fled when my archers had appeared. I could not see David of Welshpool and the other archers, but I knew they were in place and had already surrounded the castle. The villagers had fled so fast that there were animals for us to slaughter and plenty of food and wine for us. I allowed the men to drink as they had earned it after two skirmishes which had seen off two French forces and yet not really hurt us.

I gathered my knights in the largest house in the village; we barely fitted into it, "We eat first and then I want the archers relieved. I will make a watch up for the night."

Sir Ralph was eager, too eager, "And we attack on the morrow?"

"No, we do not. I told you before we started this that I intended to take these two lords, Isembart d'Azincourt and Robinet de Bournonville, but I will not lose my men to do so."

"Then let me and my men try!"

My eyes narrowed, "Obey my orders or quit France. It is that simple."

He held my eyes for a moment and then dropped his head, "Sorry, Sir William, my grief almost overcame me."

"And that is why I shall make the decisions. We shall have revenge but that is a dish best served cold. We eat well and we sleep. We rise when we feel it right to do so. While I go to speak with Isembart d'Azincourt and Robinet de Bournonville then Sir Stephen and those who were at the battle can find this sally port. We have plenty of time and I want to lose as few men as possible. In a perfect world, I would lose none for I have already lost more than I wish!"

"I can come with you to speak to these knights?"

"Aye, so long as you are as cold as a northern winter and speak only when I tell you to." I smiled, "I have not won these grey and white hairs by being foolish. I may be old, Ralph, but I am more cunning and clever than when I was young. I will use fear to win us access to the castle and, mayhap, we shall take them without losing a man."

I could see that he was disappointed in my words. He wanted a battle and he needed blood to be shed. He wanted to hack and destroy the two knights who had been responsible for the death of his son.

"Ralph, today you killed some of the men who raided the camp for Isembart d'Azincourt took many of his levy with him. Before we leave this land, we will burn the two villages to the ground so that the French will remember the price of treachery and dishonour."

That satisfied the northern knight. Before we ate, I walked the battlefield, in the summer darkness. The bodies had all been taken away since St Crispin's Day, but the field had not been ploughed yet. I dare say they would get around to it but the thought of ploughing up a body part might be too much so soon after the battle. I walked all the way to the squire's camp. The land here was grassy and would not be ploughed. Had it been daylight I might have even seen the stains where the boys had fallen. I knelt and said a prayer. As I headed back across the field, it was dry now and easy to walk upon, I spied three figures ahead. Even before I recognised them, I knew who they were. It was Rafe, James and Michael.

"Sir William, did you get a knock upon your helmet today that you wander around so boldly, after dark in the middle of France?"

I laughed, "I just thought to tax the three of you. I was saying farewell to the squires who died on St Crispin's Day."

Michael turned to look towards what had been the right flank of the English line, "Before we leave, my lord, I would say a farewell to the lads we left here. It is too dark now for me to be certain I am at the right place."

"That is good, Michael."

"And how long do we stay here, my lord?"

"That depends, James, partly upon the two French lords we come to apprehend. If they agree in the morning to come back and face trial we shall stay but a day or two longer. Enough time to convince the French that we are a nuisance worth bothering about. If they choose not to do the honourable thing then it may be a week or more. It all depends upon Stephen's memory. We need a secret way in!"

I knew that when it was daylight I would be able to inspect the castle a little more closely. I had not done so on the day of the battle. It was one thing to know there was a sally port but if the castle had a good keep, getting inside the curtain wall would avail us little.

David of Welshpool was relieved and eating his food when I reached the camp. Sir Ralph had organised the relief of the archers and my food awaited me. "Well, Captain, did any escape?"

He shook his head, "Not from the castle, my lord, but I fear that word got out for we saw two riders heading for Paris." He sounded apologetic.

Laughing I said, "Then that is perfect. The King wants the French to be aware of our presence and to draw men here. Just so long as the castle is full that suits me. The men who killed our squires came from these villages. It was their knights and the villeins who followed them that chose this path. By my estimate, the King of France and his advisers will now know we are abroad. There will be riders from Saint-Omer and Agincourt. I believe he will send immediately to Normandy for he has few men in this area. I think we have seven days, at most, before the French try to drive us hence. That means we have six days at most to capture the castle."

"And you have a plan, my lord?"

"I do. We try cunning first and break into the castle. If that fails, then we take the houses of Agincourt and demolish them. At night we pile them before their gates, soak them in oil and then burn them. That is why I want the castle full. They do not have a moat, just a ditch and they will have to use their precious water to douse the flames."

David had finished his food and he wiped his mouth. "A good plan and it might work although I have never heard of such a thing before."

"And that is why I think it might work!"

He finished his food and stood. He leaned over and said, "You did the right thing with Sir John, my lord. There are some of us who can never cease to be warriors but there are others who, when they marry, change. Sir John's father came from the land and while Sir John became a good warrior I think, in his heart, he was more like his father. You are like me, Sir William, you were born to a warrior and you will die with a sword in your hand. I will probably be the same and that should have been Captain Edgar's death and not this slow, soul-destroying end he is forced to endure."

Before we set the night guards, I told my knights and the senior men at arms what I intended. Although Sir Ralph nodded his support, along with the others, I knew that he was less than happy for he knew that there was a chance that the two killers would suffer a financial punishment when we took them to the King but that they would live and he wanted blood. He and I had the middle watch and, when we were woken to go to the main gate, I took the opportunity to speak with him.

We stood by the brazier beyond the range of the crossbows which I knew the French still had. As I spoke with Sir Ralph, I studied the gatehouse. David's description had been accurate. It was a wooden drawbridge and would be hard to take with a ram. My plan was the one which stood the best chance of success. If we destroyed the village and placed the wood and debris in the ditch, then the flames would rise and burn the drawbridge and the gate it protected. If Stephen could not find the sally port or if it had been strengthened, then I had an alternative.

"Ralph, it may well be that these men escape the death sentence for their crimes." His eyes flashed angrily at me. "Peace, Sir Ralph, and put your eyes back in your skull. Listen to my words for they are wise, and I have thought this out. If we take them for trial it will be in England and the King will be there. The trial will be before knights like yourself and I believe that they would ask for death. If they do not or the King chooses clemency, then challenge them to trial by combat."

He suddenly brightened and nodded, "And if they refuse?"

I smiled, "I do not think that they will for if we take them alive, they have a journey to Calais, across the sea and thence to London. Do you think that the rest of our knights and men at arms will not use words as weapons? They will be humiliated. I do not think that they will refuse. However, I do not think that it will come to that. I tell you this so that your blood cools before the morrow."

"You are wise, Sir William and I will heed your words."

Chapter 18

My men enjoyed a good night's sleep. There was no hurry for us to rise as any attempt to take down the village or to gain entry would have to wait until dark. I would not risk crossbows. We had men watching the main gate and the roads were guarded. Michael polished my plate and my helmet. He groomed Fire and he, Rafe and James, prepared my warhorse for war with a shining, polished chamfron. While I was being dressed, and in direct contrast, Sir Stephen and three of his men at arms were dressing in darkened clothes and oiled cloaks so that they could approach the curtain wall hidden. Four archers would be with them for protection although if they had to use their bows then my plan to secretly enter the castle would be foiled. Sir Ralph, Sir Oliver, Sir Will and Sir Abelard also had their armour polished and, at noon, the five of us with squires and banners rode to the main gate so that we could speak with Isembart d'Azincourt and Robinet de Bournonville. We took our priests with us. They would be as witnesses so that our words could be recorded and, perhaps, used as evidence in a trial.

We stopped before the gates and I sent Father John and Michael forward to open negotiations. Michael was a quick learner and we had taught him what to say. The priest spoke French and would be able to correct any errors. I could hear Michael's words and, accent apart, he was accurate.

"My Lord, William Strongstaff, Knight of the Garter and adviser to King Henry of England wishes to speak with Isembart d'Azincourt and Robinet de Bournonville."

I did not catch the words spoken but when Michael and the priest returned the look on Michael's face told me that they had agreed.

"They say it is pointless as the King of France will send men to punish you, but he will allow you to speak to them. There can be no more than four men."

"Good, that suits us. Father John, Sir Ralph, Michael, let us go. David of Welshpool, watch for treachery. Your archers can reach the walls."

"Aye, Lord."

We rode to within fifty paces of the walls. We could have stayed further away but I wanted to surreptitiously inspect the ditch as well as to show them that I was not afraid of them. As I expected it had not been maintained. My secondary plan could work and we could fill it with building debris.

Isembart d'Azincourt spoke first. I recognised his livery and I deduced that the knight next to him had to be Robinet de Bournonville. It was Lord Isembart who spoke, "This invasion of my land will not go unpunished. I have sent to the King and I have no doubt that there are men already on their way here to destroy you and your handful of bandits."

None of us wore helmets and I knew that while Sir Ralph would heed my words about remaining silent, his eyes would be eloquent, and I saw the two knights shifting uncomfortably as he stared at them.

"The two of you have a strange sense of honour that you call us bandits. You were the ones who acted without honour and slew pages and squires! You are the ones who forgot the oaths you swore when you were first given your spurs. You were the ones who killed our squires and sons!"

I saw that my words stunned them for they did not think that this was personal. They now knew the reason for my chevauchée; I was there for justice, "What is it that you want?"

"Surrender your castle and come with Robinet de Bournonville to England to stand trial before a jury of your peers."

"We have done penance already!"

I laughed, "Giving some of the treasure that you stole to the Duke of Burgundy hardly counts as penance. There are the souls of dead boys who seek justice." I raised my voice so that the last word echoed along the walls. I knew that, within the castle, the ordinary folk were listening. "If you do not surrender then we will use force to break down your walls and every man we find will be killed. Any who do not die defending your walls shall be hanged. We will destroy every building except for the churches. It is your decision."

He shook his head, "With this handful of men? You have no siege machines and we are well provided with food. Do your worst. We shall be relieved before you have built a ram!"

I nodded, "That is your last word?"

"It is."

I gestured with my right hand, "This is Sir Ralph of Middleham Grange. You killed his son. He would challenge you, Isembart d'Azincourt and you, Robinet de Bournonville, to single combat. Will you oblige him and save the lives of all those in the castle?" It was their one chance to emerge with any kind of honour and in their rejection of the offer, they both signed their own death warrant.

"I am sorry that your son died, Sir Ralph, but he was on my land without my leave. We will await the King and neither of us will fight you."

I looked at the walls and said, solemnly, "May God have mercy for we shall have none!" I turned and we rode away.

Sir Ralph said, "See, they are beyond redemption."

"And not only Father John heard their rejection of our offer but every man woman, child and priest, inside the walls. We spoke fairly and they have shown their true character. Now let us see what Sir Stephen has discovered."

By the time we reached Tramecourt Sir Stephen and his men had returned. They looked elated and were busy speaking with the other men at arms we had left guarding our camp.

"Well?"

"It is as I remembered, Sir William. The sally port is at the south-west corner of the castle and is on a steepish slope. The church is just forty paces from the wall at that point. The wall is overgrown and almost hidden for some trees have rooted there. Had we not found it from within when we searched for treasure, we would have missed it. The masonry on the wall there is poorly mortared, and I do not think that they have maintained their walls."

I nodded, "But they have a keep. I saw that when we spoke with them."

"They do but the entrance is at the ground level and there is just a gate. When we were looking for the sally port, we could hear the villagers from Agincourt and Tramecourt, they are camped in the bailey. The gate will not be barred and if we make an attack they will try to get in the keep."

I was satisfied. I could see how this would succeed. I turned to Sir Will. "I want you to take the knights, men at arms and archers. Begin to demolish the houses to the east of the castle. Stay away from their crossbows and do not yet put the demolition material in the ditch, that will be the work of this night. David of Welshpool, you and your archers can help and keep their bows ready in case they oblige us and sally forth!"

Sir Ralph said, "You have a plan?"

"I have; tonight, we will enter the castle through the sally port. Oswald, you have been there before and you can guide us. You, Ralph, our squires and my men at arms will enter. The rest, under the command of Sir Will and Sir Stephen, shall start to fill the ditch with

201

the demolished timbers and inflammable material. I want to draw the eyes of those within towards the front gate."

"And do we fire it?"

"If you have completed enough to do so then aye. When we have gained the castle bailey and men have secured the gate to the keep, I will send men to open the main gate. If you hear a commotion from inside then do not fire the gate. I hope you shall not need to do so."

Sir Oliver asked, "And when we have the gate opened, what then?"

My face became a grim mask, "Then we do what I promised, every man in the castle shall be killed. If they flee then that is the will of God but if they fight, then they die."

"And the two knights?"

I looked at Sir Abelard who had asked the question, "We take them prisoner if we can, but I would not have another of my men die because of them." We eat and then begin our work. I want all but a handful working on the demolition. Harold of Derby and five of my men at arms will watch the sally port."

While the others ate, I gathered the group who would attack. "We will not need shields, but I need you, Harold of Derby, to bring an axe. Michael, you will be at the rear and if things go awry then you will need to get to Sir Will and tell him."

I saw the look of horror on his face. He was used to success, but I knew that this attack had the potential to go wrong. I did not want him risked. If this was my time to die, then so be it but those with families and a future deserved the chance of life. Sir Ralph was the exception, but he was driven!

Rafe and James ensured that I ate well. Rafe said as he poured another beaker of wine, "James and I could come with you lord. It isn't as though you will be moving quickly is it?"

I smiled, "And what if your leg let you down at the wrong moment? Michael might be torn between saving you and saving himself. No, Rafe, James, it is a noble offer, but I have lived long enough and if I can help Sir Ralph to rid himself of the spectre of his dead son then I will be happy."

The look they exchanged told me that they were not convinced.

The men took great delight in destroying the houses close by the castle of Azincourt. It seemed fitting that the villeins who had helped to kill the boys on St Crispin's Day would be punished. The lath and timber were soon demolished, and the thatch would burn when we fired it. That the French in the castle knew what we were doing was obvious and the walls were lined with those whose houses were dying as they cursed us and waved fists and old swords impotently at us. We piled the demolition material two hundred paces from the walls. That did not stop them from using their crossbows to deter us but the men who moved the material had mail and plate. The bolts clattered off both. David of Welshpool's archers soon discouraged the crossbows by raining arrows upon the walls. Thus far they had expended few missiles. As darkness fell the night watch closed up to watch the walls while the men at arms began to carry the demolition material to the ditch. I left to join Sir Ralph. The work on the ditch would be long and slow. The men who carried the demolition material would need protection and so men at arms carried improvised pavise. They took it slowly for there was little need for haste. As I went, I saw that the walls facing my men were filled with armed men. That meant we would have fewer to face when we gained entry.

I made my way back to the camp where Oswald was waiting to take me to Sir Ralph and others. They had left as soon as it was dark. "The others are in position and we just await you and Michael, my lord."

Michael held my helmet, but I shook my head, "My coif and my arming cap will suffice." Few knights wore the caps but I liked the comfort it brought.

It took, perhaps half an hour to reach the sally port and I was aware all the way of the noise from the main gate. The back wall seemed silent. I knew that was an illusion. There would be families who were camped there. None would be asleep. I hoped that the noise from our attack would make them gravitate towards the keep. When I reached the curtain wall, I saw that the gate was almost invisible. I nodded to Sir Ralph and they began to tear away the ivy and other climbers. It took an effort to remove it and, as they did so, I took off my manifer to examine the mortar. The ivy had eaten into it and as the roots were pulled out so the mortar, what little remained, also came out. I pushed on the stones and they moved. It took a further half-hour for my men to silently remove the ivy and I went to the door. The wood was soft. This was the original door and time and nature had softened and weakened it. Harold raised his axe and I shook my head. We would not need it. I mimed, instead, for them to lean against it and break in that way.

My men at arms were large warriors and they all wore plate. Four of them placed their combined weight on the door and pushed. At first, nothing appeared to be happening and then the rotten wood and mortar creaked, groaned and then cracked open a little. Suddenly it gave way and the four who had pushed found themselves sprawling on the ivy, brambles and nettles. To us, outside, the noise had sounded very loud but, as we peered in I saw that the families who were camped were a good thirty or forty paces from the overgrown section of the wall and none appeared to have noticed. Nat and Harold were the first to react, and then Gilbert. They leapt to their feet and ran to the invitingly open gate of the keep. It was just eighty paces from us. Sir Ralph and the rest of my men at arms quickly ran and I tried to keep up. Harold and Nat, along with Gilbert, Peter, Jack and Garth were to go to the gate and open it. They had with them their own spearmen. The rest of us, Sir Ralph, his men at arms and spearmen along with his squire, ran to the keep.

Of course, it was impossible to do so either silently or to be unseen and the women and children screamed in terror as they saw us, and they ran as fast as they could for the keep. I cursed my age for I knew that I would be behind the others and, more importantly, Sir Ralph. He would not attempt to take the knights alive and, equally important, would risk death to achieve his ends. The door to the keep was ours but until Nat and Harold had the gates open then the handful of men who were in the castle would be in danger for we were seriously outnumbered.

As I stepped into the dimly lit keep, I saw the dangers. One of Ralph's men, Osbert, lay to the side of the door clutching a cloth to his thigh. He gave me a rueful look as I passed. I counselled him, "Keep the pressure on the wound, Osbert, and pray to God."

"Aye, Sir William!"

I could hear fighting above me. Looking around, as I ran up the spiral stairs, I saw that Michael was close behind me. The walls of the keep muffled any noises from outside and I just hoped that we had the main gate open and that we were flooding the castle with my men. There was blood on the stairs which added another hazard and then I passed the body of a French spearman which explained it as he had been gutted and bled out. Sir Ralph had entered the keep with six men and his squire. Osbert lay downstairs and I now saw another two who had been wounded. Fighting in the close confines of a castle was harder than fighting in the open. There were fewer places to run and often a battle was won by the one who was able to manoeuvre better and quicker. There were the sounds of fighting from inside the chamber and that suggested more Frenchmen. This was the floor which contained the lord's bedchamber and the quarters of his bodyguards. As I ran down the corridor towards the door to the first chamber, I saw a man at arms lunge at Ralph's squire who was sprawled upon the ground. If I had not been wielding a hand and a half sword then he might have died. As it was the last handspan of my sword's blade hacked into the wrist of the Frenchman. I must have severed a tendon for the sword dropped from his hand and Ralph's squire, from a prone position, swung his sword two handed to take off the man's leg.

Even though Ralph's men were outnumbered I saw no sign of him. I shouted, "Where is Sir Ralph?"

His squire pushed himself to his feet and pointed to the ladder which led to the top of the keep and the fighting platform. "He followed the two knights upstairs. These men appeared from nowhere." Even as he spoke another of Sir Ralph's men fell.

"Michael, help these and I will go to Sir Ralph's aid."

Before he could answer a French man at arms and a spearman ran to get at me. Michael only had a spear, but he did not hesitate. He rushed at them and rammed the spear into the unprotected leg of the man at arms whilst swinging the butt of the spear into the groin of the spearman. The two men fell, and Sir Ralph's squire ran to Michael's aid. "Go, Sir William, we will hold them until the others arrive." I saw that the Frenchmen had no mail and I prayed that the squires could fend them off.

I climbed the ladder and heard the clash of steel above me. When I reached the top, I saw that Sir Ralph was cornered by Isembart and three of his men. Sir Ralph was wounded but Robinet de Bournonville lay dying. He had had his thigh sliced open to the bone and was bleeding to death. The keep had a pointed roof in the centre and there was a wide fighting platform all around it. The fight was on the opposite corner of the keep.

I yelled, "Turn, treacherous dog and face my wrath! You shall have no more of my men."

I was a greater prize than a wounded Sir Ralph who was slowly sliding down the wall. Isembart and two of his men at arms advanced. I picked up the sword of Robinet de Bournonville. I was an old man and with odds of three to one it was unlikely that I would survive but the longer I held on the more chance there was of Sir Will and Sir Stephen leading my men to our aid. I backed myself towards the northwest tower which was as far away from Sir Ralph as I could manage. I would use the two corners to protect my flanks. And then, as they closed to end my life a white-feathered arrow soared from the bailey and smacked into the side of the head of one of the men at arms. Two to one were better odds.

The French knight laughed, "When you die, I will be accorded great honour for you have ever been the bane of the French! You should have died many times!" He pointed to the south-east, "The new Constable will be here within days! Your attempt to raid this land has come to nought for he was in Paris raising an army when we heard you had landed!"

205

"Do not talk, fight, for I grow weary of your cockerel crowing, murderer and defiler of boys!"

He launched an attack on me and brought down his poleaxe towards my head. This time there was no helmet to protect me and I slashed at the head of the poleaxe with the sword of Robinet de Bournonville. Although I deflected the blow, the man at arms swung his war hammer at my knee. The plate did its job and stopped him shattering the kneecap, but it not only hurt, I also found that I could barely stand for he had seriously wounded me. The French knight saw his chance and raised his poleaxe for the coup de grace. I could not move and the French man at arms was also raising his war hammer to end my life. As I raised my sword to block the poleaxe, I hurled the sword of Robinet de Bournonville at the man at arms. He had pulled back his war hammer and stepped a little too close. He intended to smash my skull in. Luck was with me or perhaps God decided that it was not my moment to die. The tip of the sword entered the eye of the man at arms. He dropped his war hammer and, screaming, clutched the ruined orb. This time my sword blow had more power and I bit into the shaft of de Bournonville's poleaxe below the langet. Splinters of wood flew from it and he lost his balance. My left hand was now freed, and I used my sword two handed to smash into the side of his cuirass. I was lucky as I hit the strap which bound the back and front plate together. As the strap was sheared the edge of my sword bit into his gambeson and I drew blood. I did not think that I could move my left leg as the kneecap burned with pain. Instead, I used it to pivot and swing and bringing my right leg forward I swung again at his side. This time the blow was so hard that the front and backplate fell apart.

My luck then deserted me as the French knight fell backwards, for his axe head caught the damaged poleyn on my left knee and not only tore it away but gouged deeply into the flesh. I forced myself to ignore both the pain and the blood dripping down my leg. I could not show him that I was hurt. "Yield, for you are beaten!"

"Never!" He brought the poleaxe around and I made the mistake of trying to step out of the way. My left leg gave way and I tumbled to the ground. As I did so I saw that Sir Ralph was now slumped in the opposite corner to me, but I had drawn all of his opponents to me. I could hear Michael's voice, but he was still ascending the stairs. Isembart d'Azincourt stood over me, his legs straddling my body, and raised the poleaxe to split my skull in two. I did the only thing I could do, I lunged upwards with my sword. It was a long sword and it drove up into his unprotected groin. His scream sounded like a vixen in the night. I kept pushing as he stood frozen above me. He could not control his body and I was showered by his bodily fluids, but I kept pushing until my manifer met flesh. He tumbled to the ground.

It was then that Michael and Sir Ralph's squires clambered up to the fighting platform. Michael ran to me and I smiled, "I fear this surcoat is beyond redemption."

He looked serious, "Is this your blood, my lord?"

Shaking my head, I said, "No, but my knee is hurt. Help me to my feet and then see to Sir Ralph. Give me your spear. I will use it as a crutch." He handed me the spear and I added, "How goes the fray?"

"The castle is ours although I fear many have fled. Sir Stephen is below."

"There have been enough deaths. It is over. See to Sir Ralph."

I used the spear to help me to the side of the castle wall and rested my back against it. I could barely bear the pain from the wound, but I had to stay alert.

Michael ran back to me, "Sir Ralph lives but he is sorely wounded."

"Shout for a healer!"

He went to the corner of the keep which faced our point of attack and yelled, "We need healers here. Sir Ralph and Sir William are hurt!"

A sudden shooting pain raced up from my knee and I slumped to the ground. I had been hurt in battle before but never like this. I must have bled more than I had thought for the world became dim and then became black as darkness took me.

Chapter 19

When I came to, I was lying in a chamber with the two healers Sir Henry had brought with him peering at my wound. Michael, Sir Will, and Sir Stephen stood looking too. I looked at the ceiling and deduced that I was in the chamber of Isembart d'Azincourt. I heard their voices and realised that they did not know I was awake.

"It would be safer to take the leg off now, while he is asleep. If we take it off above the knee, then he might live."

Stephen of Morpeth snorted, "Are you healers or leeches? Had you tended to Prince Hal at Shrewsbury we would now have a different king. The wound has no malodorous smell and I have seen far worse injuries."

"Sir Stephen, it is his age. Taking the leg is safer and his days of fighting are gone. My colleague and I are agreed. We have saved Sir Ralph's life; let us do the same for Sir William."

"Sir Ralph just needed fire and stitches. It was the loss of blood which incapacitated him. Sir William just had a sabaton of blood was all! Heal him or I will draw my sword!"

I spoke, "Stephen, they are healers and mean well let them alone. They can tend to the others who need their craft, but they will not take my leg!"

My two knights and squire turned with such unbounded looks of joy that I was touched that they were so concerned with an old warhorse.

One of the healers shook his head, "My lord, heed our advice."

Shaking my head, I said, "The only one I would trust is John Bradbury and he is in England. Get you hence. Sir Stephen is right, you are leeches. I will heal myself." My voice was filled with anger and they fled. "I would rather die than lose my leg and be a cripple." They left the room so quickly that their feet barely touched the ground. "Let me know what has happened and how long I have lain here."

Sir Will spoke, "You have slept for many hours, lord, and we have taken the castle. The men at arms, crossbowmen and spearmen were all killed. Many of the men of the two villages also perished but more than fifty escaped. We did not want to pursue them for we had wounded to tend to."

"And how many died?"

"Six, lord; five of them were Sir Ralph's men."

"We will need to leave by the day after tomorrow at the latest."

"Why, my lord? We have won and we have few losses."

"Stephen, the new Constable is in Paris and that is but a three-day march from here. He will have had the news two days ago and he could be but a day away. Ask David of Welshpool to send some of his archers down the Paris road to spy them out. Then have the men prepare the two villages for firing and when all that is done send Rafe and James to me."

Sir Stephen and Sir William were just grateful to have something to do and they left. I smiled at Michael, "You did better than well today. The way you dealt with the man at arms and spearman was impressive."

He smiled, "Rafe and John taught me that move." His face became serious, "You take too many chances, my lord. When you raced after Sir Ralph, I thought we had lost you."

"Sir Ralph was my squire and his father was my friend; I could not let him die."

"And now it is over."

"Not quite but soon it will be. Did you take your share of the treasure?"

"I have sat by your side since we brought you here."

I could hear Rafe and James as they ascended the stairs. "Then go now for I have company and they can tend to my needs. There will be plate and mail on the fighting platform where the knights fell."

He waited until they had entered the chamber and then obeyed me. The bedsheets were covered with blood and I saw a look exchanged by my two former men at arms. "The blood is nothing, but I need your advice and your help."

Rafe frowned, "Advice, lord?"

I nodded, "I was struck on the knee with a hammer head and then my leg was cut. Have a look at the wound. The leeches have left but they wanted to cut the leg off."

Realisation dawned on the face of Rafe, "Aye, lord, and they tried that with me. You would not let them and Father Matthew at Weedon healed me."

He took the candle to help him look at the wound. He shook his head, "They have not even stitched it!" He clucked his tongue in disgust and then looked at me, "Do you mind if I have a poke, my lord?"

I nodded, "Aye, but before you do, James, find me some wine."

209

He found me a beaker and filled it with wine. I drank it in one and held it for it to be refilled. He did so and I drank that one as quickly as the first. "Do your worst."

Rafe had suffered a similar wound to me and I hoped he would remember what the priest had done to heal him. He tried to be gentle. I knew that from the apologetic looks he gave to me when he was too rough. When he had finished, he said, "It seems that your kneecap has a crack in it. Bone knits but mine took a long time and I moved on it too much which is why I am lame. Father Matthew told me I should be immobilised. We will get the cut stitched and then see about rigging something up so that you can travel in a wagon." He saw the look on my face and shook his head, "There is no use looking at me like that, my lord. The choice is to go home in a wagon or…" He looked down at his leg.

"Then when James has refilled my beaker you can stitch the wound."

To be fair to Rafe he was as gentle as a father with a new-born babe. It still hurt. James went to tell the others the news and we held a council of war in the chamber when it was cleansed and stitched. "My plans are in tatters. There may well be men drawn from Normandy, but we do not have as much time as I thought. Also, I will encumber and slow you. For that, I apologise."

Sir Ralph was not with us. He was in a different chamber. David of Welshpool shook his head, "It does not matter, my lord, at what speed we can travel. You and Sir Ralph will be well protected."

"Then we leave before dawn. It will take Rafe and the others that time to make the wagon suitable for Sir Ralph and me. We fire the buildings and head for the coast. We made this journey in three days and thanks to me it will take more than that to return. David of Welshpool. Have your scouts returned?"

"No, my lord, and I take heart from that. If they had returned, then the French would be closer than we hoped."

"Good. Michael, go to Sir Ralph and tell him what we plan."

"Aye, lord."

I smiled, "You all did well but now I must rest."

I ate but a little as the wine had made me sleepy. When I woke it was in the night and my bladder was bursting. The candle showed me where lay the garderobe. As soon as I moved Michael was by my side. "My lord!"

"I need the garderobe."

In answer he brought forth a large pot, "Rafe said for you to use this."

"Who rules here, Rafe or me?"

"Until we see Lady Eleanor it is Rafe. We have all agreed so no argument and they will come for you within the hour to put you and Sir Ralph in the wagon. They are adapting it now."

I could not get over how confident he was now. All diffidence had gone, and he was assured. I would go along with it, for now. After I had got over the embarrassment of urinating before my squire, he helped me to dress. After the fight, they had taken my armour from me and now I was dressed in a simple tunic.

Michael tried to put my boots on for me but he could not manage the left one without hurting me. Luckily, Rafe, James and Oswald came to carry me down the stairs to the wagon. Rafe nodded. "There is an art to it. James, help me to hold the leg. Oswald and Michael work as quickly as you can but do not jerk the master."

It did hurt but I gritted my teeth and bore it as I knew that there was no alternative. Then they carried me down the stairs. The spiral staircase made it hard and James and Rafe had to squeeze together with Oswald supporting my upper body. We were preceded down the stairs by Michael. All of us were sweating when we reached the ground floor. The bodies had all been cleared; they had been replaced by faggots and pieces of broken buildings. We left by the keep's gate to the wagon. I was to be the first one in. I saw that they had rigged a covering to give us shade and shelter from any rain. I had already worked out that we would not leave it again until we reached Calais and I could be seen by a good physician. Rafe had used his own experience well. There were some cereal bags upon which I both sat and rested my leg. They had been arranged so that my left leg was supported by two bags. The jolting would still hurt but the leg would have minimal movement. Michael had brought some of the cushions from the French lord's bedchamber and I would be comfortable.

The three of them were about to leave to fetch Sir Ralph when I asked, "Where is my sword?"

Rafe shook his head, "You will not need it, my lord."

"Michael, bring me my sword or we do not leave!"

My squire grinned and said cheekily to the others as he leapt over the wooden side of the wagon and raced towards the next wagon, "Told you!"

I looked around and it felt eery. Where were my men? I could hear them working but not see them. Michael brought my sword back and I laid it next to me. He then tied my horses to the rear. He placed a jug of wine, bread, cheese and ham inside too. He mounted his horse and then waited. When they brought Sir Ralph, I saw that the bed they had made for him meant that he would travel on his back. They laid him in asleep. I cocked a questioning eye at Rafe who shrugged, "The doctors treated Sir Ralph on the ground floor. There was so much blood that they thought he would die before they could tend to him. They have learned that your men are as tough as you. They have given him a potion to make him sleep. They tried to give it to you too, but Sir Stephen was having none of it."

I resolved then never to use healers I did not know. They had been presented to me as skilled men and they were patently not.

Once Sir Ralph was placed next to me Rafe and James climbed up on to the drivers' seats while Oswald ran to tell Sir Stephen that we were ready. The first jolt almost made me scream in pain and I heard Rafe curse, "Sorry my lord, once we get going it will not be too bad."

I heard the crackle of flame and, as we crossed over the drawbridge, I saw Tramecourt begin to burn. Of Azincourt village, there was little sign of buildings except for some stone foundations. The church and the castle were all that remained. I saw the first flame leap up from the keep as the faggots there were ignited. Now I knew why I had seen so few of my men They were obeying my orders and setting fires. Sir Stephen and Sir Will were by the gate. They rode with me towards the road to Calais and spoke as we rode. "Christopher White Arrow and Jack Gardyvyan have half of the archers down the road. They will clear it of any Frenchmen. David of Welshpool leads the rearguard. The French are less than thirty miles from us. You have fulfilled King Henry's command. We will be hunted."

I nodded, "And are we well-provisioned?"

"We have spare horses and that is good. We intend to keep moving and to stop for an hour at a time. You and your moving hospital will not stop."

"When you stop then so will I. We will all share the dangers." I was facing the castle for the first part and I watched as flaming brands were thrown into the ditch. The drawbridge began to burn. The castle would not be destroyed but it would be so badly damaged that it would take a great deal of coin and manpower to repair it.

By the time dawn came, we were well on the way north to Calais. With sixty mounted archers before us, I was not worried about an ambush, but horsemen could catch us. Therein lay the danger for we had lost men at arms and others had been wounded. The second of the three wagons had more wounded men as well as some of the treasure we had taken. We stopped at noon so that the horses could rest, and the men could eat. I made water again in the clay pot and the noise of it made Ralph awaken. He looked up at me and I saw how thin and drawn he was.

I shook my head, "You could not wait for me and you had to face the two of them alone!"

He laughed and I saw that it hurt him, "I thought you would persuade them to surrender. I did not want that!"

"There was no danger of their surrender, Ralph, but we are now a pair of cripples, at least for a while and if we are attacked then we will be helpless bystanders."

Ralph's squire had placed his sword close to hand and Sir Ralph said, "I can swash this about! It might help!"

The journey was slow for Rafe and James commanded the pace. Before us were the knights and men at arms. They might have gone faster but Rafe kept the same steady pace. He was doing so to avoid inflicting more pain upon Ralph and me.

I had misjudged the knight who commanded at Saint-Omer. We had hurt him and his men, but he had not simply gone back into his castle and hunkered down. Jack Gardyvyan rode back, and I saw him speaking with Sir Stephen. Unlike Sir Ralph, I could see over Rafe. I shouted, "If you are going to speak then have the goodness to do so where I can hear!"

The knights and Jack rode back. My archer pointed over his shoulder, "The French are waiting for us on the road just a mile ahead. They have made a barrier across the road."

Stephen, Will and Oliver had been good men at arms but they had spent their lives following orders. They would learn to give commands. Abelard was young. I saw on their faces that they did not know what to do. Had I not been there they would simply have charged the barrier.

"Are there other roads we can use to go around them?"

"Aye, Sir William, we passed one a mile back we could turn around the wagons and follow it. It will add twenty miles to our journey."

Shaking my head, I said, "Thanks to Rafe here we have moved too slowly as it is and there are knights from Paris chasing down the road after us. If we can shift these men, then we can move at a faster pace and outrun those who pursue us. They have a barrier across the road, you say? And they have none in the woods?" Jack nodded. "Fetch archers from the rearguard but leave enough there with David of Welshpool to warn of pursuit. We will use these wagons as bait. Jack, have the archers dismount and use horse holders. Take them into the woods and fields on both sides of the road. Will, take the knights and your men, not Stephen of Morpeth and his, and attack their left flank when the archers rain death. Harold of Derby, take the rest of the men at

213

arms and attack their right flank. Stephen of Morpeth, we advance as though we intend to attack."

"But Sir William, neither you nor Sir Ralph wear armour!"

"And we need none for the French use crossbows. They cannot hit us for we are above their sightline and the wagons will protect us." I saw the doubt on their faces. "The French did not see how many archers we had when they attacked us. This will come as a shock. Now we waste time! Do this!" I had trained all of them and they obeyed. As we moved, I added, "Rafe and James, don your helmets and use these two shields to protect your sides." I handed my shield to Michael who passed it to James and then I handed the other to Ralph's squire who gave his to Rafe. "And Rafe, from now on do not worry about my knee. I would rather have pain than lose a single man because you were being considerate!"

I heard the resignation in his voice, "Aye, Sir William."

I almost regretted my command as, now that he was ready, he whipped the horses and the wagon jolted. To take my mind from the pain I gripped my sword. I saw that Sir Ralph had done the same. I doubted that we could even defend ourselves but the thought of accepting death without defending myself never entered my head.

From my slightly elevated position and as I peered between Rafe and James I saw the barrier. It was just a couple of carts dragged across the road, but they had dismounted men at arms behind it and, further back, horsemen. They sounded the horn as we approached, and I hoped that it was not a signal for others to attack from the flanks or rear. "Michael, keep a watch along the flanks."

"Aye, Sir William."

My hurried plan had not allowed for a coordinated attack. Christopher and Jack would command the two sets of archers on the flanks to loose as soon as they were in position. Any confusion could not be helped. Our archers had not used many arrows yet and they released so fast that it looked like two rain clouds had appeared over the French. Those at the barrier sent their bolts at Sir Stephen and his men at arms. The bolts might have penetrated mail, but Stephen and his men not only had the finest of plate but also good shields. With mailed horses, they could endure the short flurry of crossbow bolts. Stephen and his men urged their horses on to close with the barrier knowing that it took time to reload a crossbow. I was just grateful that they had not targeted Rafe and James. When they neared the barrier, I saw Sir Stephen and his men dismount and begin to climb the barrier. It was frustrating to simply lie and watch. My hand gripped my sword and I cursed Isembart d'Azincourt! There were two roars as our men at arms and knights ran from the flanks, behind the barrier. All that I could see were the swords and axes raised behind the barrier. Behind them, I saw the knights of Saint-Omer and when I saw the standard waved, I knew they would attack but the noise of the battle was too great for me to be heard by my men. Rafe and James had stopped the wagon just behind Sir Stephen's horses and they drew their swords while they pulled their borrowed shields before them. Michael and Ralph's squire had their shields on their outside arms and were peering into the flanks for danger.

I saw the line of French knights, there looked to be ten of them, as they charged. They did not complete their charge for sixty bodkin arrows plunged down followed by another sixty and another. One hundred and eighty deadly arrows, as the French discovered on St Crispin's Day, would penetrate armour and mail. I heard the screams of men and horses as our arrows harvested a metal crop. They disappeared from view. When Sir Stephen appeared at the top of the cart barrier with a surcoat covered in blood, gore and the detritus of battle, he raised his sword and roared, "Victory!"

We had won.

It took more than two hours to clear the road. It was not a delay we could afford but we had to ensure that the road was clear for the wagons. The carts were not just removed, they had to be demolished. The French had chosen a good site for an ambush. There were hedgerows along both sides. I knew that this meant they were trying to delay us.

"Michael, ride to the rearguard and tell them that I think the pursuit is close!"

He turned and galloped off. We had not lost any knights but a couple of men at arms had fallen. We put their bodies in our wagon and covered them with their cloaks. None would be left behind. My men had also stripped the dead of their plate and mail. That was not simply greed, the bodies were easier to hurl into the fields that way. Not all had perished in the skirmish and more than half of the knights and men at arms had fled. We had gained horses, but the delay meant that we could not afford to stop again.

Sir Stephen rode to me, "We are ready, my lord. We have another six horses now!"

"Good, then we do not stop again and Rafe, spare neither our horses nor our wounds. There are dead men in this wagon now and that is down to me! I wish to take living men home and not corpses!"

He obeyed me and for the next twenty miles, I endured such pain as I had never experienced before. Darkness fell and still, we rode. Men

215

ate as they rode. The doctors and the priests complained that we had to stop but my men at arms silenced them. We were forced to stop, just before dawn, in order to change horses. We put the two hackneys of Sir Ralph and myself in the traces to pull the wagons. The heavy horses which pulled the wagon were exhausted. Men took the opportunity to make water and their horses to drink and greedily graze. Ralph had managed to sleep during the hours of darkness and after sitting up to make water he remained in that position.

"Have we outrun them, Sir William?"

I shrugged. I had not slept, and I was not sure of anything any longer except that I hated being in the position I was. Others would have to do the fighting for me, and I did not like that! "I am not sure, but we have done all that we can. The King will be happy for we have drawn men to us, and you have your vengeance so we should be satisfied and yet I am not."

The two hackneys were not trained to haul a wagon and they took some time to be placed in the traces and it was dawn before we began to move again. Rafe was in a positive mood, "The animals have all had a rest and it is just twenty miles to Calais."

"Just drive the wagon, Rafe, and do not tempt fate!".

"Aye, lord," he said, cheerfully.

We made just five miles before archers galloped up shouting, "The French are here! Defend yourselves!"

David of Welshpool was too wise a leader to panic and if he shouted such an order then we were in danger. There was little point in trying to outrun them and so I shouted, "Make our wagon fort! Sir Stephen, fetch back the archers! We fight here!"

Rafe wheeled the wagon so that it formed one side of the fort and the other two blocked the road and made the third edge. I saw empty saddles as our archers galloped up. What I did not see was David of Welshpool. Will Straight Shaft reined in next to the wagon, "Captain David is dead, my lord! The French sent hobelars ahead of their main column and ambushed us. He and six others fell."

There was no time for recriminations. I had to be thankful that they had not attacked the wagons. "Place your men behind the barriers."

Even as I gave the order, I saw the French knights, hobelars and men at arms as they galloped up the road. I would mourn David of Welshpool later, for now, we had been outwitted and we would have to fight for our lives. I would not die sitting on my backside. I used my sword to push me on to my right leg and when I was upright put the dagger I had used to cut the ham into my left boot. Rafe had strapped my left leg so heavily that I could not bend it even if I tried and so I gingerly rested it on one of the cereal sacks. It hurt but not as badly as I had expected.

Rafe shouted, "Sir William!"

I waved my left hand in irritation, "Defend the wagon! Men at arms and knights, dismount!" This was my retinue and we would fight and die under my orders!

We had a natural enclosure. The archers filled its centre and then, as the French galloped up the road, my knights and men at arms clambered up on to the wagons. We formed one side, close to an open field of wheat. The one facing the enemy was the one with the mail, plate, weapons, and the treasure! Sir Abelard clambered aboard my wagon along with Nat, Harold and the rest of my men at arms. They stood shoulder to shoulder with me. The French numbers were hard to ascertain but some had lances and spears.

Christopher White Arrow took charge and shouted, "Loose!" It was a blind volley for the wagons hid the French from view, but their constant rain would have to have an effect.

And then they hit us. I saw Oswald skewered by a lance. Sir Stephen swung his sword two handed and hacked into the neck of the knight who had slain his man at arms. The hobelars and men at arms filtered around the wagons. Rafe and James held my pole weapons and Rafe wielded my poleaxe as well as I had done on St Crispin's Day. Sir Abelard defended his side and I knew that all of my men were defending me. They would all give their lives for me and I did not want that. Harold blocked one blow from a French spear, but a second lance was thrust at him. I could not move but my sword was long enough for me to hack down and sever the end of the wooden weapon. The jagged, splintered end was pulled back and rammed into the face of my man at arms. I think that he was blinded by the strike, but he launched himself at his killer and with a sword in hand knocked the horse and rider to the ground. A spear from behind ended his pain. Kit Warhammer stepped next to me and swung his war hammer to smash into the helmet and skull of the man who had killed his friend. This was a battle without any hint of surrender from either side; men were no longer thinking about victory and defeat but vengeance and survival.

A spear came at my middle and I barely managed to deflect it; without mail, I would have been dead had it struck. The arrows from my archers were now being sent on a horizontal trajectory and the spearman who tried to skewer me had his head transfixed by a red flighted arrow. That would be Jack Gardyvyan! I saw Rafe knocked from his perch. He fell between the horses. We were losing. We had fought and won on St Crispin's Day, but we had lost more on this unknown day already! I suddenly remembered Michael. He had been next to the wagon and, as I swept my sword to keep the French at bay and as Kit Warhammer crashed his weapon into the skull of a horse I saw my squire with the broken shaft of his spear, defending himself from a hobelar. A second was coming at his blind side and I was helpless to aid my brave squire. Then I remembered my boot and the dagger tucked in the top. I drew and threw it in one motion. It had been one of the first skills Red Ralph had taught me and I had not forgotten it. It struck the Frenchman in the neck and he fell from his horse. Michael took the opportunity to hurl his shattered spear at a knight. The knight had a hounskull helmet and he simply did not see the hastily thrown missile. It clattered into him and must have disorientated him for when Michael boldly rode up to him, he did not react. As the knight turned his head to see whence the weapon had come, Michael rammed his sword tip into the eye hole of the helmet and drove it into the skull of the Frenchman who fell dead. Was this the turning point?

Stephen of Morpeth and his men came from the north of England. There the Vikings had reigned supreme for many years and York still felt more Viking than English. Even so, I was surprised when Stephen and his men suddenly leapt from their wagon into the mounted Frenchmen. They were reckless and seemed immune from the blows rained down upon them, John of Thropton struck a blow at a French horse's leg which had so much power that it sheared the animal's leg and the falling horse and rider created so much confusion that Stephen and the others were able to carve their way through the disorganised Frenchmen!

Behind me, I heard Jack Gardyvyan shout, "Archers to me!" I watched them race by the wagons. They had arrows nocked and they sent them into plated knights and men at arms at less than six paces. Each one was fatal. The combination of Stephen of Morpeth's berserker attack and the archers' assault made the French flee but we had paid a high price. Harold of Derby would no longer have to worry about gambling. He had staked his life for the last time. Robert of Weedon had also fought for me one last time.

Then, as my men began to search for wounded, I heard James shout, "Riders! Ho!" Every hand went to a weapon and I looked. Enemies, there were none. It was a column of men coming from Calais. The constable had kept his promise, but it was just an hour late for some of my men.

Epilogue

We spent two weeks in Calais, waiting for a favourable wind and ensuring that those who had been wounded were fit to travel. They had a better doctor in Calais than the ones brought by Sir Henry, and he complimented Rafe on his skills. The bone was knitting. Indeed, the fortnight we waited helped the process as the doctor refused to let me move. Ralph too, showed signs of recovery but it would be a long process. We buried our dead in the cemetery in Calais. It made the port even more special to us. None of us would mind service in France so long as we could land in Calais and tend the graves of the dead. As a chevauchée, it had proved highly successful. We were all richer. Michael even had a French warhorse he had taken as well as plate for he had slain a knight. My more experienced men took the opportunity of investing in goods to take home and either give to loved ones or to sell.

The ship which took us home had come from Harfleur where the Duke of Bedford had totally destroyed the French fleet and the siege had been relieved. Perhaps we had not needed to create a diversion, I would never know. What I did know was that the squires who had died on St Crispin's Day had been avenged and I felt more at peace. Michael would be an able replacement for Walter but for Sir Ralph, there would always be a hole which could never be filled. Such was war and such was the life of a knight. We would be home by September and the campaigning season would be over. We would have peace…until the Spring at least and then King Henry would return to win the Kingdom he felt was his due. When he gained the crown it would be at a cost; the blood on the crown would be the blood of the men who would fight and die for this most charismatic of kings and I knew that I would follow him for that was my appointed task!

The End

Glossary

Aketon- padded garment worn beneath the armour

Ballock dagger or knife- a blade with two swellings next to the blade

Barbican-a gatehouse which can be defended like a castle

Bastard Sword- two handed sword

Besagew- a circular metal plate to protect the armpit

Bodkin dagger- a long thin dagger like a stiletto used to penetrate mail links

Brigandine- padded jacket worn by archers, sometimes studded with metal

Chamfron- metal covering for the head and neck of a warhorse

Chevauchée- a raid by mounted men

Cordwainers- shoemakers

Cuisse- metal greave

Dauentre-Daventry

Esquire- a man of higher social rank, above a gentleman but below a knight

Familia – the bodyguard of a knight (in the case of a king these may well be knights themselves)

Fowler-a nine-foot-long breech-loading cannon

Galoches- Clogs Gardyvyan- An archer's haversack containing all of his war-gear

Gardyvyan- archer's war bag

Gules- a heraldic term for red

Houppelande -a lord's gown with long sleeves

Horsed archers-archers who rode to war on horses but did not fight from horseback

Hovel- a simple bivouac, used when no tents were available

Jupon- Short surcoat

Laudes- the first service of the day (normally at around 3 a.m.)

Langet- a metal collar protecting the top part of a pole weapon

Mêlée- a medieval fight between knights

Pele or peel tower-a simple refuge tower with access to the first floor via an external ladder

Poleyn- a metal plate to protect the knee

Pursuivant- the rank below a herald

Pyx-a small, well decorated and often jewelled box used to take the host to those too sick or infirm to visit a church

Rondel dagger- a narrow-bladed dagger with a disc at the end of the hilt to protect the hand

Sallet basinet- medieval helmet of the simplest type: round with a neck protector

Sennight- Seven nights (a week)

The Pale- the lands around Dublin and Calais. It belonged to the King of England.

Historical Notes

For the English maps, I have used the original Ordnance Survey maps. Produced by the army in the 19th century they show England before modern developments and, in most cases, are pre-industrial revolution. Produced by Cassini they are a useful tool for a historian. I also discovered a good website http: orbis.stanford.edu. This allows a reader to plot any two places in the Roman world and if you input the mode of transport you wish to use and the time of year it will calculate how long it would take you to travel the route. I have used it for all of my books up to the eighteenth century as the transportation system was roughly the same. The Romans would have travelled more quickly!

A poleaxe such as Sir William might have used. (Author's drawing)

This is a work of fiction but almost everything which happened from Southampton to the return to London happened the way I wrote it. As I often say I cannot make this sort of stuff up! It was the Earl of March who told the King of the plot and the three were executed. If it seems improbable then all that I can say is that is the way it is reported to have happened. More than two thousand men died at Harfleur from disease and another two thousand had to be sent home. A challenge to the Dauphin was issued by the King. The key part of this novel, in terms of my story, is the slaughter of the squires. I made up the last section where Strongstaff and Sir Ralph have vengeance. I think the squires deserved it but they were killed and it went against all the rules of war.

Sir John Oldcastle is the character on whom Shakespeare based Sir John Falstaff and he did lead the Lollard rebellion.

There will be another novel in this series for King Henry has not finished but the struggle for a crown will go on for more generations to come.

Books used in the research:

- The Tower of London -Lapper and Parnell (Osprey)
- English Medieval Knight 1300-1400-Gravett
- The Castles of Edward 1 in Wales- Gravett
- Norman Stone Castles- Gravett
- The Armies of Crécy and Poitiers- Rothero
- The Armies of Agincourt- Rothero
- The Scottish and Welsh Wars 1250-1400
- Henry V and the conquest of France- Knight and Turner
- Chronicles in the Age of Chivalry-Ed. Eliz Hallam
- English Longbowman 1330-1515- Bartlett
- Northumberland at War-Derek Dodds
- Henry V -Teresa Cole
- The Longbow- Mike Loades
- Teutonic Knight 1190-1561- Nicolle and Turner
- Warkworth Castle and Hermitage- John Goodall
- Shrewsbury 1403- Dickon Whitehead
- Agincourt- Christopher Hibbert
- British Kings and Queens- Mike Ashley
- Agincourt 1415- Matthew Bennett
- Ordnance Survey Original series map #81 1864-1869

For more information on all of the books then please visit the author's web site at http://www.griffhosker.com where there is a link to contact him.

Griff Hosker
May 2020

Other books by Griff Hosker

If you enjoyed reading this book, then why not read another one by the author?

Ancient History

The Sword of Cartimandua Series
(Germania and Britannia 50 A.D. – 128 A.D.)
Ulpius Felix- Roman Warrior (prequel)
The Sword of Cartimandua
The Horse Warriors
Invasion Caledonia
Roman Retreat
Revolt of the Red Witch
Druid's Gold
Trajan's Hunters
The Last Frontier
Hero of Rome
Roman Hawk
Roman Treachery
Roman Wall
Roman Courage

The Wolf Warrior series
(Britain in the late 6th Century)
Saxon Dawn
Saxon Revenge
Saxon England
Saxon Blood
Saxon Slayer
Saxon Slaughter
Saxon Bane
Saxon Fall: Rise of the Warlord
Saxon Throne
Saxon Sword

Medieval History

The Dragon Heart Series

Viking Slave
Viking Warrior
Viking Jarl
Viking Kingdom
Viking Wolf
Viking War
Viking Sword
Viking Wrath
Viking Raid
Viking Legend
Viking Vengeance
Viking Dragon
Viking Treasure
Viking Enemy
Viking Witch
Viking Blood
Viking Weregeld
Viking Storm
Viking Warband
Viking Shadow
Viking Legacy
Viking Clan
Viking Bravery

The Norman Genesis Series
Hrolf the Viking
Horseman
The Battle for a Home
Revenge of the Franks
The Land of the Northmen
Ragnvald Hrolfsson
Brothers in Blood
Lord of Rouen
Drekar in the Seine
Duke of Normandy
The Duke and the King

New World Series
Blood on the Blade
Across the Seas
The Savage Wilderness
The Bear and the Wolf

The Vengeance Trail

The Reconquista Chronicles
Castilian Knight
El Campeador
The Lord of Valencia

The Aelfraed Series
(Britain and Byzantium 1050 A.D. - 1085 A.D.)
Housecarl
Outlaw
Varangian

The Anarchy Series England
1120-1180
English Knight
Knight of the Empress
Northern Knight
Baron of the North
Earl
King Henry's Champion
The King is Dead
Warlord of the North
Enemy at the Gate
The Fallen Crown
Warlord's War
Kingmaker
Henry II
Crusader
The Welsh Marches
Irish War
Poisonous Plots
The Princes' Revolt
Earl Marshal

Border Knight
1182-1300
Sword for Hire
Return of the Knight
Baron's War
Magna Carta

Welsh Wars
Henry III
The Bloody Border
Baron's Crusade
Sentinel of the North
War in the West

Sir John Hawkwood Series
France and Italy 1339- 1387
Crécy: The Age of the Archer
Man At Arms

Lord Edward's Archer
Lord Edward's Archer
King in Waiting
An Archer's Crusade

Struggle for a Crown
1360- 1485
Blood on the Crown
To Murder A King
The Throne
King Henry IV
The Road to Agincourt
St Crispin's Day

Tales from the Sword

Conquistador
England and America in the 16th Century
Conquistador (Coming in 2021)

Modern History

The Napoleonic Horseman Series
Chasseur à Cheval
Napoleon's Guard
British Light Dragoon
Soldier Spy
1808: The Road to Coruña
Talavera

The Lines of Torres Vedras
Bloody Badajoz
The Road to France

The Lucky Jack American Civil War series
Rebel Raiders
Confederate Rangers
The Road to Gettysburg

The British Ace Series
1914
1915 Fokker Scourge
1916 Angels over the Somme
1917 Eagles Fall
1918 We will remember them
From Arctic Snow to Desert Sand
Wings over Persia

Combined Operations series
1940-1945
Commando
Raider
Behind Enemy Lines
Dieppe
Toehold in Europe
Sword Beach
Breakout
The Battle for Antwerp
King Tiger
Beyond the Rhine
Korea
Korean Winter

Other Books
Great Granny's Ghost (Aimed at 9-14-year-old young people)

For more information on all of the books then please visit the author's
web site at www.griffhosker.com where there is a link to contact him or
visit his Facebook page: GriffHosker at Sword Books

o contact him.